THE NEXT CRUSADE

BOOK FIVE OF
THE LUNAR FREE STATE

John E. Siers

Theogony Books
Coinjock, NC

Chris Kennedy/Theogony Books
1097 Waterlily Rd.
Coinjock, NC 27923
https://chriskennedypublishing.com/

Publisher's Note: This is a work of fiction. Names, characters, places, and incidents are a product of the author's imagination. Locales and public names are sometimes used for atmospheric purposes. Any resemblance to actual people, living or dead, or to businesses, companies, events, institutions, or locales is completely coincidental.

Cover Design by Shezaad Sudar.

Ordering Information:
Quantity sales. Special discounts are available on quantity purchases by corporations, associations, and others. For details, contact the "Special Sales Department" at the address above.

The Next Crusade/John E. Siers -- 1st ed.
ISBN: 978-1648552670

To Bill Webb who, after I'd spent 20 years writing in my hermit cave, dragged me out into the real world of published authors.

Prologue

*N*orseman kept station quietly in the empty space near the hyper limit of the nondescript red dwarf—a star that didn't even have a name, only a catalog number. The cruiser's officers and crew had been briefed generally on the mission. They knew they were here to meet someone in the outer reaches of this lifeless system. The mission fell under the broad umbrella of a series of highly classified Fleet operations. Only Commander John O'Hara, *Norseman's* captain, knew exactly why they were there and who they were supposed to meet. His calm, unruffled expression showed no hint of surprise when seven ships dropped out of hyperspace less than a light-minute from *Norseman's* position.

"Hyper signature!" Lieutenant Sandra Fiorelli sang out. "Seven bogies in tight formation... one of capital ship mass, the others... destroyers maybe, or lighter escort vessels. Range fifteen point four million klicks, bearing three four seven up one. They've gone passive... if they light up their drives, we should get a better read on them."

"Acknowledged," O'Hara replied.

Fiorelli's good, he decided. The young lieutenant had joined the ship as Assistant Navigation and Tactical Officer less than a month earlier. *Kind of reminds me of another junior NTO, aboard* Lewis and Clark, *on the mission that started this whole operation.* O'Hara had some less than pleasant memories of the *Lewis and Clark* mission, including a frustrating personal relationship (or lack thereof) with the junior NTO in question. He hadn't thought about her in some time, but now, the memories came back. *Wonder how she's doing. If things had been just a little different...*

"They're moving in-system, Captain," Fiorelli advised. "Analyzing drive profiles. Sir, those are Otuka ships! Looks like one of their big home ships and six parasites!" She brought up her active search and targeting systems, anticipating a call to battle stations.

"Ping them for IFF, Lieutenant." O'Hara's calm directive took her by surprise.

"Sir? The Otuka..."

"Go ahead and challenge them, Ms. Fiorelli. You might get a surprise."

"Yes, sir." Fiorelli turned to her console and issued the coded challenge. Seconds ticked by as the signals sped toward the unknown ships. Fiorelli's eyes widened in surprise when the red icons on her display changed to green.

"I'm getting a response, Captain, but it's a Fleet code I don't recognize."

"I see it," O'Hara advised. "Bravo Oscar seven seven seven... and that, Lieutenant, is exactly the code we're waiting for. Acknowledge with our ID please. Mister Renault, open Fleet channel fifteen alpha and stand by for a data dump. Engineering, prep the boat bay for incoming visitors. Oh, and let's go to Condition Yellow. We're supposed to be able to trust these people, but I'd prefer to have our defenses up and our weapons ready."

Forty minutes later, as the Otuka matched vectors with *Norseman*, a small craft detached from the huge home ship and headed directly toward them.

"This is… weird," Fiorelli remarked, but her captain only chuckled.

"I imagine it's just as weird for them, Sandra," O'Hara said, "but so far, all is according to plan. By the way, people, just for the record, you never saw those ships, and we were never here. Got it?"

"Yes, sir," a chorus from the bridge acknowledged.

"What ships, Captain? And where are we, anyway?" Lieutenant George Renault was something of a smartass, but this time, even O'Hara smiled as his remarks eased the tension on the bridge.

It was, O'Hara had to admit, a strange encounter for both sides. The Otuka were a race of voracious carnivores who considered human beings the best-tasting meat in the galaxy. Nearly 40 years ago, the Lunar Free State had found a primitive human population on a planet in the Rothstein system they'd called New Eden. It was a planet that had, until then, been a private hunting preserve for the Otuka. The ensuing conflict had resulted in a bloody defeat for the Otuka, whose survivors had vanished into deep space and were never seen again near New Eden.

The Otuka were mostly nomadic pirates who traveled as clans, usually with a clan home ship accompanied by smaller parasite warships. Over the years, LFS Fleet ships had encountered them many times in various places, but the usual result was the Otuka fleeing in panic. A clan group like this one would be unlikely to take on a single LFS destroyer, let alone a heavy cruiser like *Norseman*.

The Otuka were not just pirates. First and foremost, they were traders, and they were always looking for ways to make a profit, whether by piracy or by more civilized methods. After the New Eden encounter, one of their clan leaders had even sought to trade with the Lunar Free State. The volume of trade had never been high, but they had stayed with it over the years, and a few of the alien traders had become well-known.

Some of them have giant brass balls, O'Hara reflected. *They're not afraid to sail right into a hostile system and try to do business with people who are willing and able to kill them. Somebody at Fleet Command came up with a brilliant idea on this one.*

Eight years earlier, the deep-space survey cruiser *Lewis and Clark* had discovered a pre-industrial human civilization on a planet in a star system 47 light-years from Luna. O'Hara had been part of that mission, first as *Lewis and Clark's* NTO, then later as Executive Officer after the captain and several other officers became casualties in a battle that followed the discovery.

When they surveyed the planet, which the local humans called *Tatanna*—"Home of the Goddess" in their language—the LFS cruiser discovered an alien presence. The insectoid Ay'uskanar were not native to the star system. The oxygen-nitrogen atmosphere and cold climate of the planet were a hostile environment for them, but the planet had mineral resources the insects wanted. For over a century in local years, they had ruled over the human population and used human labor to mine the resource. They had also suppressed human attempts to develop any sort of industry or technology.

The Ay'uskanar were not cruel. If anything, they were completely devoid of emotion. They took what they wanted from the planet, including forced human labor for their mines, but otherwise left the humans to manage their own affairs. They were also merciless and would brutally suppress any perceived resistance to their rule, including wiping out entire villages of humans they suspected of conspiring against them or interfering with their mining operations.

Lewis and Clark had put a team of Marines down on the planet, and those Marines had made contact with local human authorities. The Ay'uskanar—the "Bugs" as humans came to call them—detected the cruiser's presence and attacked. The ensuing battle had been brutal. *Lewis and Clark* had survived only because an LFS battle group had arrived in time to intervene.

They had returned to Luna, leaving the Bugs to reclaim Tatanna. The entire mission had been classified, and all involved had been sworn to secrecy. Even the name of the star—Sacagawea, given as an historical nod to the discovering ship's namesake—was classified. The Lunar Catalog of Astrography still referred to it by its catalog number, NLC72917.

But the Lunar Free State was not about to allow a native human population to be dominated by off-world aliens. The "Moonies" had come to the rescue of humans on New Eden decades earlier, and they had established themselves as champions of the oppressed. They had gotten a lot of grief from the nations of Earth as a result. Some thought an immediate response was needed, but cooler heads in the Directorate and Lunar Command had realized that the Ay'uskanar were not a pirate rabble like the Otuka had been. Before going to war with them, they had wanted to know more about the Bugs... a lot more. Over the next several years, the LFS Navy had probed the limits of Bug space, gathering intelligence about the strength and capabilities of the prospective enemy.

It had also been necessary to maintain contact with the humans on Tatanna. For one thing, the LFS had to determine whether the people of Tatanna wanted to be free of the Bugs—wanted it enough to risk a bloody conflict to gain their freedom.

Fleet had been running a covert operation on Tatanna to maintain contact with the locals and lay the groundwork for a revolt against the Bugs. To do that, they'd had to find a way to insert the team—a couple of diplomatic people and some specialists with a Marine security force—and keep them supplied for the long term. After the *Lewis and Clark* mission, the system had been heavily reinforced by the Bugs. Warships could have been sent in to distract the Bug forces while the necessary contacts were made, but that would have violated the secondary objective—to lull the Bugs into a false sense of security where Tatanna was concerned and ultimately cause them to reduce their forces in the system. Fleet had been willing to risk it for the initial insertion of the team and an occasional mission after that, but the fewer LFS warships that entered the system, the better. That was where the Otuka came in.

Gypsum, the mineral the Bugs found so valuable on Tatanna, was quite common on Earth. The Otuka had been promised shiploads of the stuff for free. All they had to do was go to Tatanna, contact the Bugs, and sell it to them. Terra Corporation—the commercial arm of the Lunar Free State—would obtain and supply the gypsum and would also pay a substantial fee to the Otuka for services rendered. It was a pure-profit venture, an offer the alien traders could hardly refuse.

In return, however, the Otuka had to resupply the LFS team on Tatanna and carry encrypted messages back and forth between the team and Luna. Resupply was tricky, but most drops could be accomplished using a stealth drone—also supplied by the LFS—on a one-way trip down to the planet.

It was a perfect mission for a bunch of interstellar pirates, and the Otuka had agreed. They'd had few dealings with the Ay'uskanar, who were notoriously hostile to intruders in their territory, but the potential profits were huge, and they had been willing to risk it. Their first contact had been successful, and, for more than five years, they had been transporting shipments of gypsum to the Bugs' orbital facility at Tatanna. They never disclosed what the Bugs were paying them, but it was obviously enough to keep them interested. They also made the necessary supply drops and collected reports from the covert LFS team on the planet.

After a run to Tatanna, the Otuka would head for their own territory to further profit from whatever the Bugs had given them. Along the way, they would stop at this lifeless red dwarf system to hand off the reports. For more than five years, LFS warships had been coming to collect those reports. Their crews never knew why they were doing so, nor did they have the keys to decrypt the information they received. *This time it's different,* O'Hara thought. This was the first time *Norseman* had been sent on the mission, and the ship had been chosen because her captain already knew the story behind the operation. He was one of the officers Lunar Command had assigned to the top-secret Tatanna project known as Operation Blue Orchid. *We're about to find out whether it's all been worthwhile.*

"I'm going to the boat bay." O'Hara rose from his command chair. "Mr. Dormeyer, you have the bridge."

"Aye, sir. I have the bridge," Alton Dormeyer acknowledged. Dormeyer had also been one of *Lewis and Clark's* officers on that first mission. O'Hara had been impressed with his performance and had been happy to get him for the XO slot aboard *Norseman*.

* * *

O'Hara watched as the small Otuka shuttle settled into *Norseman's* boat bay. As expected, three people— humans, not Otuka—debarked from the craft and headed for the hatch, escorted by a pair of *Norseman's* Marines. All three wore LFS Marine field dress, but only one had Marine markings with a major's rank tabs. The tall, heavy-set man leading the group wore field gear with a Diplomatic Corps emblem and the rank of commander. The third member of the group was a slender woman with a pleasant, weathered face and an unruly mop of gray hair. Her field gear bore no markings other than a patch with the logo of the Lunar Research Institute. O'Hara greeted them as they came through the hatch.

"Ambassador Michaels, I presume." He extended his hand to the man. "I'm Captain O'Hara. Welcome aboard *Norseman.*"

"Thank you, Captain." Michaels grinned at him. "Can't tell you how happy I am to be here. This is Doctor Swarovski, our team's anthropologist—" he indicated the gray-haired woman, who shook hands with O'Hara, "—and this is our Marine commander—"

"We've already met," the Marine interrupted. "Permission to come aboard, sir."

Still a ramrod-straight Marine. O'Hara noted that the major had come aboard in proper military fashion, first saluting the ship's colors displayed on the bulkhead, then saluting him. He returned the salute with a smile.

"Permission granted, Major, and yes, we've met, though it has been a while. I seem to recall you were a second lieutenant when last I saw you."

"I was a second lieutenant when last I saw Luna, sir," Nova Sakura replied. "I've received two sets of promotion orders by Otuka mail since then."

"Commander O'Hara was our XO aboard *Lewis and Clark*," she advised Michaels, who looked at O'Hara with surprise.

"For the record, Commander," O'Hara told him, "I'm a member of the Blue Orchid team and am authorized to discuss your mission with you, but no one else on the ship is cleared. There is one other veteran of the *Lewis and Clark* mission aboard. You'll recall Dormeyer, Major, he's now my XO, but he's not Blue Orchid cleared, so if you encounter him, you'll have to limit your conversation to reminiscing about old times aboard *Elsie*."

He turned to Michaels again. "I don't know what sort of time you've been keeping, but ship's time—Lunar Standard Time—is 1545 hours. I thought you and your team might like a couple of hours to settle into your quarters and then join me for a private dinner tonight. I'm anxious to hear about your adventures."

* * *

"It was great to eat real Luna food again." Michaels looked satisfied as the stewards cleared away the remaining dinner dishes and poured coffee for the diners. "Didn't realize how much I missed it."

"Nothing special," O'Hara told him. "Just roast chicken, the usual trimmings... not exactly five-star cuisine."

Michaels looked around, made sure the stewards were gone, then turned back to the table.

"It may be 'just chicken' to you, Captain," he said, with a wry grin, "but there are no chickens on Tatanna. That niche on the local menu is filled by a furry creature that looks a lot like a very large rat. Not saying it isn't tasty, you understand, but it's not chicken."

"Actually," Swarovski remarked, "I've grown rather fond of Tatannan food. I don't suppose there's any more of that ice cream around..."

"I think we can find some." O'Hara chuckled. He tapped an icon on the table pad, and a steward appeared immediately.

"Sir?"

"Seconds on the dessert for Dr. Swarovski," he ordered.

"And for Major Sakura as well!" Nova held up her hand. "Always had a weakness for ice cream."

"None for me, thanks," Michaels said, "but I would *love* to have another cup of coffee. That's another thing I haven't had in a long time."

"Right away, sir." The steward departed and returned less than a minute later with two large bowls of the requested treat and a full pot of fresh coffee. O'Hara waited until he was gone, then again turned to Michaels.

"So, are the Tatannans ready to be liberated from the Bugs?"

"They're as ready as they're going to get," Michaels replied. "Are *we* ready to liberate *them*? The dispatches I've received from Lunar Command don't give me a warm, fuzzy feeling."

"Well, that's the question." O'Hara shrugged. "I've been on the project since the beginning. Apparently, HQ thinks I have some useful knowledge about the Bug's capabilities. I haven't missed many meetings over the years, and I don't have a warm, fuzzy feeling about the situation either.

"The Directorate established a commission to oversee the project, and it includes a mix of directors with different views on the subject. One faction believes we should send the Fleet, take on the Bugs, and liberate the planet. Fleet's willing, and our best military assessment is that we can do it. We've had ships probing the edges of Ay'uskanar space for more than six years, and we have a pretty good idea where their home worlds are and what capabilities they have.

"There's another faction that says we need to keep trying to make peaceful contact with the Bugs and work out a deal with them. A couple of the directors on the commission are TerraCorp people and are the most vocal of that group. They would actually like to establish trade with the Bugs."

"I was told we tried to make peaceful contact and failed," Michaels said. "The reports didn't give any details, but I've been wondering. Obviously, that would be the ideal solution."

"Yes, it would," O'Hara agreed, "and we tried. We've tried three times, and each time, the Bugs came out shooting. On the first attempt, we lost a freighter with seventeen crew and two diplomatic people, but we kept trying. After that, we made sure our envoy ship was covered by an appropriate escort. On the second attempt, we got out with defensive action only, but on the third, we got into a serious dust-up with the Bugs—casualties on both sides."

"Why can't we contact them the way the Otuka are doing it?" Swarovski wanted to know.

"We would, if we knew how," O'Hara said. "We've asked them, and they've flat out refused to tell us. We don't know how they made first contact, we don't know how they're delivering the shipments to the Bugs or what the Bugs give them in return, and we don't know how they've managed to make the supply drops to you without upsetting the Bugs."

"Why should they tell us?" Nova shrugged. "If we knew, we wouldn't need them. They'd lose a very profitable contract."

"Exactly," O'Hara agreed, "but it may be simply that the Otuka came to them as unknowns, whereas the Bugs have already identified us and our ships as an enemy. That brings us to the third faction on the commission, the one that says we should just walk away—pull our people out, stop subsidizing the Otuka, and let the Bugs have the planet. They say the Bugs aren't so bad. They're not slaughtering humans by the thousands, and they certainly aren't *eating* them like the Otuka were doing on New Eden.

"Those commissioners are quick to point out that 'liberating' Tatanna is only the beginning. Assuming we do that and somehow manage to avoid a prolonged interstellar war with the Bugs, we would then be stuck with the problem of administering the planet, protecting the natives, and leading them toward 'civilized' society. They talk about the burden New Eden has placed on the resources of the LFS and question whether we want to take on yet another Lunar Protectorate. They also remind everyone that it would likely put even more strain on our already piss-poor relations with the nations of Earth, particularly the Confederacy. Bottom line, they think we should shut up, close the book, and forget we ever discovered humans living in the Sacagawea system."

Michaels looked shocked. "Can't say I agree with that, Captain, and not just because I've spent the last six years working toward a different solution. The Bugs are no longer as passive as they were when the original survey found them. They've stepped up their presence on the planet. They run constant satellite surveillance over the countryside and send patrols into the cities and towns. Nobody seems to know what they're looking for, and they kill anyone who gets in their way. There have been mysterious disappearances, as many as a dozen people at a time, who just vanish and are never heard from again.

"They've also opened five more mines and impressed whole villages into mining service. When they march people off to the mines, they level the abandoned village with a kinetic strike. Any villagers who avoid capture and stay behind get vaporized. Anyone who says the Bugs 'aren't so bad' hasn't been living on Tatanna for the last few years."

"As for 'administering the planet,'" Swarovski joined the discussion, "Tatanna is *not* New Eden. It has its own government and a significant infrastructure of towns and villages, roads, and waterways. All we would need to do is protect it from external influence and let the locals develop on their own. They already have everything in place for self-rule, assuming we can keep the Confederacy from insisting their feudal society needs to be restructured as a socialist pseudo-democracy run by an army of bureaucrats."

"Right," Michaels said. "Besides—and I'll admit this is a bad attitude for someone from the Diplomatic Corps—I've always been of the opinion that anything that pisses off the Confeds is a good course of action."

"I think you'll find a lot of people on Luna who feel the same way." O'Hara chuckled. "You can count me in that group. The Confederacy represents too much of what our founders came to the Moon to escape.

"Personally," he continued, "I think the 'liberate Tatanna' group will prevail. I think one of the reasons you've been recalled is to help them convince the others, but I also think we are six months away, probably closer to a year, from being ready to take on the Bugs."

"I can live with that," Michaels replied. "It's certainly better than 'give up and walk away.' I'll need to get back to Tatanna before the action starts. King Algar has been praying for the Bugs to be gone for most of his life, and we've given him hope it will finally happen. Unfortunately, I haven't been able to tell him *when* it will happen, and I think his patience may be wearing thin. I'd love to be able to give him an actual date to look forward to."

He continued with a sigh, "If the decision goes the other way, I'll still need to go back. If we're not going to get rid of the Bugs, somebody needs to tell the king to his face. Hopefully, he won't call me a charlatan and throw me into his dungeon."

"If he does, I'll be in the next cell." Nova Sakura grinned crookedly. "Either way, I have to go back as well. I left two squads of Marines plus a couple of Navy techs and engineers back there, with a Master Sergeant in charge. I wonder how Fleet's going to get us back to the planet. Are we going to be guests of the Otuka again?"

"*That* was a strange trip." Swarovski shook her head. "Not sure I'd want to do that again. The centaurs locked us away in a separate part of the ship, gave us a bucket for a toilet, and passed food to us and took away waste—including the bucket—through a little hatch next to the door. We hardly saw them, except when we boarded the ship and when we departed. We had bunks, a couple of chairs, and a table, but all of it looked like something they'd built out of whatever materials they had on hand."

"Well, given their anatomy, I'm pretty sure none of their furniture would have worked for us," Nova said. "And, given their eating habits, we're better off not socializing with them. If they invite you to dinner, they're probably thinking of you as the main course. Fortunately, Tatanna is much more hospitable; it's not a bad place to live. It'll be even better if we can kick the Bugs out."

"As I said, I think that's going to happen," O'Hara replied. "Not tomorrow, but I think we're in the final phase."

* * *

*I*t's going to happen but am I going to be part of it? he wondered. With the buildup of the Lunar Fleet and the shortage of experienced officers, promotions had come quickly. At just 41 years of age, O'Hara had heard a rumor that he was on the list for promotion to commodore. The LFS rank structure did not include the old Earth navy rank of "captain," and his current rank of commander was the highest "non-flag" officer rank. There were only seven single-ship command slots for an officer of that rank. Only battlecruisers—the flagships of the Fleet's seven battle groups—rated a commodore in the captain's chair. That person would also serve as flag captain to the admiral who commanded the group. O'Hara wasn't sure one of those slots would be available if he got promoted or whether he would get one if it was.

He might get a destroyer squadron, whose squadron commander usually doubled as captain of the squadron flagship. Again, there were only a few independent attack squadrons, and Fleet gave preference to officers with extensive destroyer experience when choosing a commodore for that position.

If he didn't get one of those, his promotion would mean a transfer to Fleet Headquarters and a staff position or command of a non-mobile facility like the TransLuna Fleet Anchorage. *After all this preparation, I'd hate to sit this one out back on Luna.*

* * * * *

Chapter One

LFS Marine Corps Training Center, Luna

"You are here today because someone thought you might have what it takes to become Lunar Marines."

Gunnery Sergeant Jesus Martinez looked over the fifty recruits standing in five ranks of ten in front of him. He did not smile, and he noted with approval that none of them were smiling either.

"For some of you, it will be my unfortunate duty to prove that someone wrong," he told them. "I will be very much surprised—pleasantly surprised but surprised all the same—if all of you complete the next twelve weeks of training.

"It appears that most of you meet the minimum physical requirements," he noted. "Some of you may even exceed those requirements."

In the rearmost rank, Darius Jefferson tried very hard not to smile. Martinez had been looking directly at him, and Darius was pretty sure the last remark was intended for him. He was big, nearly two meters tall with a mass of 120 kilos, and none of it was fat. He had excelled in the physical sports in high school. He had also done well in martial arts, making up for his lack of speed with balance, technique, and the ability to take punishment. He had confidence in his ability to handle any physical challenge the Marines threw at him.

Martinez continued, "You will find that size, strength, and endurance will not be enough to make it here. You will need teamwork, discipline, and plain common sense. You will need to put your brains in overdrive because you will be studying and learning new things with an intensity that will make all the schooling you've had so far look like play time in kindergarten. If you give it your all, without a break, for 12 weeks, you might make it through, but if you screw up badly enough for even one second, you may find yourselves out of here so fast, you won't know what hit you."

Darius winced, even though he expected it. Upon learning that Darius was planning to join the Corps, his high school history teacher, Mr. Merrick, a Marine veteran, had told him, "You're smarter than people make you out to be, Jefferson. If you apply yourself in Basic Training as well as you've done here in school, you'll be all right. Most recruits who wash out don't listen, don't learn what the instructors teach them, or don't pay attention to orders. Think of it as though you're still in school. Study hard, and when you pin on the Shield and Stars—not if, but when—I expect you to drop me a note and tell me I was right."

Darius was sure he could do it, but he was 12 weeks away from pinning on the coveted Marine Corps emblem. A lot could happen in that time. Meanwhile, Martinez was still lecturing.

"I'll bet most of you came here because you want to be warriors." He scowled at them. "If that is to be your assignment in the Marines, so be it. There are no finer warriors in this part of the galaxy, but if you think that means you will be sitting around on your dead asses waiting for a war to come along, you are in for an unpleasant surprise.

"Some Earthworm nations produce forces they call Marines, and most of them are warriors, but unless they have a war to fight, they lose their edge. They go soft. They do a little training here and there, but mostly they just sit around waiting for something to happen. Eventually, their governments decide they don't need to keep paying them to do that, so they start cutting back—on people, on equipment, on everything Marines need to function.

"That's not the way the Lunar Free State does it." Martinez smiled sardonically—the first time they had seen any sign of humor. "If there's no war going on, we'll find something else for you to do." He began to walk slowly up and down the ranks, inspecting them closely, ready to pounce on anyone who relaxed, turned to look at him, or showed any sign of slackness or inattention.

"You might come out of here and get shipped right to Advanced Combat Training, then get packed aboard an assault carrier and shipped out to the far end of nowhere. If so, congratulations, you're a warrior, and you will be seeing action soon. Fleet doesn't lock and load those carriers unless they need to dump a whole can of whoop-ass on somebody.

"You might get assigned to Air Wing, repairing, maintaining, arming, and otherwise supporting the planetary attack craft, air-superiority fighters, or assault landers the Marines use to get the job done down on the surface. If so, you are in for many more weeks of serious technical training.

"Or, you might finish basic and get picked for one of the Special Services units. Those of you who grew up on Luna know Marines serve as TerraNova's police department. It, coupled with our swift and sure justice system, is why Luna has a lower crime rate than just about any place on Earth. Marines are also responsible for all other First Responder services down there, including EMT, fire, rescue, and disaster response. We provide the same services for East TerraNova, Farside Research, TransLuna Station, New Eden, and the Mars Project.

"If you get selected for one of those services, I don't want to hear any bitching. They are considered elite units. When they have slots available, they get first pick of our graduates, and they don't want any but the best. It is considered an honor to be picked to serve in one of those units. It also means you will be in for some heavy-duty training that will make this place look like a picnic in TerraNova Park."

Darius blinked in surprise. He hadn't even considered that he might wind up in one of the Special Services, but he decided he wouldn't mind. He'd been attracted to the Marines by the oft-repeated mantra of the Corps. Lunar Marines were the shield, the protectors of the nation. They told the citizens of Luna "nothing will hurt you tonight, not on my watch." That was exactly what the Special Services people did. They just did it a lot closer to home... sometimes. The New Eden Protectorate was many light-years from Luna.

He might end up one of the best-in-class and get picked for that kind of duty. His teacher's remark about "smarter than people make you out to be" was on the mark. Darius was smart, a good student, and a fast learner. People thought otherwise of him because he liked to hang out with people who were even smarter than he was—the superbrains, the kids who got into quantum physics when they were in grade school, who designed and built robot surveyors that could survive on the surface of Venus for a school science project. He admired those kids but noticed they were often socially challenged. They were geniuses when it came to science and technology, but, as he discovered when he started hanging out with them, they were totally naive about human nature and easy marks for bullies and scam artists.

Except when Darius was around. It didn't take the bad actors long to realize that messing with his friends could be hazardous to their health. There were a couple of incidents that could have gotten him into trouble, except his teachers were savvy enough to know who was who, and what was what.

Darius became the self-appointed protector of the dwerks, who recognized the value he brought to their group and were patient with his limited knowledge. Though his social life might have suffered a bit, he had learned a lot and had managed to develop a more-than-friends-but-not-quite-intimate relationship with Jin Yi, one of the girls in the group.

That was pretty much over now. She was off to Luna University on a well-earned scholarship to study exobiology, and he... well, he was here, trying to become a Lunar Marine.

His reverie was interrupted when Martinez stopped directly in front of him and looked him up and down. He braced himself for a dressing-down, but the drill instructor just turned and moved on down the line. He returned to the front of the group and faced them again.

"Now that I've blown all that sunshine in your ears, let's talk about reality," he told them. "Most of you will come out of here, go through Advanced Combat Training, and then be assigned as regular Fleet Marines. You will be sent to a unit aboard some warship. Battlecruisers carry a full company of Marines, cruisers a platoon, but you might wind up aboard a destroyer, which carries a single squad with no officer, just a noncom squad leader. Your primary mission will be to stand by in case the ship's captain decides he needs Marines for something. You might get dropped on some miserable, stinking hell of a planet for a recon mission, or you might get sent out to board a surrendered pirate or other hostile ship. Whatever comes along, if the captain decides it's a job for the Marines, you will be expected to do it in an orderly and proficient manner.

"Warships do combat in space, and that's where your secondary mission comes in. In space combat, Marines are responsible for damage control. Your job will be to repair battle damage, do search-and-rescue for combat casualties, and generally do whatever is necessary to keep your ship in action. We do not expect you to do the jobs of trained Navy technicians, but there will be many jobs that require strong backs, common sense, and a basic familiarity with the ship's systems. You will find that your training will continue and will often involve assisting the Navy with general ship's maintenance and repair jobs as requested. It has been my personal experience that the Navy usually reserves the dirtiest, nastiest jobs for the Marines, but you may console yourself with the thought that the day may come when your ability and willingness to do such jobs might save the lives of those Navy people."

Darius decided Air Wing was all right, though he would rather be in a combat unit or in Special Services. Unfortunately, it sounded like that was less likely than any of the new recruits imagined. Regular Fleet service didn't sound like the stuff they put in the recruiting flashes. The idea of being cooped up in a small ship like a destroyer with only 10 Marines aboard sounded awful. He resolved to work and study hard over the coming weeks to try his best to get one of the Special Services billets.

* * *

12 December 2111, Lunar Command HQ, TerraNova City

Kim Jong Pak stood at the window of his office, looking out at what was arguably the best view in TerraNova. Fifty meters below, the city's main concourse stretched across the huge green space of TerraNova Park, with its walking trails and water features designed to provide a pleasant, Earth-like setting in the underground city. The domed ceiling was lit to simulate a sunny afternoon, and the information display at the park's entrance advised visitors that a light rainfall was scheduled for early evening. After that, the forecast called for a clear night, meaning the park's planetarium system would produce a night-sky image on the dome with a starry vista that would rival the darkest clear-sky sites on Earth.

Hundreds of people were on the walkways of the concourse, while others enjoyed lunch or looked at merchandise in the shops and restaurants that ringed the park. The idea of the nation's Chief Executive standing at a window overlooking such a public place might have concerned his security people, but the panels were set for one-way transparency. Kim could enjoy the view, but the people passing below couldn't see him. In addition, the crystal-clear polymer panes were well beyond bulletproof. They were designed that way, not for security but for safety, specifically for pressure integrity. If some natural or man-made catastrophe cracked open the dome over the park, exposing it to the harsh lunar environment, the surrounding sections of the city would remain pressurized and comfortable.

It was unlikely to ever happen. The city was built into a mountain. Though the park was at its topmost level, the ceiling that arched over it was topped by several hundred meters of solid rock. The only portions of the city even close to being exposed were some of the outlying commercial areas, including the penthouse suites of the Luna Hilton and the city's most notable restaurants. Tourists always wanted a view of the Lunar surface, even if they had to look at it through ten centimeters of radiation-shielded polycrystal.

Still, Kim reflected, *one couldn't be too careful.* In its short history, the Lunar Free State had been under nuclear attack by Earth nations twice. It could happen again, given the current sad state of relations between the LFS and certain prominent nations down on the home planet.

Nuclear-tipped missiles had been replaced by kinetic weapons for use against surface targets. They were less expensive and easier to build than fusion bombs but every bit as destructive. Unfortunately, they were available to every nation or group that had any sort of space capability. The huge TransLuna orbital facility at the first La-Grange point between Earth and Luna was more than a port of entry for the Lunar Free State. It defined the official borders of the lunar nation and was the staging point for the LFS Fleet, whose defensive mission included the directive that no ship or other object not under TransLuna's direct control be allowed to pass within those borders. In simple terms, no ship or small craft not flying the LFS flag could land on the Moon. Cargo and passengers bound for the lunar surface had to travel aboard an LFS ship or transfer to one at TransLuna. There were no exceptions.

This was a source of irritation to many Earth nations, particularly those of the Confederacy, who reciprocated by banning the landing of any LFS ships within their borders on Earth, but the LFS had long ago secured a free port in the western United States and another on Cheju Do, an island province of the Republic of Korea. The U.S. and Korea were "non-aligned" nations that refused to join the Confederacy after the collapse of the old United Nations in the first half of the 21st century. Lunar heavy lifters landed with impunity at both ports and departed with cargo shipped in from all over Earth. The LFS also had arrangements with Japan, Australia, and the United Kingdom that allowed landing rights at the major commercial spaceports in each of those nations.

There was no point in explaining to anyone that the restrictions on lunar space were a simple security measure. More than a century had passed since terrorists had used ordinary commercial aircraft to kill almost 3,000 people in the United States in a single day. Since then, terror attacks from the air had happened many times, though none had been as deadly, but Luna's critics pointed out that no other nation had banned all commercial air traffic within its borders.

None of them are living in a single city inside an air bubble under a lunar mountain, Kim thought with a snort. *An aircraft crashing into a target on Earth is limited to atmospheric flight speeds. A spacecraft crashing on the Moon knows no such limits. Granted, we've come a long way since the early days. We're more spread out and dispersed, but we've still got way too many eggs in one basket.*

Kim had come to Luna from Korea as a boy, when his father had been recruited to head up the newly-formed Lunar Free State Marine Corps. The family had arrived before the Second Battle of Luna, so he had first-hand knowledge of how things had been in those early days. What had been a simple network of tunnels within the mountain was now a multi-level city with three major sections connected by broad underground concourses several kilometers in length. It would take more than one direct hit—kinetic or nuclear—to completely wipe out the Lunar Free State of the 22nd century, but a single weapon could still cause more damage to Luna than to any Earth nation.

There was also the New Eden enclave on the second planet of Rothstein's Star, over seventy light-years from the Sol system. The Lunar Free State had built a small city in a remote corner of the planet's largest continent—remote, as in "high in the mountains of the frozen north." In short, it was a place New Eden's aboriginal natives considered unsuitable for habitation, but it was fine for people who were used to living on the Moon. From their perspective, the fact that you could step outside the city without a pressure suit and radiation shielding made it a really nice place to live.

The enclave was called Eden's Gate. It was the site of the planet's only spaceport for regular surface-to-orbit traffic. Heavy-lift ore freighters landed at four remote mining sites—also located in uninhabited areas—but all other traffic to those sites was via atmospheric flights from Eden's Gate. The enclave was the headquarters of the NEP's Aboriginal Services Division. ASD's primary mission was to prevent, or at least minimize, cultural contamination of the native population—the "Edies"—through contact with off-worlders. Its secondary mission was to promote advancement of the Edie civilization in ways that would not violate the primary mission.

Simple enough at first glance, Kim reflected, *but the devil is in the details.* ASD's mission required it to ensure that no advanced technology be given, sold, or bartered to the Edies. ASD used such technology extensively to provide medical services to the natives, including airlifting seriously ill or injured Edies to the primary hospital at Eden's Gate or transporting personnel and supplies to a dozen clinics at local population centers.

The Edies had been forced into a nomadic hunter-gatherer life-style when the Otuka controlled the planet. With the aliens gone, their civilization was on the rise again, and they were building towns and villages, cultivating fields, and raising livestock. They were also creating hand-crafted products of interest to off-worlders, and Terra Corporation operated three trading posts on the planet where native crafts could be exchanged for ASD-approved off-world products or raw materials. One of the TerraCorp mining sites produced iron ore which was boosted to a solar-powered orbital smelter facility. Some of the refined metal was then shipped back to the surface and bartered to native blacksmiths for handcrafted metal items that were popular back on Earth. It was a small part of the commercial picture, but it was profitable for all concerned.

That was another point of contention between Luna and the nations of Earth. All trade with the New Eden natives—all access to New Eden's resources, for that matter—was controlled by Terra-Corp, which was controlled by the Lunar Free State's government. According to TerraCorp's charter, Kim, as CEO of the Lunar Free State, was Chairman of the Terra Corporation Board.

In short, the Lunar Free State was more than a sovereign nation, it was a major player in the commercial infrastructure of the entire Sol system. It had major interests in asteroid mining as well as mineral extraction on Mars. It also controlled an interstellar trading fleet that did business with several alien races over many light-years. It held a total monopoly on the resources and produce of New Eden's entire star system.

That was enough to upset even the unaligned nations, but they continued to do business with the LFS. The Confederacy, however, had decreed full economic sanctions, forbidding its member nations to engage in any commerce whatsoever with Luna. All of them gave lip service to the sanctions, but many managed to circumvent them by dealing with TerraCorp subsidiaries in Japan, the U.S., or Korea. The Lunar Free State was a small, but prosperous, nation that provided a lucrative market for Earth-made goods of all sorts, but it had many enemies and few friends back on Earth.

We're not going to make any friends with the Tatanna initiative, Kim thought with a sigh. *Just like New Eden, there isn't much our enemies can do about it... except build more warships.*

Over the past few decades, Earth's political scene had gotten... complicated. The Confederacy had spread from its roots in the European Union and now included all the nations of South and Central America as well as Mexico. Technically, Russia and India were also members, though neither was an active participant in Confederacy affairs.

Virtually all of Africa and the Middle East, as far east as India's border with Pakistan, was under the loose control of the Islamic Federation, which also extended its influence into much of Southeast Asia. At the same time, some of the Federation's nations professed membership in the Confederacy, which they could do because the Islamic Federation presented itself as an alliance of nations whose predominant religion was Islam, rather than as a governing body of any sort. In practice, most of its members were Islamic theocracies, which were far more loyal to the I.F. than to the Confederacy.

The remainder of the world consisted of unaligned nations, each of which was an independent entity, but even among the members of that group, there were alliances, sub-groupings, and virtual pockets of power. Canada, Australia, and New Zealand had again joined with the U.K. in a bond reminiscent of the old British Commonwealth of the 20th Century. The U.S. had extended its influence into the oceans, holding sway over many Caribbean nations and Pacific Islands as far west as the Philippines. China had never regrouped after World War III, and many of its eastern provinces were now under Japanese influence, while others were closely tied to Korea. Mongolia was considered part of Russia. Britain had reclaimed its dominion over Hong Kong.

The Confederacy had significantly increased its military presence in space. Technically, its space forces were made up of units built or purchased, crewed, and maintained by individual member nations, but overall command was held by Confederacy Space Command in Amsterdam. While some of the independents, most notably the Americans, British, and Japanese, had substantial space forces, the combined units of the Confederacy far outnumbered any other military force in space, except for the Lunar Free State.

Twenty years ago, just one of our battle groups could have wiped out everything they had in a stand-up fight, Kim reflected. *Today, if they put their whole fleet under competent leadership, the outcome would be far less certain. Still, it's that 'competent leadership' issue that makes me feel a lot better.* While the Confederacy Fleet theoretically operated under a strict chain of command, its individual units often gave first loyalty to the nation from which they had come.

Kim was not a military man, though as Chief Executive he wore the traditional Fleet Admiral's uniform on formal occasions. His father had been the first commandant of the LFS Marines, but Kim Jong Pak had graduated from Luna University with a degree in business management and had gone to work for TerraCorp as a strategic market analyst. Years later, Kim had been tapped by Lorna Greenwood, the second CEO of the Lunar nation, for her personal staff.

Greenwood had come up through the military ranks to command the LFS Fleet before becoming CEO, and she had considered her lack of business experience a weakness. She had relied heavily on Kim during her term, but when Michael O'Hara had succeeded her in the CEO position, Kim had returned to the business world as a TerraCorp executive. He eventually became TerraCorp's Chief Operating Officer, and when O'Hara retired, the Directorate had picked him as the Lunar nation's fourth CEO.

While serving on Greenwood's staff, Kim had come to realize that Luna's military strength was vital to the overall success of the nation. He regarded the LFS Navy and Marines as instruments of Luna's policies in the commercial sector, as well as the diplomatic arena. He was somewhat less comfortable with the idea of his nation being the champion of oppressed human civilizations in other star systems, but a precedent had been set with New Eden, and his advisors—military and civilian—had convinced him that liberation of Tatanna from the Bugs was another worthy cause.

So, like the Crusaders of old, we're about to go off to a distant star system to rescue the locals from the forces of evil. I wonder when the Confeds, or somebody else on Earth, will decide to challenge us.

Despite the secrecy that surrounded the project, Kim was certain some of Luna's enemies must have had knowledge of it. Operation Blue Orchid had been eight years in the making, and there were too many people involved in its preparation. He might expect the military people to keep it secret, but the Lunar Directorate had been briefed early in the project, and a few Directors had served on the planning commission. Kim believed in the adage that three people could keep a secret only if two of them were dead, but he would also have added the proviso that none of them were Lunar Directors.

In theory, Luna didn't have a political class. Directors were selected from the ranks of the Lunar citizenry by direct vote of their peers, but in Kim's experience, those who came from the commercial sector—usually executives of TerraCorp—tended to regard Luna's national interest as secondary to their own bottom line. The nations of Earth were still Luna's most significant trading partners, and Kim had few illusions about what sort of information some LFS "businesspeople" might be willing to trade to advance a particular deal.

Somebody down there knows what we're about to do, Kim told himself with certainty, *but for whatever reason, they've chosen not to make an issue of it.*

"Sir, Admiral Ling is here."

Kim smiled at the reminder that he was never completely alone. The soft, polite voice seemed to come from mid-air, as the Artificial Intelligence known as Mike made optimum use of the office's state-of-the-art sound system.

"Send her in, please," he told the AI.

A moment later, the door to the office opened to admit the commander of Luna's combined fleets. Just 155 centimeters in height and massing about 50 kilos, Amy Ling was not physically impressive, but she carried herself with a commanding presence that went beyond the uniform she wore. Her Asian features showed the maturity of middle age, with streaks of grey in her dark hair and a few lines around her brown eyes with their pronounced epicanthic fold.

With the latest anti-aging treatments, "middle age" had acquired a new meaning. Ling was one of the Original Citizens who had established the Lunar nation on the Moon. A few months ago, she had celebrated her 100th birthday.

"You sent for me, sir?" Ling's salute was precise and properly respectful, but Kim couldn't shake the feeling he ought to be saluting her instead. *Maybe when I get to be that age, I'll be able to project authority the way she does.*

"Yes, I did, Admiral. I want to discuss a few things with you. Come in." He motioned toward the informal seating area at one end of the office. "Have a seat, and to use one of your own expressions, 'smoke if you've got 'em.'"

Ling paused for a moment, then took the indicated chair.

"It's pretty bad when my personal habit has even come to the CEO's attention," she remarked. Nonetheless, she slid a thin case out of a pocket in her uniform tunic, took out a cigarette, and lit it. "Are you sure this won't bother you?"

"Not at all," he replied with a grin as he pushed an ashtray across the coffee table toward her. "Mike assures me the ventilation system can be adjusted so I won't even notice. He says it's a trick he learned from Sonja."

Ling almost choked on the first puff of smoke and glanced sharply at Kim. Sonja was the AI for the battlecruiser *Sorceress*, Ling's flagship. As such, she had plenty of experience dealing with Ling's habit.

"Anyway," Kim continued, settling into another of the comfortable armchairs, "I've read all the reports, but I need to hear it from you directly: Are we ready for Blue Orchid?"

Ling leaned back in her chair to consider the question. Kim was known for his analytical skills. If he said he "read all the reports" that meant he had considered the details of the extremely complex plan of operation. It also meant he wasn't looking for vague generalities or cheerful assurances. *In other words, time to get serious.*

"Sir, we are as ready as eight years of carefully considered preparation can make us. We've thoroughly scouted the Bugs, we know where their home star system is located, and we know the extent of what they consider to be their territory. They have a presence in seven star systems beyond their own but have established settlements in only two of those. They only establish colonies on hot, heavy-gravity planets that have a methane atmosphere, just like their home world. In the other five systems, they have set up industrial operations to extract and process local resources for shipment back to the home worlds. To our knowledge, Tatanna is the only such outpost on a world with native intelligent life. It also happens to be the most distant one from their home worlds.

"The Sacagawea system is about a dozen light-years closer to their home world than it is to Sol. If it comes to a long campaign, they've got shorter supply lines than we have, so we're hoping to make it a short campaign. We need to take the system away from them, hold it against counterattack, and convince them not to press the matter."

"I understand the plan," Kim said. "Do you really think we can convince them to give up what they obviously consider a valuable resource?"

"I wish I could give you a solid affirmative on that, but I can't," she admitted. "We know our military tech is better than theirs in many ways, and I'm sure we can take the system from them and hold it. Beyond that, well, they're an alien race, and our best guess about how they think is just that—a guess.

"From what we know about their interactions with the Ta-tannans, they seem to operate on cold, hard logic. We are going to try to give them good, logical reasons to cease hostilities and with-draw. We will plan no offensive action against them anywhere out-side the Sacagawea system. Even within that system, we won't engage them unless they threaten Tatanna."

"I thought the plan called for attacks in several other systems—diversions before the actual Tatanna offensive goes in. Won't that send them the wrong message? Mind you," Kim cautioned, "I'm not criticizing the plan, and it's a little late to start making changes. I'm just playing Devil's Advocate at the 11th hour."

"'Attack' is too strong a word," Ling replied. "What we've planned are incursions or probes into two of the Bug 'resource' sys-tems that are farthest from Sacagawea. The objective is to get the Bugs' attention without engaging them in battle. The forces involved will be fast units—mostly destroyers—that can go in, tweak the Bugs' noses, then stay away from them while taunting them with their presence.

"There is some risk, and the commanders involved will operate under rules of engagement that allow them to take whatever action is needed to defend themselves, but their priority will be to disengage and evade the enemy.

"We're sending them in early—weeks before we launch the actu-al assault on the Bug forces at Tatanna. The hope is that we can get the Bugs to divert resources to the 'threatened' systems, resources that will then be unavailable to send against us when we go for the real objective. As soon as we've secured that objective, we will with-draw from the other systems and cease harassing them. We hope the

Bugs will get the message that we have what we want, and we will not bother them further if they leave it at that.

"We're also prepared to bribe them. If they come back after we've taken the system, we're prepared to offer them large quantities of the mineral they've been mining on Tatanna. You will recall that we tried that early on, as an alternative to armed conflict, but we couldn't get them to communicate with us, let alone accept our offer. The hope is they will be more open to such an offer after we've kicked their butts and denied them Tatanna as a source. We're prepared to use the Otuka as intermediaries if they won't deal with us directly.

"That's the plan—" she shrugged, "—but it's exactly that: a plan. No plan can be expected to match the reality of actual warfare. I'm reasonably confident it's a *good* plan, but if it doesn't work exactly as we expect, we will have to improvise, adapt, and overcome."

She stubbed out the remains of her cigarette and took out another without thinking about it. Medical science had eliminated the detrimental health effects of tobacco use. Smoking had once again become popular, but in the closed environment of the Lunar Free State, few indulged to the same degree as the Fleet's supreme commander. Kim didn't object since Mike's ventilation adjustments were obviously working. The smoke was hardly noticeable.

For a moment, he felt a twinge of guilt over the use of the AI for such mundane, personal comforts. Mike not only served as his personal assistant but also as the primary information asset for Lunar Command, the Lunar Research Institute, and Terra Corporation. He was the nation's primary keeper of records and the supervisor of operations for the lunar capital's infrastructure. His control of the ventilation in Kim's office was just a tiny part of what he did to maintain the environment of the underground city.

Kim pulled his thoughts back from the momentary distraction. Ling was looking at him, waiting for his reaction.

"All right, Admiral, you're right. It looks like a good plan, and procrastination won't make it any better. Mike will confirm the orders to you through the usual channels, but I'll give them to you verbally now: Commence Operation Blue Orchid."

"Yes, sir." She put the cigarette aside and acknowledged with a salute.

"The only thing I still have to figure out is how Earth—the Confeds in particular—are going to react," Kim muttered. "They haven't said a word, but I can't believe we've gotten this far without their noticing something is going on."

Ling gave him a wry grin. "That, sir, is what falls under the heading of Somebody Else's Problem. I have my mission, you have yours… and I don't envy you for it."

Kim gave her a dark look. "Be careful. You know where that 'problem' ends up if something happens to me."

Ling's grin disappeared. If the CEO died or became incapacitated while in office, the LFS Constitution required the highest-ranking officer of the Lunar military—currently, Amy Ling—to assume the office of Chief Executive. It was a constitutional provision that had always provoked criticism from the "enlightened" governments of Earth.

"That, sir," she told him sincerely, "is why your health and welfare are matters of constant concern to me."

* * *

Tempête de Neige, A Private Resort in the Swiss Alps

The five men meeting in the heavily secured conference room spoke English, though it was not the native language for any of them. One of the unspoken rules of their association was that none might have advantage over the others.

"The Moonies have become an obstacle to our progress," Andre DuMorne insisted. "I believe the time has come for direct action."

"I disagree," Huang Chang Li replied calmly. "I think 'obstacle' overstates the case. They are simply a factor that must be considered."

DuMorne turned sharply toward Huang but paused as Gerhard Richter held up his hand. As usual, they had drawn lots upon entering the meeting, and Richter was chairman for today.

"I am inclined to agree with you, Andre," he said, "but I understand Chang's position as well—his reluctance to disturb the Golden Goose."

"It has been a most profitable relationship," Huang admitted. For over a decade, his shipyards in Korea, Japan, and China had supplied major structural elements for the Lunar Free State's ever-expanding TransLuna facility, as well as sub-assemblies for the Lunar Fleet's shipyard.

"I don't expect our actions to change that much," Richter continued. "We aren't looking to destroy the Lunar Free State, only to… change its course a bit. Is that not correct?"

"We aren't looking to destroy them yet," DuMorne replied, "but ultimately, our cause will benefit if they cease to exist as an independent nation. The Confederacy, with its huge bureaucracy, is better suited to our needs and is far easier to control."

"So, we could do as well by convincing the Moonies to join the Confederacy," Butos Kimba said, with a hint of a smile.

"Hah!" The exclamation came from the fifth member of the group, Mohammed Al Sharif. "I would have a better chance of converting them to Islam and recruiting them for the Jihad. The typical Moonie can't say the word 'Confederacy' without spitting on the ground."

Richter glanced sharply at him. Al Sharif had little regard for the Confederacy, though several major Islamic nations were members of the group. While the Confederacy was Richter's primary area of responsibility, the German would not have taken any action involving those Islamic members without first consulting Mohammed. It was a delicate dance in which the two of them were very careful not to step on each other's toes.

"All the same," Huang rejoined the argument, "my own position would be much simpler if they did. It would also be helpful if the Confederacy would spend as much money building up CircumTerra as the Moonies have spent on their spaceport facility."

"We have been over all of this before," Richter declared. "The Confederacy does its share to enhance your bottom line, Chang. Today, we are here to discuss what the Moonies are doing and how it will impact our future decisions. What is the latest from your sources?"

"Unfortunately, I can add little to what we already know." Huang's frustration showed in the sour look on his face. "The Moonies are playing this one very quietly. About all we can say for certain is that one of their ships discovered another human-habitable planet with an indigenous human population. We don't know what they plan to do about it. We don't even know the location of the star in question. My contacts are executives of Terra Corporation, and some are even members of the Lunar Directorate, but none are members of the select group the Directorate formed to study the issue. Officially, they don't even know whether such a group exists."

"In other words," DuMorne grumbled, "we know little more than we knew eight years ago when this new human population was discovered. Surely, no government can keep secrets *that* well against all the resources we have at our disposal."

"My contacts are businesspeople." Huang shrugged. "It would be helpful if we had military sources. Surely the nations of the Confederacy must have intelligence assets in that regard. Gerhardt, do your sources have anything to add?"

"Most Confederacy nations have no idea how to do military intelligence," Richter replied. "The Americans and the Russians might have something, but the Russians give nothing away. As for the Americans..." He lifted an eyebrow in DuMorne's direction.

"We work through Wall Street." DuMorne shook his head. "I have very few contacts in the American government and none in their military intelligence agencies. We do have contacts in Terra Corporation, including some Moonie directors. Hopefully they're not the same ones you have been cultivating, Chang. I would hate to get into a situation where they play us against each other."

"Yes, that would be unfortunate," Huang mused. "We must compare notes on that, Andre, so that if it ever happens, we can turn it to our advantage."

DuMorne looked very smug. "It was one of *my* Directorate contacts who first gave us information on this subject. The information came from a Moonie military officer who was part of the mission that made the discovery."

"You have a contact in the Lunar military?" Al Sharif was skeptical. "So…"

"Unfortunately," DuMorne replied, "the officer in question incurred the disfavor of the Lunar high command. His patrons saved his career, but he was shuffled off to their commercial fleet. He is still useful—it is good to know what TerraCorp's traders are doing out among the stars—but he can't provide us with any new information on the present topic. We have also been cultivating someone high in the Moonie Diplomatic Corps who knows of their contact with this distant human world, but so far, he has been unwilling to tell me where that world is located."

"There is one thing I can tell you," Huang advised. "My people keep me informed about what is happening at TransLuna. From those reports, I expect that whatever the Lunar Free State is going to do will be soon. There has been a significant increase in activity on the military side, with virtually every docking slip occupied by their warships and a constant flow of equipment and supplies. They are preparing a major Fleet operation, and it looks like they will be launching it soon, perhaps within days. They could be preparing for something totally unrelated to this mysterious human-inhabited world, but it appears to be far too extensive for another anti-piracy operation, so…"

"A valid point," Richter conceded. "If they were expecting an attack by anyone against Earth or Luna, they would notify the unaligned nations. They would even notify the Confederacy. They also give notice if they are planning major Fleet exercises, allegedly to avoid unfortunate misunderstandings."

"This isn't an exercise," Huang insisted. "One of my sources said they were loading their fleet colliers with live ordnance, and it appears they are provisioning their warships for an extended campaign. The use of the colliers suggests a campaign in another star system."

"Whatever they are doing," DuMorne interjected, "we are not in any position to do anything about it, except, perhaps, to take advantage of the long-term absence of a large portion of their fleet from our neighborhood."

"Hmmm... yes," Richter mused. "If we agree that it suits our interests to promote continued antagonism between the LFS and the Confederacy, perhaps it would be a good time for the Confederate Fleet to conduct significant exercises of their own. I think the CSF high command would be amenable to the idea of a few drills to test their readiness, with no advance notice to the Moonies."

"We could take a few lessons from history," Huang noted. "The Americans and Russians played such games regularly a hundred years ago."

"I'm sure you favor anything that encourages both sides to build up their military forces," DuMorne replied with a snort, "but we really must consider the long term. What is our goal with respect to the Moonies?"

"Is there really any question?" Kimba inquired with a feral grin. "Our goal is the destruction of the Lunar Free State. In simple terms, death to all Moonies."

* * *

In the silence that followed, Kimba studied the faces of the other four. Huang's Asian features gave no hint of what he was thinking, but Kimba sensed strong opposition. *The golden goose*, he thought. At the same time, he sensed support from Al Sharif, but the expressions of both Richter and DuMorne registered shock. Finally, DuMorne spoke.

"I was thinking more in terms of control than destruction," he said, carefully. "The Moonies are both volatile and powerful. Any attempt to actually destroy them could have… unfortunate consequences."

"I have no fear of them," Kimba replied with a sneer. "They are a cat in a tree, hissing defiance at the wolves on the ground."

"More like a tiger in a tree," Huang told him, "who chooses not to engage the wolves because they are no more than an annoyance."

"Chang is right," Richter agreed. "I can persuade the Confederacy to annoy them because most of their fleet is otherwise occupied. Were they not, they could wipe out everything the Confederates have in a day. If you don't fear them, you should."

"Besides," DuMorne added, "they have built a city on the Moon, an amazing facility at the L1 point, and a merchant fleet that trades profitably among the stars. We don't want to destroy all of that, we want to take it for our own."

"I don't fear them because I don't plan to fight them… not directly," Kimba insisted. "If you want a snake's skin, you need only cut off its head. We remove the head of the Lunar government in such a way that no one on Earth can be blamed, and within a year or two, they will be meek and manageable members of the Confederacy."

"Kim?" DuMorne looked doubtful. "I will admit, the man has not lived up to our expectations. We used every bit of our influence to get him elected, thinking his TerraCorp background would make him more amenable to our point of view.

"Unfortunately, he seems to have developed a stubborn streak of patriotic nationalism. He never knew we were involved, and it won't do to have him discover our influence now. What we really need is an LFS Chief Executive who already knows he is in our debt.

"I don't think we are in a position to press for that now," he continued, "but I will agree that Kim needs to be removed. I presume, Butos, you were thinking of something sudden, direct, and permanent."

Kimba's grin became even more feral. "I was," he admitted. "Surely, with the resources at our disposal, we can come up with something like that."

"I'm sure we can," Richter growled, "but I don't think that would serve our purpose. Have you forgotten? The Moonie constitution specifies the succession if a Chief Executive dies or is incapacitated.

"Do you really want Ling in the CEO's chair? If she suspected, for a moment, anyone on Earth had a hand in Kim's demise, we might be digging ourselves out of rubble by the end of the day. The woman is a warrior, and, to her, the only good enemy is a dead enemy."

"You might be digging out," Al Sharif said with a smirk. "We know she hates the Confederacy, but the Jihad is only a shadow, Butos is only the dictator of one small country, and Huang and DuMorne are just... businessmen as far as she is concerned. We would have to do this in such a way that no blame could possibly fall on the Confederacy.

"Besides, she is a narrow-focused military officer. She might be much easier to manipulate than Kim has proven to be."

"Mohammed has a point," DuMorne said, looking directly at Richter. "She is a simple-minded warrior—has been since the earliest days of the Lunar Free State. Kim, on the other hand, is far too clever. Left in place, it may only be a matter of time before he discovers some of his people are far more beholden to us than patriotic Moonie citizens ought to be."

"You may be right," Richter admitted. "I want to stress that this must be done carefully. She may be a 'simple-minded' military officer, but she's very good at her job and commands enough firepower to sterilize the Earth three times over. The good news is that she must be near retirement, and she has shown no inclination toward wanting the CEO position. It won't be more than a year or two before the matter is back in the hands of the Directorate. Maybe, by then, we will have found a candidate who is more amenable to our control, one who is 'in our debt' as you say, Andre.

"So," he continued, "it appears we agree on a general course of action. Are any of you of a different mind?" He looked at Huang, the only one who had not commented, but the Asian wore his usual emotionless mask and chose not to speak up.

"Very well." Had Richter been holding a gavel, the moment would have been appropriate for its use. They'd decided and set a course. All that remained was to work out the messy little details and execute the plan. As Kimba had noted, with the resources at their disposal, something could certainly be arranged.

* * *

11 February 2112, TransLuna Station

Major Nova Sakura, LFSMC was a combat veteran, but she felt a nervous flutter in her stomach as she sat on the auditorium stage. *Not my usual area of operations,* she reflected. Since graduating from the academy eight years earlier, she'd gotten comfortable with small-unit command, oversee-ing her own troops. Granted, for the last few years, she'd been on detached duty at a remote station some 47 light-years from Luna, commanding just 20 Marines in support of a diplomatic mission, but it had been an interesting and challenging assignment, and she had been the ranking Marine on station.

This time, she was in the spotlight and feeling very out of place because she was the lowest-ranking of the 100 plus officers present. Even the destroyer captains in the back row were lieutenant com-manders. *Including Blondie.* Sakura smiled when she recognized her old friend Lorna Greenwood in the last row. Of the remaining officers, she recognized no one except Fleet Admiral Amy Ling, Ambassador Michaels, and Commodore John O'Hara who shared the stage with her. A hush fell over the group as Ling stood and approached the podium.

"Louis, is the room secure?" she asked, glancing at the ceiling as she spoke.

"Yes, Admiral. All doors are sealed, all persons in attendance have been verified, all communications links have been terminated. Security systems are now activated." The voice of TransLuna Sta-tion's AI came over the room's sound system, clearly audible to all in attendance.

"I shouldn't need to remind any of you," Ling addressed the au-dience, "that everything you see and hear from this point on is Code Alpha and not to be discussed with anyone outside this room. You will be able to advise your people about the details of the mission once the force is in hyper en route to the objective.

"I do not intend to rehash the details of the mission today. You've had plenty of time to review the plan over the past month and to discuss it in previous meetings. For the past five days, you've all been on 12-hour alert status for departure. I'm here to tell you that you will be departing tomorrow, in battle order, beginning with Second Fleet, Second Battle Group at 1600 hours. Diversionary operations have already been initiated in two star systems far from the objective. In other words, Operation Blue Orchid is on, people. I'm satisfied all preparations are in place, and there's nothing more to talk about.

"I'm going to ask the three people up here with me to step up in turn and offer some final words of encouragement in the hope that they will help you focus on the mission. Ambassador Michaels has spent the past several years in contact with the human inhabitants of the planet Tatanna. He's going to tell you about those people, their society, and what they've had to endure under Bug rule.

"Commodore O'Hara will offer his insights regarding space warfare with the Bugs. He was the Executive Officer aboard *Lewis and Clark* on the expedition that discovered Tatanna and had the first combat encounter with the aliens. Since then, as captain of *Norseman*, he has participated in several recon-in-force missions that probed Bug space and Bug capabilities. Much of what was learned in those encounters has already been factored into the Blue Orchid battle plan, but I thought it would be useful for him to share his experience directly with you.

"Major Sakura has the distinction of being the only Marine officer who has ever engaged the Bugs in surface combat, which she did on Tatanna during that same *Lewis and Clark* mission. In addition, she has been on the planet with Ambassador Michaels for the past several years, observing the Bugs and helping prepare the Tatannans for what is about to happen. She is here today to give you a first-hand account of that experience.

"All three of these people will be with you on the mission. Ambassador Michaels will rejoin his liaison group in contact with the Tatannans. Major Sakura will be attached as advisor to General Sherwood's staff aboard *Omaha Beach* and, at your discretion, Sam—" she nodded to Major General Samuel Sherwood in the front row, "—will be in the first assault wave to land on the planet."

Rather be there than speaking in front of this group, Nova thought.

"Commodore O'Hara will be attached to Admiral McGruder's staff aboard *Nike*—" she nodded to Rear Admiral Charles McGruder, commanding Second Fleet's BG-2, also in the front row, "—where he will serve as advisor on the space combat side."

"OK, I'm done," Ling declared. "Listen to these people, pay attention to what they have to say, then let's go out there and get it done."

She returned to her chair and sat down, waving a hand to Michaels as she did so. The Ambassador rose and stepped up to the podium.

* * * * *

Chapter Two

Castle Boroson, *Algar Shektal* (King Algar's City)

"Ready on the firing line!"

Twenty crossbows snapped up to the ready position. Master Sergeant Moira Bouchard, LFSMC looked out over the range that had once been a huge stable space within the castle walls but was now a training area for the King's Guard.

"Take aim!" she commanded. "Fire!"

Twenty bowstrings snapped forward in unison, and an instant later, twenty bolts struck the targets downrange with a peculiar crunching sound.

"Cease fire! Rest your bows!" Bouchard ordered. The bowmen lowered their weapons to touch the dirt floor in front of them.

"Well, Your Highness?" Bouchard shot a questioning glance at the young man standing beside her.

"You've proved your point," Prince Arne T'Boroson conceded. "The new bolts can penetrate Bug armor, but we are still helpless against their weapons. They have longer range and can kill many men in the time it takes to reload a bow."

"True," she agreed, "but it is not our intention to put your people into a pitched battle against the creatures. We expect you only to defend the palace and the king if the Bugs choose to come here. We hope they will not, that they will see my people as the enemy and engage only our forces. None of our staging points are near the

King's City. The Bugs know you cannot fight them, and we hope they will do the logical thing and leave your people alone."

"We could defend ourselves much more effectively if we had just a few of your magic weapons," the prince persisted. "Why can't you provide them to us?"

"That, Highness, is a decision above my pay grade." Bouchard shook her head. "You can speak to Major Sakura or Ambassador Michaels when they return but…"

"Your father understands their reasoning, Highness." Ramis D'Mala spoke up for the first time. "They are thinking beyond the battle with the Bugs, to the time when Tatanna is free of the creatures, free to resume our path toward a better civilization. They are concerned that if we acquire powerful technology—magic, if you prefer—before we are able to understand and control it, it will bring us great harm."

"My father trusts the off-worlders," the prince replied, "because he believes this is our only chance to be rid of the Bugs. He would do anything to accomplish that end. I do not mean to disparage your people, Lady Moira, but I cannot be certain we will succeed."

"The more reason to keep your people out of the conflict, Highness." Bouchard shrugged. "If nothing else, the Bugs are logical. They will know their enemy is not of this world. No matter the outcome, they will have no reason to punish you if your people have no part in the conflict."

"I agree with Lady Moira, Highness," Ramis said. "This is the best course for us."

The prince relaxed a bit and favored the two of them with a wry grin.

"Ramis, you always agree with Lady Moira. Don't you know men are supposed to be masters of their women?"

That brought an answering grin from Bouchard, and Ramis blushed. The prince was well aware the two of them were lovers.

"Lady Moira is a most exceptional woman," he muttered.

"Indeed," the prince agreed, "and we are fortunate to have her and her people, but now that the time is drawing near, I grow restless.

"Soon, we will either be free of the Bugs, or our dreams will be shattered forever. I am inclined to believe what Lady Moira and Major Sakura have told us, for they have actually fought the Bugs and won, but one can never know the future until it becomes the past."

"*T'Anna marsin tei*," Bouchard replied in the language of Tatanna. *As the Goddess wills it.*

* * *

*N*ever imagined I'd be having dinner with a king and a prince, Bouchard thought, *but for once, I'm not the only woman here.* She smiled across the table at Myrel, Prince Arne's wife of just two months. His first wife, she reminded herself. Polygamy was common on Tatanna, particularly among nobles who could afford more than one wife. So far, the prince only had one, but in his exalted station—heir to the throne of all Tatanna—he would probably end up with several more, some for political reasons. *If we do liberate these people from the Bugs, they're going to have to deal with our scandalous ideas of gender equality.*

Some Tatannans—including the king and his son—were already having to deal with them, thanks to Bouchard and Major Sakura. The concept of women soldiers was totally alien to the planet's patriarchal society, but they had proven themselves years ago in combat against the Bugs.

Bouchard found it a bit strange that a culture so dominated by men should worship a female deity. Tatanna's universal religion was monotheistic, dedicated to the worship of the Goddess described as the "Mother of All Men." *I guess all these heavy-duty testosterone-driven types are just a bunch of Mama's Boys.*

"So, Lady Moira—" her reverie was interrupted when King Algar addressed her directly, "—it would appear the hour of our liberation is at hand."

"Perhaps not quite at hand, Majesty, but within no more than a crossing if the message holds true."

Bouchard had become fluent in the planet's common language, but she still had to think a bit to translate Tatanna's calendar and length of day into Lunar standard. A "crossing" was the length of time—about 33 local days—it took for the planet's smaller, inner moon to overtake and pass the larger, outer satellite. Crossings were the Tatannan equivalent of months, but the Tatannan year was based on typical seasonal markers of solstice and equinox and worked out to be 380 local days, or about 11.5 crossings. With the ten-day Tatannan equivalent of a week and a day that lasted around 26 hours, "no more than a crossing" was as close as she could get to the expected date without doing some serious calculation.

According to the dispatch from HQ, Fleet would arrive in force in about 20 Earth days—which meant they had already started by the time the dispatch arrived, since transit from Luna required about 24 days in hyperspace.

It would then take several more days for the force to reach the inner system. She wasn't sure how long because it would depend on the planet's orbital position and other factors best left to Fleet navigation specialists. After that, all hell ought to break loose when the Marines landed on the planet.

The landing was also subject to delays due to battles with the Bugs in the outer system, delays in securing the orbitals so the ground forces could be launched, or general delays caused by screwups while trying to put a massive battle plan into action. On second thought, Moira decided, her estimate might be a bit optimistic.

"The message said Ambassador Michaels will return when the event happens," the king continued, "but there was no mention of Major Sakura."

Bouchard winced. In addition to the message she'd given to the king, she'd received a private communication—a set of orders—from her commanding officer. She wasn't particularly happy about those orders, but it was on her to carry them out.

"I have word the Major will be returning to Tatanna," she replied, "but she will be with one of the forces fighting the Bugs. I am directed to remain here and use my Marines—with the help of Your Majesty's own—to keep the palace secure. Our ships will be watching from the sky and will send help if they see any indication the Bugs are moving this way.

"We don't expect the Bugs will," she tried to reassure the others with a smile. "We expect they will have many other concerns to deal with at the time."

Yeah… our ships will send help, she thought, *while I try to hold off the Bugs with twenty Marines armed with combat knives and swords and a bunch of leather-armored troops with crossbows.*

Under the table, Ramis put a hand on her thigh and gently squeezed it. They'd been lovers long enough that he was tuned in to her; he could sense her concerns about the coming conflict.

She noted he'd also gotten over his initial shock and awe of her. She was no longer the alien warrior woman he feared and worshiped from afar. She was the woman he loved, who just happened to be a warrior from another world. She wanted very much to kiss him, but she decided that would not be appropriate at the king's dinner table, so she settled for placing her hand over his and returning the gentle squeeze.

Down the table, Arrimas D'Norr was watching them with a frown. Another of the king's stalwart advisers, he had been there in the early days when the Marines had been hiding in the wilderness under the king's protection, trying to avoid detection by both the king's enemies and the Bugs.

Arrimas was a good enough man, Bouchard decided, but definitely *not* a proponent of gender equality. He had never accepted the idea of women soldiers, and he disapproved of her relationship with Ramis. *Doesn't matter,* she thought. *Ramis has the king's ear, Arrimas is irrelevant. It will all be over in a little while, one way or another. Either way, Ramis and I won't have to worry about royal politics anymore.*

* * *

The dinner had been a dull and dreary affair. *As usual,* Arrimas thought, *the king allows himself to be led by the off-worlders. He listens to them, listens to women as if they were men.* Arrimas hated the Bugs as much as any Tatannan, but he was by no means sure the star people could defeat the monsters. If they did, they would be the ones playing the tune to which King Algar must dance. For the most part, the people loved Algar, but Arrimas would prefer to serve a king with a stone heart and an iron fist. Fortunately, he knew where he might find one.

When he returned to his quarters, he took pen and parchment and prepared a letter. With luck, he would pass that letter to a trusted contact tomorrow, and it would reach its intended recipient in a few days.

* * *

House Corsa, Province of North Coast

"Calm yourself, Ronor," Asral T'Corsa advised. "I believe there is a solution, but time is short, and we must move with purpose."

"Calm myself?" Ronor T'Korval, Duke High Reaches slammed his cup down, spilling wine on T'Corsa's fine, snow-white tablecloth. "How can I be calm when the world we know is about to end? No matter which side wins, we lose. If the off-worlders prevail, the king will have powerful allies to consolidate his rule. If the Bugs win, they will punish all of us for conspiracy against them. They will enslave those they need to work the mines and kill everyone else."

"No, that will not happen," T'Corsa insisted. "Not if we convince the Bugs that we can give them victory without fighting."

T'Korval stared at him in disbelief. "Are you mad? Give the Bugs victory? I detest the creatures and would happily see them gone if I could convince them to take King Algar with them, but I don't see how we can possibly influence the outcome. I imagine a mudrunner whispering 'I can help you win' in a bull *targon's* ear as he faces another bull in the rutting season. The only place a mudrunner should be under those circumstances is far away from the conflict, hiding in a deep hole. The Bugs can rain fire from the skies, and I've no doubt the off-worlders can do the same."

"Your Lordship has a gift for words." Ersin T'Corsa favored the young duke with a crooked grin. "A mudrunner and a targon… I shall have to remember that one."

"Ronor! Please, hold for just a moment and listen to what I have to say." Asral almost shouted the plea as T'Korval rose from his chair with a snarl and turned to face Ersin.

Asral wished that, for once, his half-brother would learn to keep his mouth shut. *My most clever spymaster, and a skillful assassin, but give him a cup or two of wine, and he chooses to antagonize exactly the wrong person at the worst possible time.*

The son of their father's second wife, Ersin held no noble titles and stood to inherit nothing from the wealth of House Corsa unless Asral and all his sons died without heirs. As Duke North Coast, Asral was aware of the threat his half-brother posed, but he had turned Ersin into his ally by giving him what he wanted most: not wealth and title, but power.

To be sure, he also rewarded Ersin's efforts with enough copper to satisfy his prodigious tastes for wine and women, but, more importantly, he allowed him free reign to do what he wished anywhere in the province and anything he could get away with outside the province. He was a spymaster, assassin, and enforcer who carried out all the messy tasks that needed to be done, without soiling the hands of his noble brother. He carried no papers of authority and had no title or official standing, but he was known and feared throughout North Coast and was high on King Algar's list of the Crown's enemies.

Unfortunately, that power only fueled Ersin's contempt for nobility, but Asral had hoped he would have sense enough not to display that contempt tonight. Ersin might be a clever assassin, but his brutal enforcements were usually carried out by his gang of thugs. In a face-to-face physical confrontation, he would be no match for T'Corval. The volatile Duke High Reaches was known for his skill with a blade, as well as for his short temper.

At Asral's urgent signal, a servant appeared to mop up the spilled wine and present the younger duke with a fresh cup.

"What I am trying to tell you," he explained, "is that one of my informants—a man *very* close to King Algar—has given us a way to take charge of the situation. We must move against Algar now, or in the very near future, when the conflict begins."

"Move? Against Algar? Hmmph!" T'Corval snorted with contempt. "What would you do, make a contract with the Assassin's Guild? Or send Ersin's people sneaking into the heart of Castle Boroson to do the deed?"

"Of course not," Asral insisted. "The Guild owes its existence to Algar's grandfather and is sworn never to move against the king. If you try to hire them to assassinate Algar, they'll take your money and kill you instead. As for Ersin—" he turned to his half-brother with a glare, "—he will be the first to tell you that his very best men cannot do the job. In fact, most of them could not survive anywhere in the King's City as they are all on the High Sheriff's 'kill on sight' list."

"True, including myself," Ersin admitted with a grin that suggested he took pride in the fact.

"Well, then…"

"I am not thinking of mere assassination. I propose an armed force, sufficient to overwhelm Algar's palace guard and take the throne. Algar will need to die, and Prince Arne as well. We are fortunate the king has but one heir."

"You are mad." T'Corval slumped back into his chair, picked up his refilled wine cup, and took a long drink. "The Bugs do not permit open conflict among us. They will destroy your forces, rain fire on your house, and leave Algar to distribute your lands among his favorite nobles."

"No, they will not," Asral replied, calmly, "for two reasons. First, they will be busy with more important matters—fighting the off-worlders—and, more importantly, they will finally have proof that what we have been telling them is true: Algar conspired with the off-worlders against them."

"Aha!" The younger duke spotted the flaw in the plan. "What makes you think the off-worlders will not come to Algar's defense? Even if they do not, what happens if they win? After they have disposed of the Bugs, they will come for you."

Asral sighed. "No, my friend, they will not, and that is what my informant has discovered. The off-worlders plan to keep their forces far away from Algar Shektal because they don't want to give the Bugs any reason to destroy the city. They have studied the Bugs well enough to know the creatures are cold and logical—they do not kill or destroy for no reason. Besides, the off-worlders will be busy fighting the Bugs and will not expect an attack on the king by his own subjects.

"Most importantly, according to my source, the off-worlders have made it clear they are only fighting the Bugs because the people of Tatanna want them to do so, but the only people of Tatanna they have talked to are Algar and his closest advisors. They have repeatedly made the point that this is our world, to be ruled by our king and nobles. They have even said they will not fight the Bugs; they will abandon the effort and leave us alone if the human rulers of Tatanna—Algar and his people—simply ask them to do so. If Algar is removed, and they find themselves dealing with the new rulers of our world…"

Asral stopped speaking and waited. High Reaches was no fool, though his volatile temper and outspoken nature caused many to underestimate his intelligence. He would need to work through what Asral had told him, to look for flaws in the logic. Hopefully, he would ask questions because that would mean he thought there was some merit to the plan. At that point, Asral would be certain of victory. He had never failed to manipulate the fiery young duke to his will, once he got Ronor thinking in the right direction.

"Your informant must be very close to Algar if he has told you all this," Ronor said skeptically.

"Oh, he is indeed," Asral assured him. "He was one of Algar's earliest contacts with the off-worlders years ago when they first appeared here."

That much was true. The source of Asral's information was an agent who had spent time living with the off-worlders when the Bugs were hunting them, and Algar had given them refuge in a remote camp on the Little Kilder river. The man had been on Ersin's payroll before that, but neither Algar nor the High Sheriff had suspected him. *He's a most useful spy,* T'Corsa reflected, *but not clever enough to realize that he, too, is being played.* The man had no direct contact with Ersin or Asral. He believed he was being paid by Ronor T'Corval, Duke High Reaches.

I don't think I'll mention that to Ronor, Asral decided. *Just another security measure. Any spy can be caught eventually, and any man can be made to tell what he knows. Can't have Algar thinking North Coast is anything but loyal to the crown.*

"So we take the throne from Algar and then tell the off-worlders we don't want them here any longer." Ronor clearly had doubts about the plan. "What if they have been lying about their intentions? What if they go ahead and destroy the Bugs, then come back and announce to us that they are now our new masters?"

"I don't believe that will be the case," Asral replied. He had considered the possibility, but it seemed unlikely. "If that was their intention, why go to the trouble of soliciting Algar's support? We have nothing that can help them defeat the Bugs, and we can't hinder them in any way, so they don't need our support or approval.

"As for the plan," he continued, "I'm not sure we should ask them to leave. I hate the Bugs, and the off-worlders may have much to offer us. We should leave our options open and concentrate on our objective—removal of Algar and the end of the Boroson dynasty."

"So," Ronor replied, "you remove Algar and his son, declare yourself to be King of Kings, and then—"

"Goddess!" Asral exclaimed. "Whatever gave you that idea? I have no desire to be king!"

"But you said—"

"I rule North Coast by fear. Ersin and his men keep my subjects in line using methods that make him the most hated man in the province, but I'm sure they hate me almost as much. I could never command the love and respect those simpering fools in the crown lands express for Algar, or the loyalty of so many of the other dukes, especially Algar's current allies. No, my friend, our next king must be a man who is respected for his open opposition to Algar, a man known for the courage of his convictions, and that is why I have asked you to come here tonight. If I wanted you to support my bid for the throne, I would have made the three-day journey to your house instead."

He paused for a moment and watched the young duke's face. First he saw shock, as the meaning of Asral's words registered, then suspicion, tempered by the realization that he might really take the throne and rule all Tatanna's realms. Then came the look of hunger, desire, greed. It was obvious T'Corval wanted the throne, and the power and respect that went with it—wanted it more than he had ever wanted anything in his life.

Ronor is so transparent. So easy to predict, to manipulate, Asral thought. *The only challenge is to make sure no one else has access to him.*

Suspicion again. "What do you gain from this?" Ronor challenged. "You, who have always claimed no deed is worth doing unless it be to one's profit."

"Oh, I fully expect to profit when you are on the throne," Asral admitted. "I expect to be first among the dukes in your favor, the man who always has the ear of the king. Once Algar is gone, there will be many adjustments to be made. Some will rise, some will fall. I expect to rise at the expense of those who fall."

"Hmmm, perhaps, but none of that can happen until the conflict between the off-worlders and the Bugs has been decided. You say we might cast our fortune with the off-worlders, but what will happen to your precious mines if we do? Will the off-worlders pay copper for those worthless rocks the way the Bugs do? I know you tax the miners heavily, and the loss of that revenue would surely be missed. Have you thought of that?"

"I have." Asral shrugged, as if it meant little to him. "I am sure Algar has thought of it as well, since he taxes me on that very same revenue. It would certainly be a matter for the new king to discuss with the off-worlders."

"Yes, I suppose it would." Ronor smiled for the first time. "The new king…"

Asral felt a flash of triumph. *He's accepted it. He will do whatever I ask, take any path as long as it leads to the throne. All we must do is carry it out.*

That could prove far more difficult than expected. If the plan failed…

It will fall on him; I've already made plans to erase any sign of my involvement.

In truth, Asral wanted the throne for himself. He wanted to be king, to rule with an iron hand, but he had no stomach for the consequences of failure, which would no doubt involve a meeting with Algar's executioner.

* * * * *

Chapter Three

"Here they come, ma'am. Thirty-seven degrees, up nine. Range... one point two meg. I see fifteen point sources. Three of them look to be cruiser-size."

"Acknowledged." Lieutenant Commander Lorna Greenwood nodded to her Navigation and Tactical Officer. "Helm, maintain station."

To those on the bridge, Lorna was the image of an experienced, nerves-of-steel warship captain, but inside, the legendary Shepard's Prayer—supposedly uttered by 20th-century astronaut Alan Shepard as he waited to be launched into space—was running through her head. *Dear Lord, please don't let me screw this up.*

LFS *Lynx* was Lorna's first command, and she was quite aware of her status as the most junior captain in Destroyer Squadron 12, the battle-hardened "Cat Pack" under the flag of Commodore Rebecca Ling. As Lorna contemplated the many ways the prayer might fail her, Ling's orders came over the squadron net.

"I'm taking *Jaguar* to meet the threat. *Leopard, Cougar*, you're with me. *Dragon, Hydra*, close behind my group, formation delta. *Lynx*, I need you to maintain station and cover left. Acknowledge."

Lorna waited patiently while the other four ships, in the order named, acknowledged.

"Acknowledged," she said at last. "*Lynx* maintaining station."

She watched as the other three destroyers broke formation and went out to meet the incoming Bugs, with the two light cruisers close behind. At first glance, the LFS forces appeared to be at a disadvantage; in reality, the Bugs were seriously outmatched. *Dragon* or *Hydra* alone could have taken the three Bug cruisers, and the Bugs' 12 light attack craft were no match for three *Predator*-class destroyers.

The Bugs must have known that. Either the attack force was all they could deploy against the incoming LFS group, or they had something else planned. This attack might be a feint to draw the defenders away from the ship they were supposed to protect—the assault carrier *Iwo Jima,* with an entire division of LFS Marines plus their equipment, as well as planetary landing and attack craft. The carrier represented half the ground force tasked with taking Tatanna away from the Bugs. The other half was inbound aboard the carrier *Omaha Beach*, with its escort of cruisers and destroyers.

"Mr. Merrill," she told her comm officer, "advise *Iwo Jima* we will be launching drones."

"Mr. Frisbee—" she turned to her NTO, "—I need three recon birds. Put the first one two hundred thousand klicks dead in front of the carrier, the others a hundred thousand above and below her."

"Programming for launch," the NTO advised.

Senior Lieutenant Casimir Przbyzienski had come to Luna from Poland as a teenager and spoke standard English with a noticeable accent. Lorna had to resist the urge to smile when she called him by his self-inflicted nickname.

"Please call me Frisbee, ma'am," he had told her at their first meeting. "It saves much embarrassment and pain to my ears when people try to pronounce my name. Otherwise, most would just call me 'Ski.'"

Lorna quickly discovered everyone on the ship called him Frisbee. Enlisted and noncoms called him Mr. Frisbee, with proper respect for his rank. She also learned he was very good at his job. He would understand exactly what she was doing—placing the reconnaissance probes in the positions vacated by *Jaguar* and the two cruisers. Commodore Ling had set up their formation for a reason, primarily to give her a good look at anything that might be coming their way. Lorna was leaving the rear guard position—formerly held by LFS *Leopard*—uncovered, but with the inbound vector they'd already built up, there was no chance of an enemy overtaking them from behind.

She hoped the Commodore would agree with her logic. Recon drones were expensive, and *Lynx* only carried six. Given the mission profile, she probably wouldn't get a chance to recover them.

Other junior captains might have been upset at being left behind when Ling went out to take on the Bugs, but Lorna wasn't. The Commodore was leaving the defense of the carrier—in essence, the fate of the whole mission—in her hands. On one hand, it ramped up her already high level of nervous tension, on the other, she felt a glow of pride.

Twenty minutes later, the Bugs provided ample justification for her tactics.

"Contact! Multiple contacts!" Przbyzienski sang out. "Bearing three three nine, up twelve. Range seven hundred thirty thousand, inbound direct for intercept. I see nine sources. Looks like two cruisers, and seven light attack ships."

The data, Lorna noted, was coming from the leading drone, which was 250,000 kilometers in front of the carrier.

"Time to missile range?" she asked.

"Eighty-three minutes with present vectors, ma'am. Closure rate approximately one hundred forty kps and steady."

"Contact *Iwo Jima*. Advise them of the incoming bogies and request a course change, starboard twenty, up five."

"Yes, ma'am," Merrill acknowledged.

Commodore Ling would have simply ordered the carrier to change course, but Lorna was a lowly Lieutenant Commander. The carrier's captain would most likely comply since *Lynx* was his only escort, but Lorna was relieved when *Iwo Jima* accepted the request without question.

"Helm, when they turn, we turn with them. Maintain separation but put us directly between the carrier and the Bugs. Adjust acceleration as needed."

"Aye, ma'am," the helmsman acknowledged.

The turn would give the LFS ships better fields of fire against the incoming Bugs, as well as a better defensive position. The assault carrier packed significant firepower and excellent missile defenses. Its primary weaknesses were a lack of maneuverability and heavy armor. *Lynx* didn't have much in the way of armor either, but she was fast and deadly.

The turn would also take them somewhat closer to where Ling's group was already engaging the first incoming Bug force. Lorna didn't know whether the Commodore would be able to free up any ships to assist her, but this would make it easier to do so. The Bugs, she noted, had reacted to her course change and were accelerating. They must have realized they'd been spotted, and they wanted to close the distance as quickly as possible. Przbyzienski updated the information on Lorna's display as she keyed her command channel.

"Flag from *Lynx*. We have incoming. Nine hostiles including two heavies. We are adjusting course toward you, preparing for engagement in approximately forty-seven minutes. Transmitting tactical data to you now."

"*Lynx*, Flag, are you requesting assistance?" Ling's query came back after the few seconds of transmission delay.

Lorna hesitated. It would be nice to have some company, but Ling was facing a larger threat.

"Not at this time, Flag," she responded, "but I won't be upset if you decide to send some."

"Understood." The Commodore's voice held a hint of amusement. "We'll see what we can do."

Lorna checked her tactical displays again. The incoming Bugs were still boring in, but *Lynx* was now positioned as she had ordered, directly between the carrier and the threat. She checked her other display and found that Ling's force had taken a bite out of the first attackers. There appeared to be only two Bug cruisers and seven of the light attack craft still in action, but LFS *Leopard's* icon was flashing yellow, indicating significant battle damage, and was dropping back out of the action. As Lorna watched, LFS *Dragon* disengaged as well and turned back toward the carrier. *Dragon's* icon glowed the clear green of an undamaged, combat-effective ship. Apparently, Ling had decided to send reinforcements. A moment later, her command channel came to life again.

"*Lynx, Dragon*, we'll be joining you shortly," Commander Marcus Liddy, *Dragon's* captain advised. "Your present line looks good. We should be able to match vectors before you engage."

"Acknowledged, *Dragon*. You're the SO, Commander. Tell me how you want to play it."

"I like it just the way you have it set up, *Lynx*. You can move up a little to clear the carrier's field of fire, and we'll slide in low. *Dragon* will run the tac net, and we'll take 'em as they come."

"Roger that," Lorna replied. With only two ships, they didn't have the tactical edge Ling had in the first engagement. If they took it to the Bugs, any survivors that got by them would have an open shot at the carrier. *Iwo Jima* was not exactly helpless, but any battle damage she took could seriously impair the mission. Their best option was to stay tight, cover each other, and concentrate fire.

This would be Lorna's first combat engagement as a warship captain, but it was not her first encounter with the Bugs. She'd been the Navigation and Tactical Officer aboard *Lewis and Clark* eight years ago on the first mission to this star system. The cruiser had taken serious damage in that encounter, and nearly a quarter of her officers and crew had died. Lorna had gotten her baptism by fire and earned a Heart of Luna for the injury she had taken during the battle. *Eight years,* she thought, *and finally it's payback time, not just for* Elsie's *people, but for those villagers down on the planet.*

* * *

"Jefferson! Heads up, there! You OK?"

"Yessir! I mean, yes, Sergeant!"

Darius had never in his worst nightmares imagined space combat would be like this. He and Sergeant Hobbs were alone in the tiny compartment, sealed in with nothing but a damage control status board and the ship's comm system to give them any clues as to what was happening. The only thing they knew was that LFS *Lynx* was at battle stations and about to engage the enemy.

They were dressed in Marine DCR gear—environment suits with light body armor, which were significantly tougher than the shipsuits worn by the Navy crew, but nowhere near as tough as full combat armor. Neither had any sort of weapon. Instead, they were equipped with a variety of rescue tools, including laser cutters, heavy axes, and pry bars, all of which would be of no use to them if the enemy hit their part of the ship. The damage control station was deep in the ship's hull, about as well-protected as anywhere on board, but that didn't mean much in a lightly-armored ship like a destroyer.

Good news is we'll never know what hit us, Darius thought. *Bad news is we'll never know what hit us.* Somehow, the meager attempt at humor made him feel better. He managed to relax a bit and turned his attention back to the tool inventory checklist on the DC status display in front of him.

"Relax, kid." Hobbs grinned and punched him in the shoulder. "Just another wonderful day in the Corps. You ain't in boot camp anymore, so 'Sarge' will do."

No, I'm not in boot camp, he told himself, *and I'm not in one of those special services units. I guess I should have been more careful of what I wished not to get. Karma's a bitch for sure.*

No one in Darius' recruit platoon had gotten a special services billet. There had been rumors Fleet was working up to a big operation that would require a lot of Marines for combat units and warship duty. Two-thirds of his fellow recruits—those who made it through boot—had been assigned to combat battalions aboard one of Fleet's two assault carriers. There'd been a scattering of Air Wing assignments, also to units aboard those carriers, but Darius had found himself headed for Second Fleet, Charlie Company, Third Platoon, etc., which turned out to be the single squad assigned to LFS *Lynx*.

Up to this point, it hadn't been bad duty, just a lot of damage control drills, plus occasional small-unit combat training of the kind that could be conducted aboard a ship as small as a destroyer. He was starting to feel pride in the snarling wildcat patch he wore on his shoulder. His more-experienced shipmates made sure he knew that DesRon 12—of which *Lynx* was a part—was one of the Navy's elite combat units. From the serious chatter he was hearing on the command channel, they were about to prove it.

* * *

Battlecruiser LFS *Nike,* Inbound for Tatanna

"Your thoughts, Commodore O'Hara?"

John O'Hara looked up in surprise from the notes on his data pad. While he had no problem conversing with an Admiral—his father was a three-star—he still hadn't gotten used to being called "Commodore." He was technically a flag officer, though he had no command of his own. *I drew a staff assignment,* he mused, *but at least they sent me where the action is.*

"My first thought, Admiral, is that Von Moltke was right. Time for Plan Bravo."

Prussian Field Marshall Graf von Moltke was a 19th-century military strategist best remembered for his famous remark that no battle plan survives first contact with the enemy.

Admiral McGruder's look was sour, but he nodded because the citation was appropriate. The plan had called for Fleet's heaviest units—the battlecruisers *Nike* and *Amazon*, each supported by three heavy cruisers and screening destroyers—to engage the enemy in the outer system during the opening phase. The idea had been to draw whatever forces the Bugs had in the Sacagawea system to what appeared to be the most significant threat; however, the Bugs hadn't responded in force. The LFS heavies had encountered nothing but light picket forces that had fought fiercely but had led the attackers on a lengthy chase before being defeated without being reinforced. McGruder had been tempted to believe the Bugs had no heavy forces in the system, that they had been drawn away by Fleet's diversionary actions elsewhere.

Then the fast cruiser force sent to secure Tatanna's orbitals ran into a hornet's nest. Not only had the Bugs held heavy forces near the planet, they had also turned their orbital processing facility into a heavily-armed and well-defended fortress and had deployed hundreds of hard-to-detect robot weapons platforms in planetary orbit.

The plan had called for the LFS to assault the planet before the Bugs could organize a defense, then mop up the remaining Bug units in space. The Marine Assault Carriers *Iwo Jima* and *Omaha Beach*, with relatively light escorting forces, were supposed to get in quickly and take up station over the planet as soon as the orbitals were secured. They had been forced to slow their approach because the cruiser force was still heavily engaged. Worse, the Bugs had apparently had enough units clear of the planet to launch attacks on the carriers as well.

"Unfortunately," McGruder said with a sigh, "our only Plan B is even older than von Moltke's theorem; it goes back to Nelson at Trafalgar. Forget the fancy maneuvers, just go straight at them."

Nike, Amazon, and their consorts were doing just that—heading in-system toward the planet at maximum acceleration—but it would be twelve more hours before they could support the forces there. Meanwhile, McGruder had a decision to make. General Sherwood, aboard *Omaha Beach,* was requesting permission to take the carriers in on the theory that it was better to unload his forces under fire in orbit than to hold back in open space with Bug attack craft taking shots at them and their escorts. With light-minutes between them, McGruder couldn't have a face-to-face conversation with the Marine force commander, but he could sense the frustration of a hard-core warrior who wanted to get into the fight.

"All right, Jerry," he told his Chief of Staff, "message to *Omaha Beach* and *Iwo Jima*: Carriers to proceed with escorts to low orbit and commence drops. Godspeed and good luck."

"I guess the Bugs have learned a few things." He turned back to his staff around the conference table. "Every other time we stuck our nose into one of their systems, they came at us with everything they had, but now, when it's not a probe, when we're coming at them for real, they change up and hold their heavy stuff in reserve."

"We know they can adapt." O'Hara shrugged. "Their combat tactics have evolved over the years. We've seen less tendency to charge in blindly with guns blazing, more feints, and more attempts to flank or envelope. Fortunately, we've seen no such evolution in their hardware. They're still using the same ship types and weapons they used eight years ago when *Lewis and Clark* first encountered them here."

"Ours haven't improved much, either," McGruder reminded him. "Our ships are a little faster, and our missiles have longer range, but we haven't come up with any anti-Bug super-weapons. Ship-for-ship, we can take them easily, but they've got us outnumbered about three to one at the planet, and I've just sent the carriers into the middle of it. If any of you have any ideas other than a mad dash to reinforce them, speak now."

He looked around the table, but nobody spoke up.

* * *

LFS *Lynx*, Inbound for Tatanna

Darius expected some relief after the first battle. He thought things would get better, that there would be a break or some celebration of victory. He was disappointed.

He'd listened to the terse order-and-response dialog on the command channel—point defense active, incoming, commence missile fire, commence graser fire, target callouts, maneuvering—but none of it made sense because he couldn't see the tactical displays on the bridge. He felt a sudden lurch and heard a deep, ringing sound resonating through the ship's hull like a gong, followed by the terse call, "hit portside, hull breach on Bravo Deck, Frame 32." The damage control displays in front of him lit up with urgent red and yellow messages and flashing icons. The large deck plan displayed on the bulkhead showed a red band that went clear across Bravo Deck, indicating breached compartments and pressure loss.

He remembered a pre-battle briefing where they'd been told the Bugs used missiles with no warheads, just solid kinetic penetrators that relied on velocity at impact to inflict damage. Battlecruisers would suffer the least from such weapons since most of the penetrator's energy would be expended getting through the heavy battle armor, if it could get through at all. Cruisers and other medium-to-heavy ships would suffer most because their armor wasn't heavy enough to stop the penetrator, which would expend most of its energy inside the ship's hull.

Destroyers, they said, would suffer less damage than their heavier brethren because they had very little armor. With a broadside hit, the penetrator would pass cleanly through the ship, without expending all its energy, and would keep going. Like a bullet through a paper target, they said. Just one little hole. *Which is fine if you're not standing behind that paper target,* he remembered thinking at the time.

He looked at the display in front of him and decided they were right—whatever hit them had gone clear through the ship. More importantly, it apparently hadn't impaired Lynx's combat capabilities. According to the command channel, the Bug responsible for the hit had been taken out by the destroyer's grasers.

"Jefferson! You're up! Get back to Bravo Six and assist with damage repair and casualties as needed."

Sergeant Hobbs' order reminded Darius that he was supposed to be doing something other than staring at displays. He checked the seals on his suit as he got up. The compartment in question would be in vacuum—due to a large hole in the hull—and he would need to cycle in through a pressure lock. A quick look at the display showed Bravo Six was one of the port side missile batteries, normally manned by two crew members. He grabbed his rescue medkit and heavy multi-tool and headed out.

Halfway to his objective, he received a call from Hobbs telling him to forget Bravo Six—the Navy had everything under control there. He was to proceed to the Boat Bay on the starboard side of the ship, directly across from Bravo Six and in the missile's path, and help the Navy clear wreckage. There were no casualties because the boat bay wasn't normally manned during battle stations—the large compartment was normally depressurized in combat to prevent air loss if it was breached.

He arrived to find the bay doors holed in several places. The ship's Utility Boat—the only small craft the destroyer carried—had been torn loose from its docking clamps and lay in a heap against the doors. The Navy crew needed to clear the wreckage before the doors could be repaired and the compartment sealed. The boat was a total loss.

Darius pitched in. The repair would not have been a priority while the ship was under attack, but the battle was over. Captain Greenwood had ordered a stand-down from battle stations. Hobbs came by a few minutes later and told him to continue helping until the Navy petty officer in charge of the detail released him, then to get chow and some rest.

"Take a break while you can," Hobbs told him. "You never know when you'll get another chance."

Darius looked around. *My first time in combat, but everybody else is acting like it's no big deal, business as usual.* He wished, for about the 99th time, that he was aboard the carrier they were escorting, getting ready for a battle in which he could fight back.

* * *

"*L*ynx took one hit and one crew casualty, non-fatal. We lost one missile tube on the port broadside and had peripheral equipment damage. My people say it will be repaired within the hour. My U-Boat is a total loss, and the boat bay is out of service pending repair. No impact on combat-effectiveness."

Lorna looked at the array of captains on her screen as she reported to Commodore Ling. She was pleased her ship had done well in the first clash with the Bugs, but she was even more pleased that *Iwo Jima* had taken no damage. *Lynx* and *Dragon* had kept the attackers off the carrier until the rest of Ling's ships returned and swept the enemy out of space.

LFS *Leopard* had taken a couple of serious hits in Ling's earlier engagement and had lost three crew members. Her crews were still working on repairing the damage, but she was keeping up with the formation and had reported 90 percent effective in response to Ling's query. For the most part, the escort was still intact and the carrier untouched, but they'd been put on hold for orbital deployment because the advance force was still dealing with Bug problems around the planet.

"All right, people," Ling told them, "we just got word from Admiral McGruder. We're going in. Recon shows the Bug ground forces are still concentrated around their mining installations. Fleet wants to land the Marines before the Bugs get the bright idea of moving into human-inhabited areas and using the locals as shields.

"Be advised that the orbitals are still not secure. The carriers will be making their drops under fire, so we need to keep them covered as best we can. We will maintain Formation Alpha going in, but once *Iwo Jima* reaches orbit, I want to put most of our strength between them and the planet. The advance force says most of the opposition is coming up from below. I'll have deployment orders for you on approach. Any questions?"

Lorna had none, and apparently none of the other captains had any either. Commodore Ling always made a point of giving her officers the best available information. Sometimes, the reasoning behind an order was obvious, but, given time to explain, she never left that to chance.

* * *

Darius was most of the way through a light lunch when the "All Hands" announcement came. To his relief, it wasn't an immediate call to action. Captain Greenwood was giving everyone advance notice. They were headed in-system to put the carrier in orbit around the planet. Unfortunately, the orbitals were still "hot," and heavy resistance was expected. Barring any encounters on the way in, *Lynx* would be going back to Condition Red at 1400 hours. All off-watch crew was advised to get as much rest as possible until then.

Darius glanced at the chronometer on the bulkhead—1223, ship's time. He had about an hour and a half to grab… what? A nap? One of his instructors in Advanced Combat had told him that a Marine needed to learn how to sleep anywhere, anytime an opportunity arose.

Guess that's one combat skill I haven't learned yet. His nerves were still on edge from the first battle, and the prospect of another battle wasn't doing anything to calm him down. He looked around the crew's mess and saw some Navy types starting a card game at a nearby table. Others were swapping conversation, while a few had their pads out to read books or seek other entertainment. With a sudden flash of inspiration, he got out his pad and started composing a message to his sort-of-girlfriend back home. There wasn't much privacy in the mess, so he decided to text the message rather than doing a video chat. He did slap a quick shot of himself on the front end, so she could see what he looked like in his Marine BDUs.

Hey Jin. Feels kind of strange to be writing a text like this and not knowing when it will get to you. I'm a lot of light-years from Luna, and it's like we're back in the Dark Ages when people used to write letters to each other. I guess you won't get this until the ship drops out of hyper on the trip back home and connects with LunaNet. Anyway, this will be a long message since I can't just say "Hi how R U" and wait for an instant reply.

Suddenly, it occurred to him that his message might never get to her. He was in the middle of a war zone, and there was no guarantee the ship would ever get back to Luna. He'd been told mail was copied to the flagship whenever possible for just that reason, but that wouldn't happen unless he finished this message and sent it before they got into combat again. He turned back to the task with a greater sense of urgency. *We've been in a space battle, so I guess I can really call myself a Marine now.*

* * * * *

Chapter Four

LFS *Omaha Beach*, Inbound for Tatanna

"OK, Major, you're up."

Sherwood nodded to Nova Sakura and stepped away from the podium. Nova got up and quickly checked her uniform before stepping in front of the camera. This was Commander's Call—the last briefing before combat drops began. Every Marine aboard *Omaha Beach* would be looking at her. Since Sherwood was in command of the entire assault group for this operation, those aboard *Iwo Jima* would see her as well, but the second carrier was approaching the planet from the other side, several light-minutes away, and would receive the briefing with a delay dictated by the laws of physics.

"Thank you, sir," she began. "Marines, the general has just told you I'm the only officer ever to engage the Bugs in ground combat. That's correct, but don't expect me to give you some magic words that will guarantee victory. That engagement was over eight years ago, and I was a green second lieutenant with a single squad of Marines. Our primary objective was to disengage, evade, and escape from a superior Bug force that was hunting us. We did that, but it took several days, and we lost two Marines.

"The engagement was in this system on the planet that is our present objective, and we learned a few things. That information has already been factored into the mission plan, so I'm going to tell you things you've already heard, but they bear repeating, so listen up."

"For those officers who outrank me," she said with a hint of a smile, "*please* listen up, sir, or ma'am, as the case may be."

Nova couldn't see her audience, but a chuckle from General Sherwood convinced her that her attempt at humor had succeeded.

"To begin with," she said, putting on her serious combat face, "you people can walk around on that planet with nothing more than I'm wearing now." She stepped back to display the basic Battle Dress Uniform she was wearing.

"The Bugs can't do that. For them, it's a hostile environment. They're methane-breathers, and oxygen is toxic to them. Every Bug you encounter down there will be wearing a sealed environment suit or will be inside a sealed vehicle. Break those seals, and they're dead.

"What's more, methane burns when it meets oxygen. Break those seals with something hot enough, and you get a very satisfying explosion. We dropped a mortar round on top of a grounded Bug assault lander and witnessed a nice fireworks display. We used our one-and-only Scorpion to take down a Bug gunship with similar results. The Bug ground troops wear suits that look to be armored, but my sharpshooter took out several at over 400 meters with a standard 7mm sniper rifle—one shot, one kill. All it takes is one hole in that armor.

"That's the good news. Here's the bad. Bugs do not know fear, do not retreat, and will continue to attack until they achieve their objective or are called off by their superiors. From what we've discovered—from both space and ground encounters—their superiors consider all units expendable in pursuit of the objective. In short, they don't seem to care if they lose a thousand Bug soldiers killing ten of ours, unless they decide those thousand can be expended somewhere else with better results. They're cold, they're logical, and they obey orders to the death."

Nova paused for a moment to let that sink in, then she went on.

"Twentieth-century American General George Patton once said a wounded enemy soldier was worth more than a dead one, because it not only took that soldier out of action but also two others who went to his aid and carried him back from the lines.

"Don't count on the Bugs for that. A wounded Bug will continue to fight until it dies, and the other Bugs will ignore it if it is no longer contributing to the battle. I don't think the Bug Order of Battle includes any medics. That, ladies and gentlemen, is what we are up against.

"On the brighter side, that same narrow-minded determination can work against them. Bugs will march right into a minefield and keep going, simply because it's the most efficient way to clear the mines. If the mine field is big enough, they'll keep going until their entire force is wiped out, unless they are called off by orders from above. We set tripwires and mines behind us along our path of retreat. The Bugs kept walking into them until they were called off when the Navy came to our rescue and blew them out of space— which was a good thing because we would have run out of Claymores before they ran out of Bugs.

"I wish I could tell you more, but it was a squad-level engagement spread over two days. I hope I've given you some information you can use. Most importantly, I hope you understand that this is an enemy that can be beaten. They're big, and they're armor-plated, but they are not invincible, and their strengths can be used against them and turned into weaknesses. In about two hours, we're going to get a chance to prove that. Keep your heads together, cover each other, watch your six, and give 'em hell.

"Semper Fi."

* * *

Castle Boroson, *Algar Shektal*

"Lieutenant…"

"Yes, sir, I've seen it." Moira Bouchard held up her transponder, which showed three green lights and was identical to the one Ambassador Michaels was showing her. The transponder was typical of the tech gear available to the team—small, easily concealed, and not easily identified. It was designed to look like a small stone talisman worn on a leather thong around the neck. Bouchard and her people had no high-tech weapons, no communication or surveillance equipment, nothing that might cause anyone they encountered to suspect they were offworlders. As far as most of the castle staff were concerned, they were emissaries from a far corner of the kingdom who spoke with a strange accent that was common in their lands. Even the king's guards Bouchard was training thought she was a mystic female warrior from their world—a member of a strange cult of the Goddess who believed women should be primary defenders of the faith. In the beginning, she'd been forced to prove herself by knocking the stuffing out of the biggest and strongest of them in hand-to-hand combat, but she was an LFS Marine, and she got it done.

Michaels had returned to the castle three days ago. He had been dropped into the secret supply zone by a stealth courier that had arrived with the earliest Fleet units, then brought to the city in a closed carriage under the High Sheriff's protection. He'd delivered the news that the liberation of Tatanna was imminent but confirmed that Major Sakura would not be returning to the castle until after the dust settled. Bouchard was in charge of the Marine and Navy detail for the duration. Michaels had also delivered a temporary field commission, countersigned by Major General Sherwood, bumping her up to Second Lieutenant, but Bouchard would have traded it in a heartbeat for a platoon of fully armed, combat-ready Marines.

The transponder—their only source of information other than the messages delivered with their supply drops—could only convey standard coded messages and could only be activated by a pulse sent by a ship in Tatanna orbit. The display beneath the green lights showed a three-character code Bouchard had already decoded: *Operation in progress. Proceed per orders.* More importantly, the message meant friendly forces were already somewhere overhead.

"Have you talked to the king?" she asked.

"Yes, and I've told him it's happening. I advised him to lock down the castle as you suggested, but he says no. He wants no hint of anything out of the ordinary here until the Bugs are defeated. Business as usual; he'll even be holding audiences in the throne room today. He placed the guards under your command for the duration—and forced the Captain of the Guards to acknowledge it—but he won't allow any obvious defensive measures."

"Damn! That doesn't mean much if I can't deploy the guards or Marines for an in-depth defense. I'll need to assemble them in the stable and wait for the sentries to pass the word if the Bugs start acting up. I hate that—it's a reactive strategy that lets the enemy control the action. Do you suppose he'd get upset if I double the guards around the throne room? Four extra men shouldn't be too noticeable, especially if they're his House Guard and not Marines."

"It sounds reasonable to me, but His Majesty's a bit on edge today. Understandable, I guess, but it seems to bring out his stubborn streak. I'll ask him."

"Please do. Meanwhile, I'm going to double the guard at the main gate, without asking permission, in case we need to close it in a hurry. I'm also going to put a couple of my Marines on the walls. Damned glad we've got binoculars, though I could wish for a full suite of surveillance gear.

"I guess we'll have to make do. Bug weapons are pretty potent—" she looked at the ambassador with a crooked grin, "—but those walls are two meters of solid stone."

When she said it, she knew she could only hold the place for a limited time against a conventional assault by Bug ground forces. An airborne assault or kinetic strike from above could wipe out the defenders or take the entire castle off the map in a heartbeat. She was counting on the LFS Navy and Marines to keep that from happening.

* * *

LZ Alpha One, North Coast Province, Planet Tatanna

"Well, Major, does it look familiar?"

"Yes, sir, it does," Nova replied to the General's query. They were standing on the ridge overlooking the Bug mining site where her people first encountered the Bugs back in '04.

"It's been a few years, and there are a lot more Bugs this time, but it's definitely the same place. The mine has been extended to the northwest—following the ore, I guess. That Bug military equipment compound wasn't there, but we know they've been building up on this planet for years."

We should have hit them years ago, she reflected. *It's going to be harder now.*

The good news was that there appeared to be only twelve Bug installations on the planet. The Bugs only built near their mining sites and rarely ventured far from them because of the hostile—for them—environment. The huge ore processing and shipping station in synchronous orbit over the primary continent was presumed to be their command-and-control center, and the LFS Navy had already taken the station out of play. It was up to the Marines to clean out the Bug sites on the planet. That had to be done with some care, since most of them had communities of human miners living nearby.

This was the largest of the sites, and Sherwood had chosen it for his primary landing area and HQ. The Bug equipment compound was already a junkyard of twisted wreckage, thanks to air strikes sent in well before the general and his staff landed with the first wave of Marines. Nova was thankful there were no humans working the mines. Apparently, the Bugs had shut down mining and sent them away before the assault started. The area looked deserted—by both humans and Bugs.

The Bugs had had enough warning to redeploy some of their forces in the wilderness to the north. The Marines were heavily engaged in that area, and another air strike had been called in. As she watched, a pair of Marine Raptors delivered a low level strike that cut a swath of destruction across the forest on the other side of the mine.

Any locals still in the area must think Armageddon has arrived, she thought with a grim smile. The village to the west wasn't deserted when the Marines landed, but the villagers didn't seem inclined to come out to see what was happening. Generations of living under Bug rule had convinced them curiosity was not conducive to a long life. She hoped they would stay in their homes. If they fled across the countryside, they might well wind up in somebody's field of fire.

"Your observations regarding Bug air capability are holding true," Sherwood remarked. "As long as the Navy can keep them from hitting us from orbit, we appear to own the skies."

Nova had spent years on Tatanna gathering intelligence. Ambassador Michaels had spent his time learning everything he could about Tatanna's human society, but her primary concern had been the Bugs. Early on, she'd noticed they seemed to lack any atmospheric transport or attack capability. Whatever they needed—including ground assault troops and any support they required—was always dropped in from orbit.

"That's true, sir, but I hear the Navy's finding the Bugs a bit more difficult than expected."

"Yes, they are. They're pulling in the heavies from the outer system. It appears the Bugs didn't take the bait and are keeping everything they've got here, around the planet. The Navy's got *Omaha Beach* covered, but they're having a rough time keeping the Bugs clear of *Iwo Jima*. Bradley's getting his drops off, but his escorts are having a hell of a time."

Nova sighed. *We'll get it done, but it's not going to be the walk in the park Lunar HQ made it out to be. I tried to tell them, but...* She wondered if her heartfelt desire to rid this lovely planet of Bugs hadn't made her sugar-coat her assessments a bit. *No,* she decided, *I don't believe I ever did that. I guess somebody up there wanted to do this as much as I did.*

The mention of *Iwo Jima's* escorts brought another thought to her mind. *Blondie's up there. Wonder how she's doing.*

* * *

Castle Boroson, *Algar Shektal*

Ronor T'Korval waited impatiently in the hall outside Algar's Throne Room. Duke High Reaches was an honored guest who had been granted a royal audience without question. As a nobleman of the realm, he was not kept waiting with any degree of discomfort. He sat with his aides in an alcove with comfortable chairs and a table. Servants brought them food and drink while they waited.

Still, he had to await the king's pleasure, and Algar had not yet opened the door to petitioners. Until that happened, Ronor could not relax. He looked around the hall, trying to judge the mood, looking for anything that might hinder him in reaching his goal.

Most of the waiting crowd were commoners, primarily merchants seeking the Crown's justice or support in commercial matters. A few others were landed gentry with minor grievances for redress. Scattered among them were some who carefully avoided any appearance of recognition or attention to the duke—twenty of his best guardsmen, disguised in simple journeymen's clothing. He smiled at what he perceived as a sign of the Goddess' favor. The cold, early-fall weather allowed them to dress with enough bulk to conceal weapons without arousing suspicion.

He had visited this hall many times in the past to present his opposition to some policy or decree he didn't like. Algar always received him cordially and listened patiently but seldom granted his petition. Today would be different. He smiled at the thought of putting his monarch to the sword and seizing the throne for himself.

If the usual patterns were followed, the doors would open, and he, as befitted his noble status, would enter first with his two attendants, who also concealed arms, to be presented directly to King Algar. The other petitioners would be allowed to enter but would be stopped behind the row of tables where the king's clerks would take note of their grievance and bid them wait to be called.

Ronor's intention was to engage Algar in a presentation of one of his usual complaints to delay him until all his men were in position. At a secret signal from him, they would attack the clerks and create mayhem. This would draw the attention of the guards to the rear of the hall, leaving Ronor inside the king's defenses. He would strike, and the king would be dead before any could intervene.

His men should be sufficient to take the king's guards and deal with any others in the throne room who looked to be a problem. He would have to move swiftly to his next objective, finding Prince Arne, so Algar's only heir could be sent to join his father. His agents had told him Arne was somewhere in the palace and had not been outside the walls for several days. They had also supplied him with diagrams of the palace, including the royal residence suites where Arne was most likely to be found.

All depended on swift, bold action, but Ronor was prepared and confident. By the end of the day, he would rule Tatanna!

He felt a momentary twinge of anxiety as two more of the king's guards appeared to supplement the pair standing beside the Throne Room door, but no more appeared, and he knew those outside wouldn't be a factor once his people were inside the doors. Even if the guards inside were also doubled, they would only be four against his twenty.

He forced himself to relax and settled back in his chair to await Algar's convenience.

* * * * *

Chapter Five

Assault Force Bravo, in Tatanna Orbit

On the bridge of LFS *Lynx*, Lorna Greenwood felt a lessening of tension. The latest wave of Bugs had been decimated without scoring a single hit on *Iwo Jima*, and now, there was only one Bug left. It was twisting and turning in a complex evasion pattern, but Lorna was confident *Lynx's* gunnery would deal with it before it could get past her. *Frisbee's tracking it, and he'll let it have the full graser broadside as soon as he's dialed in. Serious overkill, but why take a chance?* It looked like the Bug was trying to go over her, and she ordered a slight roll to port to give her tactical officer a clear shot.

* * *

The Bug pilot was a Level 4 Tech-Warrior. As such, it was allowed a certain amount of discretion within mission parameters. The mission was the destruction of the very large human ship, one of two such behemoths currently in orbit that were unloading ground forces and support equipment to the planet below. It was understood that no single attacker could accomplish the mission, but each was expected to inflict what damage it could in support of the goal.

The Bug had already expended its four missiles to no effect. The smaller ship had formidable missile defenses, and the one that got past them had been destroyed by the target's defensive fire. The only remaining option was to ram the target, and the Bug was prepared to do so. The certainty of its own death played no part in the decision. The mission required it.

All four of its wing mates had already been destroyed. Three had been hit by the smaller ship's primary beam weapons, the first one before it had fired all its missiles. The last one had almost gotten past the smaller enemy, only to be hit by heavy fire from the target. Logic told the Bug there was no chance its final attack would succeed, but that would not in any way stop it from trying.

A Level 4 was not a mindless robot. It reasoned that if it could damage or destroy the smaller ship, future attacks would have a greater chance of success since the large one would be less well defended.

* * *

At *Lynx's* tactical station, Senior Lieutenant Przbyzienski suddenly sat up and stared at his displays. The Bug had almost reached the point where he planned to open fire on it as it went by, but it had made a radical course change and was heading directly toward the destroyer! Flashing warnings told him the sudden, unexpected maneuver had caused his grasers to lose lock, and he knew he wouldn't reacquire the target in time.

He stabbed an icon on the defense systems panel to designate the Bug as an incoming missile. The fast-tracking point-defense lasers locked on immediately and opened fire, but it wasn't going to be enough. The lasers were designed to recharge quickly and deliver rapid, precision fire on much smaller targets. They would damage the incoming Bug ship, but it was unlikely they could destroy it completely or stop its headlong charge. There was no doubt about the enemy's intention—it was going to ram them.

"Ma'am!" He turned to Lorna with a helpless look.

"Helm! Hard starboard now!" she ordered.

It was a desperation move, an attempt to twist out of the Bug's path, but it was too late. The destroyer had just begun to turn when the Bug slammed into her starboard side just aft of midship where her fusion plant was located.

LFS warship power plants were designed to take battle damage and to fail as safely as possible. If it were hit, the core of star-hot plasma vented to space rather than consuming the ship in a nuclear fireball. The bulkheads fore and aft of the reactor containment were the strongest transverse structures in the ship, and both the keel and dorsal spines were heavily reinforced above and below the plant. LFS *Lynx* was not consumed and did not break in half when her fusion plant took the impact, but nearly a third of her crew died in an instant, and what remained of her aft section when the fireball faded was little more than a skeleton of burned and twisted structural members.

Amidships and forward, structural damage was surprisingly light, though extreme stresses on the hull breached several compartments. Most of the crew had been at their stations, wearing their shipsuits and secured in shock-resistant seats. There were few serious injuries among the survivors. Most of the ship's systems were no longer functional, and others would remain in service only until emergency power sources were depleted. Emergency seals activated, and all compartments that remained airtight were on limited internal life support.

On the bridge, now illuminated by red emergency lighting, most of Lorna's command displays were dark. Those that weren't only displayed bad news. Internal communications were working, but she wasn't getting any reports aft of frame 52 amidships. She tried not to think about how many people she'd lost, including her Executive Officer and the backup command team in Auxiliary Control. She needed to focus on the survivors and what she needed to do to save the ship and keep them alive.

Save the ship? She felt a crushing sense of defeat as she realized that wasn't going to happen.

* * *

"No communication with *Lynx*, ma'am. Her emergency beacons have triggered, but she's going down, and we're not going to reach her."

"Acknowledged." On the bridge of LFS *Jaguar*, Rebecca Ling had already reached the same conclusion. *I left them out there on the sharp end of the stick.*

Yes, you did, her cold, analytical command sense told her. *You had no choice, and she did well the last time. For that matter, she did well this time, but fortunes of war. Karma. Whatever. Too late to do anything about it.*

They'd inserted *Iwo Jima* into the very low orbit required to deploy the Marines, then Ling had been forced to split her forces to meet multiple threats. The heaviest had come from the planet's larger moon. She'd sent the two light cruisers to meet that threat, then taken *Jaguar* and *Cougar* to deal with an enemy force coming up behind them. She'd deployed the battle-damaged *Leopard* ahead to watch the front door and left *Lynx* in a lower orbit to guard against anything coming up from the planet. She'd known it was a likely threat axis, but she'd put a lot of faith in her most junior captain.

She did a damned fine job, Ling thought bitterly. *Five to one, and she got four of them before the last one got her.*

Standard procedure called for supporting ships to move in on the crippled destroyer and remove any injured crew, then tow it to a secure area, but *Lynx's* final vector was taking her down from orbit, and she tumbled slowly as she fell toward the planet. The tumbling would stop when she reached the tenuous upper atmosphere, and aerodynamic forces came into play, but the ship was not designed for atmospheric flight.

She wouldn't burn up like a typical de-orbiting satellite because her reentry speed was too low. "In orbit" was a loosely applied term where gravity-powered ships were concerned. The assault force had been hovering over the deployment point on the planet, its orbital velocity held to the planet's speed of rotation. With its non-aerodynamic design, *Lynx* would break into several very large pieces on the way down, and those large pieces would make very large craters wherever they hit.

Get them out of there, Greenwood, Ling pleaded, hoping fervently someone was still alive to hear her plea.

* * *

One external video display was still working, and the ship's slow rotation gave alternating views of the planet below and deep space above. The navigational position display that was functional told the story, and Lorna had reached the same conclusion as her commodore. Thankful the "All

Hands" icon was still lit on her console, she touched it and gave the most painful order of her career.

"All hands, this is the captain. Abandon ship. Repeat, abandon ship. Officers and NCOs, account for your people and get them to the lifepods. Launch at local discretion. Do not wait for further orders. Damage control, sweep the ship. Make sure no one is left behind. I say again, abandon ship."

"Mr. Frisbee," she ordered, getting up from her command chair, "the bridge crew is your responsibility. Get them to the lifepods. I'm going forward to help DC with the sweep. Don't wait for me."

"Ma'am—" Przbyzienski started to protest, but Lorna held up her hand.

"Don't worry, Cas, I'll be along. I'm pretty sure Morrison's gone, and that makes you my exec. Get everybody off."

She rarely used the diminutive of his first name, but it had the desired effect, and he saluted her sharply.

"Yes, ma'am, will do."

She gave him a grim smile that lacked any trace of humor. "Besides, it's my job to be the last one off."

* * *

"Let's go, Jefferson, we're up!" Hobbs was already on his feet, checking his gear. Darius was trying to make sense of the displays in front of him.

"Simple sweep from the bow aft," Hobbs told him. "You take Alpha Deck, I'll take Bravo. Internal gravity's on emergency power, only about a quarter gee, so move carefully and use the handrails."

Darius looked at the deck plan on the forward bulkhead. The fore end compartment on the upper—Alpha—deck was the chase cluster, the 40-cm graser battery, and its associated equipment. The compartment was not manned unless maintenance or repair work was needed, but he would check it anyway. On the lower—Bravo—deck, Hobbs would start at the forward loading racks for the two chase missile tubes. The racks were automated, but the compartment would normally have two missile techs to watch over the loading process. By now, all forward compartments should be empty, or emptying, as crew members headed for the lifepods, but it was their job to see that nobody stayed behind.

"How far aft do we sweep?" he asked.

"Lifepod clusters at frame thirty-six," Hobbs replied. "Midships DC should get everything from there back to the lifepods at forty-eight, and they'll also check aft, as far as they can."

"Sarge, do you think there's anybody back there?" Darius pointed at the display for the aft part of the ship. Most of the sections were flashing a red message, "No Data Available."

"Honestly, kid, I think the fusion plant got dumped. I don't think there's a ship back there."

* * *

"Sir, they've deployed lifepods! I see ten, no, there's one more. Make it eleven, and they're all at retrievable altitude."

"Acknowledged." Lieutenant Commander Rogers studied the display as LFS *Leopard* closed the range. Like the ship that had spawned them, the lifepods were skimming the upper reaches of the planet's atmosphere, but unlike *Lynx*, they were light enough for *Leopard's* grav tractors to pull them up to orbital level where they could be retrieved.

That wouldn't be true much longer, though. Any that didn't get out in the next minute or two would have to take the long ride down to the planet's surface. The lifepods were designed for that, but it would then be up to the Marines down there to locate and rescue the occupants.

Eleven pods, no, make it thirteen. Two more had just separated from the tumbling hulk. The LFS standard lifepod could carry eight people, so as many as 104 survivors could have gotten clear so far. A *Predator*-class destroyer had a full complement of 130 and carried 24 pods, an excessive number, to allow for possible battle damage.

Doesn't mean there will be that many survivors. I'd be surprised if there were. He studied the image of the shattered destroyer and decided they'd be lucky if even half the ship's crew were still alive. *We can hope for eight, but it only takes one person to launch a lifepod.*

It looked like *Leopard* was the only ship that would reach the scene in time to do any good. His people had already acquired tractor locks on the first two pods.

The good news is that Jaguar *and* Cougar *are coming and are close enough to get in the fight if the Bugs show up again. This rescue is going to keep us busy for a while.*

He studied the display, willing more lifepods to appear.

* * *

Lorna was headed forward on "A" deck when she met Jefferson coming aft. He assured her he had not missed anyone, so she stayed with him the rest of the way back to Frame 36. There they found one pod launching while Lieutenant Przbyzienski, Ensign Mary Jane McGill, and Sergeant Hobbs loaded the last four stragglers into another one.

"Everyone aft of here is already gone, ma'am. We launched ten pods aft and four from here so far. This is it," the acting exec told Lorna.

She looked at the remaining group and realized they would need one more pod, which was not a problem since there were three more at this station with green status displays. Przbyzienski wanted to put his captain in the first one, but she wouldn't have it.

"Get out there and take charge, Mr. Frisbee. You too, Sergeant."

She waved Hobbs aboard, then turned to Darius and McGill.

"I'm with you, ma'am, otherwise my sweep's not complete," Darius said before she could speak. He surprised her with his stubborn audacity.

"I'm with you as well, ma'am. Plenty of room in this one." McGill had already opened the hatch on another pod and was starting the pre-launch check.

Lorna shook her head, then turned to Przbyzienski.

"Close it up and go," she ordered. He nodded, tossed her a salute, and climbed aboard. The hatches closed, and the green lights showed a good seal, then they felt the heavy vibration as the pod launched. The three of them were, as far as they knew, the last survivors still aboard *Lynx*.

* * *

"M a'am?" McGill was looking at Lorna, who had taken a step toward the waiting pod, then stopped, a look of sudden concern on her face.

"Stand by. I need to check something below."

"Huh?" It was hardly an appropriate response from a Marine Private to an order from his captain, but Darius was taken by surprise when Lorna turned suddenly and went through the nearby hatch and down the ladder. He turned to McGill, who looked equally surprised.

"Go with her, Marine. She may need help with… whatever it is," McGill ordered. "I'll finish prepping this thing, but I'm not leaving until the two of you get back."

* * *

L orna didn't have far to go. The crew's mess was just forward of Frame 36 on Bravo Deck, and when she ducked through the hatch, she saw her concern had been valid. The module mounted on the aft bulkhead showed two steady green lights and one flashing amber. It was sealed and powered up but running on internal power because the ship's power systems were down.

They forgot Bob! Lorna thought with dismay.

Cats had long been the favored pets of the Lunar Free State. The first citizens had brought cats with them when they settled on the Moon, and the cats flourished there because they adapted well to living in a sealed environment, whether on Luna or aboard ship. Nothing in Fleet regulations permitted or forbade having them aboard LFS warships, and having a cat aboard had become a Navy tradition. A small ship like a destroyer usually only had one, while capital ships might have several. So, there was no way a destroyer squadron that called itself the Cat Pack would be without, and no way a ship called *Lynx* would have one named anything other than

"Bob." Bob was a tabby-patterned Maine Coon, who might have been mistaken for a small bobcat were it not for his long, fluffy tail.

In battle, humans were protected by shipsuits and strapped into shock frames at their duty stations, but somewhere back in history, Fleet had decided that feline "crewmembers" needed protection as well. The life support module had been provided so Bob could be secured inside when the ship went to battle stations. Bob accepted his confinement without a fuss, knowing that when he was released, the crew would make it up to him with special treats and attention.

How could they have left him?

Lorna knew the bitter answer to that one. The crew from Main Engineering had made themselves Bob's self-appointed keepers. When the reactor lost containment, it was unlikely any of them survived. Nobody was on duty in the mess during combat, and whoever checked the compartment aft of it had only looked for human survivors.

She thought about taking the cat out of the module but rejected the idea. If he got nervous or upset, he might bolt. She had no desire to chase after a furry creature that knew every nook and cranny aboard. Fortunately, the module designers had planned for situations in which the module needed to be moved. Lorna pulled the three locking pins, disconnected a single cable, and lifted the entire module away from its mount. It was light and compact, and Bob didn't mass much more than seven kilos. With internal gravity down to a quarter gee, she had no problem handling it.

* * *

The doomed ship was now several kilometers deep into the tenuous upper atmosphere of Tatanna. In reaction to the thin airflow, she had stopped tumbling and assumed a semi-stable attitude. The pressure of flowing air wasn't much, but it was enough to flex her aft hull structure and stress the already weakened structural members to the breaking point. A huge chunk of the aft section broke loose, upsetting the delicate balance and causing the hulk to slew violently to one side before swinging back and restabilizing with a slight change of attitude.

* * *

Lorna was crossing the mess hall with the module in hand when the sudden lurch swept her off her feet and sent her sliding across the deck. Instinctively, she wrapped her arms around the module. She gritted her teeth at the sudden pain as her left shoulder struck a column that supported one of the dining tables. An instant later, her head struck the bulkhead, and she lost consciousness.

* * *

Darius had just turned to enter the mess hall when he was also swept off his feet. His back struck flat against the opposite side of the corridor, and the impact knocked the breath out of him for a moment but caused no injury. On the less violent rebound, he caught the edge of the mess hall hatch and secured himself until the motion stopped. To his dismay, he saw the captain down on the deck, still clutching the module with one hand.

What the hell is that thing? His damage control training had not included the module as a vital piece of equipment. *Whatever it is, Captain Greenwood thought it was important enough to go back for it.* He reached Lorna's side and tried to check her for injuries. Her suit's readout showed good vital signs, but she'd taken a knock to the head and wasn't responding. He hated to risk further injury, but he had to get her out of there and take that crazy box with him as well.

Lorna was as tall as Darius, but nowhere near as heavy. In the reduced gravity, he found it easy to sling her over his shoulder. That left one hand free to grab the module. Thus burdened, he headed out the hatch and back to the ladder to "A" deck. By the time he reached it, she was beginning to wake up and seemed to be feeling some pain.

Darius put down the module and eased her down to the deck, noticing for the first time that the captain was an attractive woman. She was a bit older than he was... well, to be honest, more like ten years older, but...

She came awake and winced in pain as she tried to move. Darius jerked himself back to reality. *She's your captain, damn it! Get it together, Marine.*

"Ma'am, are you OK?"

"Shoulder," she said, waving at her left side. "Don't think I can use this arm."

"We've got to get you up this ladder, ma'am," he said.

"Low grav," she responded. "I think I can make it with one hand."

"OK, just wait one," he replied. "I'll get help, just in case, ma'am."

He grabbed the module and went up the ladder. *She's right,* he decided, *no problem doing it with one hand in this gravity.* He set the module down on the deck above, then called out.

"Ensign McGill, are you OK?"

"I'm OK," she replied, appearing at the hatch a second later. "Nasty ride, but I was sitting down in the pod. Where's Captain Greenwood?"

"Down there. She's hurt but not bad. We've got to get her up here. This—" he waved at the module, "—is what she went back for."

"Dear Lord!" McGill gasped. "It's Bob! They forgot Bob!"

Suddenly, Darius got it... *the ship's cat!* "Well, OK, he's safe now, so let's get the captain up here, ma'am." He had to keep reminding himself that McGill was an officer. He had also noticed that she, too, was an attractive young woman. *Younger than the captain, but not quite as good-looking. Damn it, Marine, get it together. You picked a hell of a time to let your hormones loose.*

They finished the task in an orderly manner, despite Darius' reluctance to put his hands on the captain's attractive stern aspect to help her as he followed her up the ladder. In less than a minute, they were inside the pod, strapping in and securing Bob's module, while McGill initiated the launch sequence. The pod separated from the destroyer's hull with a heavy lurch and started the long, downward journey.

"We're clear, ma'am," McGill reported, "but we're too low for orbital retrieval. Our beacon's on, and I tried the comm, but I can't contact anyone. I think we're in the ionized layer of the atmosphere. Nobody's going to hear us—won't even pick up the beacon. How's the shoulder? Is there anything we should be doing for it?"

"I'm pretty sure it's dislocated. That can be fixed, but I don't think I can do it myself."

"I can do it." Darius surprised himself again by volunteering. "Saw it done a couple of times to guys on my high school z-ball team. You play that rough in zero gee, and sometimes something gets jerked out of place."

"That makes you the closest thing we've got to an expert," Lorna told him. She turned to him and presented her injured shoulder. "Have at it."

Darius swallowed hard, suddenly reluctant. He hoped he remembered what he had seen. Fortunately, his coach had been talkative and had explained what he was doing to anyone who happened to be watching. *Let's see, I think he put his hand about here and pressed, then he grabbed the arm like this and...* He gritted his teeth and pulled the arm in what he thought was the right direction. The captain let out a sharp exclamation of pain. Under his hand, Darius felt the joint pop back into place.

Lorna took a deep breath and let it out, then looked directly at Darius.

"Good job, Marine... damned good job." She moved the arm tentatively and winced again. "It'll hurt for a while, but I've got my arm back. Let's check on Bob."

* * *

The cat proved to be uninjured and surprisingly unruffled. Like the ship they'd left behind, the lifepod was maintaining minimal internal gravity, but that didn't seem to bother Bob. He'd been through low-gravity drills before. He perched himself on a vacant seat and looked expectantly at them.

"Sorry, Bob," McGill told him. "We forgot to pack the cat treats. Can I offer you a protein bar instead?"

To her surprise, the cat accepted the offering and nibbled at it in apparent satisfaction. McGill turned to Lorna with a smile that faded at the look of cold desolation on her captain's face.

"Ma'am…"

"My ship," Lorna said. "I've lost my ship… and so many good people…"

Until then, it hadn't been real to McGill. In the heat of battle, in the rush to get everyone off the ship, she'd kept herself frantically busy, which gave her no time to consider what had happened. When she saw the look on Lorna's face, everything came down on her like a crushing weight. Tears came, flowing freely. She bent her head and tried to stifle the sobs that forced their way out.

* * *

Lorna put her good arm around the younger woman's shoulders but said nothing. There was nothing to say, and she couldn't shed her own tears yet. She was the captain. She had to maintain, to persevere, to overcome, even if these were the only two left to see it. Later, sometime when she was alone, she would let herself go, but for now, these two were her responsibility, and they were not yet safe.

The pod would free fall partway to the surface but would eventually power up its grav thrusters to keep the approach velocity low. Its landing system was fully automated, and it would conserve power so it could maneuver at low altitude in the hope of finding a suitable landing zone. Eventually, its power cells would run out, and it would have to land somewhere, but it would be about two hours before that happened.

* * *

"We retrieved fifteen pods, ma'am," Rogers reported, "for a total of eighty-one survivors. Unfortunately, neither *Lynx's* captain nor exec appear to have made it out. Her tactical officer was aboard the last pod we picked up, and he told us the captain and two others were supposed to be in a pod right behind him, but we watched until the ship started to break up, and we didn't see any more pods. I suppose there could have been some, but I doubt it. We wouldn't have been able to retrieve them anyway, so they'd have to make planetfall."

Damn! Damn, damn, damn! Rebecca Ling could find no words to express her feelings. *Greenwood was good! She would have hoisted her own flag someday, I'm sure of it. Worse, she's the end of a legendary line. Her grandmother mentored my mother and was one of my heroines back in the day. I'd hoped to do the same for her, pay it forward for what inspired me.*

"I'll pass the word to the Marines, just in case." Ling managed to maintain her stoic command face as she replied to *Leopard's* captain. "Looks like the wreck is going down along the east coast of the primary continent. If there are any more pods, they'll end up there as well."

"You've done well, Phil," she added. "Don't beat yourself up. You saved all that could be saved. I need you to link up with *Iwo Jima* and transfer the survivors. The carrier has more space and better facilities than you do. When you're clear, take up the point position again. I'm going to put *Dragon* in the low guard slot."

If Greenwood could tear up the Bugs so thoroughly with a destroyer, a light cruiser ought to really ruin their day.

* * * * *

Chapter Six

Castle Boroson, West Tower

Sword in hand, Moira Bouchard climbed the long spiral stairs. Her face showed no emotion; she felt only a cold determination, a deadly purpose. Nothing she could do would restore what she had lost, but she didn't pause or slow her quick and purposeful steps. She was on a mission.

She had been on her way to check the sentries at the front gate when a panicked crowd erupted from the main doors of the palace. They ran straight at her, and it took her a moment to realize they were running for the gate behind her. They wanted out, to escape from the castle walls as quickly as possible.

"*Ko ita?*" she demanded, grabbing one by the arm. *What's happening?*

The man was a short, overweight merchant, who was stumbling along and gasping, already out of breath. He jerked away from her and screamed words that chilled her to the bone.

"Murder! Murder in the throne room!"

She yelled orders to the guards to close and seal the gates, to let no one pass in or out. She bucked the fleeing crowd and ran into the palace toward the outer chamber and the throne room beyond.

When she arrived, she saw carnage. Three guards and two other men were down at the door, lying in spreading pools of blood. The fourth guard was inside, dead from a knife wound to the back. She worked her way around the dead bodies piled in front of the throne and noted that they included the rest of the king's guards. She raced up the steps and stopped suddenly as she tried to grasp what she saw before her.

King Algar was dead. So were several of his advisors, who had been sitting at tables beside the throne. All had been brutally hacked to death with edged weapons, but the king had been beheaded as well, and his head had been left on the seat of the throne.

"Moira…"

Bouchard heard her name, a bare whisper to her left, and turned to confront her worst nightmare. Ramis was still alive, but she knew as she took him in her arms that his wounds were mortal.

"Who did this?" she asked, trying to look at his face through her sudden tears.

"The duke…" He struggled to speak. "High Reaches… Ronor T'Corval…"

He coughed blood, then clutched her sleeve.

"The prince," he whispered. "Save the prince." His hand fell away from her arm, and his head rolled to the side as he died.

She held him for a moment, then kissed him gently for the last time and laid him down on the floor. She stood up.

Moira Bouchard was an LFS Marine whose first combat specialty had been sniper. Given a high-tech modern rifle, she could take out an enemy at a thousand meters with a single shot, but like all combat Marines, she'd been trained to use a blade as well. For the last several years, she'd been posted on Tatanna, where the sword was the high-tech weapon of the realm, and she'd honed her skills against the best swordsmen in the king's service.

They'd been reluctant to accept her because she was a woman. Nothing was held back in training, and even with wooden practice swords, injuries were common. She'd been forced to insult some of the men to the point of anger before they would take her on, but she'd proven herself and was now an acknowledged mistress of the sword.

The Marine Combat Sword, issued for dress as well as field use to officers and NCOs, was the product of thousands of years of swordmaker's craft on Earth combined with the advanced metallurgy of the 22nd century. In form, it resembled a Japanese *katana*, but unlike the legendary single-edged sword of the Samurai, the forward third of its spine was a razor edge. Its point was sharply tapered to produce a weapon that was as good for thrusting as it was for slashing. Though light and fast, it was far stronger than the heavier blades produced on Tatanna. Bouchard had worn the sword in public and practiced with it in private, but no Tatannan had ever seen what it could do.

The prince... save the prince...

Prince Arne seldom attended his father's daily sessions in the throne room. He would be in the west tower, the Royal Residence, with his wife.

Her mission clear, Moira Bouchard moved with a purpose. She drew her sword as she left the bloody scene of the assassination. On her way out, she noted without feeling that Ambassador Michaels, lying near the front door, was another victim of the slaughter.

* * *

Bouchard moved upward at a steady pace, balancing the need for haste with the need to conserve energy for the battle she was sure lay ahead. The attackers had encountered feeble resistance on the way up. She had already passed the bodies of several members of the palace staff and two palace guards. From the sounds ahead, she judged there was resistance at the door to the prince's chambers.

She arrived and found a dozen men, led by one she assumed was the duke, engaging two surviving guards. The duke's minions were dressed in common clothing, though each wore a scarlet band around one arm, presumably so they could identify each other in the melee. The duke wore full court regalia, including, she noticed, a shirt of well-polished chain mail.

The guards were holding for the moment. They had backed into the door's alcove, where they could only be reached if the attackers stood directly in front of the opening, but one appeared to be wounded, and she knew they would fall soon. She strode forward in silence, but one of the killers must have sensed her approach. He spun around and died before he could raise the crude battle-axe he carried. The next one started to turn, but she cut him down as well. His scream of anguish alerted the others to her presence.

Two of the attackers at the front continued to deal with the last guard. The rest turned to face her, with weapons that ranged from long daggers to short-handled axes. Except for the duke, who'd worn his long sword in an ornate scabbard across his back; they'd been forced to bring weapons they could conceal under their clothing.

One lunged forward with a knife, only to fall back with a scream as his arm, the hand still grasping the knife, landed on the stone floor with a thud and a clatter. Bouchard followed the downward slash with an upward thrust to the left that earned her a bonus. She impaled not only the nearest attacker but also the man who had pressed in too closely behind him. Her right leg snapped up in a kick that took another under the chin, broke his neck, and hurled him backward into his cohorts. She retrieved her bloody sword and dropped into a guard position as they fell back. One heavy brute tried to edge around her to the left, and she locked eyes with him as she stepped in his direction. For a moment, they stared at each other, then a look of horror appeared on his face.

"Muh-Rah!" he shouted to the others. "Muh-Rah has come for us!"

A stab of anguish pierced Bouchard's icy calm. In the theology of Tatanna, Muh-Rah was the Angel of Death. She was the warrior handmaiden of the Goddess, who sent her to slay evildoers and hurl them into the coldest depths of Hell. When they had first met years ago, Ramis had called her Muh-Rah, a play on her first name and a tribute to her warrior skills. Ramis, the gentle scholar with whom the warrior woman had fallen deeply in love.

"Yes!" she hissed in a voice of pure venom, "Muh-Rah has come for you."

With a shriek, the man dropped his sword and hurled himself through the stained-glass tower window. It was an unfortunate choice for an escape route, as his flight came to an abrupt and fatal end on the stone-paved courtyard 30 meters below.

She turned and leaped forward, taking two more of the marauders down before they could react. She was cold. She was death. She felt nothing. She planned nothing. She saw an opportunity and struck without thinking. One bent forward, and she beheaded him with an upward stroke.

By then, the remaining attackers had broken through the door into the prince's chamber. Led by their duke, they charged inside and across the outer sitting room toward the bedchamber beyond. The last one in tried to close the door, but Bouchard kicked it open and knocked him backward. Before he could recover, she cut him open from shoulder to hip and stepped over him as he fell. With another slash, she cut down the hanging curtain that closed off the bedchamber and dropped it on an attacker who had hidden behind it, hoping to take her in ambush. She impaled him before he could get clear of the falling curtain and stepped into the room.

Prince Arne stood beside the bed, holding an ornate buckler and short sword, taken from a wall display, with trembling hands. Myrel, still in her dressing gown, huddled behind him on the bed as the duke, bloody sword in hand, faced her husband.

Two more details to take care of. Bouchard saw an opening, and her blade took one of the attacker's arms off as it cut halfway through his upper torso. The other attacker held a long spear, an infantryman's pole arm taken from one of the palace guards. He tried to use it to block Bouchard's overhand slash, but he died anyway when her blade sliced through the wooden shaft without slowing. The duke raised his sword, preparing to batter down the prince's meager defense.

"High Reaches!" Bouchard shouted, summoning her best Marine Master Sergeant's parade ground voice. "You stand in dead man's boots!"

It was a Tatannan colloquial expression she'd picked up somewhere, and it was nothing more or less than a direct threat, as in "I'm going to kill you now." It produced the desired effect. The duke whirled to face her. For the first time that day, Bouchard took the time to assess the threat. *Big guy, for a Tatannan, anyway. Skilled with that big two-hander, I'm guessing.* An historical weapons expert from Earth would have called the duke's sword a claymore without giving it a second thought. *He's not afraid of you, either.*

* * *

The duke assessed the woman. Until now, he'd focused on his goal of killing the prince and hadn't paid much attention to the mayhem among his forces to the rear.

A woman? A freakishly tall woman, even taller than I am, but with a woman's slender build. None of the mass required of a true warrior; not even half my weight. That sword—long, matched to her height, but too thin to stand up to heavy steel in real combat. It must be sharp, but... He suddenly realized none of his men were left standing and that no one was holding her at bay. *She must have taken them from behind. My men wore only light leather armor. A blade that light will be easily turned by my mail, assuming she gets to wield it.* He had seen what his sword could do to an unarmored opponent. He favored the woman with a look of contempt.

"I am the new King of Kings," he declared, ignoring the still-living prince behind him. "Kneel to me, woman."

"I kneel to no king," she replied with equal contempt. "I am not of this world."

Ronor laughed. *Does she really expect me to believe she is Muh-Rah?* Duke High Reaches was not a religious man and had little regard for ancient superstitions.

To his surprise, she didn't wilt before him. She continued to look at him with her intense, strangely alien eyes. His laughter faded as he realized the truth. For the first time, he was face-to-face with an off-worlder, one of the strange and magical sky-people who had come to conspire with Algar and replace the Bugs as masters of the world. She was the real enemy.

Enraged, he sprang forward and brought his blade down in a flashing arc to cleave her in two. He expected her to twist aside to avoid the stroke, but it didn't matter. She could not stand against his attack, and she could not evade him for long. She would die and then he would deal with the prince.

She made no effort to dodge the blow. She brought up her blade in a flash, and his blade stopped, hard blocked in mid-stroke, as if struck against stone, with a horrible ringing sound that seemed to linger in the air. He tried to draw it back, but it wouldn't come; it was held by some unseen force. Finally, he wrenched it free and stared at it in disbelief. There was a notch in the middle of his blade, nearly a finger-width deep, where her sword, that incredibly thin, frail-looking thing, had bit into the finest steel Tatannan swordsmiths could produce.

He was still staring at his sword when that thin blade slid through his chain mail as if it were nothing but parchment and pierced his heart.

* * *

LZ Alpha One, North Coast Province

"Looks like the Navy's having a rough time up there," General Sherwood remarked, as he scrolled through the message he'd just received. "They've lost a ship."

"Lost?" Colonel Olson, his chief of staff looked skeptical. The LFS Navy hadn't lost a ship—had one destroyed—in quite a few years. Some had taken serious battle damage, but...

"Lost, as in knocked out of orbit and falling to the planet in pieces," Sherwood replied. "That's why they gave us the heads-up." He stepped up to the large map table in the command post.

"According to this, we can expect falling wreckage anywhere along a line from here—" he indicated a point on the map due south of their position, "—to here." He indicated a second point due east, along the coast. "It actually extends further, but anything beyond this line will drop into the ocean."

"Hmmm." Olson studied the map. "We've got no operations in progress anywhere along the line. Could be a bad day for civilians in either of these two villages, but there's nothing we can do about that. Do we know which ship it was?"

"One of *Iwo Jima's* escorts." Sherwood consulted the message pad. "A destroyer, LFS *Lynx.*"

"Major?" Colonel Olson heard Nova's sharp indrawn breath and saw the look of concern on her face.

Nova shook her head, sharply. "Nothing, sir... just... her captain's an old friend of mine. Academy classmate. Do they mention casualties?"

"Not specifically—" Sherwood looked at the message again, "—but I'm guessing not everyone got off. They're asking us to be alert for lifepod beacons. Can we do that, Senior Tech?" The last question was addressed to the Navy communications technician manning the long-range comm equipment that kept them in touch with the ships in orbit.

"Yessir," the tech replied. "Standard Navy E-Comm band. This gear monitors that channel automatically, but we won't pick up a signal at any distance, especially if the source is below our horizon." He turned to his console in response to another incoming message, then turned back immediately.

"Sir, I've got a coded transponder message here, relayed to us by *Omaha Beach.*"

"A lifepod? That's a timely coincidence."

"No, sir," the tech responded. "According to the header, it's from the Diplomatic Mission in the King's City."

* * *

Castle Boroson, LFS Command Post

"Who sent this?" Bouchard demanded.

She held up the transponder, which showed red lights, indicating an outgoing message. Again, there was a three-character code, "Under attack. Need assistance."

The three Marines and one Navy tech looked at her blankly. The other person in the room raised his hand, tentatively.

"Uh, I did, Lieutenant." The young man wore the rank of Ensign with the insignia of the Diplomatic Corps on his uniform. He had arrived with Michaels to serve as the Ambassador's assistant, but Bouchard suspected he'd been added to the TO as an afterthought. His only qualifications seemed to be whatever Michaels had told him on the trip out. He hadn't yet learned to speak more than a dozen words of the Tatannan language.

Bouchard gritted her teeth. Ensign Bunker was holding up another transponder, which he must have retrieved from Michaels' body after the Ambassador was killed. Bouchard had the only other such device, and by tacit agreement, neither of them was supposed to use it without the other's knowledge and consent short of Armageddon.

"At best, Ensign, that was premature," she told him. "At worst, you may have compromised our mission entirely."

"It's my decision." Bunker bristled, probably realizing he and Bouchard were equal in rank, and hers was only a field commission—a very recent one at that. "Tend to your Marines and let me handle the diplomatic mission."

"Listen carefully, Ensign." She took a step toward him. "You have just made it my concern. Thanks to your ill-considered message—which our limited communications capability gives us no way to retract—the Marines will most likely dump a heavy assault force on our heads in very short order because they think the Bugs are attacking us. That's something Ambassador Michaels wanted to avoid at all costs because deploying forces here will attract the attention of the Bugs. Once the Bugs realize the king is in league with us, they just might make leveling this city a priority, which would put an end to your precious diplomatic mission. Is there any part of that you do not understand, Ensign?"

The Navy tech was trying to shrink into the woodwork, having never witnessed an argument between two officers, but the Marines stood fast, their faces devoid of expression. As far as they were concerned, Bunker wasn't a real officer. They knew who was in charge, and Bouchard had just delivered a typical Marine officer's 'Prayer Meeting' to a green recruit who had seriously screwed the pooch.

Bunker looked like he was about to jump back at her, but the door behind Bouchard opened. She whirled and drew her sword so quickly, none of them saw it leave the scabbard.

"P… p… please, Milady," the trembling serving boy stammered in formal Tatannan, "the prince… uh… that is to say, the king, requests your presence… in the meeting chamber."

Bouchard relaxed. "Tell his Majesty I am at his service," she replied in the same language, "and will be there in a moment."

The youth fled. She turned back to a suddenly pale Bunker who had not understood a word of the exchange, then she sheathed the sword in a fluid motion and pointed at the novice diplomat.

"You know nothing of the situation. Stay here," she ordered. "Do nothing."

With that she turned and was gone, slamming the heavy door behind her.

Sergeant Manfred "Manny" Walker stepped up to Bunker and glanced down to see whether the Ensign might have wet his pants.

"LT's in kind of a bloody mood today," he remarked in a conversational tone, "and she's just sent about a hundred bad guys to the Tatannan version of Hell with her sword. If I were you, sir, I might consider that pissing her off is not the smartest thing you could do right now."

Wish I'd been there, he thought, fingering the hilt of his sword. He'd been posted on the walls when all the action happened, and he'd missed it, though he did get a nice view of a bad guy flying through the tower window and splattering on the courtyard.

* * *

LZ Alpha One, North Coast Province

"Those are your people, Major, and you know the locals. What does this look like to you?"

"Sir, there are only two people authorized to send a signal like that: Ambassador Michaels and the senior Marine, Lieutenant Bouchard," Nova told the General. "If either of them is calling for help, the situation must be critical."

"I figured as much," he agreed. "I've picked your brain since we left Luna, but now that we've engaged the enemy, you're less useful here than you would be at the castle. I need you to take a platoon and get over there. I don't think we can wait for morning."

"Let me see." He checked his status board for available units, then turned to Olson. "Brad, call Colonel Chang and tell him I need one of his Force Recon groups. I want Bravo Company, First Platoon. Tell him to turn them out for immediate deployment because I'm sending Major Sakura over there to take charge of them for a special mission. Call the staging area and tell them to warm up an Archangel for platoon transport—range to LZ about 250 klicks. We'll also need a couple of Raptors for close cover, and you'd better add a Firefly for stealth recon."

"You'll need that," he told Nova, "to look things over before you make a blind drop at night. We've got nothing in the area—we're specifically avoiding it—but I'll ask *Omaha Beach* to get orbital imagery and pass it to you ASAP.

"As for the mission, with what we know now, I can't give you specific orders. Let us know what you find, and we'll respond accordingly. Any questions?"

"No, sir, I'm on my way." She popped a sharp salute, then scooped up her gear bag from the command post rack.

"Major..." she paused when the general spoke again. "You've had lots of experience with squad-level recon on this planet. Nobody knows the land and the people like you do, but you've never commanded a full platoon in combat. I picked that platoon because it's led by a young officer—a lieutenant by the name of Ashcroft—who has impressed me, both personally and in the way he runs his unit. He's a resource; make use of him."

"Yes, sir, I understand. I'll take all the help I can get."

"Good. Carry on."

* * *

On the King's Road, North of the City

Something had gone horribly wrong.

When he saw Duke High Reaches enter the castle, Arrimas had been certain his labors on the duke's behalf were about to bear fruit. He had not been told of any plan, but the timing was right. His last message, delivered by hand to the duke's agent, had stressed that the off-worlders were about to move against the Bugs. He feared his message had reached the duke too late.

He'd been present that morning—as one of the king's trusted advisors—when the off-world Ambassador told Algar the attack on the Bugs had begun. It occurred to Arrimas that the off-worlders were distracted, and it would be a perfect time for the duke to act. He had wanted to let High Reaches know, but he dared not approach or show any sign of recognition. He had never dealt with the duke directly, only with his agent in a little village to the north. After all was done, he would reveal himself and accept whatever reward the duke—the new king—chose to give him for his efforts.

King Algar was dead. His death had been publicly announced to the anxious crowd that gathered outside the gates as rumors spread throughout the city. Ronor T'Corval, Duke High Reaches, was dead as well. No public announcement had been needed since the duke's head was displayed on the end of a pike atop the castle's main gate. In case there was any doubt as to why it was there, a nearby sign that appeared to be written in his blood declared him a kingslayer.

Prince Arne had immediately assumed the throne. Arrimas felt a cold chill of fear when the newly crowned king summoned him, certain his allegiance to High Reaches had been discovered. His terror subsided when Arne gave him a sealed letter addressed to Duke Middle Plains, one of the crown's most steadfast allies. The king had ordered him to depart immediately to deliver the letter in person. The High Sheriff had insisted two of his guardsmen ride with him in case of trouble and directed him to follow a specific route to avoid the areas where the off-worlders and Bugs might be in conflict and the Bug mining sites, where the creatures conducted most of their operations.

He'd been relieved to find the route would take him through the village of Talmar, the place where he always contacted the duke's agent. It appeared none of the duke's men had escaped, and it pleased him to hear none had been taken alive, though there was little chance any of them would have known of his connection with their liege lord. Most likely, he was the only one who could deliver the news to the duke's agent and, thus, to his heirs or whoever would succeed him in ruling the High Reaches. He would have to be careful, though. The High Sheriff's two men were not stupid and would note any out-of-character behavior.

They rode at night, as the moons were both bright in the sky. They should reach the village by morning. He was away and clear, but he still looked nervously over his shoulder from time to time, expecting to find some shadowy agent of the crown on his trail.

* * *

Castle Boroson, King's City

"Your Majesty." Regas D'Narr, the Crown's High Sheriff, seemed hesitant as he presented the visitor. "This is the man whose name is not spoken, who is known only to the king and to me."

The man in question looked meek and nondescript. He wore the simple but well-cut garments typical of a prosperous merchant or craftsman, with an air of wealth acquired by his hard work. He kneeled and bowed to his new monarch.

"I am at your service, Majesty," he declared. "I am but a simple tradesman, but in the Crown's service, I am head of an ancient guild whose function is to do the king's bidding in delicate matters that must not see the light of day."

"Rise. Let us speak plainly," Arne told him. "There are no ears in this chamber but ours. You are the Master of the Guild of Assassins, pledged to serve the Crown since the time of my grandfather's grandfather. You served my father, and now, you have come to pledge service to me."

"Yes, Majesty," he acknowledged, getting to his feet, "though in truth, your father never found need of our services. He was a kind and gentle king, much loved by his people. I am sorry for your loss, a loss for all Tatanna."

"I fear," Arne declared, "I do not have my father's gentle heart. I will require your services immediately."

The master assassin raised an eyebrow but said nothing and awaited the king's instruction.

"We are at a turning point," Arne told him. "Whatever happens in the next few days—a crossing or two at most—the world as we know it will change. We must be a united people. We cannot have usurpers seeking the throne, nor allow those who conspire against the Crown to go unpunished.

"House High Reaches," he continued, "I require the entire line to be extinguished: sons, nephews, cousins, anyone who might have claim to the duke's seal. When it is done, I will claim their lands for the Crown."

"I understand, Majesty," the man replied. He had heard rumors—very wild rumors—that the Bugs were about to be gone, that Muh-Rah was among them, casting them into Hell. Other rumors said the opposite—the Bugs were running rampant, killing all in their path. He did not know which were true, but something was surely afoot. For the moment, however, none of that was his concern. He was already planning, deciding what resources would be needed to fulfill the king's command.

"It shall be done," he promised. "It will require a little time, but no more than a crossing. I will advise Sir Regas when the task is completed."

* * *

Moira Bouchard stood at the edge of the castle's broad courtyard and watched the Firefly land. Its side doors opened before the craft touched down. A half-dozen Marines in combat gear deployed in a defensive ring, followed by a figure Moira knew well, even in the dim light. The craft had come in dark, but it had passed several times over the castle, and she had ordered the torches lit around the courtyard in a clear invitation to land.

Bouchard walked forward with two of her troops carrying torches beside her. The newcomers were locked and loaded, and she had no desire to become a casualty of friendly fire. At ten paces, she stopped and popped a salute.

"Welcome back, Major," she said.

"Sergeant, excuse me, that would be Lieutenant now." Nova Sakura returned the salute. "What's your situation here?"

"Long story, ma'am, but the area's secure, so you can tell your troops to stand easy. Not too easy, but if this is all you brought, I doubt you've attracted any attention from the Bugs. Fact is, we haven't seen a Bug in or near the city for days."

"It's all I brought here," Nova said. "I've got a full platoon parked in the wilderness by the Little Kilder River, with an Archangel to deliver them and a couple of Raptors to suppress any noisy neighbors. All it'll take is a call, and they'll be here in twenty minutes. I've also got full combat gear for your Marines. If there are no Bugs, though, why the distress call?"

"Wasn't my choice to send it, ma'am. Like I said, long story. We've got a major problem, and not one we expected. King Algar's dead, and Arne is now on the throne. He'll be glad to see you, especially since Ambassador Michaels is dead as well."

* * * * *

Chapter Seven

Tatanna was a cold planet, its poles shrouded in huge permanent ice caps that extended to within 30 degrees of the equator. Its habitable zone consisted of a single large continent that straddled the equator. There were other land masses to the north and south, but they were buried under kilometers of ice, broken only by upthrust mountain peaks. Given the extreme conditions in latitudes higher than 25 north or south, most of Tatanna's population lived in an area smaller than Europe on Earth. From the coasts of the equatorial continent, a great ocean circled the globe, broken only by occasional volcanic islands that had never seen a human footprint. Given their lack of nautical technology and limited seafaring skills, Tatannans rarely ventured out into the Great Ocean.

* * *

White Cliffs, Province of North Coast

Lynx's last lifepod made what Fleet would have judged an "acceptable" landing. It came to rest mostly upright, with no injury to its occupants. It was still airtight, and its egress hatch was unobstructed, but its choice of landing site was somewhat less than ideal.

Left unguided, the pod would have come down in the ocean nearly a hundred kilometers offshore. That would have been acceptable if no other option were available. It was designed to float in any reasonably dense liquid. Its outer shell had a tough polymer coating, in case that liquid or the atmosphere was corrosive.

Its navigation and landing software preferred solid ground. The thrusters had activated when it was still at altitude, steering it toward the northeastern coast of the continent. Its travel range was limited by the need to reserve enough power for a soft landing, and it had barely reached the coast when its programming decreed it must put down. It did so, landing among a jumble of huge boulders at the base of a cliff, just fifty meters from water's edge. It did its best to level itself, but the uneven, rocky surface defeated it, and it settled with a fifteen-degree tilt to one side.

"We're down, ma'am," McGill told Lorna. "I'm reading a breathable atmosphere at nine hundred eighty millibars, temperature nine point five degrees, wind forty-four kph—windy and a little chilly—and gravity one point zero four standard. Welcome to Planet Tatanna, shall I pop the hatch?"

They'd inventoried the pod's gear on the way down, and everything was in order except for communications, which had gone offline as they passed through some sort of electrical storm. There was no reason to stay inside the pod.

"Go ahead," Lorna said. "Let's see what's out there."

McGill lifted the cover for the hatch controls and pulled the handle. There was a slight hiss as pressure equalized, then the hatch door slid sideways into its recessed housing. She sniffed the air and found the smell strange but not unpleasant, then she leaned out with care to look around. Since the pod was tilted, she had to hold an overhead handrail to keep from falling out. The steps below the hatch had deployed but were jammed against a large rock. They would have to be careful climbing out, but otherwise, the exit was clear.

In front of her, McGill saw nothing but ocean. Huge breakers crashed against the rocks not far from the pod, close enough that she felt a fine spray on her face. She started to swing out and climb down, but something next to the hatch caught her eye.

"I think I found the problem with the comm gear, ma'am." She looked at the fused and twisted remains of the antenna array and the emergency beacon module attached to it. "That lightning bolt, or whatever it was that hit us, must have taken it out. This unit's a write-off."

"Maybe it was a static discharge, ma'am," Darius said, hesitantly. "I've heard that an object moving through the air can generate a pretty heavy charge. When it discharges, it's kind of a lightning bolt in reverse."

"Good thought, Marine," Lorna told him. "Ensign, can you get a picture of that? Fleet Engineering can look at it when we get back, so the next guy who makes an atmospheric pod descent doesn't have the same problem."

"Yes, ma'am." McGill smiled. The captain must be confident they'd be rescued despite the fried electronics. They still had the handheld comm unit, but its range was extremely limited—pretty much line-of-sight—and not designed to punch through atmosphere to orbit. *Maybe something else to take up with Fleet Engineering when we get back.*

She climbed down onto the rocks and captured the requested picture with her personal pad, but as she looked around, her confidence faded. She glanced from the cliffs, then back to the sea. When the other two had climbed out of the pod, she turned to Lorna.

"Ma'am, we need to get out of here," she said.

"Why?" Lorna asked. Standard SAR doctrine advised survivors to stay at their landing site, even with communications. The pod, with its alternating brightly colored reflective stripes, was a lot easier to see than a person.

"Tide must be low right now. Do you see the high-water marks on those cliffs, about ten meters up the sides?" She turned around and looked at the ocean again. "This place has a serious tide, and it's coming in. The water is already closer to us than it was when I first looked out. It's rising fast."

Lorna nodded. "I see. I don't think we want to get back inside the pod and seal it, even if it does float."

"No, ma'am," McGill said. "It's built pretty tough, but I wouldn't bring any watercraft onto a lee shore like this. With this wind and surf, it'll be pounded to pieces in minutes, and so will we, if we try to swim."

"Sounds like you know something about it, Ensign," Lorna remarked. "I was born on Luna. I know very little about the sea."

"I was born on Luna as well, ma'am," McGill replied, "but my grandfather was a commercial fisherman out of Nova Scotia. I spent a couple of school breaks with him on the Grand Banks, and I learned a few things. He had a good boat and modern electronic gear, but he said none of that would help him if he didn't respect the tides and the weather."

"Nature always rules," Lorna acknowledged. "No matter what planet you're on. OK, we'd better gather the gear and look for a way up these cliffs."

They had to walk a few hundred meters along the cliff, but they found a route they could climb—barely. The survival gear from the pod was stowed in backpacks for easy transport, but Bob's module was not manageable. McGill fashioned a harness for him of polymer webbing and climbed the cliff with the cat tucked inside her jacket. Bob stayed quite calm and docile, and she found his soft purr reassuring as she climbed.

Before they were halfway up, the pod was afloat. By the time they reached the top, the waves were battering it against the cliff. It was damaged and taking on water.

The rugged cliffs extended as far as they could see in either direction. It was just past sunset, and daylight was fading, but they saw no lights or other signs of human habitation along the coast.

"We need to go inland," Lorna told them. "I've seen maps of this planet. Wish we had one now, but our mission wasn't supposed to require one. If I recall correctly, the only large city is a long way south, but there should be villages around here, and there's supposed to be a well-traveled road along the coast."

"Are we going to contact the local people, ma'am?" McGill asked.

"If we can find any. From what little I know of the Marines' battle plan, there shouldn't be any Bugs in this area, but there won't be any Marines here either. If we can find some locals, maybe they can put us in touch with our people."

* * *

Travel inland proved relatively easy, as the rocky cliff top gave way to sparse grasslands dotted with a few trees. In the fading light, the local flora looked less alien than it had at first. They might have been walking somewhere on Earth were it not for one noteworthy difference.

"Wow, look at that," McGill said as they topped a low hill and looked back toward the coast at the two rising moons, which were nearly full and only a few degrees apart.

"I don't think we're in Kansas anymore," Lorna remarked.

"Huh? I mean, beg pardon, ma'am?" Darius looked at her questioningly.

"Just a line from an old twentieth century vid," she explained. "My grandmother had a huge library. I used to watch them all the time… I was fascinated by the way people lived back then. Granny used them to give me history lessons."

"The moons would explain the tides, ma'am," McGill remarked. "Two moons would make for some crazy tidal patterns anyway, but when they're in close conjunction like that, you can expect to see extreme highs and lows."

The two moons also made for a very bright night, so much so that they didn't need lights to cross the open ground. They took turns carrying Bob, who seemed perfectly comfortable with the alien world around him. Occasionally, he turned his head and perked up his ears at the sound of some small wild creature in the night, but otherwise, he was content to be carried, and he encouraged them with his steady purr. McGill carried him cradled in her arms, but with Lorna and Darius, he preferred a loftier perch, so he could look over the bearer's shoulder.

According to the inertial tracker Lorna carried, they had gone about five kilometers inland, roughly westward, when they reached the road. It was nothing more than a wide dirt track, with stone markers on both sides spaced a few hundred meters apart, but it was clearly a maintained route of travel.

McGill tried the handheld comm again but got no response. With little information to go on, Lorna had chosen to head north. Her choice proved encouraging a kilometer up the road when they came upon a prominent stone marker with engraving on it. A crest of some sort was carved at the top, followed by four lines of what they assumed was text.

"Too bad we can't read it." McGill sounded frustrated.

"Phonetic alphabet," Darius remarked, quietly.

"Say again?" McGill looked blankly at him.

"Uh, they use a phonetic alphabet, ma'am. Characters represent sounds, unlike the ideographic alphabet, where each character represents a complete word."

"How would you know that? Can you read it?"

"No, ma'am, I can't. I…" Darius hesitated, but Lorna intervened.

"He's right," she declared. "Go ahead, Marine, I'd like to hear your reasoning."

"There's a limited number of different symbols, ma'am, and they get repeated often. It's like English with its twenty-six letters. You only need a few sounds to make words, but the average person speaks thousands of words. If you need a different symbol for each one…" He shrugged.

"Right." Lorna nodded. "A phonetic alphabet implies a higher literacy rate in this civilization than in others because reading and writing are easier to learn when using a phonetic alphabet. Pretty sharp observation, Private."

Darius felt a sudden warmth in his face, partly embarrassment, partly pride. Hanging out with the geeks had filled his head with many useless, but occasionally useful, bits of knowledge.

Suddenly, he found himself missing Jin. She was the one who had told him about the differences in written languages. She was proud of her Korean heritage, and she liked to tell everyone the story of King Sejong of the Choseon Dynasty, who, about a thousand years ago, had set out deliberately to create the first phonetic alphabet in Asia to replace the ideographic Mandarin Chinese that was the only written language in the region. *The captain's right,* he thought. *Jin said the king created that alphabet because he wanted the common people of Korea to be able to read and write.*

He was still thinking of Jin, wondering when, if ever, he would see her again when they rounded a bend in the road and saw the lights of a village ahead.

* * *

The Inn at Sbora's Grove, North Coast Province

Rogo D'Narus, known to all as Rogo the Fat, was a keen observer of people. He had absolutely no doubt about the nature of the strange trio that had just come through the front door of his inn. Off-worlders.

Others might have called them freaks. The golden-haired woman (very short-haired, as no Tatannan woman would ever wish to be) was more than a head taller than any man in the place, except for the huge, broad-shouldered giant who had preceded her through the door. Size was not the giant's only strangeness. His face and exposed hands were deep brown, darker than aged heartwood, almost as dark as the close-cropped jet-black hair on his head.

In contrast, the third person—also a woman—looked almost ordinary, except for hair that was more reddish than the auburn shade of most Tatannans. As she turned and looked directly at Rogo, he noted that her eyes were an amazing emerald green. With very rare exceptions, Tatannan eyes were brown. The tall woman turned to look at him, and he noticed her eyes were crystal blue.

All of them wore strange, form fitting garments—black trimmed in blue for the women, dark green for the man. Their clothing displayed subtle markings of a military flavor—badges of rank, perhaps, or regimental decor—not overstated, but obvious enough that persons of their service would recognize them immediately.

Most of the others had never seen an off-worlder. Rogo had, though it had been several years. He was a very observant man, as befit his status as the Crown's primary intelligence agent in North Coast Province.

"Quickly!" he ordered his head server, who was also his niece. "Take them to the back room with as little disturbance as possible. Draw the curtains and close the door. Urge them to be quiet and calm. Stay with them if you must. I'll be there in a moment."

He had few guests in the inn, and the only people in the common room at this hour were two old locals, who were most likely too deep in drink to notice the newcomers. Given a moment, however, even the dullest drunkard would take note of the strange creature cradled in the arms of the smaller woman, a creature whose color pattern suggested invisibility in the wilderness. As Rogo studied the off-worlders, so the creature studied him. Its strangely-shaped ears were erect, and it gazed at him with unblinking yellow eyes that could only belong to a predator.

Dear Goddess, he prayed, raising his eyes to the heavens. *What have you brought to my doorstep today?*

* * *

Village of Talmar, North Coast Province

Pleading dissatisfaction with his mount, Arrimas convinced the two guardsmen to stop in the village for the night. After taking rooms at the inn, he told them he was going to the stables to secure a fresh *kilder* for the morning departure. He walked with the stablemaster, pretending to examine the available animals, as he told his tale. Darrick, the stablemaster, was his contact with High Reaches.

"The duke did not die in vain," Arrimas insisted. "He slew King Algar and would have slain the prince had the off-worlder not intervened with her unholy magic. You must warn the duke's heir. Arne will be seeking blood."

"I will tell him what you have told me," Darrick said, his face showing none of the shock and dismay Arrimas expected. "I will also give him that packet of letters Arne gave you."

"No, you will not," Arrimas protested. "Arne does not suspect me. I will continue to serve High Reaches, but to do so, I must perform the king's mission and return. I will be leaving in the morning and—"

His protest was cut short by the arm that encircled his head from behind and the knife that slit his throat. As Arrimas collapsed to the ground, Darrick retrieved the sealed Crown packet he carried and pulled it away to avoid the spatter of blood.

"Very neatly done." Ersin T'Corsa nodded at the man holding the bloody knife. He stepped forward from the shadows and took the packet from Darrick. "We've disposed of a possible future problem and gotten this—" he waved the packet, "—as an added reward. You predicted he would come here with news of whatever happened. You have served us well, Darrick."

"Thank you, my Lord." Darrick bowed with an ingratiating smile.

"Unfortunately," Ersin told him, "there is one more detail that must be dealt with. You are the only man afield who knows of our 'High Reaches' ploy, and we can't risk the Crown learning of it."

Darrick's smile disappeared as two of Ersin's men appeared and seized his arms. The man with the knife stepped forward to deal with the last detail.

When it was over, T'Corsa and his men led their kildren from the stable and mounted. They would be far from the inn before the bodies in the stables or the bodies of the two guardsmen in their rooms were discovered. When they reached the crossroads north of the village, Ersin stopped and handed the Crown packet to his most trusted man.

"Take this to my brother, with my regards. Tell him the story the turncoat brought and let him know I will be away for a few days. If he needs my sage advice, he can send a message to Sbora's Grove, where I will be gathering information in his service."

"Yes, M'Lord." The man nodded with a knowing grin.

Ersin kept a secret hideaway near Sbora's Grove. He had an arrangement with several wenches in the village, and he often declared the best food and wine in North Coast were to be found at the inn there. It was his refuge of choice when the High Sheriff or other Crown agents were being troublesome, and sometimes, when he simply wanted to be clear of his brother's foul moods.

He'll certainly be in a foul mood when he gets this news, Ersin decided.

* * *

The Inn at Sbora's Grove

"Well, that's proof enough for me." Lorna stared at the object on the table. "These people know who we are."

She had been pretty sure of that already. As soon as they came through the door to the inn, a woman ran up to them without speaking and motioned them into a hallway. She led them to a large room that was set up for private banquets, with a long table that could seat a dozen people. She closed the door and motioned for them to sit down. She tried to speak to them, but when she realized they didn't understand, she pointed at the table, indicating they should stay there. She brought them two pitchers and some stoneware mugs, then left, closing the door behind her.

They checked the pitchers after the woman left and found that one held water and the other held some sort of fruity wine. Lorna had it on good authority that Tatannan food and drink were OK to consume, but she wasn't sure about the local water. She poured herself a mug of wine and found it to her liking. She invited the others to try it if they wanted to.

"What if it's drugged or poisoned?" McGill hesitated.

"Why would they do that?" Lorna shrugged. "We're pretty much at their mercy already."

A few minutes later, the door opened, and a man came in. They recognized him as the broad-shouldered old man they saw behind the bar when they came in. He might once have been a powerful and formidable figure by Tatannan standards, but now, he was bald, double-chinned, and significantly overweight. He pulled up a chair to the end of the table.

The chair creaked as he sat down and looked at them. He spoke briefly, but the words meant nothing to them. Lorna shook her head.

"We don't speak your language," she told him.

He nodded but said nothing. Apparently, he didn't speak their language either. He reached inside his tunic and produced a leather bag. He opened it and dumped its contents—a single item—on the table in front of him.

"Ever see one of those before, Jefferson?" Lorna inquired.

"Yes, ma'am," he replied. "I have one just like it in my survival kit. I believe you and the Ensign have them in yours as well."

"Yes, we do," Lorna agreed. "Take yours out and put it next to that one."

Darius dug in his backpack and found his LFS Marine Corps standard-issue multi-tool. He placed it on the table next to the one the innkeeper had produced. The innkeeper looked at it, then sat back, nodded, and smiled.

"Yours looks a little different," McGill remarked.

"His is the older version," Darius said. "They replaced it with this one a couple of years ago. We saw the old ones in basic training, but most field units have the new one."

"Which means he may have gotten this a few years ago," Lorna speculated. A thought struck her, and she retrieved her pad. Standard issue Navy data pads had more storage capacity than needed and included a section for the user's personal data. Like most people, Lorna carried books, photos, and personal documents on hers. She scanned through her photos, selected one, and showed the pad to the Tatannan. His reaction was dramatic. He sat back and looked at it in surprise, then leaned forward and took a closer look at the picture and at Lorna.

* * *

Rogo had never seen a photograph. He couldn't begin to imagine how anyone, even the most talented artist, could produce a painting so vivid, so true to life. It was just another bit of off-worlder magic. He looked closely at the picture. Something nagged at his memory.

There were three women in the picture. The one to the left was the golden-haired one who sat before him. The one in the middle appeared to be an older version of her—her mother, perhaps? The one on the right was strangely familiar. Could it be…?

Of course! It was the off-worlder he had first met years ago, here at the inn, the leader of the group he had sent on to the King's City. She was the woman who had given him the amazing tool and other off-world gifts. The off-world man with her spoke only a few words of the common language, but he had told Rogo her name.

He sat back with a satisfied look on his face. He pointed at the picture.

"No-Va" he said.

* * *

"**Y**es! Nova!" Lorna exclaimed triumphantly, as the man pointed to the multi-tool he had put on the table.

"Ummm… ma'am?" McGill was curious. Lorna showed her and Darius the picture.

"Nova Sakura, Marine, Academy classmate of mine. She's the one on the right. I was on the *Lewis and Clark* survey mission that came here eight years ago. So was Nova. She led the squad of Marines we dropped on the planet and then had so much trouble retrieving. She interacted with some of the locals, and he must be one of them. I think he's trying to tell us she's the one who gave him that multi-tool."

"Oh, I see. Uh…" McGill was hesitant. "No time to discuss it now, but is that your grandmother in the picture?"

"Yes," Lorna replied, with a note of sadness in her voice. McGill must have seen the huge portrait of Fleet Admiral Lorna Greenwood the First in the foyer of Lunar Command HQ or the identical one that hung in the Hall of Honor at Lunar Fleet Academy. "This was taken about a year before she died. Nova and I were in our third year at the Academy."

"Anyway—" she brought herself back to the matter at hand, "—now that we've established a real contact with these people. Any suggestions about where we go from here?"

The innkeeper spoke again.

"Rogo," he said, pointing to himself.

"Lorna," she responded with a similar gesture, then pointed to each of the others.

"Mary Jane. Darius."

Lorna smiled when she saw Jefferson's look of surprise. Apparently, he hadn't expected her to know or remember his first name. He had been one of the newest and most junior in rank of the 130 officers and crew aboard LFS *Lynx*, but she was the captain, and she was expected to know everything.

Her smile faded when she remembered that *Lynx* was gone, along with an unknown number of officers and crew.

* * *

"Lor-Na, Mari-Jayn, Dar-Yus." Rogo repeated each name, bowing to them as he did so.

"Cat." The copper-haired woman indicated the strange animal. "Bob Cat."

Rogo had been watching the off-world creature with trepidation since he came into the room. The woman scratched the animal's head and stroked its fur to show it was a harmless pet, but Bob chose that moment to yawn and stretch his front paws, displaying his impressive fangs and claws.

Rogo recoiled slightly, having confirmed his first impression—without a doubt, the creature was a predator. Nonetheless, he bowed to it and repeated the name, "Bob-Cat."

He sat back with a shrug. *I know you, and you know me,* he thought, *so what do we do now?*

* * * * *

Chapter Eight

As a group, the Bugs were an intelligent race, though individual members at the lowest level were mindless creatures who performed specific tasks for which they had been bred and trained at the direction of their superiors. Like hive-dwelling insects of Earth, they lived in a rigid society and controlled their reproduction to produce offspring only as needed, bred for the specific task at hand.

They had ventured out cautiously among the stars, seeking resources they might exploit and room to expand, but for expansion, they needed a particular type of planet—a hot, heavy gravity planet with a methane atmosphere. They were not interested in human-habitable planets unless those planets were rich in other resources they required.

The discovery of Tatanna had been their first encounter with humans. They recognized that humans were intelligent, but at their level of development, they posed no threat to the Bugs. They could be exploited to work the mines that supplied a precious mineral valued by the Bugs for hive construction.

Forcing the humans to work the mines was efficient. It alleviated the necessity of building the extensive infrastructure needed to sustain a suitable force of Bug miners in the hostile environment of the planet. For almost two Tatannan centuries, the situation continued unchanged.

Then came first contact—at Tatanna—with a new, star-traveling race of humans. They had been driven off but had since been probing nearby star systems and had engaged the Bugs many times. They had left Tatanna alone, appearing to have no interest in challenging the Bugs for the human-inhabited planet.

The ploy had not worked. Logic indicated these dangerous, star-traveling humans would be most interested in human-habitable planets, especially those already home to a native population of humans. As a result, the Bugs took an unprecedented step—they constructed a sub-hive on the planet in the remote wilderness well away from human habitation. It had taken four full planetary years to complete, but now, it could produce the military equipment and weaponry they needed to defend the planet. More importantly, with a pair of Level 18 queens in residence, it could produce the one thing no other source could provide: more Bugs.

* * *

Bug Staging Area, North of LZ Alpha One

"**D**amn!" General Sherwood peered into the huge hole in the ground. "That is an impressive piece of engineering."

The hole was the result of a precision kinetic strike on the Bug military compound, delivered from orbit by Admiral McGruder's flagship LFS *Nike*. It had leveled the large, hardened dome the Bugs had built in the middle of the wilderness, but more importantly, it had opened the broad tunnel beneath it.

"It's a Bug superhighway," Colonel Olson declared. "Second Battalion dropped a whole platoon down there wearing full armor—bottom of the hole is too hot for an unprotected trooper—and they went five klicks up the tube to the northwest. They saw absolutely nothing, no lights, no features, no change of direction, no cross-tunnels. The thing is straight as an arrow and keeps going beyond the limits of their laser ranging equipment, which means at least ten more klicks."

"I guess that explains how they kept resupplying this compound. For that matter, it explains how they were able to evac the area when they decided it was a lost cause. We thought the surviving force was holed up in the dome, but it looks like they were gone before the Navy dropped the Thunderbolt on them. Comm, get over here."

"Sir!" The corporal responsible for the field communications gear was at his elbow in an instant.

"Get me Second Division," he ordered. "Tell them to get General Mercer on the line."

Second Division, from the carrier *Iwo Jima*, was deployed to the southwest and was charged with clearing several Bug concentrations around a cluster of mines in the area. They were finding it a lot harder going than First Division's assault in the northeast.

"Mercer's still fighting them over a pretty broad front," he told Olson. "He keeps telling us they seem to have an endless supply of reinforcements. He needs to do some air recon behind the lines to find out if there's another dome like this one back there."

"That's certainly possible," Olson agreed. "I'd say it's highly likely. We didn't see this one from orbit; Bugs had it really well covered up."

"Yes, they did." Sherwood pulled out a cigar and lit it as he turned to look at the wreckage of the Bug dome around them. "Now that we know what to look for, a low-level sweep ought to find it. If so, we'll get the Navy to drop a big can of whoop-ass on that one as well."

"Most likely, we'll find another tunnel like this one." Olson was beginning to understand the implications.

"I'm sure we will," Sherwood said, "and I'm betting it leads to the same place this one does. If we can figure out where that is, we'll have a real target for Fleet to unload on."

"One thing I don't understand, sir." Olson looked puzzled. "If they can cut huge tunnels like this, why do they need human labor to mine those damned rocks for them?"

"They're mining because they need the rocks for something, their mineral content or whatever," Sherwood speculated. "Tunnelling's a different issue. Look at the sides of the tunnel—glazed over, smooth. They most likely used a plasma cutter, like the Corps of Engineers uses to cut tunnels on Luna. Turns everything in its path into super-heated gas. No debris to remove, but no rocks or minerals either. All you have to do is figure out how to vent the tunnel, so the gas can get out. Our guys usually start with a vertical shaft somewhere, then cut both ways from the middle, using the shaft as a chimney. Bet if we looked hard enough, we could find shafts like that here as well."

"General Mercer for you, sir," the comm tech advised. "Channel One."

"Right." Sherwood touched the side of his helmet. "Mark, Sam. Think I know how you can cut the Bug supply lines and keep them from slipping away like they did on this end."

* * *

Two hours later, Sherwood's Firefly landed at LZ Alpha One. As he climbed out of the craft and headed inside the modular command structure, the HQ comm tech advised him of an incoming from Second Division.

"You were right, sir," Mercer told him. "There are two domes hidden back there; one is twenty klicks behind the lines to my northeast, the other nearly a hundred klicks to the northwest. I'm glad I went for a broad sweep because my recon birds picked the second one up at the very limit of their range. Anything more I should know before I call the Navy?"

"No, just tell them to shoot straight. We don't need the whole area leveled, just take out those domes, preferably with a single kinetic. Shouldn't take more than a Level 3. That's all *Nike* used on this end."

* * *

Bug Hive, 900 Kilometers Northwest of the King's City

When the kinetic strikes hit the second and third remote bases, the queens knew the location of the hive had been compromised. Except for a few minor detours due to troublesome underground rock formations, the connecting tunnels from those bases ran straight to the hive. Given the attacking humans' level of intelligence and technology, they would find it simple to plot converging lines on a map to locate the source of those tunnels.

The hive was much larger, deeper, more complex, and better protected than the remote bases, but a rain of kinetic strikes would eventually reduce it to rubble, and without control of the orbitals, the Bugs had no way of halting those strikes.

There would be no help from the homeworld. Even before the humans arrived, a determination had been made that the resources already in place exceeded the value of the minerals the planet might produce for the foreseeable future. The Bugs had no equivalent in their philosophy for the human expression about throwing good money after bad, but they understood the concept. The queens in the Tatanna Hive knew they would either win with what they had or perish. With that in mind, they began to prepare for a final battle in which they would hold back no reserves.

Bugs hatched from the egg went through a larval stage that lasted the equivalent of three Earth months, then they went into a pupa stage that lasted two more. Once it emerged from the pupa stage, a Bug could assume its function in society within days, even at the higher levels. A Level 1 soldier could be ready to send against the enemy within hours of its emergence. Since the hive was built years earlier, the queens had been producing eggs and larvae for military needs. The larvae had been allowed to develop to the almost mature pupa stage, then had been placed in frozen stasis until needed. It was time to thaw them out.

The additional workers needed to maximize production of war machines, weapons, and equipment had been thawed when the human attackers first arrived and had already fabricated a vast reserve of all that was needed to equip the warriors. The Bugs were efficient; the next few days would see the arrival of exactly enough warriors to make use of everything. There was no point in thawing any more than that because the fabrication effort had depleted their supply of raw materials.

* * *

The Inn at Sbora's Grove

Mary Jane McGill woke up slowly, savoring the remnants of a pleasant childhood dream. She'd been on vacation with her mother at her grandparents' comfortable home on the coast of Nova Scotia. It was a chilly night, and she was cuddled up in her mother's arms in the big four-poster bed, wrapped in a warm quilt and surrounded by the smoky smell of a wood fire. In her youth, fireplaces were still used in Nova Scotia to provide supplemental heat in early fall when the weather turned cold. Such things were illegal now, as the Canadian government had fallen in line with the global crusade against carbon emissions. Her grandparents' house had been torn down long ago to make way for a condominium development.

She slowly realized where she was—on a planet 47 light-years from Earth, sleeping at a primitive hostelry in a medieval civilization. It was a bit chilly, and she could smell the remnants of the fire in the outer room's hearth. It was the only source of warmth nearby, and she decided that was what had triggered the dream.

She bolted upright when she realized she was sharing the bed with someone and was huddled close against that person.

* * *

"Did you sleep well, Ensign?" Lorna inquired. She'd been awake for several minutes but had been reluctant to disturb McGill. She sat up, withdrawing her arm from under McGill's pillow. She'd been surprised when the younger woman had snuggled close in her sleep, and she'd envied McGill's carefree, childlike slumber. It reminded Lorna that she was responsible for these people. McGill, *Lynx's* most junior officer, had shown a sometimes annoying tendency to idolize her captain. She trusted Lorna to get them safely home.

McGill turned away from Lorna, but not quickly enough to hide the deep blush that colored her normally pale complexion.

"Sorry, ma'am, I didn't mean to... I mean, I just..."

"Nothing to be sorry about, Ensign," Lorna told her, cheerfully. "It was cold in here. That there is warmth in numbers is a basic survival tactic in a cold environment."

"Yes, ma'am, I guess so." McGill still sounded embarrassed.

"We Moonies live in a controlled environment," Lorna told her. "We're not used to temperature variations like this. I feel sorry for Jefferson. He didn't have anyone to keep him warm."

* * *

Rogo had quartered them in a little two-room suite that featured a good-sized bed in the back room—good-sized by Tatannan standards, but a bit short for Lorna's nearly two-meter height. The front room had a sitting bench that folded down into a bed. It looked pitifully small for a man of Jefferson's size, but he had looked at the arrangement and quietly remarked about the back room being "officer country." In his mind, it wasn't just a matter of privacy for the women.

Lorna had examined the stout bar that secured the outer door and declared that they wouldn't need to stand watch at night. The suite was on the inn's second floor, and the three small windows in the outer room didn't appear large enough to admit an intruder. Nonetheless, Jefferson felt it was his duty as a Marine to sleep near the door and windows in case the place needed to be defended.

Despite Lorna's comment, he hadn't been totally without a companion to keep him warm. He woke up with the first light of dawn and found Bob curled up in a warm, furry lump on his chest. He hadn't wanted to disturb the officers, so he'd been as quiet as possible as he stoked the fire in the hearth and added one of the logs the innkeeper had stocked for them. The logs had a strange color and texture, but they burned well.

It was their second night at the inn. The night they arrived, Rogo had put them in some sort of storeroom and given them thick mats to sleep on the floor. That room had not been as secure, and they had kept watch in three-hour shifts. The next morning, Rogo had moved them to the comfortable suite they now occupied, which had just been cleaned and prepared. Despite the small size of the rack, Darius had slept well and was ready for whatever the day might bring.

They had made a lot of progress the day before. Rogo had brought them a hand-drawn map that was almost a work of art. He had spread it on the suite's table and pointed out the King's City (designated by a crest like the one they had seen on the road sign the night before), the roads, the villages, and the location of the inn. The large city might have been a thousand kilometers away or just over the next hill but, judging by the distance between the inn and the coastline, Lorna estimated it was no more than 200 kilometers distant, assuming the map was to scale.

They had played charades of a sort, trying to communicate with each other using gestures and some simple drawings on a sort of chalkboard Rogo provided. The LFS people had picked up a few words of the local language, and Rogo had learned a few of theirs.

After a couple of hours, Rogo had departed to attend to his business, leaving them to themselves for the rest of the day.

* * *

They had just finished breakfast when Rogo returned for another visit. This time, he showed them a picture that seemed to indicate a person riding some sort of animal between the inn and the King's City, but the animal looked strange, nothing like a horse. McGill copied the drawing, just the animal without the rider, pointed to it, and looked questioningly at Rogo.

"Kilder," he said.

He got another questioning look in return, so he went to the door and spoke to the woman who waited there, the same woman who had shown them to the banquet room the first time and who now seemed to be assigned to care for them. She nodded and went down the stairs. When she returned a moment later, Rogo motioned McGill to the window.

"Kilder," he said again.

McGill looked out the window and gasped. Darius went quickly to the window and peered over her shoulder. A stable boy had led a large beast that looked like a cross between a rhinoceros and a crocodile into the yard below. The boy fed it a bundle of grass, so it was an herbivore, but its heavy tail and lumpy, scaly skin were very reptilian. As they watched, the boy threw a saddle over its back and cinched it in place. He added a pair of large cargo bags behind the saddle. Apparently, the creature was a beast of burden and a heavy hauler.

Lorna joined them at the window, and she nodded at the scene below.

"OK, now we've seen a kilder," she said.

"Kilder," Rogo repeated, holding up one finger. He held up two, three, and four fingers in succession. "*Kildren*," he said, with emphasis on the second syllable.

"I think he's trying to tell us that kildren is the plural of kilder," Darius said.

"I think you're right," Lorna agreed. "It appears he's suggesting that some person is going to ride a kilder to the King's City. Could he be talking about sending a message to someone there?"

"Hmmm…" McGill went back to the chalkboard, picked up the chalk, and made motions as if writing on her hand. She mimicked passing the message to the mounted figure in Rogo's drawing.

"Yes," Rogo said with a smile, demonstrating that he had learned at least one English word. He pointed at McGill and made the same writing motion.

"I think he wants us to write a message to our people, ma'am," Darius said.

"That's a good idea." Lorna nodded. "If nothing else, it will prove the message is valid. How's your handwriting, Ensign? Mine's been described as barely readable at times."

"I got decent marks in penmanship in school, but it hasn't gotten much use since then."

"Hmmph…" Lorna snorted. "At least you grew up on Luna, where they still teach it."

It was a valid comment. With the proliferation of keyboard and keypad devices in the modern world, schools in most civilized nations on Earth, particularly in Europe and the Americas, no longer taught cursive writing. College students in fields such as history and archeology studied it so they could decipher ancient documents, but the standing joke on Luna was that most Earthworms didn't know how to sign their own name.

"How about you, Marine?" Lorna turned to Darius. "Can you write clearly?"

"Actually, ma'am, I did calligraphy as a kind of hobby for a while. I was told I'm pretty good at it, though I haven't done any for about a year…"

"Private, you never cease to amaze me," Lorna told him. "You need to be careful, though. If people find out how knowledgeable and talented you are, sooner or later, somebody is going to decide you should be an officer."

Darius didn't know what to say. Less than two months out of basic, and his commanding officer was already telling him he had a bright future in the Marines. *Assuming we ever get back to the real world.*

The thought brought him up short. Back on Luna, Jin was a big fan of medieval fantasy role-playing games, and he had spent many hours with her in imaginary battles with swords and sorcery. *It feels like I'm in the middle of one of those games, especially after seeing that kilder critter.*

"I think we need to use one of our pads," he said, looking at the parchment, stylus, and ink pot Rogo had put on the table. "That would be further authentication for whoever gets the message."

He dug into his survival pack and produced the standard-issue Marine Corps multi-purpose writing pad and pen. It looked a lot like the writing pads humans on Earth had been using for over a century but was actually a sophisticated product of modern technology. Its "paper" was fireproof and almost indestructible, though it could be cut with a very sharp blade. It was intended to survive just about any hostile environment, as was the pen. The pen would even write in zero gravity in a hard vacuum. Navy and Marine EVA suits had a special exterior pocket for the pad and pen to allow for communication if electronic methods failed or—in the case of Marines—if a strike team was operating in silent mode.

"Ready to copy, ma'am," Darius reported.

"All right. List our names and ranks, followed by 'downed survivors of LFS *Lynx*, northeast coast of Tatanna's primary continent.'"

It took about five minutes for Lorna to dictate and Darius to neatly print the message. It was brief but covered the important details of their situation. Lorna took the sheet, folded it, and handed it to Rogo. He accepted it with a bow, then pointed again to the drawing of the kilder-mounted rider heading for the King's City. He rolled up the map, collected the chalkboard, and left the room.

* * *

Later that afternoon, the woman had returned, bringing them dinner. The main course was a stew that was rather tasty—strange, but tasty all the same. There was no point in asking what was in it since they wouldn't have understood her answers anyway. There was a meat component, which Bob sniffed out and devoured with apparent relish. McGill worried that the cat might not be able to digest the native food, but Lorna pointed out that they had nothing else to offer him, and they would have to rely on his instincts.

Realizing they weren't going anywhere and had no pressing duties, Lorna suggested they spend the evening telling each other about themselves. She kicked it off with a story about her first trip to Copper Hills, an Akara world where her grandmother had held a very large estate. McGill then talked about fishing with her grandfather off Nova Scotia.

Darius was hesitant at first. Until now, he'd never been off Luna, but Lorna encouraged him to talk about his experiences in Marine Corps basic training, and he quickly warmed to the subject. He stopped abruptly a couple of times, when he realized some colorful bit of language he'd quoted from one of his drill instructors wasn't intended to be repeated in the company of officers, particularly female officers.

Lorna laughed and shot back an equally colorful quote from her grandmother, who had been dubbed "The Iron Maiden" by her Navy troops. The Marines, she told them, usually called granny "The Babe on the Horse"—a reference to the hull artwork on her flagship, LFS *Valkyrie*.

The storytelling took them well past sunset, then they took turns using the small bathroom that was part of the suite to clean up and get ready for bed. They'd been amazed to find that the inn had indoor plumbing, and McGill vowed to ask Rogo about it when next they saw him. She suspected water was supplied from a tank on the roof but had no idea how it was pumped down. While the toilet wasn't exactly like an Earth or Luna commode, it appeared to function on the same siphon principle and was connected to some sort of waste disposal system, perhaps a septic tank or field.

The one thing the inn lacked, however, was hot running water. There was a small tub for bathing, but anyone who wanted a hot bath needed to heat the water over the hearth in a large iron pot provided for the purpose. As a result, it took a couple of hours for all three of them to finish cleaning up for the night. All things considered, though, they agreed that being marooned on Tatanna had not proven to be a terrible ordeal so far.

* * * * *

Chapter Nine

Battlecruiser LFS *Isis*, in Tatanna Orbit

"Where in hell are they getting these reserves?" Commander Jerry Murtaugh, McGruder's Chief of Staff wanted to know. For the past several hours, the Task Force had been under attack by wave after wave of warcraft launched from the planet. The Task Force was slaughtering the Bugs by the thousands, but they were taking damage as well. The attacks were concentrated on the LFS capital ships. Both *Nike* and *Amazon* had taken hits, and the heavy cruiser *Spartan* was no longer combat-effective.

"I'd be more interested to know why they didn't use them when we were trying to take the orbitals," John O'Hara remarked. "That was a critical point where they could have made a difference." O'Hara's old command, LFS *Norseman*, had taken damage as well, but it was still in the fight.

"That is strange," Admiral McGruder agreed. "The Marines were right about one thing—all of these attacks are being launched from the area they want us to saturate with KWs. Looks like they really do have the Bugs' main base pinpointed."

"We'll have to conduct that bombardment under heavy fire," Murtaugh complained. "It's a damned good thing the carriers have pulled back."

"That's another strange thing," O'Hara said. "We've pulled the carriers back because they've unloaded everything the Marines need

161

on the planet. Again, the Bugs could have made it a whole lot harder if they'd thrown all this hardware at us while the carriers were still unloading."

"So, what are you thinking, John?" McGruder asked.

"I believe they seriously underestimated us, sir. They sent forces they thought could handle us, and they were wrong. They've seen their mistake, but it's too late. Every time they launch against us, we pinpoint another launch site to take out. I think this is a last ditch effort. If we get past this one, they're done."

A soft chime sounded in the briefing room.

"Yes, Nadia?"

"Captain Jacobs for you, Admiral." The soft contralto voice of *Nike's* AI surrounded them.

"Put him on. Yes, Mark?"

"Locked and loaded for the fire mission, Admiral. *Amazon* reports ready as well." Commodore Mark Jacobs was *Nike's* captain, which made him Flag Captain for the Task Force. "It doesn't look like the Bugs are going to give us much time. The survivors from the last run are regrouping, and there's another batch coming up from the planet. I don't think we'll complete the entire course of fire before we have to switch back to Vipers. Any changes to targeting?"

"No, we'll go with the Marines' priorities first. I think the Bugs are going to run out of attack craft soon, so the launch sites won't matter. If you are ready, you may commence fire."

"Aye, sir," Jacob's acknowledged. "Commencing fire."

Seconds later, they felt the familiar shiver as *Nike's* mass drivers launched a full broadside from her starboard tubes—ten KWs on their way to targets down on the planet. The kinetics required the larger-bore missile tubes normally reserved for the long-range Viper anti-ship missiles. They still had the eight short-range Broadswords available, but if the Bugs came at them in heavy numbers, they would need all their firepower to handle the attackers.

Their priority was the Bugs' heavy equipment staging areas—targets that hadn't been revealed until the first Marine units had moved into the area and found a dug-in defense in place. After that, they would use additional KW strikes to open up the Bug base. At some point though, they would have to cease fire and leave it to the Marines to finish the job.

* * *

First Division Forward HQ
60 Kilometers South of Objective

"Navy says incoming, General," the comm tech sang out. "Ninety seconds."

"Pass the word to all units," Sherwood ordered. "Heads down until the shock waves pass."

He disobeyed his own order, stepped out of the HQ module, and walked the twenty meters north to the crest of the ridge. His smart-fabric uniform jacket protected him from the bitter cold, but he could understand why few Tatannans lived this far north. It was less than 5 degrees Celsius, with a 20-kph breeze blowing... and this was supposed to be late summer in the northern hemisphere!

The nearest target was 40 kilometers away. The shock wave would take some time to reach him and would be pretty much spent by then. He took the precaution of putting on his light-reactive goggles. Like a nuclear blast, kinetic strikes flashed brilliantly, but they were much cleaner, with no direct radiation or residual fallout.

On cue, a line of brilliant fireballs marched along the horizon from east to west. They were not evenly spaced, but neither were the Bug staging areas. Sherwood was confident the Navy's shooting had been accurate. From the size of the fireballs and the volcano-like pyroclastic clouds they threw up, he guessed the KWs had been pretty much maxed out. As weapons systems go, they were quite simple, nothing more than massive, solid projectiles mated to a high-output short duration gravitational propulsion unit. Most of the technology in them went into the guidance system that enabled them to hit their targets with precision.

Their effectiveness was based on a simple principle of physics—the kinetic energy of a moving object depended on mass and the square of the velocity. When the weapon struck its target, all the energy would be instantly converted to heat, with devastating results. With the gravity drive, the velocity of a KW could be controlled, so the same weapon could be used to take out a fifty-meter chunk of highway to stop vehicle traffic or to wipe out an entire enemy base, leaving a glowing-hot crater two kilometers wide. The Navy had been asked to take out the Bug staging areas, so what Sherwood was looking at was a series of big crater strikes.

He felt the first ground shock and decided it was time to take cover. Ground shocks traveled faster than air shocks, so things were likely to get rather breezy in a minute. He ducked back into the HQ module and started issuing orders, preparing to get what he hoped would be the final offensive under way.

* * *

Bug Hive, 900 Kilometers Northwest of the King's City

For the Bugs, the end appeared to be near. They had expended almost all their attack craft, without significant effect on the enemy fleet in orbit. All the exposed surface installations around the hive had been leveled, enemy ground forces were advancing, and kinetic strikes had already breached the uppermost level of the hive. When the environment failed in a section, any workers remaining there died, either poisoned by the oxygen-rich atmosphere of the planet or killed by the cold. No environment suits were available for workers within the hive, so they simply perished at their stations.

Deep within the hive, the queens considered one remaining option that might bring victory. This option offered little chance of success, but every possibility had to be explored. Several years earlier, the Bugs made contact with an individual who apparently held some rank among the locals. The individual indicated a willingness to serve as an intelligence source and had been paid well for his efforts. When the first off-world humans came to the planet, the informant insisted the intruders were conspiring with the king of the humans. At the time, the Bugs found no evidence to support this claim, but now, it appeared the informant had been right. The off-world invaders had come here at the king's invitation.

More recently, the informant had made another claim. It was absurd from a logical standpoint, but the Bugs had learned long ago that humans did not always act logically. He told them, if the human king were killed and replaced by another, one sympathetic to the Bugs, the new king would be able to banish the off-world invaders. The informant insisted the invaders would respect the authority of the local king, who was, after all, a human like them, to manage his hive and deal with the Bugs as he saw fit.

If that were true, and the Bugs doubted it was, there was still a chance. By the very nature of the hive mentality, the Bugs never lied about anything, but they knew humans did. They did not trust the informant, but at this point, they had nothing to lose.

There was one remaining remote facility, connected to the hive by a long tunnel, that had not been discovered by the invaders because it had not yet been used. It would allow the Bugs to send a small force—all they had left—to a place near the human hive where the king resided. The invaders appeared to have no forces near that hive, so the Bug force should be able to accomplish its objective— removal of the current king.

One other thing would be needed. They would have to contact the informant and require him to replace the king. The Bugs had no idea how a human king was created, but the informant had assured them it could be done. It was time to put him to the test.

They assembled the task force and sent it on its way. They prepared a message in the human language to tell the informant what was required of him. A pair of Level 6 messengers were to carry the message, accompanied by ten Level 3 ground force warriors. This group had a much shorter trip to make but would need to go down one of the already compromised tunnels to an area near one the now-abandoned mines. The human invaders had already wiped out all Bug forces in that area and had moved on, but there was always the chance some of the enemy remained. From there, they would need to move cross-country through wilderness terrain, but their chance of encountering enemies would be much diminished. The messenger group was instructed to avoid enemy contact at all costs. Their only mission was to deliver the message.

Once clear of the tunnels, both the attack force and the messenger group would need to operate in environment suits, which could only support them for a limited time. They needed to remain alive long enough to accomplish their missions—to remove the king and to advise the informant to act. After that, they could die.

The limiting factor was the length of time the hive could hold out. The mission would fail if the informer took the throne after the last queen died, but the hive was deep, extensive, and very tough. They would hold it as long as they could and wait for word of success or failure. The attack force was already twenty kilometers down the tube when the messenger group started toward its destination: House Corsa, home of the informant, Duke North Coast.

* * *

The Inn at Sbora's Grove

Rogo's face showed happy surprise, followed by a welcoming grin as the man came through the door. His carefully controlled features gave no hint of the hatred and disgust he felt. He had been expecting this visitor.

"My Lord!" His voice was loud and cheerful. "Once again, you honor us with your presence."

"Rogo!" Ersin T'Corsa returned the grin. "A cup of your best *tenali* wine for me and my companion." He waved to indicate the brutish-looking fellow who had entered ahead of him.

"Pour a cup for yourself, as well," T'Corsa insisted. "The day is young, but it is never too early to enjoy it." He threw down a copper coin worth three times the price of the drinks.

"Alas, the Goddess has not smiled on us this year," Rogo lamented. "The trees have yielded poor fruit, but I believe I still have a bottle of last year's excellent vintage."

He selected the bottle from the rack behind him, set three stoneware cups on the bar, and filled them. He waited, allowing T'Corsa and the other man to select their cups first. Ersin had to nudge the other man, who was looking suspiciously around the common room, as if expecting some threat to spring out of the walls. He turned back to the bar, grabbed one of the cups, and swallowed the contents in a single draught. Rogo picked up the last cup.

"Good fortune, My Lord," he proclaimed and drained his cup.

Ersin smiled and lifted his cup but took only a small sip before setting it down.

Rogo wondered what it was like to live in such fear of being poisoned that you could not take food or drink until others had tasted it first.

Knowing that you were coming, he thought, *I could have had you. You always take the cup farthest from your hand, and that miserable excuse for a bodyguard always takes the nearest. I know poisons for which even a sip is enough, though you might not know you had been murdered until the next day. Yes, I could have had you, and maybe someday I will, but not today.*

"Always so peaceful this time of year," Ersin remarked. "That's why I come here, but I would find it tiresome to live here all the year. Your food and wine are good, Rogo, but nothing exciting happens here. The highlight of your season is the passing of a merchant convoy on its way from one busy place to another. Other than that, I imagine you rarely see any strangers pass through." He gave Rogo a sly and expectant look.

"Well now, My Lord, that is usually the case, but as it happens, we saw the arrival of some very unusual people just two days ago. I had intended to send a messenger to your Lordship's esteemed brother to ask him what to do with them, but since you are here…"

Rogo had known this was coming. When Ersin arrived at his cottage near Sbora's Grove the previous afternoon, he immediately summoned two young women who were his favorite local playthings. One was a kitchen maid in Rogo's inn and a notorious gossip. She was Ersin's primary source of information and would tell him all that was happening in the village to curry his favor. Rogo often used her to misdirect Ersin and passed along information the Crown wanted him to have. It was largely through those efforts that Ersin now believed Rogo to be a loyal servant of Duke North Coast, though he once suspected otherwise.

The other girl had once been an acolyte of the Goddess until the senior priestess had cast her out of the local temple for immoral conduct. She made a meager living doing odd jobs for farmers and merchants, and she seemed to be doing well despite the small money she earned at those jobs. Most villagers assumed she was selling her favors, and not just to the duke's half-brother.

She was earning a stipend from the Crown at Rogo's request, and she was his primary information source about local affairs, including the comings and goings of Ersin T'Corsa. She was very good as a spy and managed to conceal the fact that she hated Ersin and would cheerfully cut his throat in the night—would have already done so, had not Rogo convinced her it served their mission to keep him alive.

That girl had come to him in the early hours of the morning, while he was still preparing to open the inn. The night she had shared with Ersin and the other girl had produced some disturbing news, including the claim that King Algar was dead. According to Ersin, Algar had been murdered in his sleep by his own son, Prince Arne, who now sat upon the throne. "You will hear stories from the city that someone else is to blame," he had told them, "but do not believe them. It was Arne who did the deed, so he could seize his father's crown."

Rogo would not have believed that claim even if it had come from a more reputable source, but it was obvious something had happened. Hopefully, he would get news from his contacts in the palace. The second report the girl brought him was equally disturbing.

Despite all attempts to keep it secret, his kitchen maid had apparently discovered that Rogo was keeping some strange visitors hidden away, and she had shared that information with Ersin T'Corsa. The duke's half-brother had been very interested and had pressed the girl for every detail she knew.

Rogo was glad the Crown's Express Rider had come through yesterday and was now carrying Rogo's report and the off-worlders' message to the High Sheriff, but it would be three more days before the message got there. With the report of the king's death, Rogo had no idea what the current situation in the palace was. All he could do was hope his message reached the right person, who would take appropriate action.

Meanwhile, he had hastily written a message to Asral T'Corsa—Ersin's brother—telling him of the strange visitors and asking what to do with them. He had not sent that message. He was holding it as proof of his "good intentions" when Ersin came to question him.

"They came walking through the door, bold as you please, after sunset day before last," he told Ersin. "There's been no post rider headed for House Corsa this tenday, so I was going to have my grandson take this message to his Lordship."

He showed Ersin the message. "I was thinking, perhaps, you might want to take it to him yourself or send your associate to do it."

"I'll do better than that," Ersin declared. "I'll take your visitors to the duke directly. I'm sure he'll be most interested to meet them. You have a coach and driver for hire, do you not? For such important services, I'm sure my brother will pay you twice your normal rate of fare."

"An excellent idea, My Lord!" Rogo smiled broadly. He rubbed his hands together as though he were anticipating the large purse Ersin promised, but inwardly, he was raging. His last feeble hope of keeping the off-worlders here had been taken.

"Margol," he told his niece, "go to the stables and tell Jarl to get himself and the coach ready. He will be leaving shortly to carry some passengers to House Corsa. He should be prepared for three, perhaps four, days on the road with his return included."

"My Lord—" he turned back to Ersin again, "—you should know these people are really strange. For as long as they have been here, they have not spoken a word of the common language."

"They are mute? They say nothing at all?" Ersin's brow wrinkled in puzzlement.

"Oh no, My Lord. They speak many words, but they are strange words that seem to have no meaning. I have had SouthWesters come to the inn before, and their speech is very strange, but if you listen carefully, you can puzzle out the words. I have not understood a word these people have said, but they have a manner about them that seems to say they are people of importance, especially the tall woman, who seems to be their leader."

"Woman?" Ersin favored Rogo with a lecherous leer.

"Two of them are women, and one looks almost like an ordinary woman, but the other… well, you will need to see her for yourself, My Lord. The third one—the man—is twice the size of your associate and looks like he is made of stone. They also have an animal—not a very large one—but… well, you'll have to see it as well. Truthfully, I find them disturbing and will be happy to be rid of them."

"Are you sure they are people, not some spirit-beings sent by the Goddess?" Ersin's smirk told Rogo he was joking. *I'm sure he has little faith in the Goddess,* Rogo decided, *else he would walk in fear of being struck dead for all the evil he has done. The Mother of All is patient, and someday he will come to judgment.*

"No, My Lord, they are just people. They eat the food I put before them, and from what we have seen when cleaning the suite where I put them, they seem to have other ordinary human needs as well. They are strange, and they wear strange clothing, but they are people."

"Well then, I think, perhaps, it is time I meet these strange people. Take me to them."

* * *

It was nearly midday when the coach departed, carrying the three off-worlders and their gear, with Ersin and his thug riding their mounts alongside. As he watched them go, Rogo felt sick to his stomach.

He had, by gestures, smiles, and words he knew they did not understand, persuaded them to gather their gear and go with Ersin. He had shown deference to Ersin, portraying him as a person of importance who would help them reach their people. They might even have thought the coach was taking them to the King's City.

Rogo had no idea what the duke would do with them. Maybe he would treat them properly and return them to their people, seeking to curry favor from the off-worlders. If the king were dead, and the Crown's people in confusion, he might seek to hold them until he could use them to his advantage in some other way.

Over his years of covert service, Rogo had learned that Duke North Coast never did anything out of altruism or from a sense of what was proper. Whatever action he took would be the one he perceived to be most advantageous to House Corsa. If he could find no advantage and saw the off-worlders as a threat to his plans, they might well disappear and never be seen again. In that case, Ersin might return to dispose of Rogo, but that was a secondary consideration. Rogo considered himself more than a match for Ersin in a contest of wits over brutality, but the off-worlders had trusted Rogo, and he felt as if he had betrayed that trust.

He went to the kitchen, found Ersin's plaything, and sent her off on an errand that would take the rest of the day. With her out of the way, he sent for his grandson and told him to prepare for a long, hard ride. While the boy was getting himself and his mount ready, Rogo wrote the message for him to carry.

He had no idea what the situation in the city was. For all he knew, the sheriff might be dead or imprisoned or simply have more to worry about than a few lost off-worlders. Being cautious had kept Rogo alive for many years in the dangerous game of covert intelligence. Given a choice, he would have waited for more information before acting, but in this case, time was critical.

He read the message over once more, then folded it, sealed it with wax, using a special stamp the sheriff would recognize, and placed it in a courier pouch. His grandson's precious plains-bred kilder was the fastest animal in North Coast Province, and the boy could ride like no other. Carrying nothing but minimum supplies and Rogo's message, he could reach the King's City in less than two days; he might even overtake the Express Rider carrying Rogo's first message.

Unfortunately, the coach and its passengers would reach House Corsa by nightfall.

* * * * *

Chapter Ten

House Corsa, North Coast Province

When they first left Rogo's inn, the *Lynx* survivors assumed they were being taken to the King's City, but Lorna had her doubts after they had gone only a few hundred meters and turned right at the crossroads. Several kilometers later, she shared those doubts with McGill and Jefferson.

"We're going west," she told them. "According to the map Rogo showed us, the road to the capital runs almost due south. I don't think Rogo was very happy about our leaving, nor do I think he was particularly fond of our host." She waved a hand toward the window of the coach, where Ersin T'Corsa rode beside them. Rogo had introduced them at the inn, but the only thing they learned was Ersin's name.

"I'd have to agree with that," McGill replied. "Rogo smiled and acted like all was sweetness and light, but I think he was trying to warn us about something. Didn't much like the way this Ersin guy looked at me, either."

"Not much we can do at this point," Lorna told them. "Just stay on your guard."

They reached their destination, an imposing castle at the top of a hill, at sunset. There was nothing surrounding it that could be called a city, though they had passed through a small village a few kilometers back. Ersin's man, whose name had never been mentioned, had ridden ahead nearly an hour ago, presumably to announce their arrival. The carriage rolled in through open gates, then they disembarked, and Ersin showed them into a large chamber where a number of people were already waiting.

* * *

"Why do I feel like we're living in a Kafka novel?" McGill's question to Lorna was just above a whisper.

"*The Trial,*" Lorna replied. "I'm getting the same impression."

They stood in the center of the chamber, which vaguely resembled a courtroom, facing a man in rich-looking attire who looked down on them from a bench that was elevated almost a meter above the floor. His ornate, upholstered chair was flanked by a pair of gilded statues of hooded men with axes in hand. Their appearance suggested executioners rather than guards or soldiers.

To the left and right, at a lower level, four men in dark crimson robes sat behind smaller, less ornate benches. They stared at Lorna and her companions in silence. Ersin stood beside the man seated on the upper bench. The two of them appeared to argue, though Ersin smiled and laughed throughout the exchange. The other man—the one in charge—never smiled.

Finally, he turned and spoke to them, still wearing an angry look. Lorna tried to answer, to make them understand that none of them spoke the local language. One of the men to the side rose and barked some sort of command in words they did not understand. Again, Lorna tried to speak, but the man ignored her and spoke instead to the man in the center.

From that point on, no one listened to them, even though Lorna raised her voice several times, trying to tell them their names. Finally, she turned to McGill.

"Think you nailed it, Ensign," she muttered. "We're in Kafka Land."

* * *

"You drive me to the edge of insanity, Ersin," Asral T'Corsa told his half-brother. "First, you send an underling to bring me news of the debacle with High Reaches and then you drop this pile of kilder-dung on my doorstep."

"Ah, but I did take care of some messy details with the High Reaches affair, my brother." Ersin wore that familiar smirk that Asral found so annoying.

"Yes, I'll grant that was done well and timely, but this is another matter. I want no part of these freakish creatures, especially now that everything else is so unstable."

"The innkeeper spent a pair of days with them, and he assures me they are quite human, that the differences between them and us are merely superficial. Further, it appears these are castaways, off-worlders who were in some way defeated by the Bugs and fell from the sky, lost and helpless.

"That's speculation on the part of the innkeeper," he hastened to add, seeing his brother's expression. "They don't seem to speak a word of the common language, but Rogo insists they have a language of their own, that those sounds they make have meaning and are not mere gibberish."

"Of what possible use is that?" Asral snarled. "We can learn nothing from them if we can't understand them!

"You!" he said, pointing at the tall, golden-haired female freak. "What business do you have here? Why do you trespass in my domain?"

The strange woman spoke—or made sounds that seemed to be directed at him, though he could not understand a single word.

"Kneel to His Lordship, devil-witch," Asral's chamberlain shouted, "and keep your eyes down when you speak to him!"

"M'Lord," he insisted, "these are demons, not people. Kill them and burn the remains."

"I agree, M'Lord," the Provincial Sheriff said. He did not get up from his chair, and his voice had a bit of a tentative quaver.

"Spineless *tembri*," Ersin muttered, naming the furtive little scavengers that infested dwellings in the northern provinces. "Three wretched shadows of the off-worlders, and they are ready to run and hide in a hole."

"What of that thing with the yellow eyes," Asral inquired. "Did the innkeeper convince you that is human as well?" He pointed at Bob, cradled in McGill's arms, who stared at him with a typical cat's unblinking lack of respect.

"A pet, perhaps." Ersin shrugged. "Hardly a demon familiar, as these superstitious cretins would have you believe. Brother, you need to find some advisors with functioning testicles."

"What am I to do with these creatures?" Asral demanded. "Tell me that, if you can."

"Oh, I don't know, brother." Ersin still wore the annoying smirk. "That's your choice, which is why you are the duke and I your humble servant. Perhaps you might consider selling them back to their people for some outrageous ransom."

"I want nothing to do with the off-worlders!" Asral snarled. "Not until we know what has come of their war with the Bugs. To help them, to even shelter them here, might bring Bug lightning down on us! In truth, the chamberlain and the sheriff may have the right of it, but that, in turn, might bring similar wrath from the off-worlders. You've brought a bag of yellowtails into our midst, and we may be stung no matter which course we take."

"Such a difficult decision," Ersin said. "Fortunately, I'm not the one who must make it. Consider this, my brother. Would you rather I had told the innkeeper to send them to the king? To King *Arne*, that is, since Algar is no more."

Asral stopped. He had no answer, had not even considered the possibility. He needed time to think things through.

Ersin was already headed for the door, no doubt to his own rooms to sample more of his brother's fine wine and congratulate himself on his cleverness. He paused at the door for one more comment.

"If you can't think of anything to do with them, my brother, you might send the little one to my chambers. I'll wager I can speak to her in a language she'll understand."

He ducked out the door and was gone. Asral turned and regarded the off-worlders again.

"Seize them," he ordered his guards. "Take them down to the sheriff's cells and lock them away until I decide what to do with them."

* * *

L orna winced when the guard grabbed her injured left arm.

OK, enough of Kafka, she thought. Existentialist writer Franz Kafka's protagonist, Josef K, went to his death because he never questioned or resisted the authority of his tormentors. He never knew who they were. *I don't know who these people are, but I'll damned sure question their authority.*

Lorna pulled her arm away, but his grip wasn't particularly strong.

"Take your hands off me," she ordered.

The guard grunted and tried to grab her again. Lorna rammed the heel of her right hand up under his chin, snapping his head back and sending him stumbling backward two steps before he fell flat.

* * *

J efferson blinked when his captain decked the guard but took it as a cue to follow her lead. Another guard had attempted to seize his arm, but Darius simply stood there. The guard might as well have tried to grab a stone statue, until the statue turned, clamped its huge hands under his ribs, lifted him off his feet, and hurled him across the room.

He didn't mass more than 60 kilos, Darius decided. During workouts in *Lynx's* tiny gym, he usually pressed twice that.

McGill had been standing between Darius and Lorna. Alerted by an angry, animal sound, Darius turned and delivered a solid kidney punch to the man who tried to grab McGill from behind. As the guard's knees buckled, Darius reached out and peeled a hissing, squalling Bob off the man's face, leaving a bloody trail of claw marks behind. McGill delivered a sharp kick to the guard's groin, causing him to curl into a fetal position. She held out her hands, and Darius handed Bob to her. The cat retracted his claws and settled again into McGill's arms but continued to warn off their attackers with a high-pitched growl and a hiss.

Darius looked at Lorna and again took a cue from his captain. He drew his sidearm and turned his attention to the remaining guards.

* * *

The Beretta M27 was a recent product of the Sol System's oldest firearm manufacturer. It was the standard-issue sidearm of the LFS military, and the lifepod survival pack had included two of them, with standard belts and holsters. Lorna had been a competition-level pistol shooter since childhood and had taken one without a second thought. She had given the other to Jefferson, knowing his Marine training made him better qualified than McGill.

"Hold your fire, Marine," she ordered.

"Aye aye, ma'am," Darius acknowledged.

A half-dozen other guards and a dozen civilians, including the four next to the bench, were in the room. The civilians retreated to the walls and tried to edge toward the door, while the guards stood their ground with drawn swords. His Lordship, as Lorna thought of him, remained in his chair behind the bench, still looking down on them with an angry scowl. He barked an order, and the guards began to inch forward, cautiously.

"Continue to hold fire," Lorna warned Darius. "I'm going to give them a warning shot."

In outward appearance, the M27 looked very much like the standard military pistols of the early 21st century. Its internal function wasn't much different than that of semiautomatic pistols of the past 200 years, most of which were descendants of John Moses Browning's famous 1911 design. Where the Beretta differed was not so much in the gun as in the ammunition.

The M27 fired a "caseless" round, a 5-centimeter long tube that tapered to a point at the front end, which was a solid projectile like the bullets of old. The rear end was a hollow tube with a cast grain of propellant. In effect, it was a miniature rocket that would continue to burn propellant and build velocity after leaving the barrel.

The M27's 7mm caseless round carried a 160-grain projectile which would reach nearly 1000 meters per second approximately two meters in front of the muzzle. Lorna spun around and faced His Lordship's bench at a range of about four meters. The Beretta had an internal suppressor to reduce the noise, but in the confined space of the room, her two shots must have sounded to the Tatannans like thunderbolts from Hell.

* * *

Duke North Coast's heart nearly stopped as the two thunderous shots rang out, and the statues on either side of his chair exploded, showering him with stone fragments. His breath caught in his throat when he realized the demon bitch's weapon, whatever it was, was now pointed directly at him.

Despite his terror, the expression on his face did not change. He still stared directly at her, wearing the angry frown with which he had issued his last order. Asral T'Corsa prided himself on his control of his facial features. He was always aware of his expression and how he looked to others. That ability made him a formidable opponent in games of chance and served him well in the manipulation of others.

Unfortunately, he had less control over certain other bodily functions, as evidenced by the warm, wet feeling spreading through his breeches. *Thank the Goddess I'm sitting behind the bench*, he thought. *They'll never notice if I don't stand up.*

"Hold your positions!" he ordered. "Do not approach them. Put your weapons away."

He pretended not to notice that his guards were doing anything but approaching the off-worlders. They were scrambling away from them toward the door. They stopped at his command, however, and quickly sheathed their swords. That was sufficient for his purpose. The chamber became very quiet.

The off-world woman spoke again, words that meant nothing to him, but she was smiling. The smile didn't reach her strange blue eyes, however, and her weapon never wavered. He recognized the look of a predator. It wasn't very different from the look on the face of the strange beast the other woman held in her arms.

* * *

"Now, shall we try this again?" Lorna said with a smile. "I'm Lieutenant Commander Lorna Greenwood of the Lunar Free State Navy. We're the people who are trying to free you from the nasty Bugs. We're shipwrecked, and we'd appreciate your help getting back to our people."

She paused for a moment.

"Nothing to say, Your Lordship?" she inquired.

"Guess he doesn't speak English," she remarked to McGill, "but I think we got his attention."

* * *

"Chamberlain!" T'Corsa turned to the man cowering behind the lower bench to his right. The white-faced functionary looked up at him and made a croaking noise that sounded vaguely like a response.

"Apparently, our guests are unhappy with the proposed accommodations. Tell your people to prepare the Green Suites for their use. Prepare them for royalty, as if the king, himself, had come to visit."

"Yes, M'Lord," the chamberlain managed to mumble. "It will be done immediately." He stood and began to edge toward the door, trying to watch both the duke and the off-worlders. T'Corsa sniffed the air and detected a cesspool odor. *At least I only wet myself,* he thought, taking some consolation from the fact that the chamberlain needed to change his soiled linen.

"You!" he ordered the sheriff. "I want you to persuade our guests to go to their new quarters. I would strongly suggest you be careful, lest you upset them."

He looked left and right at the shattered statues, art objects that had been in his family for generations. "I'll hold you personally responsible if they break anything else of value."

* * *

"I think we made our point," Lorna told her people, "though I don't know what we've accomplished in doing so."

The guards had put up their weapons, and most of them wore please-don't-shoot-me expressions. Some of them even made a point of displaying their empty hands. His Lordship spoke, and one of the crimson robes beat a hasty retreat out the door. A second one, a stout bearded man who wore a chain of office around his neck, got to his feet and moved cautiously in front of them, holding up his hands, so they could see he was unarmed. He made sweeping gestures, seeming to indicate they should move toward the door.

Darius scanned the room, alert for additional threats, but Lorna continued to look at His Lordship, who nodded and made a similar gesture, indicating they should follow the other man.

Earlier, they'd carried their gear bags into the chamber and set them down. Lorna picked hers up and slung it over her left shoulder. The Beretta never left her right hand, and she brought her left around in a two-hand combat grip, with the gun pointed at the ceiling.

"I'll take point," Lorna ordered. "Jefferson, you've got our six. Stay sharp, people."

"Aye, aye, ma'am," Darius acknowledged. He gathered his gear, as well as McGill's, handling the double load with ease and leaving her free to manage Bob. He nodded to the captain. *Ready to move out.*

Damn! She's supposed to be a Navy officer, he thought, *but she sounds like she'd be just as comfortable leading a squad of Marines. Hell, if we had a full squad, she'd be hoisting the LFS flag over this stupid little castle by now.*

"Maybe we should put Bob on point, ma'am," McGill remarked with a chuckle. "He seems to be really good at recognizing the enemy, and he's not shy about taking action."

"No, I'll keep him with you, in reserve," Lorna replied with a chuckle. "I'm thinking about putting him in for a commendation, maybe a Marine Close Combat ribbon. What do you think, Jefferson?"

"No question, ma'am," Darius replied. "Bob's a Marine, all right."

Despite the casual banter, they scanned their surroundings as they cautiously followed the scarlet-robed man toward the door. Lorna and Darius held their M27s at ready. If they turned to look to the side, the Berettas turned with them. Whenever they did so, the locals scrambled backward, trying to stay as far from them as possible. At one point, Bob chose to hiss at one of them and bare his fangs. The man tripped over his own feet and fell face down, trying to get away.

They stepped out into the hallway and found it deserted except for their guide. Night had fallen, but their path was well-lit by elaborate candelabra along the walls. Darius wondered what the candles were made of, since they burned with a brilliant white light, rather than the subdued yellowish glow of typical Earth wax candles. Once again, he had that strange feeling of being in a role-playing game, and he found himself missing Jin. *She'd love it here*, he thought. He pulled himself back to reality as they started down the hall, scanning every shadow for a possible ambush.

* * * * *

Chapter Eleven

First Division Forward HQ

60 Kilometers South of Objective

"I'm having a little trouble wrapping my head around the idea that a Second Lieutenant, who was a Master Sergeant a few weeks ago, is now the Lunar Free State's primary diplomatic representative to a foreign government."

General Sherwood delivered the comment in a serious tone of voice, but his face showed a tiny hint of a smile. The other two faces on his conference screen maintained their stone-cold, serious expressions.

"Sir, I was given very little choice in the matter," Moira Bouchard protested.

"I can vouch for that, sir," Nova Sakura insisted. "When I advised King Arne that I was returning to my unit, he told me to take Ensign Bunker with me. His exact words were, 'Remove him from my presence.' He then advised me that he considered Lieutenant Bouchard the person he trusted to 'continue the relationship' he had with Ambassador Michaels."

"I can understand that," Sherwood agreed. "I've spoken with Bunker since you dropped him off here, and frankly, I'm wondering how such an arrogant little bastard ever got into the Diplomatic Corps. Must be somebody's favorite nephew. What, exactly, did he do to piss off the king?"

"I was present at the time, sir," Bouchard advised. "He needed me to interpret, since he hadn't bothered to learn the local language. He asked me to inform the king that once the Bugs were gone, we would establish a New Eden-style Protectorate, with a Lunar Governor to manage the planet's affairs."

Sherwood's eyes narrowed. "Hell! Even I know that's wrong, and I've had no more than a basic briefing on the diplomatic situation. New Eden had no government of its own. It was a tribal hunter-gatherer society, with the largest tribes having no more than a few hundred people. This planet has a fully-functional local government that's been in place for centuries."

"Yes, sir. Mr. Bunker's proposal was totally contrary to what King Algar and Ambassador Michaels had discussed. I told him that, and he expressed the opinion that a 'dark ages monarchy is not a proper form of government in the modern age.' He insisted I translate his proposal. I refused."

"So, the king doesn't know what Bunker wanted."

"The king does know, sir," Bouchard replied. "What Mr. Bunker didn't know is that Arne speaks almost perfect English. His father insisted he learn it years ago, after our first contact with them."

"Hah!" Sherwood chuckled. "In other words, the king heard not only Bunker's half-assed idea, but also your argument against it. No wonder he wants you for his ambassador."

"Sir," Nova Sakura spoke up, "you might also consider that King Arne's favorable view of Serg... Lieutenant Bouchard has something to do with her single-handedly taking out a dozen thugs and the assassin who killed his father and was about to kill him, with nothing more than a Marine Combat Sword in her hands. "

"She did what?" Sherwood looked stunned.

"It's in my report, sir. The diplomatic mission had no access to modern weapons because we didn't want them to fall into Tatannan hands. The Marines assigned to the mission carried swords and combat knives, and Lieutenant Bouchard conducted daily training to make sure they knew how to use them."

"Is that still the case?" Sherwood inquired.

"No, sir," Sakura replied. "We thought the Bugs were coming, so I brought a full load of combat gear, including LARs, LCAWs, sidearms for officers and noncoms, and a pair of 75mm tubes with appropriate ammo. I also brought the field comm gear the Lieutenant is now using, so they don't have to rely on those transponders to contact us."

"Good thinking, Major," Sherwood said. "I also agree with your decision to hold your platoon in the wilderness, out of sight. We don't want to draw too much attention, but this way we've got a quick-reaction force available if we need it. Are you good with that, Lieutenant?"

"Yes, sir. Local politics are confusing right now because of the king's death. Algar was very popular with the people, but I believe that popularity will transition to Arne as well. He was well-liked as a prince, and his father taught him well. As for us, well, we'll try to keep a low profile and not bother you until you finish cleaning up the Bug problem. Excuse me, sir…"

Bouchard turned to her right and spoke in the native language to someone off-screen. She listened to the reply, gave a short answer, and turned back.

"Sir, it appears the king is requesting my presence on a matter of some urgency."

"Go, Lieutenant. Contact Major Sakura if you need any assistance. She's there specifically to cover your six."

"Yes, sir. Bouchard out." Her window on the screen disappeared, and Sherwood turned back to Nova Sakura.

"That's one impressive young woman," he remarked. "Seriously, did she really take out the bad guys with nothing but a sword?"

"Yes, sir, she did, but there's something that's not in the report. I didn't think it was appropriate to mention it, but it might help you understand the situation. When they killed the king, the assassins also killed one of his advisors, a guy named Ramis—a nice young guy, very intelligent, and one of our biggest supporters. Ramis and Lieutenant Bouchard had a personal relationship."

"Lovers." Sherwood nodded his understanding.

"Yes, sir. Apparently, she found him still alive, and the last thing he said to her was 'Save the prince.' So yes, she had a mission. It was a valid mission in support of our objectives, and she got it done in an orderly and proficient manner. Along the way, I'm sure she collected a lot of payback.

"My concern, sir, is that she's still hurting—really hurting—but she seems to be working through it by throwing herself into her new job as de facto ambassador. I think the king knows that as well—he certainly knew of her relationship with Ramis—and he'll do what he can to help her. In other words, I would like to leave the situation as it is for now. I think it will serve the mission and be best for all concerned."

"I see," Sherwood said. "A personal tragedy, but for the moment it serves everyone's purpose to leave her in place. I don't have a problem with a Marine officer serving as ambassador, but it's not a second lieutenant's billet. Need to see what sort of field promotion authority I have under the circumstances."

"Don't know about that, sir, but I think a little 'fruit salad' for the chest might be appropriate."

"Oh, certainly that," Sherwood agreed. "I just haven't figured out how much. Twelve bad guys with a sword, saving the life of a friendly monarch... hell, that's getting up into Medal of Honor territory."

* * *

House Corsa, North Coast Province

The Green Suites were the duke's choice whenever he needed to provide guest quarters for persons of note. They were well-furnished and spacious, and they were kept meticulously clean. They were likely to impress even the most high-born and pampered visitor. Most importantly, they were arranged to allow the duke or his agents to spy on those who occupied them, to observe almost every action, to hear every word spoken above the faintest whisper.

The ceiling beams concealed a maze of listening tubes, all of which led to small rooms adjacent to the suites. Oil lamps mounted on the outer walls of each room were adorned with cut-glass crystals, one of which was the objective lens of a viewing scope that fit through a hole in the wall behind the lamp base. The gilt-framed mirror mounted on the wall in the luxurious bathing room was one-way glass, produced by a secret process known only to a master glazier in North Coast province, who sold such mirrors only to the duke, after being advised by Ersin that his health might suffer if he sold them to anyone else.

Behind the mirror, which was permanently fastened to the wall, was a hole larger than a man's head. In the tiny room on the other side of the wall, a black curtain kept any stray light from betraying the hole's presence. There were two seats in the room. One was a hard wooden stool that served for any observer who might be stationed there; the other was a comfortable, richly padded piece of furniture to be used only by one person. When the Green Suites were occupied by female guests, the little room was one of Ersin's favorite places to relax. He sat comfortably behind the hole with the curtain draped over his head.

He spent much of the first evening there after the off-worlders were quartered. He watched the huge, dark-skinned male out of curiosity, but he lost interest after determining the off-worlder was indeed human, merely a man despite his size and coloration.

The women were another matter, and Ersin watched them with burning lust as they bathed and prepared for bed. The tall one was incredibly beautiful, though very slim by Tatannan standards. Her golden hair and alien blue eyes added to her beauty, and Ersin tried to imagine what it would be like to possess her. At some point, a tiny voice in his head reminded him that she was dangerous, even without her alien magic. She had broken the jaw of one of his brother's guards with a single punch. *If the opportunity presents, I shall first have her chained to the bed,* he told himself.

Then there was the smaller one, who, at first glance, might have been mistaken for a Tatannan woman. Then one noticed the fair skin, with a light speckling of brown marks, on her arms, face, and other places. He admired her amazing, copper-colored hair, which was much lighter than the deep auburn that framed the heads of most Tatannan women. When she undressed, he confirmed that it was her natural hair color. She also had alien eyes—green rather than blue—and he found them quite attractive. Mostly, though, he liked the shape of her body. She was not as well-endowed as the tall one, but neither was she as slender. There was no fat on her, or not much, anyway, but she looked like she had more flesh on her bones than the tall one. In terms of body shape, Ersin, who considered himself an expert on the subject, rated her as near-perfect.

This one doesn't have one of those magic thunderbolt weapons, he noted. *Just have to watch out for that hideous beast that seems to favor her.* The off-worlders had finished their nightly preparations and had left the bathing room, then the beast in question had come in, jumped up onto the dressing shelf, and stared straight into the hole. As he looked at the weird yellow eyes, Ersin was suddenly struck with the notion that the creature could see him. Hastily, he got out from under the curtain and rose from his chair. *Nothing more to see here.*

He left the room and went around to the other observing chambers, particularly the ones that gave access to the bedrooms, but the view through the tiny spy-scopes was not nearly as good, and he could see nothing after the women put out the lamps and got into bed. Frustrated, he left the guest wing and went back to his chambers. *There will be tomorrow night,* he promised himself.

He would leave the daytime spying to his underlings. It would do no good to put anyone in the listening rooms, since no one understood the off-worlder language. Most Tatannans didn't even realize there could be a language other than the one that was universally spoken on their world.

* * *

"I suppose we can't complain about the accommodations," Lorna remarked. "By local standards, I'd guess this place is pretty luxurious."

"Yes, and spacious as well," McGill agreed. "Jefferson, there are two bedrooms. The captain and I could double up. Are you sure—"

"No, I'm fine here, ma'am," Darius said, patting the sofa where he had spent the last two nights, leaving the bedrooms for the women. "I know that door looks pretty sturdy, but I really don't trust these people, and this room is the logical place to stand guard."

The door was indeed solid, certainly impervious to rapid breaching by any weapon the Tatannans might have, and it was equipped with a solid bar on the inside to protect their privacy. They had discovered the previous evening that it was also equipped with several equally solid bars on the outside, apparently to keep them from wandering about the castle at night. The door was not barred in the daytime, as they had just verified, but four guards stood in the hallway outside. The guards, armed with swords and short pikes, looked as if they would rather be somewhere else. Word of certain events associated with the off-worlders arrival had spread quickly.

As for the sofa, it was large enough for Darius and quite comfortable. Its semicircular shape looked a bit unusual by Earth and Luna standards, but there were only so many ways to accommodate the seated human body in comfort, and its function was obvious. It was intended to allow several people to sit, mostly turned toward each other, and hold a conversation, as the three of them were doing now. There was a low table in the center of the semicircle that could be raised and extended toward the sofa to serve as a dining table. The table was a masterpiece of clever woodworking, considering it was made in a world where power tools did not exist.

"I don't trust them either," McGill agreed, "but I have to say the food is tasty, and there have been no ill effects so far."

They had considered the possibility that their hosts might drug or poison them, and when servants arrived bearing breakfast the first morning, they agreed that only one of them would eat the local food until they were sure it was safe. The other two would eat the field rations they brought with them in their survival packs. McGill had immediately volunteered to be the test subject.

"Ma'am, we need you 'cause you're our leader," she told Lorna, "and we need Jefferson because it's always good to have a badass Marine covering your six.

"Me, I'm expendable," she added with a grin, "and besides, field rats mostly suck. Nothing that's meant to last a hundred years in storage could possibly taste good."

The first day, they explored all there was to see in the Green Suites—a foyer in front of the door, the large central room in which they were now sitting, the toilet room, which Tatannans apparently thought should be separate from the bathing room, the two bedrooms, and a small private room with a table and four chairs that Darius called the "game room." There was also a balcony, accessible through doors at the far end of the central room. It was open to the air but covered by a substantial roof. The view from its stone rails was a sheer drop to a garden 20 meters below. It was not intended as an exit.

"Ma'am, you know, we each have about 100 meters of 200-kilo polycord in the survival bags," Darius remarked.

"Right," Lorna acknowledged, "but it's been a while since I've rappelled down anything. I think we'll save that for an escape of last resort."

Each room in the suite was well-lit by oil lamps that seemed to produce very little smoke or smell. The servants lit the lamps at sunset and refreshed the fire in the large hearth in the central room, as well as the smaller ones in the bedrooms—a necessity since the nights were proving to be very cool.

They discovered the duke's residence had both hot and cold running water. They assumed the hot water came from a wood-fired water boiler on the roof, but whatever the source was, it was welcome. They also found Tatannan soap to be an acceptable product, though it left a heavy perfumed smell when they tried to wash their clothing in it.

"As far as I'm concerned, we're prisoners," Lorna said. "It's a very nice prison, but a prison nonetheless." This was their second full day as "guests" of Duke North Coast, and they were beginning to wonder what to do next.

"They haven't taken our weapons," McGill pointed out. "I'm pretty sure we could fight our way out of here without a problem. Most of them would probably run the other way if they saw us coming."

"Uh... don't underestimate them, ma'am," Darius cautioned. "I saw crossbows on the walls when we came in. A bolt from one of those is just as deadly as a round from one of our pistols. They have decent range, and they're silent. If you don't see them before they shoot..."

"He's right," Lorna agreed. "Besides, we don't know where we are—just that we're somewhere west of the coast where we landed. I don't know where we could go. I'm still wondering about Rogo. I got the same impression you did, Mary Jane—he wasn't happy about turning us over to Ersin.

"The real question is, did he send a message to the king? If so, there's a chance some of our people will come looking for us, so I'm willing to put up with life in this gilded cage for a few more days."

* * *

Castle Boroson, the King's City

"You sent for me, Your Majesty?"

As she had always done, Moira Bouchard snapped to attention and presented the king with a sharp, Marine Corps salute. Arne reflected that it somehow seemed a far more sincere gesture of respect than the groveling, bowing, knee-to-the-floor presentations he, and his father before him, received from so many nobles.

He had once asked Major Sakura about it. *We don't kneel to anyone except God or Goddess, in your belief,* she had told him. *Marine officers are taught that salutes are something you must earn. Lower ranks will always salute you, but you will know right away whether they mean it or not, whether you have earned it.*

Lady Moira always meant it with my father, Arne decided, *and she's willing to give me the benefit of the doubt, but it may be some time before I fully earn her respect.*

"Yes, I did, milady," he replied. "Sir Regas has just brought me a message from one of his field agents in North Coast province. It tells of some of your people who came to the inn at Sbora's Grove about three days ride north of here. It was delivered by Crown messenger, and it contained this…" He held out a folded sheet of paper.

Moira took the message from the king's hand and noticed immediately that it was written on modern paper, not the parchment of

Tatanna. She unfolded it, and her eyes widened as she read the message.

"This is very good news, Majesty," she told him. "It appears these are survivors from one of our ships that was destroyed by the Bugs. Our people thought they were dead, but they landed safely and found their way to this inn you speak of. We can send people there to bring them back—" She paused as Arne held up his hand.

"There is a second message," Sir Regas D'Narr told her. "I'm afraid this news may not be so good."

* * *

First Platoon, Bravo Company
Encamped on the Little Kilder River

"Damn! Blondie's alive!" Nova Sakura couldn't keep the grin off her face. "You remember Greenwood from the *Lewis and Clark* mission? They gave her *Lynx* as her first command. They said she didn't make it out when the ship went down, but I guess they were wrong."

"I recognized the name," Bouchard replied. "Wasn't sure it was her, but how many Lorna Greenwoods can there be?"

"Well, there were two of them, but her grandmother died years ago, just before Blondie and I graduated from the Academy. So, tell me more about this second message, and why the king thinks it's a problem. We know where they were taken, right?"

"Yes. The sheriff believes they are now guests of Asral T'Corsa, Duke North Coast, the local nobleman who controls the North Coast province, an area roughly the size of France back on Earth, but not very heavily populated. He's reputed to be something of a despot, but he swears he's loyal to the king—King Algar—since none of them have been summoned yet to swear allegiance to Arne.

"The problem is that both Arne and the sheriff swear he's a lying bastard whom they suspect was involved in the assassination plot. At the very least, they're sure he was cozy with Duke High Reaches, the assassin who accidentally ran into my sword less than a tenday ago."

"Tenday?" Sakura smirked. "You really have gone native. Damn! I'm sorry Moira, I didn't mean…"

"It's OK, Major." Bouchard shook off the crushing depression that hit her. "I never know when something is going to remind me of him. Yes, you're right. Back on Luna, I would have said 'last week' but I've finally gotten used to the idea that they don't have weeks here.

"Anyway," she continued, "the sheriff is upset that our people were taken by the duke's half-brother, a guy named Ersin T'Corsa, who is apparently a really bad actor. The sheriff issued a standing order for his arrest if he's ever caught in the Crown's lands.

"They don't know what North Coast will do with our people— hold them for ransom or keep them hidden until he can find a way to use them to his advantage. They don't think he'll kill them, but he's almost certainly detaining them. The good news is he doesn't know we know he has them."

"Under the circumstances, the simplest thing would be for me to drop a platoon of Marines into his front yard and demand he produce them, with a warning that if they've suffered any injury, North Coast might be looking for a new duke. Somehow, I don't think the king would be too happy, nor would General Sherwood. You're the ambassador, what do you think?"

Bouchard gave her a sour look. "Major, you know my qualifications for that job are pretty thin. My inclination would be to tell Arne what you've just said—that we'd like to go get them, by force, if necessary, but we don't want to do anything that would cause problems for the Crown."

"Let's see what he suggests. Maybe, if we need to low-key it, a squad of Marines would be enough. The sight of a Firefly dropping into that front yard would probably make them wet their pants."

"Sounds like a plan. I'm going to pass the word to the General and see what he wants us to do because nothing's going to happen without his authorization. Talk to the king, see what he has to say, and get back to me."

"Will do, Major." Bouchard nodded and prepared to disconnect the call.

"Moira," Sakura stopped her. "Forget about rank for a minute. Girl to girl, are you OK?"

Bouchard was silent for a few seconds.

"No, I'm not, not yet," she said with a sigh, "but I'm getting better. I've started saying prayers to the Goddess if you can believe that. It seems to be helping. I get the feeling She might be listening."

"*T'Anna marsin tei,*" Sakura said. "Yeah, maybe She is, but if you want to talk to anybody else, I'm here."

* * *

Bug Hive, 900 Kilometers Northwest of the King's City

The Bugs experienced nothing that could be compared to human emotion. They knew the Hive would not be able to hold against the humans long enough for them to see the results of the final option. Through a process known only to them, they selected one of the two queens for a possible, though highly improbable, chance of survival, and the other for certain death. If, by some rare chance, the final option succeeded, they would need one queen to produce eggs for re-population and to direct the rebuilding of their presence on the planet.

The decision made, one queen, with an appropriate retinue of warriors and workers, started down the long tunnel. The other remained in the Hive to prepare for the end.

* * *

Battlecruiser LFS *Nike*, in Tatanna Orbit

"*Cease fire! Cease fire! Clear and secure all weapons systems. Set Condition Yellow throughout the ship.*"

For the first time in nearly three days, the battlecruiser stood down from Condition Red. Some of her crew would be released from battle stations for a well-deserved rest, and the crew's mess and officers' wardrooms would begin serving real meals again.

No one could truly relax until Condition Blue was set, but Captain Jacobs expected a call from the Admiral that would let him do that within the hour. If things continued to go according to plan down on the planet, Fleet's work in orbit was pretty much done. They could stand down to a defense-in-place, lick their wounds, and perhaps send some of the more badly damaged ships back to Luna.

It's been a short campaign, he thought. *Back on Luna, Fleet is just getting the very first reports we sent when we got here. Good thing we didn't need additional support because it wouldn't arrive for another month.*

They had worked through a series of fire missions that had cleared the way for the Marine advance on the Big Bug Base, as everyone was calling it. Most of those missions had been conducted under fire from a stream of Bug attack craft and surface-launched missiles, but after they'd hit the Marine-selected targets, they'd hammered the launch sites from which those attacks were coming.

About twelve hours earlier, the Bugs had finally run out of missiles and attack craft, so then it was time to hammer the Big Bug Base. The first kinetic salvos had peeled the top off the base, revealing the complexity of the structure below. They paused between strikes to let Marine air recon evaluate the effectiveness, and each time reports came back that there were more layers of tunnels beneath and more Bugs still active and shooting at the recon birds.

Finally, they decided to stop the kinetics and let the Marines do it the hard way. They'd already put way too much dust in the planet's atmosphere, and the Admiral's scientific people were telling him that any more might produce long-term climate effects.

"Sir! Message from Marine HQ. It appears they've found some survivors from LFS *Lynx* down on the planet."

"Well, that's good news," Jacobs told his bridge comm officer. "Patch that through to the Admiral."

* * * * *

Chapter Twelve

First Division Forward HQ

60 Kilometers South of Objective

"Well, sir, the king says go get 'em," Bouchard advised. "His Majesty would prefer that we speak nicely to Duke North Coast and 'politely request' that he deliver our people, but if the duke resists in any way, we are authorized to use 'whatever methods of persuasion we require,' up to and including leveling the place.

"He does request that we protect the Crown's agent, the guy who gave us the information about the survivors. He wants the duke to believe we knew where they were because of some 'off-world magic.' He also suggests we take the High Sheriff along on the mission to show that we come with the king's blessing. Other than that, he would rather we reveal as little as possible about our dealings with the Crown. As far as the duke is concerned, some of our people wandered into his territory, and we came to get them back. Period. End of Story."

"OK, on that basis I approve Major Sakura's plan," Sherwood told them. "It's low profile enough to not cause a stir, but it gives you enough resources to deal with whatever you encounter. You can go as soon as you're ready."

"I'll have to lead the mission, sir," Nova told him. "I'm the only one, other than First Lieutenant Bouchard's people, who speaks the language well enough to get the message across." She grinned at

Bouchard, whose eyes flicked self-consciously to the new silver bar she wore on her shoulder.

Sherwood chuckled when he saw the little distraction. "I'll see if I can't find a regular officer's uniform to send you with the next supply drop, Lieutenant," he said. "Honestly, we had to bump you up, since you seem to be our de facto ambassador. If nothing else, we have to show His Majesty that we fully endorse your efforts."

"Uh... yes, sir." Bouchard looked even more uncomfortable. "Admiral McGruder is asking me for a briefing on the diplomatic situation for his report back to Luna. I hope you understand, and he understands, that I'm really new to this stuff and have to kind of make it up as I go."

"None of us are professional diplomats," Sherwood said, "but if you get in a bind and don't know what to say or do, the Admiral is the guy to call. I know you're a Marine first, and you might want to call me, but he's the guy in charge of the mission."

* * *

LFS *Nike,* in Tatanna Orbit

"So, Lieutenant, I'm pleased to finally meet you." Admiral McGruder studied the image on the screen. He saw a slim, hard-looking woman in her early thirties, who was attractively feminine, despite the just-healing scar on her left cheek and the close-cropped curly brown mohawk that topped her high-and-tight-on-the-sides Marine-style haircut. She was dressed in a Marine basic field uniform, with the silver bar of a first lieutenant on her shoulder, and her sleeve showed a slightly less faded patch where her NCO stripes had been removed.

McGruder returned the salute she offered him. *Marines*, he thought, with amusement. A Navy officer wouldn't have bothered saluting him on a video call, despite his exalted rank.

"They tell me you're the only one the king will talk to, so what I need is a report on the diplomatic situation. Verbal will do for now because I've got to send my report to Fleet, but I would like you to send me a written report sometime in the next few days."

"Yes, sir." Bouchard nodded, but her thin-lipped expression betrayed the distress she was feeling.

"Admiral, be advised that I am totally out of my depth here. General Sherwood says I'm now a first lieutenant, but I still think like a Marine noncom, and I really know nothing about diplomacy. I wasn't involved in Ambassador Michaels' discussions with the king. I picked up on the general idea of where things were going from Major Sakura before she and the Ambassador returned to Luna last time, but the only instructions I had were 'try not to screw anything up while we're gone.' My normal mode of operation has always been to duck any questions about our future policy by claiming that stuff was above my pay grade."

"You didn't hesitate to shut Mr. Bunker down when he tried to talk to the king." McGruder's voice was neutral, neither accusing, nor approving.

"Sir, Arne was getting pissed, and what the ensign was proposing was nothing like what I'd heard in the past. What kind of diplomat talks down to the people he's supposed to be dealing with? He implied the Tatannans couldn't govern themselves properly, so we were going to have to take over, and he was saying it in front of the King of Tatanna!"

"Relax, Lieutenant. You may not know anything about diplomacy, but as far as I'm concerned, you got that one absolutely right." McGruder gave her an approving grin. "I spoke to that arrogant little prick after General Sherwood sent him back up here. He seems to think his authority in the matter exceeds mine, not to mention yours. He's being shipped back to Luna, and he's lucky he won't be making the trip in a warship's brig. I'm sending a report to the Diplomatic Corps that ought to set their underwear on fire, and a copy of that report is going to Admiral Ling, as well.

"Your concerns are noted. I have an idea, but right now, all I need is a sitrep—our status down there and anything that's happening that we should know about. Is that something that's in your comfort zone?"

"Yes, sir." She relaxed and produced a small smile. "A sitrep... I can do that. To begin with, most of Tatanna's nobles, and most of the people on the planet, don't have a clue what's going on. They don't know we're here, or that we're fighting the Bugs, and that we're doing it to liberate them.

"That's the Crown's big secret, though Arne told me his father sent word of it some months ago—before the task force arrived—to two dukes who were his most trusted allies, Middle Plains and Far Shores. If you have a copy of the map Ambassador Michaels took back to Luna on his last trip, you can see their territories, but I don't think either of them saw any action because they have no Bug mines on their lands and very little Bug activity."

Next to McGruder in the battlecruiser's flag briefing room, John O'Hara brought up the map on his screen and showed it to the admiral.

"We have the map, and I'll check that. Continue."

"Yes, sir. Well, as I said, most of the planet has no idea what's going on. Most don't know King Algar's dead, and Arne is on the throne, though word is spreading rapidly. Arne tells me he has dispatched riders to all the dukes and some of the lesser nobles. He hasn't told them about us, but he is telling them about his father's death because he needs them to swear allegiance to him. He's also telling them he's seizing the Duchy of High Reaches—you can check that on the map as well—in the name of the Crown, because Duke High Reaches is the assassin who killed his father."

"That's the guy you killed, isn't it?" McGruder inquired.

"Er... yes, sir," Bouchard admitted.

"Good job," McGruder said. "No wonder Arne likes you. Continue."

"Some people have noticed our assault on the Bugs because it's happening in their backyards. It's scaring the living shit... er... sorry, sir. It's scaring them a lot."

"I'm familiar with the expression, Lieutenant. Don't apologize for telling it like it is. OK, so we are scaring the shit out of them."

"Yes, sir. Riders have already arrived from Duke Five Rivers, telling the king the sky is falling, and the world is coming to an end. There are lots of Bug mines in his territory, and I imagine it was one of the primary landing areas.

"Unfortunately, I'm not privy to the battle plans, so I don't know where our people are operating, or where the significant conflicts are. It would be nice if I could give the king a general idea, so he knows what to expect."

"Yes, I can see we need to keep you updated," McGruder agreed. "That ties in with my other idea. We don't have any 'trained diplomats' up here, either, but we can provide you with a little high-level support. Anything else I need to know?"

"No, sir, except that Major Sakura is about to mount a mission to retrieve the survivors from the destroyer that went down. I'm sure they'll advise you directly."

"Yes, that's good news." He nodded. "Now, about your diplomatic problems...

"John—" he turned to O'Hara, who was off-screen from Bouchard's view, "—you have been on the Blue Orchid Project from the start. You know more about the overall intent and where we expect to go from here than anyone in this system, including me. All I know is that we're supposed to kick the Bugs' asses and then leave the rest to Lunar Command. You also have the big picture on the operation to date."

"Admiral, as far as 'where we expect to go from here' I really don't think that's been decided yet," O'Hara replied. "Assuming we do kick the Bugs out, we don't know whether they'll come back. In other words, we don't know how badly they want this planet. There have been a few ideas, including the suggestion that we might let them come and get their ore if they behave themselves, but we can't figure that out until we find a way to communicate with them.

"The only thing that seems certain is that Fleet's going to need a strong presence in this system—stronger than the one we have at New Eden—for a long time. As for our dealings with the local people, I don't think that's even been discussed yet. Ambassador Michaels was pretty much playing that by ear."

"That's kind of my point, Admiral," Bouchard interjected. "In the absence of guidance from above, do we really want the Lunar Free State's relations with Tatanna to be determined by a Marine

Master Sergeant who still has no idea why people keep calling her 'Lieutenant' or why a king would take her advice?"

"Point taken, Lieutenant." McGruder chuckled. "I think I might have a solution. John, I'm thinking about sending you down there to give Lieutenant Bouchard the support she needs. She's still going to have to take the lead with the king, but you can advise her as needed and back her up with the authority of a flag-ranked officer. What do you think?"

"Well..." O'Hara was taken by surprise. "It might work, but I presume you're not putting Lieutenant Bouchard under my command. I don't think you should as that might knock the king's nose out of joint. He trusts her and sees her as the face of the Lunar Free State. If we bring someone in above her, he might take that as a repudiation of whatever she's said and done so far. I can be presented as an advisor, not the guy in charge, and any time she feels out of her depth, she can kick the problem upstairs to me... and then I'm the one setting policy for the LFS."

"Yeah, I guess that's what I'm saying," McGruder admitted. "The king's happy because he's comfortable with her as ambassador. Fleet's happy because we've got a flag officer on the spot to guide the process. Hopefully, it'll only be temporary until Fleet, the Diplomatic Corps, the Directorate, and everybody else back on Luna get their collective heads out of their asses, which could be a long damned time, now I think about it."

"So, Lieutenant—" he turned back to Bouchard, "—how do you feel about having a Navy Commodore on your ambassadorial staff?"

"C... Commodore?" Bouchard was stunned. She hadn't been aware of O'Hara's rank, and the 'flag officer' comment had slipped by her. "Sir, I..."

"Relax, Bouchard," O'Hara said, as he leaned into view behind the admiral. "It's only me, John O'Hara. You do remember me, don't you?"

"Mr. O'Hara!" Bouchard broke into a surprised grin. "Yes, I do! You were our XO aboard *Lewis and Clark,* but I was only a corporal back then."

McGruder lifted an eyebrow in surprise. "I didn't realize you were also on that mission, Lieutenant. Can I assume you and Commodore O'Hara can work together without a problem?"

"Yes, sir, and thank you. The more I think about it, the more I like this idea. When will you be sending the Commodore down?"

"Depends on how long it takes him to pack," McGruder said. "Navy officers don't usually have to deploy on a minute's notice like Marines do, but I think you can expect him by… what's your local time?"

"Just past sunset, sir. Tatannans don't do clocks."

"I'd say some time tomorrow afternoon. Oh, and that written report I asked for, I'd suggest you let him put that together. It's the sort of thing Commodores are pretty good at, and it'll give Fleet a warm, fuzzy feeling if it has his name on it. You should countersign it, though, because you deserve the credit."

* * *

First Division Forward HQ
20 Kilometers South of Objective

"This is not making a whole lot of sense." Sherwood looked puzzled. "We crack the top of this hive open and find this crazy honeycomb underneath. It's full of Bugs, but except for a few isolated engagements, they're not fighting us. They cram themselves into the tunnels to form bug barricades, and we have to blast through them to proceed, but they're not attacking. I've got the better part of two battalions, almost 500 Marines, working their way through that maze down there, but we're not taking casualties."

"They seem to be trying to delay us." Orin Olson shook his head. "Our guys blast open a new tunnel section and vent the methane, and the first thing they run into is one of those 'bug plugs.' The bugs are already dead because they're not wearing environment suits, and they can't live in an oxygen atmosphere. Oh, and by the way, General, we have taken a few casualties, mostly accidental because somebody got careless when they opened one of those tunnels. An oxymethane light-off in a tight tunnel is not a pleasant event."

"Yeah. We've warned them about it, but..." Sherwood paused with a thoughtful look on his face.

"Maybe that's the answer," he said. "Maybe they can't fight because they don't have any more environment suits. As soon as we open a tunnel, they die, so they do their best to die in a way that's going to obstruct us.

"That still doesn't make a lot of sense, though. You'd think they'd set booby traps, IEDs, and other nasty stuff for us in a tunnel, then retreat out of that tunnel before we open it."

Olsen shrugged. Sherwood had a point, but he had no advice to offer. The good news was that the surface Bug forces in the area had been taken out. Those had fought, and the Marines had taken casualties, but the area was now clear, and Sherwood had moved his HQ to a ridge overlooking the hive less than 20 kilometers from the top of the tunnel maze. It had been several days since the Bugs had shown

212 | JOHN E. SIERS

any air or space capability, and Fleet still had him well-covered from orbit.

Second Division continued to sweep the remainder of the countryside, including the Bug mine sites First Division had cleared in their initial thrust. Mark Mercer had parceled out his ground forces to cover virtually every former Bug strong point, since they all seemed to have tunnels leading to the hive, while the air units of both divisions swept across the entire continent, looking for additional Bug facilities.

Between Mercer's troops and the air recon, they had frightened a lot of Tatannan locals. They had a large area to cover. The habitable zone stretched about 400 kilometers north and south of the equator, and the single continent was almost 3000 kilometers wide. The rest of the equatorial belt was ocean, except for a few small islands. With over a million square kilometers, most of it sparsely populated; there were still a lot of Tatannans who had no idea there was a war going on.

* * *

House Corsa, North Coast Province

"Well, that was interesting," Lorna remarked after Darius returned from the hallway and closed the door.

For the past ten minutes they had been dealing with Duke North Coast's way of establishing communications. It started shortly after breakfast, when a small, elderly Tatannan woman came into the suite, without the usual attention-requesting, permission-seeking gestures the servants usually made before entering. She simply opened the door and walked directly up to the dining table where they were sitting. She looked them over with disapproval, then started speaking loudly, her speech accentuated by various hand gestures. After nearly a full minute of loud monologue, she stopped and looked at them expectantly. When they didn't respond, she frowned, then pointed at Darius and spoke again, briefly, but even more loudly, almost shouting.

"I'm sorry, ma'am," Darius said. "I don't understand... "

He broke off in the middle of the sentence as the old woman reached out and slapped him across the mouth.

Darius looked at her, calmly. It had been intended as a serious slap, but he doubted she massed more than about 45 kilos and looked to be a century old by Luna standards. He wasn't about to take a swing at somebody's great-grandmother, so he looked to his captain for guidance.

"Who the hell are you..." Lorna started to say, then her right hand flashed up and grabbed the woman's arm to stop a slap aimed at her. She held the arm in an iron grip, until the woman panicked and tried to step back. She stumbled when Lorna released her but recovered and backed a couple of meters away from the table.

She started shouting again, as she walked around the room and pointed at various objects. She shouted a word each time, paused, then repeated the word. After a moment she stopped, then looked at them expectantly.

"I think she's... " McGill started to say, only to have the woman point at her and start shouting again. McGill turned to Lorna and raised her voice to be heard over the tirade.

"I think she's trying to teach us to speak their language, ma'am. When she pointed at the chair over there, I think she used a variation of the word Rogo used for 'sit.'"

"Someone must have told her we're deaf," Lorna remarked. The woman continued to shout. "Her teaching method sucks. Jefferson, would you please remove her from our presence? Try not to hurt her, just get her out of here."

The old woman paled when Jefferson got up and approached her. She obviously hadn't realized how big he was. She tried to shrink back as he reached out and took her by the arm. He didn't squeeze very hard, but when she tried to pull away, his grip was like an iron band. She began to shriek, but he only smiled and gestured toward the door with his free hand. He led her firmly into the hallway, where the guards stared at him, then he released her and stepped back inside, closing the door behind him.

"Drop the bar," Lorna ordered. "I don't want to see anybody else without an invitation."

The three of them looked at each other, then they all broke out laughing.

"Learning their language is not a bad idea," McGill remarked, "but they need to find a better teacher."

"I wonder if she actually is a teacher." Lorna chuckled. "If so, I'm glad I'm not a kid growing up around here."

"Now, we can relax and figure out what to do for the rest of the day..." McGill's comment trailed off as she watched Bob's antics. The cat hadn't paid any attention to the old woman. He was on the stone-topped shelf under the mirror in the bathing room. No lamp was lit in the windowless room, but McGill could see him in the dim light from the open door.

"He keeps climbing up on that shelf and looking at himself in the mirror," McGill pointed out. "I can understand that, but he only does it when the room is dark, and he always stays right in the center.

The mirror runs the full length of the wall, so what's so interesting about that one spot?"

"Cats don't usually share their thoughts with humans," Lorna mused, "so who knows what motivates them, but you're right, that is strange. They have better eyesight than we do, especially in low light."

She got up and walked to the door of the bathroom. Her shadow fell on Bob and the shelf, but he didn't look at her. Instead, he peered even more intently at the mirror.

"Oh, *hell* no!" Lorna exclaimed. "Jefferson! Find me a blunt instrument, something like a hammer or a club."

Darius glanced around, then grabbed a heavy metal candlestick from the table.

"Will this do, ma'am?"

"Perfectly," she replied. She scooped Bob off the shelf and handed him to Darius in exchange for the candlestick. She lined herself up and swung at the mirror, exactly at the spot that had fascinated Bob.

The mirror shattered inward, which didn't surprise her, revealing a large hole in the wall behind it. She bent quickly, looked through the hole, and saw a startled face looking back at her.

"Bastard!" she snarled. With one smooth motion, she drew her Beretta and fired one shot into the hole.

The shot brought a scream from the other side, followed by a crashing scramble and the sound of a door being flung open with a bang.

"Hallway, to the left!" she yelled. "Stop that son of a bitch!"

* * *

Murtax was one of Ersin's more useful minions. He was a small man with a rodent's features, who was physically unsuited to work as one of the enforcers, but he was a clever little *tembril*, good at pilfering things and listening at windows to obtain information on his master's behalf. He had been given the bathroom watch for the day, with Lord Ersin's teasing promise that he might see naked women if he stayed vigilant. He soon realized the room was seldom used during the day. So far, he had only seen the face of that strange little beast the off-worlders had brought with them. He was chewing on a bit of dried meat when he heard voices through the small listening-tube. Someone was coming into the bathing room.

He ducked under the curtain and looked through the hole, just in time to see someone pass in front of the mirror, then the candlestick crashed through. Broken glass sprayed all over his face, and the candlestick stopped just short of the end of his nose. With shaking hands, he picked pieces of glass away from his face before daring to open his eyes. To his horror, he saw the eyes of the alien woman looking directly at him. She said something in her alien language, and her intention was clear, even though he didn't understand the words.

He scrambled from under the curtain, knocked the stool over, and slipped to the floor just as the world exploded in his ears.

* * *

Darius raised the bar and flung the door open. He drew his Beretta as he charged into the hall. He looked left and saw a door open into the hallway and a man scrambling away in panicked flight. Before he could react, the man made a sharp left turn and disappeared down the stairs. Darius ran to the top of the stairs, but by the time he arrived, there was no sign of the fugitive.

Pistol in hand, he went back to the door. He noted that the guards had dropped their pikes and were not attempting to draw their swords.

"He got away, ma'am," he announced.

"Bring one of those guards in here," Lorna ordered.

Darius reached out and grabbed the nearest guard by the front of his chain mail shirt, dragged him toward the door, and pushed him in. Lorna, who was standing just inside the door, also grabbed the man by the shirt, leaned down, and confronted him face-to-face.

"Ersin T'Corsa!" she demanded. "Ersin T'Corsa here!" She pointed at the floor.

She shoved the man out the door, then watched as he mumbled something to his three cohorts, then ran down the hall in the same direction the fugitive had gone.

* * *

"So, they are requesting my presence? Is that what you think they were saying?"

"Yes, M'Lord." The guard kept his head down. "She spoke your name twice to be sure I understood. I came to you right away, M'Lord."

"You've done well. You may return to your post." Ersin waved his hand in dismissal.

He'd already heard the almost incoherent report Murtax had delivered. Apparently, the off-worlders had discovered the spyhole in the bathing room and had smashed his brother's precious one-way mirror. The loss of the mirror bothered Ersin less than the termination of his private viewing sessions. He'd spent two delightful evenings watching them and had decided he absolutely must have the smaller woman. It was just a matter of separating her from the others.

He'd considered drugging them, but the servants had told him two of them were not eating the food—they were subsisting on some sort of packaged food they'd brought with them. He also wished he could explore the wonders contained in their travel bags, but his best pilfering boy had been unable to open the strange closures. The boy had been caught in the act and thrown out the door of the suite by the dark-skinned giant.

He supposed there was nothing he could do but go and see them. Anticipating their demand, he summoned the castle's best mason and explained the job that needed to be done. He took the man with him, along with a pair of serving girls to attend to any other needs they might have. He also summoned one of his largest strongmen to accompany him.

As he approached the Green Suites, he noted that the door to the secret spy room was still open, and that it had a splintered, fist-sized hole through its solid wood center. He also noted that a chunk had been blasted out of the stone wall opposite the door. *Murtax was fortunate,* he decided. He realized it was even more fortunate the incident hadn't occurred while he was enjoying a viewing session.

The door to the suite was closed, so he rapped on it sharply with the heavy walking stick he always carried. The giant off-worlder opened the door immediately and made a sweeping gesture, inviting him to enter. Normally, Ersin didn't go through a door without sending one of his men in front of him, but this was his brother's castle, and he let his guard lapse for a moment. He stepped through the door, warily watching the giant, and was surprised when the tall woman shoved him from behind into the room. She had been waiting beside the door, and when she stepped forward, the giant moved to bar anyone else from entering.

Ersin turned to face her, an angry epithet on his lips. The words died when he found himself staring at the weapon that was thrust almost directly between his eyes. Undoubtedly, it was the same weapon used to blast the hole in the spy room door. He had a horrible vision of a similar hole in the back of his head. Like his brother, Ersin knew how to control his features, particularly in times of stress.

He smiled and shrugged, while spreading his hands out beside him. It was a gesture intended to indicate he had no idea what the problem might be but was willing to allow her to explain it.

She reached out with her very long left arm, grabbed him by the shoulder, and turned him toward the bathing room. She gestured with her weapon, and he marched forward to look into the room.

The lamp had been lit and clearly illuminated the scene. As expected, he saw a shattered mirror, the candlestick still laying on the floor, and the gaping hole in the wall. He pretended to examine it with surprise, then turned to her, shaking his head. He shrugged again as if to say he knew nothing of the matter.

"Bullshit," the tall woman said.

Ersin didn't know the word, but he understood the sentiment. She didn't believe him. It didn't matter to him. He walked to the door, which the giant still blocked, and called out for the stonemason and the serving girls. The giant moved aside to let them in, and Ersin directed them to the bathing room and pointed to the hole.

"Close that up," he told the mason. "It must be done before sunset tonight. I don't care how you do it, as long as it looks permanent, but keep in mind that we may want to open it again sometime in the future."

If I can persuade my brother to spend the copper for a new mirror.

"Clean up this mess," he told the serving girls. "When the mason is finished, clean up his mess as well. This room must be fit for bathing tonight."

He turned to the tall woman and made gestures to explain what the mason was going to do. Meanwhile, the girls had started collecting the broken glass. He must have made his point because the woman nodded to him and stepped back. She spoke to the giant, who moved aside to let him leave.

He turned to offer her a bow of farewell but stopped when he caught sight of the smaller off-world woman, holding the alien beast in her arms. He paused and gave her a long, lingering look punctuated by an unmistakable leer. He bowed to her, then again to the tall one. The alien beast hissed at him as he turned to leave. *I'll make a hat from that animal's fur,* he decided, *after I've gotten that copper-haired beauty into my bed.*

With that, he walked past the giant and out the door.

* * * * *

Chapter Thirteen

House Corsa, North Coast Province

"That sounds like… " McGill's voice trailed off as she strained to hear the distant sound.

Jefferson had been playing chess with the captain—apparently, someone at Fleet had decided a small chess set was a worthy item to include in the standard survival kit. He looked up from the board, where Lorna had just declared mate in three moves, and listened.

"That's a Raptor, ma'am!" he said. "Actually, it sounds like two Raptors!"

Jefferson had only heard Raptors in flight on training videos, but there was no mistaking the deep thrumming sound of their gravity-pulse propulsion system. The current version of the Marines' primary ground-attack craft could operate in almost any environment, from hard vacuum to a hostile, non-oxygen atmosphere.

After yesterday's excitement over the spyhole, today had been quiet. The mason had done a credible job of closing the hole with a solid brick-and-mortar plug. The servants cleaned up the mess and removed the remainder of the mirror from the wall at Lorna's insistence, but no more holes had been discovered. Everything had been done before yesterday's dinner.

After dinner, they searched the suite, looking for spy devices, holes, and other suspicious items. McGill pointed out a cabochon set into the base of a lamp holder that looked suspiciously like a lens. Further examination showed that all six of the wall-mounted lamps had the same feature. At Jefferson's suggestion, they hung an article of clothing on each one, arranged to cover the suspect feature.

None of them slept well. McGill seemed certain Ersin was still watching them, and she was reluctant to bathe and get ready for bed. Lorna kept searching for other surveillance items they may have overlooked. Darius slept fitfully, waking often when he thought he heard noises outside the door. He was blaming lack of sleep for his defeat on the chessboard, when an unexpected sound interrupted the game. He jumped up and dashed out to the balcony, with Lorna and McGill close behind.

"Raptors passed to the west, ma'am," he declared. "Two of them. I think I saw a Firefly coming in for a landing, but I lost sight of it behind the tower. Looked like it was going to set down on the other side of the castle by the front gate."

"OK, it's time to move out," Lorna told them. "Grab the gear. I don't want to leave anything behind."

They had kept their gear together in case an escape opportunity arose. It took them less than a minute to pack, and a few more seconds to find Bob, who had burrowed under the covers of McGill's bed for a nap. They were ready to move out when Darius delivered the bad news.

"Door's barred on the outside, ma'am. We're locked in."

* * *

The High Sheriff's normally sun-browned complexion had turned pasty by the time the Firefly touched down, but he'd taken the flight rather well, considering the idea of air travel was inconceivable to the average Tatannan. Other than confirming the off-worlders came with royal authority, he was to advise Duke North Coast that Arne was now king and to demand that the duke renew his allegiance to the Crown.

The sheriff had already told Nova any pledge the duke made would be worthless. The man was a liar, who, for years, had smiled and sworn his loyalty to Algar, while secretly supporting those who opposed everything the king tried to do. He was certain North Coast had known about Ronor T'Corval's plot to take the throne and had supported, perhaps even instigated, the bloody treason. If he'd had any bit of evidence to support that charge, he would have been happy to take Asral T'Corsa back to Castle Boroson in chains.

Under normal circumstances, even the High Sheriff needed to tread carefully on T'Corsa's doorstep, but Regas had seen off-world magic. He had a feeling the handful of Lunar Marines deploying in defensive formation around the craft could easily deal with anything North Coast could throw at them. He was relieved when he stepped out of the off-world craft and put his feet on solid ground again. He checked his attire, paying particular attention to the copper medallion of office around his neck, then he stepped forward to join Major Sakura.

* * *

"Showtime," Nova declared. "Sergeant Karcher, give me two riflemen. The rest of you, stay here in defensive deployment around the bird. Stay hot for dust-off if necessary."

She walked forward with the sheriff, flanked by two Marines in full combat gear with Large-Caliber Assault Weapons. The LCAW's 20mm rounds likely wouldn't do much to the stone walls of the castle, even with HE heads, but they would turn the wooden gate into splinters, without much effort. After all she'd heard about the duke and his low-life half-brother, Nova was almost hoping they'd give her an excuse for a demonstration.

They stopped about fifty meters from the front gate, just before the bridge that spanned the swampy creek that flowed around the castle like a natural moat. The sheriff hailed the castle in a voice that sounded like a Marine drill sergeant's.

"Duke North Coast! Open, in the name of the king!"

There was a scramble along the top of the walls. Several crossbows appeared, and Nova could almost feel them being aimed at her and the sheriff. *These people haven't got a clue what they're up against,* she thought, *and that could be a problem.* The two Raptors patrolling the surrounding countryside had enough firepower to level the castle if the duke's people opened fire, but that wouldn't be much consolation if they turned her into a pincushion first.

A well-dressed man, who carried himself with authority, appeared on the wall next to the gate.

"Regas D'Narr, always a pleasure to see you," the man called out in a loud voice, "but I question your authority to make such a demand, since I have been told the king is dead."

That must be the duke, Nova decided. *Let the games begin.*

"King Algar is dead," Regas replied. "Arne, his son, is now king."

"Really? Then there is truth to the rumors of patricide."

"Do not test me, Lord Duke. You know full well the name of King Algar's murderer, your very close friend Ronor T'Corval, whose head adorns the gates of Castle Boroson."

"Does it now?" T'Corsa feigned amazement. "Well, he made no secret of his hatred for the king. The only thing 'close' between Duke High Reaches and me is the border his lands share with mine to the northwest. Tell me, High Sheriff, what are the king's plans—King Arne's plans—for T'Corval's lands? I should be interested in—"

"His Majesty has not shared those plans with me," Regas cut him off. "If you wish to make a claim, you may present it at Castle Boroson in person, along with your sworn allegiance to King Arne. I have come here on more urgent matters today."

"You arrive in very strange company," the duke noted. "I presume these are the magical people from the sky we have heard so much about."

For somebody who's just meeting us for the first time, Nova thought, *you don't seem very surprised, let alone impressed.* She remembered that it was this duke's brother who had been snooping around her encampment during the first landing on the planet, years ago. *If he's as clever and treacherous as the king says he is, he's known we were here all along.*

"I am interested to know how you heard of them," Regas replied. "They are the reason we have come. The king has been told you have several of their people here in your house, as guests, perhaps. We have come to get them."

"I have no idea what you are talking about." The duke's face settled into a cold, impassive expression. Regas started to reply, but Nova touched his shoulder.

"Duke North Coast," she said, in perfect Tatannan, "do not attempt to deceive us. We have ways of knowing where our people are. We knew when they were at S'bora's Grove, but we had other matters to deal with before retrieving them. We were surprised when your people moved them, but we know you brought them here. We will assume you have treated them well, and they are in good health, but that assumption will expire quickly if you do not produce them. I hope they are not being held prisoner, because if they are, we would be forced to do whatever is necessary to free them."

* * *

Darius had suggested they try to break down the door, possibly using gunfire to knock down the bars on the other side.

Lorna vetoed that suggestion. She had seen the outside of the door, and there were no less than three solid wood bars attached that could be dropped into place and secured with iron straps. She had a better idea. She dug into her survival pack and pulled out a small, tubular object, then she headed back out to the balcony. She leaned against the rail and pointed the object over the edge of the castle roof and triggered it.

The Mark IV Distress Signal shot a red flare into the sky which detonated in a brilliant starburst that lingered for many seconds before fading. It was designed to produce a visible signal in just about any environment, including hard vacuum, but in atmosphere it also produced a very loud triple report that could be heard several kilometers away.

* * *

Several of the duke's men dropped their crossbows and fled from their posts in panic. A roared command from their captain stopped their flight, but they refused to show their heads over the wall. Asral T'Corsa glared at them. He refused to admit that the off-worlders had almost caused him to wet himself a second time. He wasn't sure where the light in the sky and the thunderous noise had come from, but he suspected his guests were to blame for them.

"Still want to tell us our people aren't here, Your Lordship?" the strange, alien woman inquired. "Are you going to open the gate, or shall I have my people remove it?"

"Wait," T'Corsa replied, "your people will be brought out."

* * *

Lorna, McGill, and Jefferson walked toward the waiting Marines, their bags slung over their shoulders. Bob rode in his usual place, cradled in McGill's arms, with his head erect, looking like the King of the Jungle. Lorna smiled when she recognized Nova standing next to a well-dressed Tatannan, who was obviously a friend, not one of the duke's people.

Ersin T'Corsa walked to Lorna's left. He had been their escort since the signal flare caused a swift unbarring of the door. As he approached the waiting group, Ersin smirked at the High Sheriff, who scowled in return. On the Crown's lands, the sheriff would have had him in irons in a moment, but centuries of Tatannan custom and tradition decreed that the king's people could not arrest a man in any duke's domain without the permission of the duke in question.

"The cavalry has arrived." Lorna exchanged salutes with Nova and broke into a happy grin. "Did I mention we're glad to see you?"

"Not as glad as we are, Blondie… I mean Commander." Nova glanced at Lorna's party but couldn't suppress a grin. "Fleet figured your number was up."

"I'll tell you all about it, but let's get out of here first," Lorna replied.

"Excuse me, Jefferson, would you mind?" McGill handed Bob to Darius. "I need to say goodbye to someone."

Lorna turned and watched as McGill went up to Ersin T'Corsa. Smiling sweetly, she put her hand on his shoulders. "It's been such a pleasure," she told him.

Ersin was amazed by the thought that his manly presence had so impressed the off-world woman. With a smile that didn't hide the leer underneath, he raised his arms to embrace her, then doubled up in agony and crumpled to the ground when she delivered a solid knee to his groin.

One of Ersin's bully boys had been walking behind them and started to step forward. He changed his mind when Jefferson got in his way, and Bob delivered a fang-bared hiss. The man crouched and tried to help his master, but Ersin was curled up in the fetal position and didn't appear to have any interest in getting up.

"That was conduct unbecoming, Ensign," Lorna said quietly, trying to suppress a smile. "Consider yourself reprimanded."

"Yes, ma'am." McGill tried to look contrite but failed miserably. "Won't happen again."

"Nicely done, ma'am," Darius remarked under his breath as he handed Bob back to her. Nova's Marines closed around them and ushered them toward the waiting Firefly. They had almost reached the craft when the pilot leaned out and called to Nova.

"Major! Red Dog One has Bugs on the ground two kilometers northwest and moving this way!"

* * *

The ten Bug warriors formed a defensive circle around the two messengers and opened fire on the human attack craft. They were armed with typical Bug infantry weapons that fired plasma bolts. The weapons were powerful and deadly but short-ranged and slow to recharge. The bolts were slow-moving compared to a typical cannon round and were easily visible in flight.

"Red Dog Two, you are taking fire," the lead Raptor pilot advised.

"Roger that, One, but these guys couldn't hit the ground with their hats, if they wore hats."

Raptors were flown by non-commissioned officers, and Master Sergeant Marcus Bailey was a veteran. He wasn't particularly concerned about his Number Two, Sergeant Alicia Martin. Ally was flying a good evasion pattern, and the Bug fire wasn't even close. The second Raptor had just made a low observation pass over the Bugs and had drawn plasma bolts from the defenders but taken no hits.

"Striker, Red Dog One, we see about a dozen Bugs on the ground, no vehicles, just emerged from the tree line. No sign of any supporting forces. We have taken fire. Permission to engage?"

"Red Dog One, Striker Prime," Nova Sakura's voice replied. "You are cleared to engage, with no restriction. Waste 'em."

"One engaging. Two, you're batting cleanup. Follow me."

Bailey popped up to nearly a thousand meters, then rolled into a steep dive that allowed him to keep the target in his sights all the way down. He triggered a three-second burst from his 20mm internal gun, a six-barreled rotary cannon that pumped out 100 rounds per second. He held the dive long enough to see the Bug formation erupt in chaos as the high explosive incendiary projectiles reached their target. He rolled out and climbed away without ever coming in range of the Bugs' weapons.

"Nice shooting, One," Martin told him. "My turn."

Bailey came sharply around and reacquired the target just in time to see it get shredded by Martin's gunnery. Martin also climbed away, adding a full roll to the maneuver.

"Ooooh," she reported, "next best thing to an orgasm."

"Alright, cease fire," he told her. "I think we got 'em, but I'm going to make a low pass to check."

"Nothing but smoking Bug parts," he reported a minute later. "Action terminated, back on station."

* * *

Once again, the alien woman stood in front of the castle gate with the sheriff at her side.

"Those were Bugs, Your Lordship," she told

T'Corsa, who was still atop the wall. His face remained impassive, though he seethed with anger inside.

He was willing to agree that Ersin deserved what he got, but the idea that anyone would humiliate a member of his family here, in the heart of his territory, was unacceptable. As Ersin's men helped him back to the gates, Asral vowed he would make the off-worlders pay for it.

For the moment, however, his attention was focused on the column of smoke rising to the northwest. He had seen the off-worlder's frightening firepower, the small explosions tearing up the ground, and what looked like a Bug, or part of one, blasted into the air.

"Curious," the woman continued. "A handful of Bugs, coming here, to your house. They're all dead now, so we'll never know what their mission was. In any case, you might want to go out there and see what happened to them… just a little lesson for those who need one."

"One more matter, North Coast," Regas D'Narr said, "King Arne requires that you reaffirm your allegiance to the Crown. Does he have it?"

"I have always been loyal to the legitimate king of the realm." T'Corsa forced himself to project an image of indignant superiority. "That you even question me is an insult. Leave now, or I shall take you to task for it."

D'Narr stared at him for a moment, then turned without another word and walked with the others back to the sky ship.

* * *

Marine Striker One, In-Flight

The Firefly was a light, fast transport that could carry a squad of Marines plus a few extra passengers. Able to take off and land in confined LZs, it often served as a command ship for larger forces in an airborne assault. For that reason, unlike the ground-attack Raptor, it was flown by a crew of two, with a commissioned officer as command pilot.

Lieutenant Joe Logan was an experienced Firefly pilot. He was confident enough in his abilities that the presence of a Marine Major and a Navy Lieutenant Commander in his ship didn't bother him. Hell, he'd carried general officers before, with the understanding that the Firefly was his command, and they were just passengers. Nonetheless, he was more than happy to oblige their request for comm traffic.

"Marine Striker One, go for Fleet Comm." The smooth, feminine contralto immediately drew his attention. *Whoa! Like to meet the face and body behind that voice.* Logan fancied himself a ladies' man, though his heavy-handed approach resulted in a low success rate. He would have been disappointed to discover that the body in question belonged to a 600-meter-long battlecruiser. The voice was that of Nadia, the cybernetic soul of Admiral McGruder's flagship, *LFS Nike*.

"Fleet Comm, information only, for appropriate distribution," he replied, in what he imagined was his best macho-seductive voice. "We are RTB with three... no check that, four... survivors from LFS *Lynx* as follows: Lieutenant Commander Lorna Greenwood, Ensign Mary Jane McGill, Marine Private Darius Jefferson, and Bob, the ship's cat. All are in good health and will be returned to Fleet as soon as transport can be arranged."

"Roger that, Striker One, that is very good news," Nadia replied, sounding very pleased and even sexier to Logan's ear. "We will pass that information to the Admiral immediately."

"Ah... one more item, Fleet Comm." Logan glanced at the note he'd been handed. "Commander Greenwood was *Lynx's* captain.

She's asking how many survivors were picked up. If you could pass that question to—"

"Eighty-one survivors were picked up," the AI replied immediately, "not counting those you just retrieved. Fleet terminated further search shortly after the ship went down, so the total number surviving is now eighty-four human crew and the cat."

Ouch, that's not good, Logan thought. He didn't know the crew complement of a destroyer, but he had a feeling it was a lot more than 84.

* * *

Lorna looked at the note the pilot had just passed back to her, and her shoulders sagged as the world seemed to collapse around her.

"Ma'am?" McGill looked at her with concern.

"More than a third gone…" Lorna's voice choked up. She handed the note to McGill, then turned away to hide the tears she could no longer hold back. Her shoulders shook as she tried to stifle the sobs that wracked her without mercy.

* * *

McGill read the note, and her tears fell as well. She started to cradle Bob in her arms, but he wriggled free and worked his way over to Lorna's lap. *OK, McGill thought, she needs you more than I do.* Without comment, she handed the note to Major Sakura.

* * *

Przbyzienski had considered legally changing his name to "Frisbee" but had decided not to for cultural heritage reasons. Nonetheless, he had been called that so often, it was a nickname to which he responded without question. He was drinking coffee with two of *Lynx's* senior noncoms when one of the carrier's petty officers came into the crew lounge that seemed to be reserved exclusively for the *Lynx* survivors. They had no assigned duties for the moment, so there were usually twenty to thirty of them in the lounge at any given time.

They had been treated well since arriving aboard *Iwo Jima*. The Marines and Navy crewmembers seemed to go out of their way to show the *Lynx* people every courtesy. The stewards in the lounge made sure their coffee cups were full and found little snacks for them at just about any time of day. In the crew's mess, the line servers gave them extra portions and the best cuts of everything. Frisbee had wondered why, until two days ago when a grizzled Marine gunny and two corporals showed up, pushing a cart loaded with cases of beer. There were several different premium brands and none of the cheap stuff. The gunny looked around the lounge and caught Frisbee's eye, then walked over and presented a sharp salute.

"Sir, are you the senior *Lynx* officer?" he inquired.

"I am. How may I help you, Gunny?"

"Well, sir, this is for you and your people, courtesy of Marine Second Division. There's a few bottles of wine in this box here, in case any of you don't like beer."

Alcoholic beverages were permitted—at appropriate times, in appropriate places—aboard LFS Navy ships, but they were not provided as part of the ship's regular fare. They had to be purchased, so somebody had paid for these. Frisbee was taken by surprise.

"We appreciate this," he said, "but why are you giving us so much? The hospitality on this ship has been excellent, but this goes above and beyond. We are just a bunch of shipwrecked destroyer sailors—"

"Not to us you aren't," the noncom insisted. "The way we see it, you people took a hit for us. The kamikaze Bug that got you had our name on it. We saw what it did to your ship, and I can't imagine what it would have done if it had hit *Iwo*. We were prepped for drop, landing craft stacked three deep in the launch bays, with a hundred Marines in each one. That bastard could have wiped out a whole battalion with one hit.

"You took him out, and we know it cost you big time, but you saved a lot of Marines. Navy people, too, but most of the people on this ship are Marines. A lot of them are down on the planet now, but they weren't then, and we were pretty damned vulnerable."

"Besides," he added, "the colonel told us he talked to *Iwo's* Tactical Officer, and he said he'd never seen a destroyer fight so well. You guys were awesome, and you covered our asses right up to the point where you got hit."

"It was our mission," Frisbee told him.

"Yes, sir, and you got it done. If it was up to me, every one of you would get a Semper Fi medal."

"Our captain was awarded the Semper Fi some years ago," Cas remembered, sadly. "She saved some Marines in a combat situation, but this time, she didn't make it out."

"I'm sorry." The Marine nodded gravely. "She ought to get another one, post."

* * *

Frisbee remembered that conversation when he saw the PO come into the lounge. The man glanced around the same way the Marine had, apparently looking for someone, then started toward their table. He pulled up short and saluted.

"Commander Pricebee... Pizeby... Przzlbinski?"

"'Frisbee' will do, Petty Officer," Przbyzienski replied, as he had done many times since coming aboard the carrier.

"Yes, sir. I have a message for you, sir." He presented the message board. Frisbee took the board, entered his personal code to open the message, and studied its contents. Suddenly, he jumped out of his chair.

"All hands, listen up!" he shouted. Startled, the *Lynx* people turned to look at him. To their knowledge, Mr. Frisbee never raised his voice, never needed to, because when he spoke, people listened. When they saw his broad grin, they relaxed.

"I've just gotten word." He raised the message pad. "Captain Greenwood, Ensign McGill, and Private Jefferson have been rescued down on the planet! They are OK and will be joining us as soon as they can get a lift to orbit."

"Yeah!" someone shouted, and that was the signal for chaotic cheering that might have been heard three decks away. It went on for almost a minute, and for Casimir Przbyzienski, it was a moment of immense relief. Until then, he had not forgiven himself for not insisting that Lorna take his place in the lifepod. He looked at the message again and saw the note at the bottom.

"Hold it, everybody," he shouted above the bedlam. "There's more. It says here they also saved the ship's cat, so I guess Bob will be joining us, as well."

If anything, the cheering grew even louder.

* * *

Alpha Company, First Battalion, Deep Inside the Hive

Through most of Earth's recorded history, men had named their sons after themselves, producing an abundance of men with "Jr." or a roman numeral after their names. Women seldom did the same for their daughters, except on Luna, where the practice had become quite common.

Sociologists speculated that it might have something to do with two other uncommon naming practices in the LFS. Women on Luna, if they married, rarely adopted their husband's surname at marriage, and children born to LFS citizens acquired the surname of their biological parent of the same sex.

Thus it happened that First Marine Division's First Battalion came to be commanded by Lieutenant Colonel Veronica Bartley II, daughter of the legendary Veronica Bartley I, Colonel, LFSMC (Retired). Troops under her command tended to attribute her hard-ass, hard-charging, hard-core Marine attitude to her need to prove that she was her mother's daughter. Veronica the First a/k/a "Rock" Bartley was one of the most decorated Marines in Lunar history, having worked her way up through the enlisted ranks to Gunnery Sergeant before finally accepting a commission. She had earned the Heart of Luna for wounds received in battle four times, and had finally retired as a full-bird colonel, with the Lunar Medal of Honor to her credit.

* * *

Bartley, along with Alpha Company's point platoon, led her troops deep into the Bug hive on Tatanna. Not one to micromanage, she never stepped on a platoon leader's prerogatives or countermanded a squad leader's directions, but even the lowest buck private was aware of her presence.

This part of the hive was still under power, with reasonably bright lighting coming from strips along the ceiling. The Marines didn't need the lights or night vision gear that had been necessary on the upper levels. They were deep below the damage done by Fleet's kinetic bombardment.

"Sorry, ma'am, more dead Bugs ahead," Lieutenant Paul Santino reported. "My guys are carefully clearing them. They haven't set any traps for us yet, but—"

"Marines don't get old by being careless," she told him. "I understand, Lieutenant. There's no time limit on this operation. Carry on."

Bartley welcomed the break. She had just returned to active duty from maternity leave, barely in time to join Operation Blue Orchid. She was trying to get herself back into pre-pregnancy physical condition, but she still had some work to do. Her hard-charging attitude was writing checks her body didn't want to cash.

"Take five," she ordered. Most of the Marines sat on the tunnel floor and reached for their canteens to hydrate, giving her an excuse to do the same. She pulled out her pad and, for the tenth time today, pulled up the picture of three-month-old Veronica III, who was back on Luna giving her grandmother a refresher course in the fine art of changing diapers.

The picture reminded her of other things in her life that needed shaping up. For one thing, she still hadn't gotten over the abrupt termination of her marriage. Unlike some Lunar couples, she and baby Veronica's father had been married, had taken out a marriage contract, though there was little ceremony. They had signed the contract in front of a certified Fair Witness, the Lunar Free State's equivalent of a Notary Public, but it had meant very little as far as her husband, Mark Morris, was concerned.

Under the laws of the Lunar Free State, marriage was a matter between two individuals and was none of the government's business. Couples of whatever gender identity could be married in a religious ceremony of their choice, or they could enter into a civil contract with whatever provisions they chose to agree upon. Marriage was not limited to couples, though polygamy, polyandry, and other three-or-more-people variations were rare. Most who decided on a civil contract chose a simple agreement to share living quarters and living expenses and to contribute equally to the health, welfare, and education of any children of the union.

On the issue of children, the LFS government did have something to say. The law made both biological parents responsible for their children until the age of 18 and required DNA testing at birth to determine beyond a doubt who the responsible parents were. That didn't mean the parents had to remain together.

Mark Morris had departed without notice when Bartley was just three months into her pregnancy. He had already signed another contract with a woman fifteen years younger than him and twelve years younger than Bartley. Nothing in LFS law prevented him from signing a new contract while the old one was still in effect, though he did send Bartley a request for termination, under a "mutual consent" clause in their contract, three months later. She agonized over it for a while, but finally signed the termination agreement just before the eve of her delivery date.

At least we're not on Earth, and Baby Ronnie isn't stuck with his last name. She looked up from her musings and stood as Lieutenant Santino approached.

"We're through the blockage, ma'am, and there's something ahead you have to see. I think we've reached the center of this crazy maze."

Bartley followed Santino through the tunnel and past the scattered pieces of Bugs left behind by the clearing operation. Ten meters beyond, the tunnel opened onto a balcony overlooking a huge chamber with a crystal-clear dome at the bottom. The interior of the dome was well lit and apparently still environmentally sealed. Live Bugs moved around inside the dome, busy with various tasks, most of which involved manipulation of the controls and displays that filled most of the chamber. *This is it,* Bartley thought, *Bug HQ, their command center.*

They were looking at the dome from the top of a long, spiral ramp that led down to the bottom of the chamber. The Bugs seemed unaware of their presence. There was no sudden flurry of activity, no sign of defenders rushing to protect the place. Suddenly, Bartley realized that a huge alien shape in the center of the dome was another Bug. It was about four times the size of the Bugs surrounding it, with most of its size coming from a bloated abdomen that lacked the hard, shiny exoskeleton armor that covered the other Bugs.

Bartley had just become one of the first humans to see a Queen Bug. Unfortunately, it was the last thing she would ever see.

* * * * *

Chapter Fourteen

At one time on Earth, it was widely believed that war with nuclear weapons would spell doomsday for the entire planet, and that belief served as a deterrent against their use. By the mid-21st century, however, the LFS had already demonstrated that nuclear weapons were obsolete for any nation with even minimal space capability. Kinetic strikes were more precise. The yield of the weapon could be precisely controlled to minimize collateral damage, the weapons were cheap to produce, and they left no radiation behind. As the nations of Earth began to move into space, they retired their nuclear arsenals in favor of cleaner, more efficient kinetic weapons.

Controlled fusion of the type used to power spacecraft and remote installations requires a steady trickle of hydrogen fuel, usually in the form of deuterium oxide. An uncontrolled fusion reaction—a nuclear bomb—requires that a large amount of such fuel be exposed to stimulation in a very brief time. The simplest way to accomplish that is to use a fission bomb, a device like the old "atom bomb" dropped on Hiroshima in 1945, as a trigger.

The largest fusion bomb ever built on Earth required less than a cubic meter of nuclear fuel. When the Bugs built their self-destruct device on Tatanna, they placed a fission bomb in the middle of a cluster of tanks that fueled the hive's regular fusion reactor. Those tanks contained hundreds of cubic meters of deuterium oxide.

It wasn't the most efficient design for a bomb—significant amounts of deuterium were dissipated by the explosion before it could reach fusion energy—but the device still produced an explosion greater than any bomb ever built on Earth. It was intended to be set off underground, twenty levels deep in the hive, the structure of which would have absorbed much of its explosive power. Unfortunately for the Marines of First Division, the top twelve levels of the hive had already been blasted open by Fleet's kinetic bombardment.

* * *

First Division Forward HQ

20 Kilometers South of Ground Zero

"I can't see... somebody help! I can't see!"

The Marine noncom stumbled into the HQ module, hands over his eyes. Pure white light streamed into the module through the open hatch behind him, but HQ was already lit by a subdued version of the same light. The module's armored windows had darkened automatically, but not enough to totally shut out the huge fireball's star-hot brilliance.

"CBR Drill, now! Pass word to all units," Sherwood ordered.

CBR—Chemical / Biological / Radiological—warfare protocols required troops to take immediate shelter and don special protective gear. It was what Marines were supposed to do if someone set off a nuclear weapon, but the best time to do it was before the weapon went off.

"All comms are down, General," the communications tech reported. "My whole console's dead. Must have been an EMP."

Must have been one hell of an EMP, Sherwood thought. Marine field electronics were supposed to be shielded against electro-magnetic pulses, even at weapon-grade levels. *It could only have been a nuke, and I've just lost more than half of First Marine Division.*

"General…" Colonel Olson wore a helpless look. "The shock wave… we're only 20 klicks away. We've got less than a minute before it gets here."

He was correct as far as the airborne shock wave was concerned, but the ground shock traveled much faster through the dense bedrock. He had barely finished speaking when it struck like an off-the-scale earthquake.

The HQ module was a durable structure, anchored in place with tie-downs connected to rods driven into the ground. When the ground shock hit, the whole structure heaved upward with a force that parted the tie-downs and uprooted the rods. Heavy armored vehicles parked nearby were tossed nearly two meters into the air. The antenna array that connected Marine HQ to Fleet and Second Division snapped its guy lines and came crashing down on top of the HQ module.

A few seconds later, the air shock arrived with hurricane force and swept the wreckage off the ridge.

* * *

Marine Striker One, In-Flight

"Major, could you plug in for a moment? We need to talk." Lieutenant Logan indicated the comm headset hanging next to Nova's seat in the rear cabin. She nodded and picked up the unit, adjusted it to fit over her uniform beret, and put it on.

"What's up, Lieutenant?"

"I'm not sure," he said. "Marine Command has just gone offline. Fleet's trying to raise them, but they're not answering. I'm getting some chatter on the tactical channels, but it's low-power stuff that is mostly lost in the noise. I think it's a Second Division unit that isn't far from here, but they seem to be having trouble getting through as well."

"Do you still have contact with Striker Home?" Nova's first concern was for her platoon, which was camped in the wilderness north of the King's City.

"Yes, ma'am, loud and clear. Their comm gear is good enough to reach us direct at this range, but they can't raise Marine Command either. I just checked."

"OK. Continue on course, Lieutenant. We'll figure it out when we get back to camp. Let me know if you hear anything more."

"Roger that, ma'am."

* * *

LFS *Nike*, in Tatanna Orbit

"Definitely nuclear, Admiral," *Nike's* Tactical Officer advised. "The signature is unmistakable. Massive EMP, extreme levels of radiation... and we've got a mushroom cloud 10,000 meters high. Anything closer than 500 kilometers due east of the site is likely to be subjected to dangerously high levels of radiation due to fallout. Anyone closer than 25 kilometers, without shielding, likely got a fatal dose from the blast. That would include Marine Command HQ, but we think the shock wave got them. It's hard to probe through all that wreckage, even with mapping radar, but it looks like the landscape has been stripped clean out to 20 kilometers."

"Thank you, Commander," McGruder replied with grim sincerity. "If you or your people come up with anything else on the situation, please pass it along to Commander Carlson."

"Yes, sir."

The young lieutenant commander's face disappeared from the screen as he signed off. McGruder turned to his assembled staff.

"I think we can assume First Marine Division no longer exists," he told them. "There may be survivors in the surrounding area, but according to Sherwood's last report, more than half of them were inside that hellhole. It sounds like Sherwood and his staff are, well, MIA at best, more likely dead. So, what about Second Division?"

"We were able to reach General Mercer." Commander Murtaugh, McGruder's Chief of Staff, looked at the notes he'd made on his pad. "He's about 400 kilometers southwest, so he's out of radiation danger, but his division is scattered all over Tatanna. He's got them broken down to the platoon level, covering all the Bug holes at the mining sites. In theory, all those holes led back to the hive, and now that it's gone—"

"Don't make any assumptions." McGruder shook his head. "We think Sherwood had all those tunnels cut at the hive end, but we didn't have the troops to explore them from one end to the other. For all we know, a damned Bug army made its way into the tunnels before they blew the hive."

"That's true," Murtaugh agreed. "I guess Second Division has to continue to watch the other ends. If we get any indication they're coming back to the hive site, we can always lay down more kinetics."

"Doesn't sound like there's anything there to go back to." Commander Evelyn Jones was McGruder's Communications and Intel officer. "We've got to get better comm gear down to Mercer. He's got nothing like Sherwood had up north, and it looks like he's now in charge of the Marines down there. We need to be able to talk to him, and he needs to talk to everybody else."

"Good point," McGruder replied. "See what you can do and get me a direct line to him ASAP. I need to give him the bad news and work out a plan. My thought is he's going to have to keep those holes covered with a minimal force, enough to sound the alarm if something shows up, and send the rest of his people north to find what's left of First Division and do SAR if necessary. He can use the landing craft from both carriers to conduct air searches, but I hope he'll sing out if he thinks of any way Fleet can assist.

"Honestly, people—" he looked at the grim faces around the table, "—I'm feeling pretty damned helpless. It's all on the Marines now."

"One thing's for sure," he added, bitterly, "any plans we might have had for making peace with the Bugs when this is over are pretty much off the table."

* * *

House Corsa, North Coast Province

"So, what have you found, Brother?"

"Pieces of Bugs." Ersin wore a sour look, his normally cheerful demeanor not yet recovered from the humiliation the off-worlder had given him. "Torn up, stinking to the sky, dripping vile fluids, unmistakable pieces of Bugs."

"And?" Asral had not failed to notice the bag Ersin held in his hand.

"And various half-destroyed Bug artifacts, some of metal and some of a strange composition like nothing we've seen before. My men are loading a wagon with the stuff to bring back. I left them to it because I could not stand the stench. Even the scavengers want nothing to do with it."

"And?" Asral gestured pointedly toward the bag.

"Oh, this." He dropped the bag on Asral's desk. "I thought this might interest you, since I've seen something like it before. Actually, I believe I saw it here, in this office. I wondered about it, but you chose not to tell me what it was."

He upended the bag, and a small box fell out. The box was made of some unknown material. It was smooth and hard as polished stone but not heavy, decorated with an intricate design that looked alien. There appeared to be no way to open it, not even a visible seam, as if it were a solid block of material.

Asral drew a sharp breath. He knew it was a message. For years, he had been secretly receiving such messages from the Bugs and sending replies by such means. The Bugs provided the magic boxes only he could open. In the past, the Bugs had given the box to a messenger at one of the Bug mines in North Coast Province. The messenger brought the box to him, and he sent another back. He had such a box, received several crossings ago, locked in his personal vault.

He looked up and saw a hint of the old, familiar smirk on Ersin's face, a look of satisfaction at having learned another of his brother's secrets.

"Yes, I know what it is," he admitted. *Doesn't matter if he knows; I'm not going to show him how to open it.*

He turned his back to Ersin and grasped the box with the unnatural two-handed grip that allowed him to touch five of the alien symbols at once. The box opened with a click, then he turned and set it on the desk so he could remove the message. The message was perfectly printed on perfect parchment, something no Tatannan could duplicate. It would disappear without a trace of ash if burned, which he had always done with such messages.

He studied the message which was written in the common language by someone, or something, not accustomed to speaking it.

Your plan has failed. King still lives. King wants off-world humans to destroy us. We are being destroyed. One chance remains. We will kill king. You must come to city and become king. Twelve days.

With a sigh, he passed the message to Ersin.

"Hmmm, twelve days," Ersin remarked, "but that would be eleven days now since the message should have arrived yesterday."

"Well, brother—" the old smirk was back in full force, "—it appears your problems are solved if the Bugs can kill Arne and if the off-worlders accept you as the new king.

"As to the first condition, the fate of their messengers leaves me in some doubt as to the Bugs' ability to fulfill it. You really should see the destruction out there—a whole group of Bugs wiped out in a moment.

"As to the second condition, I suspect our recent guests' displeasure with our hospitality leaves some doubt about how well you would be received. The off-worlders might well decide to dispatch you, along with the remaining Bugs, then find someone else to be their puppet-king."

"As usual, brother, your insights are on the mark," Asral admitted. "That's why I'm not going to be in the King's City eleven days hence, but you will be," he added with a smirk.

* * *

Castle Boroson, the King's City

Bouchard had helped John O'Hara settle into the late Ambassador Michaels' quarters in the castle, a spacious four-room suite she had unofficially dubbed "the LFS Embassy" since Michaels had used it as living quarters and an office.

Her quarters were just across the hall. Her suite was somewhat smaller, but still luxurious, but she had seldom used it while Ramis was alive. She still spent very little time there, preferring to be out among her troops, with the king's people, or anywhere but alone.

* * *

"It feels strange," O'Hara said. "I was here with *Lewis and Clark*, but I never set foot on the planet. You went down with your Marines, but we Navy types never got closer than high orbit. We saw satellite images from orbit, and we saw video from the robot surveyors, but actually being here is—"

O'Hara and Bouchard stood atop the tower, looking out over the city below. Lamps were being lit in the deepening twilight, and a chill breeze gave hints of a cold night to come.

"I had the same feeling when we first landed," Bouchard acknowledged. "We had the silly idea we could drop in with a squad of Marines, grab our busted robot, and get the hell out. Ended up spending a month down here, made contact with the locals, and…"

Her voice faded, and she turned away so he wouldn't see the tears that almost came. She was reminded of a certain local she met on that trip. He turned out to be the only man she had ever loved.

"Lieutenant, I'm sorry. I know you've just been through a personal tragedy. I didn't mean to touch on a sensitive spot."

"Wasn't you, sir," she told him. "I've got too many sensitive spots right now. I know, people die in war. Fleet says we lost over five hundred Marines two days ago with that damned Bug suicide bomb. I knew some of those people, and I spoke with General Sherwood on a video call the day before it happened.

"I guess what's really bothering me is that Ramis—my guy—wasn't a Marine. He wasn't in the King's Guard and had probably never held a sword. He was a scholar, a scientist, or the closest thing this planet has to one. He was the kind of guy Marines are supposed to protect, but his Marine wasn't there when he needed her."

She continued to stare out over the city, no longer trying to hold back the tears.

"I keep telling myself it's not my fault," she said. "That's what they tell women who've been raped. Well, I feel like I've been worse than raped, so I have to keep saying it. It's not my fault.

"Commodore—" she brushed the tears away and turned to face him, "—when this is over, I think I need to take some leave time. There's a monastery in the hills north of the city, and I may go and spend some time there, talk to the Goddess, get myself back together.

"By the way," she added, seeing the surprised look on his face, "the monks up there are female, as are all the clergy on this planet."

"Makes sense," he said with a gentle smile. "I've noticed that, here, God is female. I have a lot to learn if I'm going to be of much use on this mission."

"Seriously, sir," she assured him, "you have no idea how much I appreciate your help. Along those lines, I think you need to start learning the local language. I've got a book I've sort of been working on for about a year. You can be the first to try it out."

"Really?" O'Hara raised an eyebrow in surprise.

"Actually," she told him sadly, "Ramis was working on a book to teach English to Tatannans. I was helping him with it, and he suggested I take his stuff and turn it around. It was almost finished when…"

Her voice trailed off as she turned away to gaze out over the city again.

* * * * *

Chapter Fifteen

Terranova City, Luna

Antonio Tortorelli carried an Italian passport. His Lunar work visa listed his last city of residence as Rome. He spoke Italian with a Sicilian flavor, which seemed to match his Mediterranean complexion. He was a small, energetic man who spoke English well, though it was obviously not his first language. When required to deal with people, he maintained an agreeable personality, but nothing about him was memorable. People who met him had difficulty describing him a few hours later. He was almost an invisible man.

Tortorelli had come to Luna to work as *capo cameriere*—headwaiter—at *Frutti di Mare*, an Italian seafood restaurant in TerraNova city. It was a job for which he was eminently qualified, according to his resume and the references he carried. It was a job he was good at, though his resume, references, and passport were forgeries. Very good forgeries, but forgeries all the same.

In reality, he was not Italian, and Tortorelli was not his name. He had gone by many names in his career. His real name and country of origin were buried in forgotten records somewhere in Eastern Europe. He spoke several languages perfectly, but his present accent was as contrived as his identity.

His real employer, for the moment, was the French investment firm *Freres Le Fleur*, whose chairman was Andre DuMorne. Even the people at Freres who arranged such things knew him only as Five, a shadow operative who could be reached via a message left at a secret drop. His fee for the service they required was an obscenely large sum of money deposited in a numbered Swiss bank account. Conversely, he did not know who hired him, only that a proposal had been delivered by the agreed upon method, he had responded with a price, half to be paid on completion, and the money had appeared.

For the moment, he was Antonio Tortorelli, and he had a persona to maintain. He left his small TerraNova apartment dressed for work at the restaurant. The job gave him the time and resources he needed and a comfortable place to live, while he planned the operation. There was no hurry, no specific deadline by which the task had to be accomplished. Flawless execution was far more important than swift completion.

Five had done a great deal of research before he'd accepted the commission and come to Luna. The task would be difficult, so he set the price accordingly, but the client made the initial deposit without question.

There was a great deal of risk involved. Historically, few had ever done such a thing at so high a level and escaped unscathed. Moonie justice was swift and final for those who attempted it, so his exit strategy needed to be perfect. It was all part of the game, and he loved the game even more than the lucrative rewards it brought, else he would have retired long ago. The rewards had made him a very wealthy man.

There was always the possibility that he had been set up, that, for whatever reason, someone wanted him to attempt the mission and fail. Such things were sometimes done for political reasons. He had been used that way once, and he had barely escaped with his life. Because he was so good at what he did, those who attempted to treat him as an expendable asset were likely to find their life expectancy abruptly shortened.

He needed to take such things into consideration, though, so he began by asking why he was being sent to act against this target and what the effect would be if the person were permanently removed from his position. For most so-called "democratic" nations, removal of the nominal head of state would have little effect other than outrage for some, joy for others, and a shrug of the shoulders for most. The next person in line would step up, and it would be business as usual, for the simple reason that the deceased leader held far less power than his or her position indicated. Most real power in such nations was vested in bureaucracies. More in the way of meaningful change could be accomplished by removal of the head of a major bureaucratic agency than by removal of the titular head of the government.

That was not so for the Lunar Free State. The nation claimed to be a representative democracy and to provide a great deal of freedom for its people, but it also gave its Chief Executive a great deal of power to conduct the nation's affairs. The LFS claimed not to be a military dictatorship, though its enemies often described it as one, but there was no question its military was a powerful force that supported whatever course the Chief Executive chose to take.

The Lunar Free State's Constitution provided an orderly plan of succession should anything happen to its leader, but the plan was inflexible, allowed no intervention by the Directorate—the only government body elected by the people—and would produce a very predictable result from the standpoint of Five's clients. Removal of Kim would instantly put Admiral Amy Ling in the Chief Executive's chair, from which she could not be removed, even by unanimous vote of the Directorate, until she had served a full year. That was what his clients intended, for his instructions included the requirement that she not be a victim of any collateral damage he might need to inflict to accomplish the mission. That did not appear to pose a problem, since she rarely came down to Luna to meet Kim. She lived aboard her flagship at Luna's Fleet Anchorage.

Five noted with interest that, unlike many heads of state, the Lunar Chief Executive did not conduct business from his residence and had never done so since the founding of the Lunar Free State. The original Lunar Command offices, known to most citizens as HQ, had been near the executive living quarters in the early days when TerraNova was a small town with a few thousand people. TerraNova had grown immensely since then and was now a city. It was small by Earth standards—home to less than two million people—but it was the largest population center in the Lunar Free State. Much of its expansion had been vertical, up into the mountain under which it was built and down into the Lunar bedrock below. The city only spanned a few kilometers at its greatest horizontal extent, but its vertical structure included over twenty levels.

At some point, HQ had been moved to offices on three of the topmost levels at the edge of the large open space known as TerraNova Park. The CEO's offices, which overlooked the park, were only a short walk from the executive residence, but now there was significant vertical separation as well as horizontal.

In terms of strategy, Kim living and working in different places should have been an advantage since there were two possible target areas for the operation. From a practical standpoint, however, Five rejected both because they were too heavily secured. Assassins had attacked the CEO's HQ offices over seventy years ago, during

Greenwood's tenure. They had failed, but their attempt had caused the LFS to institute state-of-the-art security that was constantly reviewed and upgraded.

The separation of home and work could still be used to advantage because it required Kim to travel back and forth between the two. There were several routes he could take, and his security people insisted he randomize them, but there were a limited number of ways to get from point A to point B.

Sometimes, Kim went to or from the office via a walk through the park. That route involved almost 300 meters of travel through the park between the office and a secure elevator. It was the most exposed route, but Five rejected it because the security people knew it was exposed and took extra caution checking and clearing it. Besides, the park was too open for the method Five hoped to use, and its artificially generated weather—occasional rain and light breezes—would also be a problem.

That left five frequently used routes, and all of them included travel through reasonably small public spaces accessible to any citizen. During the next few days, he planned to visit each of them to gather more information.

* * *

Battlecruiser LFS *Sorceress,* Lunar Fleet Anchorage

"Well, Rob, your thoughts?"

"It's a bit early to draw conclusions, Admiral," Vice Admiral Robert O'Hara replied, cautiously.

The latest generation of LFS Navy hyperprobes could make the trip from Sacagawea to Sol in twelve days, less than half the time it took a warship to cover the same distance. Still, any reports they brought would be two weeks old by the time they arrived.

"I know," Amy Ling admitted. "It's kind of like 'Hi, folks, here we are in the Sacagawea System. Just letting you know we arrived.' They couldn't have been there more than a few days when the probe was sent. There are some indications things aren't going quite as well as we expected."

"Yes, I noticed that." O'Hara gave her a sour look. "The Bugs didn't take the bait and come out in force, and it looks like they are prepared to mount a serious defense of the planet. McGruder's bringing his heavy forces in to support the assault group."

"Do you think we need to reinforce?" she asked.

"I trust Mac's judgment, and he's not asking for help yet," he replied. "All the same, I think I'll bring First Battle Group up to readiness, just in case."

O'Hara commanded Luna's Second Fleet. He had two battle groups under his command—McGruder's Second, with battlecruisers *Nike* and *Amazon*, and his own First, with his flagship *Isis* and LFS *Valkyrie*.

"That would commit all of Second Fleet. If he needs a little help, we could send him one of my BCs with supporting units."

Ling was supreme commander of the combined fleets, but she also kept direct command of First Fleet, flying her colors aboard LFS *Sorceress*, where she and O'Hara were meeting. First Fleet also included three other battlecruisers: *Athena*, *Cassandra*, and *Medusa*.

"Your call, Admiral." O'Hara shrugged.

"I think I'll put *Cassandra* on standby, but you can bring up your First Battle Group as well. We'll decide which way to go when we get more information from Mac. Even if he doesn't need help, we'll want to send relief units after he completes the mission. We're going to need to keep a strong presence in the system for a while."

O'Hara nodded and sat in silence, while Ling made some notes on her pad. She looked up and gave him a crooked smile.

"Your son's taking it pretty hard," she remarked. "He's blaming himself because the Bugs didn't do what we expected them to."

"Yes," O'Hara replied. "I read his addendum to the summary, which Mac declined to endorse, by the way. John did a lot of the strategic analysis of our encounters with the Bugs, and the entire command team, including me, reviewed the data and agreed with his conclusions. The Bugs just picked the wrong time to change their strategy."

"Maybe they've learned something from us as well." She shrugged. "We spent nearly eight years probing their systems and testing their capabilities. They may be slow to adapt, but they're not stupid. Anyway, it wasn't his fault, and he shouldn't beat himself up. He's a solid officer, and I wish I had twenty more like him."

O'Hara decided now was the time to broach a delicate subject. "Part of it may be that he doesn't fit well into a staff position. He's got a proven track record with *Norseman*, and he really deserves another command."

"Yes, he does," Ling agreed, "but I don't have one to give him. Even if I had a battlecruiser slot available, I've got two equally qualified Commodores with seniority over him. However, I've been thinking about extending the Destroyer Squadron concept to the cruiser level, and we'd need officers of that rank for squadron command. It's been working well so far and gives us more flexibility with a variety of missions."

"Hah!" O'Hara snorted. "It's been working well, now that a certain Admiral's daughter showed Fleet how it should be done."

With her Asian complexion, Ling did not blush easily, but she did have the grace to look a bit embarrassed.

"Yes," she admitted, "Rebecca has done me proud. Here's a thumb in the eye to those who dared mumble about nepotism. The concept was mine, but she took it and ran with it. Last Fleet Games, the Cat Pack cleaned up three opforce heavy cruisers that were operating independently."

She added with a sigh, "Right now, she's out there with your son on the bleeding edge of our latest interstellar war."

There was nothing O'Hara could say in reply, so the two of them sat in silence for a moment.

"All right," Ling said at last. "Nothing more we can do until we hear from Mac again. Meanwhile, I've got to take what little we know down to Luna and report to the Chief Exec."

* * *

1 April 2112, Battlecruiser LFS *Isis*, Lunar Fleet Anchorage

"I assume you've seen the latest, Admiral..."

"Yes, and it's not as bad as I thought it might be." This time, Ling had called on Rob O'Hara aboard his flagship, as she often did when she wanted to avoid the appearance of summoning subordinates to meet with her.

"It's bad enough." O'Hara wore a grim look. "Rebecca's lost one of her destroyers, and several other ships have taken serious damage. The Marines appear to be kicking ass on the planet, but I'm more concerned about the attempted coup at the castle, in which we lost Ambassador Michaels. They're telling us the situation there is under control, but for the moment, our de facto diplomatic representative is a Marine Lieutenant—one recently promoted from Master Sergeant on a field commission."

"Yeah, that's going to require some sorting out. We sent another diplomatic officer out there to assist Michaels, and he should have taken over as ambassador, but apparently the king trusts only this—" Ling paused to consult the report on her pad, "—Lieutenant Bouchard."

"Right." O'Hara nodded. "The report's a little short on details, but Major Sakura's the ranking officer on scene. She recommends we go with the flow, and I'm inclined to let her handle it. She has more experience on Tatanna than anyone else we've got."

"Don't see that we have a choice." Ling shrugged. "I'll buck it up to the Diplomatic Corps, but there isn't much they can do until we get the military situation cleaned up. We need to focus on that, and my inclination is to send Mac some support—naval support, that is. I'll be talking to Kim later today, and I want to give him my recommendations.

"The Marines apparently have everything they need on the planet, but the Bugs could drop additional ships into the system at any time. Mac's still not calling for help, but I've never known a field commander to turn down extra combat capability when it's handed to him."

"I agree, but I don't think he needs a full Battle Group. I'd like to hold First BG to relieve him when the time comes, so… could I maybe borrow…"

"No problem." She nodded. "I'll plan on sending *Cassandra* with a pair of cruisers, an appropriate screening force, and an extra destroyer to bring Rebecca up to strength."

"You know the one she lost was *Lynx*, young Greenwood's ship, and Lorna's listed as MIA. Reading between the lines, I don't think there's much hope of recovery."

"Yes," Ling replied sadly, "I noticed. Her grandmother was one of the 'Originals.' She was pretty much my mentor and my inspiration. I served as her Flag Captain aboard *Valkyrie* a long time ago. Kind of hoped the kid would follow in her footsteps."

* * *

Lunar Command HQ, TerraNova City

"That sounds reasonable, Admiral," Kim assured her. "Do what you think best. We are committed to this operation, and I'll leave it in your hands. I'll advise the Diplomatic Corps that anything they plan to do regarding replacement of Ambassador Michaels needs to go through you.

"Just keep me advised on progress and let me know immediately if anything happens that we didn't plan for, like the assassination of a friendly monarch."

"Sir, we did not see that coming," Amy Ling said, "though maybe we should have. After this report came in, I went back and reviewed Ambassador Michaels reports to the committee over the last few years. Tatannan politics are a cesspool of intrigue that would make Machiavelli look like an amateur. About the only reason there wasn't more of this sort of thing in the past is that everyone was afraid of drawing the attention of the Bugs. Thanks to us, the Bugs now have other things to worry about." She shrugged.

"I'm not criticizing," Kim insisted. "Hindsight is always perfect. So far, I'm satisfied the people on the scene are handling the situation as well as they can. As I said, I'm leaving it with you, because there are other things I need to consider right now. Unfortunately, some of those other things involve Fleet, as well."

"I assume, sir, you are referring to the recent escalation of tensions between us and the Confederacy."

"Hmmmph, you have a talent for understatement, Admiral. Let me see…" He selected a folder on his screen. "On February 15, their Mars Squadron fired a missile at LFS *Apache*, which our ship stopped with its missile defenses. We did not return fire. They claim *Apache* wandered into the live-fire zone of a well-publicized exercise."

"Of which we received no advance notice," Ling said. "Who the hell holds fleet exercises that close to Mars? Fortunately, our ship's captain used common sense, disengaged to beyond their range, and bucked the incident back to us. Had he returned fire, it would have been nasty."

"It would have been an act of war on our part," Kim said. "That's the way the media on Earth would have portrayed it. We don't have many friends down there."

"On March 11," he continued, consulting his screen again, "we had the Confederate Commerce Patrol's seizure of LCS *Far Horizon*, en route to Ceres Station. They boarded and searched the ship and claimed they found drugs and weapons being smuggled to a terror group in the Belt. Honestly, Admiral, that one could have been handled a bit more diplomatically."

"I'm just a simple military officer, sir," she told him with a tiny hint of amusement in her voice. "In my view, a light cruiser and two destroyers are a fine example of diplomacy in action."

"Not when they threaten to blow Confederate patrol ships out of space." Kim saw no humor in the situation. "And not when they send their Marines to board a ship docked at a multi-national installation in international space."

"Sir, those Marines boarded *Far Horizon* from the spaceward side. At no time did any of them set foot in Ceres Station."

"True, but they booted the Confed CP Inspectors through the hatch and into the station, where they proceeded to scream 'piracy' and 'violation of international law' to everyone who would listen."

"Sir, you and I both know there were no drugs and no weapons. The right-wing terror group they were supposedly delivering the goods to does not exist. A terror group based in the Belt makes no sense, since there are few targets out there for them to hit and no place to hide. Everything they would need to survive has to go through Ceres or Farside, and things like guns or weapons would be noticed.

"Besides, the Confed Commerce Patrol is the most corrupt law enforcement agency in the Sol system. They extort payoffs from free miners, freighters, surveyors, and even cruise ships, but they don't usually do it to any of our ships. Our people didn't blow any patrol ships out of space, but there is no doubt they would have if they'd met any resistance, and if they hadn't complied with our request to surrender *Far Horizon*, maybe some of those CP bastards would have been forced to exit the ship on the other side, without benefit of vacuum gear."

"Yes, Admiral, you're right," Kim admitted, "and yes, I will support you on this, but I want you to understand, this is what I'm dealing with."

He turned the screen on his desk around so she could see the headline. *Lunar Navy Interferes with Commerce Patrol Drug Bust.*

"That's from an Anglo-Australian news feed," he told her. "The American media is even worse." He showed her another headline. *Moonie Commercial Ship Caught Running Guns and Drugs.*

"Those are supposed to be non-aligned nations, people who don't belong to the Confederacy. I'm sure I don't have to tell you what the European media is saying."

"Sir, I—"

He held up a hand. "No, don't say it. They're doing this deliberately, and I know it. Somebody down there has noticed we're busy. I can't imagine how they'd know, even though a third of our fleet and almost all our deep-space support capability disappeared from Luna a couple of months ago.

"Now, you're going to send another battlecruiser away, with additional ships. We know their people can count everything at the Fleet Anchorage on approach to TransLuna, so we can't keep things like this a secret. I can't help feeling these provocations would not be happening if we were at full strength."

"I have the same feeling, sir," she confided, "but if it's any consolation, I believe, with what we have left, Admiral O'Hara and I can still clean up anything the Confeds dare to send against us."

"I'm absolutely sure they won't attack us openly," Kim said with a crooked grin. "None of them have the *cojones* to take on the Dragon Lady."

Ling winced. She knew the troops called her that, though none to her face, but she hadn't expected to hear it from the Chief Executive. She decided to change the subject.

"With regard to deliberate provocations, I think we have to put *Ferret* in that category," she said.

"I thought that had been ruled an accident." He looked surprised. LFS *Ferret* was a corvette assigned to Lunar Fleet's Outer System Guard. She had been resupplying at Farside station in the Belt when a collision with a French ore freighter left her seriously damaged and two of her crew dead.

"An accident, if you believe an experienced freighter captain would mistakenly try to dock in a slip over a kilometer from the one he'd been assigned, one that was already occupied by a Lunar warship. Farside control warned him off several times, but he pleaded communications failure, which miraculously cleared up ten minutes after the collision. His ship didn't take enough damage to keep him from leaving twenty hours later, before our investigators got there. My people tell me the French authorities have not been exactly helpful regarding the location of either the ship or the captain in question."

"You're right, it sounds like another jab at us, cleverly executed so we can't respond effectively." Kim sat back with a grimace. "After further thought, I'm liking your response to the *Far Horizon* incident a lot better. So much so, you can pass my personal commendations to the captains and crews involved—privately, but put it on their records. Don't want to give Earth's news media any more fuel to throw on the fire."

* * * * *

Chapter Sixteen

First Platoon, Bravo Company

Encamped on the Little Kilder River

"I'm sorry, Blondie," Nova apologized. "I thought we'd have gotten a Fleet shuttle down here to lift you back up to orbit by now, but—"

"It's OK," Lorna assured her. "Fleet has other priorities, and the Marines…" She shrugged.

"Yeah, everybody's tied up with SAR around the nuke site. They need to figure out who's alive before they can get a tally of the dead. First Division is pretty much gone. Last I heard, they'd found less than a hundred survivors. They've confirmed that General Sherwood and his staff bought the farm in their command post twenty klicks from ground zero."

"Don't worry about us," Lorna insisted. "We're safe and comfortable here, and we're without an assignment. I've spoken to my survivors in orbit and sent my report to Commodore Ling. I've got nothing to do, and this is as good a place as any to do it."

"I'm sorry about *Lynx*," Nova said. "I'm not Navy, so I can't imagine what it's like to lose a ship, but I know how I'd feel if a unit under my command took a hit like that. If there's anything I can do—"

"Hey, you rescued us from the evil duke." Lorna managed a ghost of a smile. "About the only thing I can ask is that you take care of Jefferson. He's a good Marine, but that's just a Navy officer's opinion."

Lorna had commended Darius in her report, then advised Commodore Ling that she was turning him over to the Marines on the planet, who needed him more than she did. He didn't look happy about leaving her and McGill, but he perked up when he found out that his new unit was Bravo Company's elite Force Recon Platoon. He had quickly become very popular with the platoon, whose people wanted to hear everything about his adventures. They'd been camped in the wilderness for a couple of weeks and had seen nothing of the planet except some strange wildlife and weird-looking plants and trees.

Darius had been more than willing to oblige their curiosity, but he took a little heat from McGill, who wondered why so many of the female Marines went out of their way to wish her well. She seemed upset when she found out that Darius had told them about her parting gift to Ersin T'Corsa.

"I'll take good care of him," Nova replied. "I just wish I had a mission for my troops, but the latest word from Marine Command—that's General Mercer now—is to 'hold in place.'"

"We thought the nuke was the Bugs' last stand," she continued, "but Second Division is still fighting them. They keep popping up at the tunnel entrances near the mines. Mercer is trying to cover those sites and deal with them. At the same time, he's got to pull everything else together. I guess he figures we don't need attention right now, so if it ain't broke, don't fix it.

"You know—" she blinked as a sudden thought struck her, "—I haven't heard anything about Bravo Company. If we hadn't gotten that call for help from the palace, this platoon would have been caught up north when the Bugs blew everything to hell and gone. I would have been with Sherwood in his headquarters. Talk about karma…"

"Yeah, karma," Lorna agreed. "I'd still be in the hands of the evil duke."

"Instead, you're living in a pop-up shelter with the Marines at a remote LZ in the wilderness." Nova shook her head. "That's not much of a rescue.

"I'm going to talk to Bouchard at the castle. If they have no problem with it, I'll have Logan fly you and McGill down there tomorrow. It's only about a fifteen-minute flight, the accommodations will be better, and there's a chance Fleet will send a boat down for something the diplomatic mission needs. If so, you'll be able to hitch a ride back to orbit."

* * *

Castle Boroson, the King's City

John O'Hara looked around with a sense of the surreal. He was at a dinner for four, seated at a richly decorated octagonal dining table big enough for eight but small enough to allow conversation across the table.

Directly across the table sat King Arne, newly-crowned, aged eighteen in local years, just over twenty by Earth standards. Despite his youth, Arne looked regal, yet he was quite personable. He was dressed in the semi-formal clothing he wore for private meetings. It was less imposing than the court regalia he wore in public, and he looked comfortably at ease.

O'Hara wore his dress-alpha uniform, with the gold stars of a commodore and an impressive rack of ribbons on his chest. He had just gone through, at the king's request, an explanation of what the various uniform decorations and insignia meant. He was pleased to find that the king spoke English very well.

Bouchard sat to O'Hara's right, wearing her Marine dress-alpha uniform. The Navy shuttle that had brought O'Hara down had also delivered a supply package for her—fresh officer's uniforms with proper rank insignia, including the flashy, formal Dress Bravos, which were a bit too formal for tonight's casual dinner. Unlike O'Hara, Bouchard appeared to be comfortable dining with royalty, and she was quick to help the king with the occasional English word that escaped him. She did the same for O'Hara with Tatannan words, while making sure the fourth guest, Arne's wife Myrel, who was just beginning to show signs of her not-yet-publicly-announced pregnancy, was not neglected. Myrel, sitting to O'Hara's left, spoke very little English, but Bouchard's fluent Tatannan translation put her at ease.

In Tatannan social structure, there was no concept of queen, duchess, countess, or baroness—a female who exercised any authority as a ruler. Nobles on Tatanna rarely bothered to provide their daughters with any sort of education. They regarded them as playing pieces who could gain them a favorable alliance through marriage. Myrel was an exception, in that her father—Duke Far West—had insisted that his daughters be taught to read and write. Beyond that, she had been on her own, but when she arrived at court, she had discovered the royal library. While other young women at court spent their time with feminine crafts and gossip, Myrel had furthered her education. It was in the library that she met Prince Arne.

Now, her husband was king, and she had been drawn into the affairs of state. As O'Hara and Arne discussed Tatanna's future, she looked to Bouchard to keep her advised.

"Your presentation today was most helpful, Commodore," Arne told O'Hara after the dishes were cleared and the wine cups refilled. "We have seen nothing here in the capital, and the few reports we get from the provinces are not very useful. It is hard to imagine how extensive the fighting has been. Now that you have told me, I am still feeling like a… what is the word… spectator… yes, a spectator at a great contest that will determine the fate of my people."

"I can understand that, Majesty," O'Hara replied. "I was surprised when I heard that we had not been advising you about what was happening from the day we arrived."

"Sir," Bouchard spoke up, somewhat hesitantly, "I believe Ambassador Michaels wanted to do just that. The problem was that we had no means of communicating with Fleet, then two days after the first landing—"

"Yes," Arne interjected, "two days after your Marines made their landing, Duke High Reaches committed his foul treason and killed your ambassador along with my father. He would have killed me, as well, and taken the throne for himself were it not for Lady Moira's skill with the sword."

"For that, we are grateful," O'Hara replied, then he turned to Bouchard with an aside. "Just so you don't get blindsided, Lieutenant, be advised that Admiral McGruder has signed off on one of General Sherwood's last reports. Fleet's confirming your permanent promotion to First Lieutenant and recommending you for the LMH."

"What?" Bouchard's eyes widened, and her jaw dropped. The Lunar Medal of Honor was the highest military decoration that could be presented to a living person. "Sir, I…"

"*Ko emui?*" What's wrong? Myrel had seen the distress on Lady Moira's face and decided it must be terrible news.

Bouchard shook her head. "*Te Anna marsin tei,*" she told Myrel, then proceeded to explain what had happened in the young woman's language.

O'Hara turned back to the king.

"Majesty, there have been many things that have not gone as planned. We were not prepared for an attack on your father. We did not expect the Bugs to be so difficult to defeat. We have suffered many more losses than anticipated. There is still fighting, but I believe we can say victory is ours.

"Our efforts against the Bugs from this point forward will be mostly geared toward keeping them from returning. You will not see those efforts because they will occur in the sky, far from your world."

"I cannot imagine warfare on that scale," Arne admitted. "With the Bugs watching us, our conflicts never involved more than a few hundred men, fighting over a disputed piece of territory.

"We had conflicts, to be sure, but they were resolved in the dark of night, often by treachery in the manner of the duke's attempt to take the throne. You tell me more people died in the destruction of just one of your sky ships than died here that day. You say almost a thousand have died in the fighting against the Bugs in my kingdom, and most of those died in a single instant when the Bugs' nest was destroyed."

"That's another thing for which we were not prepared," O'Hara told him. "In our historical conflicts, defeated enemies sometimes chose suicide rather than surrender, but they never did so in such a violent, destructive fashion."

"Can your people create such destruction?"

"Yes, they can," O'Hara admitted, "but we stopped making and using such weapons decades ago. There was one war—we called it World War Three—in which a limited number of them were used, and it resulted in the destruction of many cities and the loss of millions of lives. Since then, we have put those weapons aside. We still use very destructive weapons, but they are more precise. We do not kill everyone in a huge area just to destroy a small target."

"And yet," Arne reminded him, "we know the Bugs have done exactly that. They have often destroyed whole villages to demonstrate their power when they thought we needed to be reminded."

"Yes, I know," O'Hara replied. "That was one of the primary reasons we decided to come and free you from them."

* * *

Lorna."

"Good evening, sir." Lorna turned from the parapet and acknowledged John O'Hara's greeting with a salute. He frowned as he returned it.

"We're off duty," he said. "No need to be so formal."

"You're still in uniform—" she shrugged, "—and so am I. I have nothing else to wear, except for the robe the king's people gave me to put on while they washed my uniform, but at least it's clean."

"I'm sorry about your ship," he said. "You and your people did a fine job up there. Admiral McGruder is recommending *Lynx* for Sword of the Fleet. That pretty much guarantees the name will remain in service, probably assigned to the next new destroyer that comes out of the shipyards. It also means you and your crew will be able to wear the ribbon permanently."

"Those of us that survived," she said, bitterly.

"Lorna, it's war. We lost just as many people aboard *Elsie*, fighting the same enemy."

"Yes, I know," she replied, "but I wasn't in command. I was just an ensign who got bumped into the NTO slot by mistake."

"It wasn't a mistake. You were good then, and you're even better now. The Marines think you and your crew are heroes. You got hammered hard, but not one Bug missile got past *Lynx*. Look at it from their point of view. They were packed elbow-to-elbow in their drop ships, waiting to launch. They knew the carrier was under attack, and their worst fear was that they were going to take a hit and die before they ever got into combat.

"You lost 46 people," he added, "and I'm sorry for that, but if one missile had gotten past you, it could have killed a hundred Marines, and if they had gotten hit the way *Lynx* did, with a kamikaze Bug…"

She didn't reply, and for a while, they stood in silence, watching the two moons rise over the city. Behind them, Sacagawea had just set in the west, bathing the sky in a deep purple glow.

"It's a very pretty planet," Lorna said, at last. "I wish all those Navy people in orbit could see this, so they'd know what we're fighting for."

Another long moment passed in silence, then O'Hara finally got up the nerve to say what was on his mind.

"I've missed you."

She looked at him sharply.

"That was years ago, John, and yes, I've missed you, too," she admitted, "but nothing has changed."

"Everything has changed," he insisted. "You wanted to get your career started, and you have. You've moved up in rank, and now, you've had a command of your own. I've moved up as well, had two commands, and now I've got my own flag, but in all those years, I haven't met another woman I'd like to spend my future with. I'm not getting any younger, and—"

"You're 42 years old," Lorna interrupted. "I think enough of you to remember that. Your birthday was two months ago. Don't try to tell me you're getting old.

"As for my career—" she turned back to gaze out over the city, "—I came up in rank very quickly, and I was given command of a destroyer ahead of a number of available Lieutenant Commanders senior to me. Even though my grandmother's dead, people still talk about favoritism. Admiral Ling was one of granny's protégés, and now they think I'm hers. Even more eyebrows went up when I got *Lynx* and was assigned to the Cat Pack under her daughter's command.

"I lost my ship and a third of my crew on our very first combat mission." O'Hara heard the bitterness and pain in her voice. "You know how Fleet bends over backward to avoid any hint of patronage, matronage, nepotism, favoritism in any form, and yet it happens.

"Maybe some people did push for me, and maybe I didn't deserve what I got. Maybe some good people are dead because I wasn't good enough. One thing's for sure; nobody in Fleet is likely to trust me with another command. At best, they'll shake their heads and say I need more experience, and maybe I'll get an exec slot on a support ship. At worst, they'll find a staff job for me somewhere. No, maybe that's not the worst. Maybe I'll be court-martialed and get booted out of the service altogether."

"Lorna, that's not going to happen," he said. "I've seen the reports. You did well up there. You were on the bleeding edge, and you paid the price, but you got the job done. That's what the reports say, and that's the way Fleet will look at it."

"Maybe," she replied, "but that's not the way it feels. Maybe I have a career left, maybe not. Either way, I can't plan for the future until I have a better idea of what's going to happen. I'm not going to think about my personal life until I get my professional life straightened out."

She lapsed into silence, and he made no reply, mostly because she had touched on something that bothered him in terms of his own career. *Yeah, right. Had two commands, and I've got my flag, but no ship to fly it and no prospects for a command any time soon. Patronage? Her grandmother's dead, but my grandfather's still alive, and my father's a Vice Admiral.*

Like Lorna, John O'Hara was the grandchild of one of the Lunar Free State's most noteworthy original citizens. Michael O'Hara had been the longest-serving Chief Executive in the nation's history. He had retired at the age of 117 and then gone to live on New Eden and returned to his roots as an engineer. Under the auspices of the New Eden Protectorate, which had been founded during his term as CEO, he was now teaching the native "Edies" how to build bridges, roads, and other elements of their developing civilization's infrastructure. Meanwhile, his son Robert—John's father—had risen through the Fleet ranks to Vice Admiral in command of Second Fleet.

After the Lewis and Clark *affair, there are plenty of people who think I've been coasting along on patronage, and maybe nobody in Fleet wants to trust me with another command.*

During the *Lewis and Clark* mission, the ship's captain had been a casualty of battle, and John O'Hara had declared the executive officer unfit for command and relieved him of duty under a seldom-used article of military regulations. On return to Luna, the former exec had filed charges of mutiny. An investigation had been opened, and it had looked as though O'Hara was headed for a court-martial, but because of the discovery of a new human civilization on Tatanna, Fleet had clamped a lid of secrecy on the situation. When the final investigation report came out—classified secret—it looked very much like a whitewash. No charges were brought against anyone, and O'Hara had moved on to an exec slot on a heavy cruiser.

Officially, nobody knew there had been a charge of mutiny, but O'Hara couldn't shake the feeling that the whole affair was haunting his career. He would only be convinced otherwise if they gave him another command, and right now, that didn't look likely.

Maybe she's right, he thought. *Maybe my professional life needs attention even more than hers does.*

* * *

"What a beautiful creature." Myrel looked at Bob with awe, and he returned her gaze with the fearless curiosity so typical of cats. The king's wife had come looking for Moira and had found her in the guest suite, talking to Mary Jane McGill, while Bob sat on the table between them.

"Is he... may I touch him?" Myrel was enraptured by the haughty feline, who regarded her with a total lack of respect for her royal station.

"It is said that cats choose their humans rather than us choosing them," Bouchard responded. "If you hold out your hand, he may come to you. I make no promises."

Myrel held out her hand, and Bob immediately got up and walked forward to investigate. Myrel did not flinch, though she had been told of the cat's attack on one of Duke North Coast's men who had dared to lay hands on McGill. Bob moved with lazy grace and didn't appear threatening.

After probing the royal hand with his nose, the cat began rubbing his head against it. Taking the cue, Myrel turned her hand over and began stroking his back. Bob rewarded her with a very loud purr.

"That means you have been chosen, my Lady," Bouchard said with a grin. "You are not only permitted to pet him, you are required to do so whenever you are in his presence."

"That sound he makes... it is so soothing." Myrel was smiling but then she shook off Bob's influence and turned to McGill with a slight bow.

"Excuse me," she said in heavily-accented English. "Not want to intrude but must speak to Lady Moira."

"Of course, Your Highness," McGill responded with a slight bow.

Myrel turned immediately to Bouchard and switched back to her native Tatannan.

"Duke Middle Plains arrived today, with his oldest son. His Majesty is telling them all about... well, everything... and, as you can imagine, the duke is very upset. He will get over it, however. He was always King Algar's strongest ally. In any event, His Majesty thinks it would be good for him to meet some off-worlders in an informal setting, where he can see you and judge for himself that you are the friends we say you are."

"He wants all of you to join us for dinner. Middle Plains is a young man, a few years older than my Arne. Though it is said he never strays from his wives, he has an eye for beautiful women and fancies himself charming. My husband thinks that you, Moira, along with Lady Mary Jane and Lady Lorna, will do more to calm his concerns about off-worlders than any discussions with Commodore O'Hara could possibly do."

"We're not diplomats," Bouchard protested. "As I have often told His Majesty, we are military officers with little knowledge of affairs of state. Besides, Commander Greenwood and Ensign McGill don't speak your language."

"I know," Myrel acknowledged with a smile. "His Majesty knows that as well. He says he doesn't want you to be diplomats. For tonight, he just wants you to be women."

* * *

"Seriously? The king wants us to be eye candy at dinner tonight?" Lorna found the idea amusing. "Did anyone tell him what happened to the last guy who wanted to look at us?"

"I think he wants to show the duke we are human," Bouchard replied. "If he finds you attractive, so much the better."

"That might be true for you two—" McGill shook her head, "—but nobody ever offered me a job as a fashion model."

"Actually, Ensign," Bouchard said, "by Tatannan standards, you are the most attractive of the three of us. I'm a head taller than most local men—which tends to call attention to this very unfashionable Marine hairstyle—and Commander Greenwood tops me by about ten centimeters. Besides, we're both a little too thin. Tatannan males like their women a bit more... shapely, or maybe I should say sturdy."

"You mean, my fat ass is actually an asset?" McGill grinned at her. She was not fat, though she was shorter and a bit wider in the hips than either of the other two.

"It's all about making a favorable impression," Bouchard told them. "I'd almost suggest we take Bob along, based on the reaction he's received from just about everybody in the castle who's seen him. He's a real charmer, but I'd hate to think about what might happen if he doesn't take a liking to the duke."

"You have no idea." McGill chuckled. "You have to see him in combat mode to believe it. I was really surprised to find out that Tatannans don't keep pets. You would think there would be animals around here that are analogs of dogs or cats."

"They do have working animals." Bouchard shrugged. "You've seen what kildren look like, but for some reason, the Tatannans don't seem to have developed the concept of an animal as a companion. It's just another reminder that we really are on another planet."

* * *

The Last Bug Installation, West of the King's City

Of the twelve Bug operational sites identified and engaged by the Marines, six were too small and remote to be worth direct tunnel connections to the hive. For those that did have such connections, the Bugs had gathered whatever warriors remained in the hive after the first queen departed and sent them into the tunnels with instructions to seal the tunnel behind them at the hive end. They already knew what was going to happen to the hive, even though the human bombardment was just beginning.

The humans invading the hive after the bombardment encountered only worker Bugs, who could not fight back and could only try to block the hive corridors and die in the process. It was simply a delaying action while the warriors traveled down the long tunnels. They were instructed to continue to the far end and emerge to fight any humans they encountered. The installations there would already have been captured by the humans, and the warriors were not expected to recapture them or even inflict significant damage on the enemy. Their mission was nothing more than a delaying action and diversion.

The seventh tunnel—the one whose existence the humans had not discovered—was how the final mission would be accomplished. Constructed years earlier, the tunnel led to a large, environmentally-sealed Bug installation deep underground near the edge of the human king's city. It contained supplies and support equipment not only for the queen, but for as many as 50 workers and 300 warriors. With calculated Bug efficiency, that was exactly the number of Bugs that accompanied the queen to the installation.

Like the diversionary groups, the mission force sealed the tunnel behind them at the hive end to prevent any blast effects from traveling down the 900-kilometer-long tube. It was also intended to keep the humans from following them, but that wasn't really an issue. In the aftermath of the blast, the hive ends of all the tunnels were buried under many tons of radioactive rock.

The surviving queen and her minions had reached the sealed installation days earlier. They knew, through the empathic sense Bugs had among themselves, that the hive and the other queen were no more. They would wait a few more days for the diversionary forces to fully engage the human forces.

* * * * *

Chapter Seventeen

Terranova City, Luna

Kim Jong Pak was a creature of habit. His security people tried to make him vary his movements, but they overlooked certain things. When he followed one of his favorite routes from office to home, he always walked to the right side of the minor concourse, the side where the small shops were located. Sometimes, he paused to look at the window displays, but even when he seemed to be in a hurry, he walked to the right. It was a minor consideration in Five's planning, but worth noting.

Likewise, Kim never took the route through TerraNova Park on Wednesday. That was the big public event night in the park, usually involving a concert or some other entertainment program. Anything from festivals to live theater to special planetarium programs were displayed on the dome. The decision to avoid that route on that day was made by Kim's security team since the park was always crowded then.

There were noteworthy points on Kim's other routes of travel as well. Five had spent a lot of time reviewing the video collected by the self-contained micro-cameras he had placed along the routes. The video was also intended to verify the other feature of his plan—the facial recognition software that put a special tag on the video when Kim came into view.

The information about the park was key, however, since that was the only regular route that was not suited to Five's plan. Wednesday would have to be the day of execution. His camera studies provided a time window with which he could be reasonably confident. Exact timing wasn't necessary, but any deviation from the window could cause problems with his exit strategy.

Kim's choice of route didn't matter, as long as it wasn't through the park. Five would cover all the other possibilities. With the date and time window selected, he started his final preparations. Tomorrow was Wednesday, and he did not want to wait another week.

* * *

LFS *Sorceress*, Lunar Fleet Anchorage

"Mac doesn't pull any punches, does he?" Rob O'Hara remarked.

"No, he doesn't," Amy Ling replied, "but based on the content, I think his conclusions are valid."

"You honestly think this Ensign Bunker was sent out there to deliberately sabotage our relationship with the Tatannans? I mean, he'd have to know we'd have his ass in a sling once he returned. His career's done, finished, end of story. He might have gotten away with it if he'd kept his mouth shut with Sherwood and Mac, if he had just claimed this crazy Marine Lieutenant totally misinterpreted what he was trying to say, but…"

"But he didn't." Ling nodded. "He sounded off on this half-assed 'Colonial Governor' idea as though he believed it was the way the Diplomatic Corps wanted him to play it. Maybe that's because he did believe it, which implies he's a dupe and somebody set him up."

"That implies somebody in the Diplomatic Corps, high up in the Diplomatic Corps, who's been in on the Blue Orchid Project from the beginning is… what?" O'Hara threw up his hands. "A traitor? A power player? Somebody who decided to go off on his own, in defiance of the program that's been vetted throughout the project and signed off on by the CEO?"

"I'm actually hoping it's the latter," Ling told him, "because if it's a traitor, somebody down on Earth—someone in the Confederacy—knows where we are and what we're doing out there. In any case, Mac's report went to DCHQ and should have landed on Admiral Hutchins' desk. I've dropped a copy on Kim's desk, as well. I expect the shit is about to be sucked into somebody's turbine, and for once, it's not Fleet's."

* * *

Corporate Offices of Frères le Fleur, Paris, France

"I am holding a call from a man named Thomas Hutchins, Director. He is calling from our resort in Mexico, in English, on your private line, audio only. He insists he must speak to you."

"Our favorite Moonie diplomat," Pierre DuMorne muttered.

"Shhh." Andre DuMorne waved at his younger brother to be silent. "I will take the call, Michelle."

"Hello, Tom," Andre said when the call was connected. He mentioned neither rank nor last name. His private calls were supposedly as secure as any in the world, but he trusted no form of electronic communication. "I hope you are enjoying your vacation."

"Well, I was," Hutchins replied, "until I got a message from my office back on... back home." It appeared that he, too, was wary of saying too much on a call. "That man we sent on that special mission has failed. Worse, they are sending him back, and somebody is going to be asking where he got his instructions."

"Explain this, please. How did it happen?" DuMorne demanded. "He was supposed to stay there and cause problems without revealing anything. 'Subtle sabotage' was what you called it, I believe."

"Yes, that was the plan." Hutchins still sounded agitated. "We warned him not to trust the ambassador and to work in the background, but something came up. The ambassador is... well... out of the picture. Our man tried to take over and decided to go with what we told him we wanted. He went too heavy-handed, and some military bastard stepped on him and sent him back to Luna. He should be arriving in a few days."

"I see." DuMorne said. *So much for not providing any identifying information.* DuMorne rolled his eyes in frustration. "What can I do about this? How can I help you, my friend?"

"If they start grilling him, it's going to fall on me. You need to help me get out of this. I've arranged to... uh... preserve my assets, but I can't go back to Luna, and people will be looking for me. They have agents on Earth and... Anyway, I'm sure you can fix me up with a comfortable new life somewhere."

"To be sure," DuMorne replied. "We can arrange that, but it will take a little time. For the moment, stay where you are and relax. You will not be expected to pay for anything, and you might ask the concierge about special entertainments on the Blue List. You may be surprised by what is available to our particular friends.

"If someone comes looking, they will be told you have gone somewhere else. We will send them 'chasing the wild goose' as the Americans say. I will make sure our local management understands."

"Fine, but I won't be happy until you come up with the arrangements. Remember, it's in your best interest to make sure they don't find me."

"I understand, *mon ami*. We will be in touch." DuMorne ended the call.

"I cannot believe he actually said that." Pierre wore a crooked grin. "He's right; it's in our best interest to make sure they don't find him."

"Yes, it is." Andre returned the grin. "You know what needs to be done, and it doesn't need to be subtle, just quick and permanent. We've already gotten all we need from him, including the location of this far-away star system where the Moonies have found another human civilization. Imagine what that information will be worth to our associates."

His grin faded to a thoughtful frown. "This operation was a long-term, subtle ploy intended to discredit Moonie colonialism. In the grand scheme, it is nothing, but unfortunately, we will have to dispose of a well-cultivated asset high in the Moonie organizational structure."

"Quick and permanent," Pierre repeated, "and I presume you don't mind if it happens in public, as long as there is no connection to us."

"Correct. An 'accident' would be nice, but I leave that to you. Just make sure you account for any personal communications devices he might have. Otherwise, I don't care if I see it in the newsfeeds a few days from now. Besides, if our other operation succeeds, the news media will soon have a much bigger story to work on."

* * *

Terranova City, Luna

Wednesday, 6 April 2112, 1400 Hours LST

Five traveled light. He had nothing with him, except the clothes he wore and his personal pad with the appropriate electronic identification documents—passport, Lunar work visa, and credit account drawn on the Bank of Luna. In short, nothing he wouldn't be carrying for a day of work or leisure in TerraNova City or a tourist excursion up to TransLuna spaceport on his day off to get a beautiful view of the stars, the Earth, and the Moon from the L1 point.

He reserved a seat on a late afternoon shuttle to the station, with a return trip later that evening. He also made a reservation at First LaGrange, a five-star restaurant on the station that claimed to provide "the most incredible view in the explored Universe."

He did not expect to enjoy that view, nor would he be returning in the evening, or ever, if things went according to plan. Instead, he would board a French cargo carrier that had just arrived from its latest run to the asteroid belt and stopped at TransLuna to pick up a small amount of cargo on its way to the Confederacy's CircumTerra station in synchronous Earth orbit. Once aboard, he would assume a new identity and become a French crewman who had arrived with the freighter and had never set foot on Luna. He would have all the right documents, including a verifiable 20-year membership in the Merchant Spacer's Guild, and the captain and crew of the ship would swear he had been with them the entire trip and hadn't gone ashore at TransLuna. He would also make some significant adjustments to his physical appearance just in case a random camera somewhere had seen him.

Given the amount of public camera surveillance in TerraNova, he was quite certain he would eventually be identified as the perpetrator... or Antonio Tortorelli would.

That would be after the fact when Antonio Tortorelli no longer existed.

* * *

1430 Hours LST

Kim Jong Pak rubbed his temples, feeling the onset of a headache he attributed to the pressures of the job.

There had been three more incidents, clear provocations of Lunar Fleet or OSG ships by Confederate warships—provocations that could have gone badly if Luna's people hadn't kept their heads. He'd issued stern warnings to the Confederacy's Council of Nations in Brussels, but those warnings had been ignored.

Instead, that same Council had issued a summons for him—Luna's Chief Executive—to appear before them on charges that the Lunar Research Institute's scientific station on Mars was "engaging in wanton and deliberate contamination of the planet's ecosystem."

Mars didn't have an ecosystem. Fossilized remains of microscopic life had been found there many decades ago, but those fossils were millions of years old. No evidence had been found of anything currently living on the planet, other than Earth organisms in the immediate vicinity of every established site on the planet, including those of the Confederacy. Most of the sites used simple septic systems that disposed of human and other waste products in tanks and fields under the Martian soil. The Confederacy's mines on the planet disposed of their mining waste products and processing chemicals imported from Earth by simply dumping them out in the open.

Yet somehow, an attempt by Lunar scientists to develop variations of Earth plants that could grow in the raw Martian environment was—in their view—"contamination of the ecosystem."

Kim had no intention of appearing before the Confederacy's kangaroo court, but he hadn't yet figured out how to say "screw you" in polite, diplomatic language. As a precaution, he sent a quick message to Admiral Ling, requesting she drop a "suitable Marine force" for field exercises on Mars close to the LRI station, just in case the Confeds decided to take direct action against the scientists.

He didn't think the Confederacy really wanted a war. They were just pushing to see what they could get away with, and, as far as he was concerned, they'd reached their limit. He made a point of telling Ling the Marines should avoid a confrontation, if possible, but under no circumstances should they allow the Confeds to interfere with the LRI people in any way.

He turned to the latest reports from Operation Blue Orchid. He was pleased that Fleet appeared to be getting the military job done but was troubled by the number of casualties reported.

In sheer numbers, New Eden had cost far more, and most everyone agreed that the sacrifice had been worth it to liberate an entire planet from alien oppression. New Eden, however, was decades ago, not on Kim's watch.

The diplomatic news was troubling. This time, Luna was not liberating a planet with small tribes of humans living as hunter-gatherers. Tatanna had its own system of government, headed by a king who had been a strong proponent of liberation from the Bugs. Now that the king had been assassinated, along with Luna's ambassador, the king's son had taken the throne and was reported to be of the same mind as his father, but no one seemed quite sure whether the situation was stable.

That was followed by the disturbing news that the remaining Diplomatic Corps representative on the planet had suddenly tried to push an unacceptable agenda on the new king. After reading the report, Kim put a call through to the Diplomatic Corps, where staffers told him Admiral Hutchins was vacationing on Earth.

Luna didn't have an officially designated Foreign Minister or Secretary of State, but Hutchins was the top officer in the Diplomatic Corps, and he reported directly to the CEO. Kim didn't recall authorizing Hutchins' leave, but it might have slipped by him in the myriad of tiny details that crossed his desk every day. In any case, the staffers insisted that Hutchins had been notified of the problem and would be returning to Luna as soon as possible.

Kim sighed. Impasse on all fronts. Nothing he could do at the moment.

"Mike, what do I have scheduled for tomorrow?" he inquired.

"You have the meeting of the LRI Board tomorrow afternoon, but your morning schedule is presently clear, sir," the AI replied. "The Confederacy's envoy has not responded to your request for a meeting."

Kim gritted his teeth. The Confederacy had recalled their ambassador a month ago, pleading a need to reevaluate their diplomatic posture with the LFS. That left only an envoy in their embassy, a minor functionary with no authority to do anything but refer everything back to Brussels. Still, he was the only one available to hear Kim's concerns, and now, it appeared that he wasn't answering calls.

"I think I'll go home early tonight, Mike. Advise Lieutenant Mandrake I'll be leaving in about half an hour."

Kim hated to spring sudden schedule changes on his security detail. He knew they went to great lengths to protect him against all threats, real or imagined, and he didn't want to make their job any more difficult.

* * *

Arnold "Red" Mandrake looked a bit old for his rank of First Lieutenant, but that was due to a rather unique requirement. To be an officer in HQ Security, one had to serve four years as an enlisted member of the detail and two years as a noncom. Then, and only then, could he or she apply for one of the special slots at Lunar Fleet Academy, spend the usual four years there, and be commissioned a Second Lieutenant in the Marines, with the understanding that the next four years would be spent assigned to the Fleet HQ Security Force. All of Luna's police and law enforcement services were special units of the Marines, but HQ Security had been an elite unit since it was formed after an assassination attempt on the CEO in 2045.

Mandrake wasn't the head of all HQ Security, but he was the ninth officer in charge of the CEOs personal detail in its 67-year history. Another year would certainly bring a promotion, and his choice of a command spot anywhere in Lunar law enforcement, unless, like some of his predecessors, he chose to move to a spot in Fleet Marine Forces. Either way, he had a promising career ahead of him.

After the heads-up from Mike, he dispatched an advance party of three Marines to sweep the route through Concourse Charlie on Level 15, a simple straight route from the HQ elevator bank, which only went down to 15, to the residential lift system. According to his private method of reckoning, that was Route 3, and he had selected it for today by his usual method, a roll of the dice—or rather a single die since there were only six routes to choose from. The first roll had come up with a single dot, which would have indicated Route 1, a trip through TerraNova Park, but today was Wednesday, and the park would be crowded.

He almost considered it anyway because of Kim's early departure, but there was a live theater performance scheduled for tonight, and there would be a lot of people setting up stages and making other early preparations. He rolled the die again, and it had come up with a 3.

The advance detail reported all clear just as Kim came out of his office. Mandrake arranged the rest of his detail and nodded to the CEO.

"Ready to go home, sir?"

"Yes, I am," Kim acknowledged. "Lead on, Lieutenant."

* * *

The device was not large, and it wasn't tiny. It was about the size of a portable data pad, what people once called a "cell phone" for reasons that were lost in history. In other words, it was about a centimeter in thickness, seven centimeters wide, and twelve centimeters long. It had an additional centimeter-thick foam pad on the back, but that was compressible to allow it to conform to just about any surface. Once the backing was removed from the adhesive it would stick to just about anything.

The case had no external features except a tiny port that allowed a control device to plug in for programming and activation. It also had a chameleon polymer on its external surfaces that could be programmed to any color to match any surface on which it was placed. The entire assembly was non-metallic and produced no electronic emissions unless triggered.

It had been a challenge to find suitable places for three or four of the devices on each of the possible routes. If the route was in a confined area, such as Concourse "C" on Level 15, the device only needed to be within twenty meters of the target's expected path. In more open areas, it needed to be triggered within 10 meters of the target to guarantee success.

Those were Five's conservative estimates. It was more likely any of the devices would cover a fifty-meter radius in even the most open areas, though it might take a few seconds for the effects to spread that far. Beyond that, the agent would continue to disperse, and it would still be effective hours later and hundreds of meters from the trigger site. Given TerraNova's typical pedestrian traffic, there would probably be a great deal of collateral damage.

Five had placed the devices so the tiny camera would have a view of the target's approach, but in an unobtrusive location where it was unlikely to be noticed or disturbed for the few hours needed to complete the task. Once placed, it couldn't be easily removed, but security might be alerted if anyone got too curious. He was momentarily amused by the thought that the discovery of one of the devices might lead Kim's detail to change to another route, one where other devices had been planted but not detected.

If one of the devices was triggered, it would automatically trigger those nearby on the same route. Any that were not triggered would go off automatically approximately eight hours later. If none of them triggered within the expected time frame, Five planned to go back down to Luna, disarm them, rework his plans, and try again.

* * *

1511 Hours LST

Level 15's Charlie Concourse ran along the edge of one of the upscale housing warrens, accessible through three portals that came into the concourse along the left side of Kim's route. The right side was lined with various shops, a delicatessen, and two small restaurants. The entire concourse was only 200 meters long and closed at both ends with large double airlocks that were normally kept open.

Mandrake was in position, 20 meters in front of the four Marines surrounding Kim. Pedestrian traffic was light on Concourse Charlie at this time of day. Lunar citizens were an easygoing bunch, and most would step to the other side of the concourse when they saw the flashing blue armbands worn by the close-in detail. When they figured out what was going on, they would typically smile and wave at the CEO.

Occasionally, some preoccupied citizen would fail to notice what was happening. Mandrake would politely call attention to the approaching detail and ask the person in question to step aside. He rarely encountered a problem sufficient to cause him to stop smiling or use an authoritarian tone. As for the shopkeepers along the way, they were used to seeing the detail since this was one of Kim's regular routes. Mandrake knew all of them by sight, and they recognized him as well. They offered a cheery wave and directed their customers to stay inside until Kim went by.

Mandrake glanced back and paused as Kim stopped to admire something in the window display of a little antique and curio shop. He often stopped there and occasionally entered to buy something, but tonight, he only stopped for a moment then continued.

Mandrake started to move but spun around when he heard a strange noise behind him, followed by a shout from one of his team.

* * *

The face ID software acquired a match and instantly triggered the mechanism. A tiny valve opened, allowing small amounts of two chemicals to combine. The two chemicals reacted instantly, producing a large amount of gas. The gas was harmless; its function was to serve as a propellant for the contents of a much larger chamber, one that occupied over 90% of the total volume of the device. The few ounces of liquid shot out of the device through a ruptured pressure seal and vaporized instantly. The result was a rapidly spreading cloud of the deadliest nerve agent ever produced—one that didn't need to be inhaled, just contact exposed skin. The cloud was colorless, odorless, and almost instantly fatal.

* * *

Corporal Ligget, at the front right corner of the square formation around Kim, heard a very loud *pop* from the base of an ornamental dragon sculpture that flanked the door of the Thai restaurant ahead. He also heard a hissing sound, but he didn't waste time looking for the source. He had been on the CEO's security detail for more than two years, and his trained bodyguard reflexes kicked in. With no visible threat, he didn't waste time reaching for his weapon. Instead, he spun around and started pushing Kim away from the source of the sound.

"Get back, sir!" he shouted into the startled CEO's face. "Get..."

His shouted command cut off suddenly, and he dropped to the ground, stiff and unmoving. The nerve agent caused instant tightening of every muscle in the body, including the heart. Victims stiffened and went down immediately. With no fresh blood bringing oxygen to the brain, death occurred in less than a minute.

Kim and the other three Marines dropped an instant later, without ever knowing what was happening to them. Twenty meters up the street, Mandrake failed to notice the sound of the other device triggering behind him. He managed to take three steps toward Kim before the nerve agent took him down, as well.

By all rights, everyone in Concourse Charlie should have died, and that would have happened if TerraNova's internal systems had been monitored and controlled by humans. In the Lunar city, though, those systems were managed by Mike, the first and most capable Artificial Intelligence created by the Lunar Free State's cybernetic scientists and engineers. The AI had incredibly fast parallel processing abilities, and his queue was normally loaded to capacity with thousands of tasks. TerraNova was a sealed city, surrounded by the harsh, unforgiving environment of the Moon. Security and emergency response were always Mike's top priorities.

Mike had cameras covering virtually every public area in TerraNova—high-resolution cameras with built-in infrared lighting that would allow them to function if regular lighting failed and would reveal details in normal light that were not visible to the human eye. So, he saw the clouds of deadly vapor the devices produced and saw the humans touched by it instantly stiffen and fall.

A human might have taken seconds to realize what was happening, more seconds to decide what to do, and still more to act. Mike took nanoseconds. Lieutenant Mandrake had not yet fallen when the strident alarms sounded, and brilliant red strobe lights began flashing in Concourse C.

Five seconds after the alarm began, pressure doors slammed down, sealing off the shops, the three portals into the residential sections, and the larger portals at both ends of the concourse. Mike would have preferred not to wait the five seconds, but that was a hard-wired, mandatory delay to give anyone crossing a threshold time to get clear before the doors came down.

Mike's action saved many lives. The owner and two customers inside Kim's favorite curio shop survived as the shop door sealed less than a second before the cloud reached it. The same was true of thirty-two people inside five other shops. Uncounted numbers of people outside the concourse and in the attached residential areas were safe because the closing doors kept the deadly nerve agent in Concourse C.

The owner, two employees, and three customers died in the Thai restaurant. The first device had been triggered in the restaurant's doorway, and those inside died just as Kim and his bodyguards were overcome. The same was true of four people inside a clothing store whose doorway hid the second device, the one that killed Mandrake.

The third device was attached to the base of a floral planter at the far end of the concourse. It triggered as well but killed no one inside any of the shops. The nearest business was an art gallery that was closed for the day. Its owner had planned to come in that evening to set up for a local artist's show that was to begin the next morning.

The only other casualty inside a shop was the owner of a small bookstore, one that specialized in old books printed on paper, as well as new ones, though few were published that way anymore. She had been setting up a display near the door and had left a small cart full of books parked on the yellow and black striped area that marked where the pressure door would come down in an emergency. She had gone to the back of the store for just a moment when the warnings sounded, and five seconds was not enough time to move the cart out of the way. The door was power-driven and crushed the cart down to ten centimeters, but the door could not seal, and the deadly vapor invaded the shop ten seconds later.

In addition to Kim and his Marines, twenty people died on the concourse, including one woman who stepped out of a shop instead of in when the alarm sounded. Most died less than thirty seconds after the first device was triggered, though two, who were near one of the residential portals, lived almost a full minute before the nerve agent reached them.

By then, Mike had already sealed the entire city as a precaution and had activated the emergency response teams.

* * *

TerraNova Shuttle Terminal, 1515 Hours LST

Five, who was sitting with the rest of the waiting passengers, looked up in surprise when the alarms sounded and the pressure doors closed, sealing off the lounge from the rest of the terminal. The TransLuna shuttle was still listed as incoming on the status display, and he had expected another hour's wait before it would be ready to take on passengers. He had arrived early, anticipating delays, but there had been no hassle, nothing more than a cursory security scan and ID check.

The Lunar Free State's Customs and Immigration people were mostly concerned with people arriving on Luna rather than those departing, but when the alarms sounded, Five realized that might change at any moment. If he was right, those alarms meant he had completed his contract to the satisfaction of his unknown employers. What he had not done was make good on his escape.

* * *

LFS *Sorceress* at Lunar Fleet Anchorage

"Seriously, Mom, are you ever going to retire?"

Amy Ling smiled at the image of her son on the screen. George Mackenzie Jr., PhD was the Director of the Lunar Research Institute's Information Technology division. He had been asking the same question for nearly fifteen years, since his father had died at the age of 87 while still on active duty with the Lunar Marine Corps. George Senior had reached the rank of Brigadier General and had been in good health when he died in the crash of a Marine landing craft during a training exercise.

"I'll retire when I get old," she told him. "Right now, I'm too busy trying to figure out what I want to be when I grow up. Besides, the Navy gives me all these neat toys to play with."

"Well now, there's the problem," George replied. "What can I get my mother for her birthday that could possible match... what's that? There's some kind of alert..."

George's image disappeared from Ling's screen and was replaced by Sonja's familiar Sorceress avatar.

"Ma'am, I'm sorry to interrupt," the AI said, "but we have a Code Red situation. I have a message from Mike on Luna. Mr. Kim has been assassinated. Per the Lunar Constitution, you are now the Chief Executive."

* * * * *

Chapter Eighteen

Battlecruiser LFS *Sorceress*, Lunar Fleet Anchorage

Best known for her hard-driving, no-nonsense command style, Amy Ling also knew how to delegate—to select people who could get the job done, then stand back and let them do it.

"Rob, as of right now, the Fleet is yours. That may or may not be a temporary command, but somebody just dumped the CEO job on my head, and that obviously needs my full attention."

"Understood, Admiral." Rob O'Hara wore a grave expression, as would most Lunar citizens in the days to come. Their Chief Executive had been assassinated in a horrible act of terror that had killed many of their fellow citizens as well. Their nation was at war, and they had no idea who the enemy was.

"I've already got Blue Orchid and the rest of Second Fleet, but have you any specific directives for Home Fleet at this time?"

"You can stand everybody down from Condition Yellow," she replied, "but I want Fleet-wide Security Blue in effect until further notice. I'm not expecting anybody else's fleet to come looking for a fight, but until we find out who did this, I want tight control over who comes and goes aboard any of our ships, and I want grav nodes hot, and all ships on one hour standby.

"I've advised my Home Fleet staff that they now report to you, so touch base with them. As for me, I need to get acquainted with Kim's staff ASAP."

"Roger that, ma'am." O'Hara managed a reassuring half-smile. "You do what you have to do, and I've got your back."

"You always have, Rob," she replied with a grim smile. "We'll get you that fourth star eventually. For now, if anybody doesn't behave like you already have it, let me know."

She broke the connection and looked at the empty conference table in front of her. It was a rare occurrence in the Flag Briefing Room aboard *Sorceress*. As she'd told O'Hara, her Home Fleet staff was now assigned to him, and she had to jump into the CEO's job without them. She would, however, require assistance from Kim's people on Luna, and she was not going to waste time bringing them up to the Fleet Anchorage to talk. In the aftermath of the assassination, it was not a good idea to gather too many high-level people in one place.

"Sonja, please set up a conference call. I need Mike, Admiral Lavoisier, General Tucker, Admiral Ivanova, Admiral Moskowitz, and Admiral Hutchins."

"Admiral Hutchins has still not returned from leave on Earth," the AI replied. "His staff has been unable to contact him."

"Understood. Add the second-in-command at the Diplomatic Corps to the list."

"Yes, ma'am. I'll advise you as soon as I have contacted them."

"Thank you... and by the way, young lady, I am invoking Executive Privilege. As long as I remain aboard—and I don't know how long that will be—you are still my Executive Assistant, so plan to be on that call."

"Yes, ma'am," she acknowledged, "but be advised that Mike has served in that capacity for every CEO since the founding of the Lunar Free State."

"Good, then I'll have two of you. Besides, I have other things for Mike to do right now."

Sonja chose not to point out that multitasking was second nature to every Artificial Intelligence. Like her sister battlecruiser AIs, she considered Mike her "father" and welcomed the opportunity to work with him.

* * *

I f Mike were human, he would be experiencing frustration on several fronts.

He had confirmed that the lethal nerve agent, which he identified as CPX-B—an agent that had originally been developed in Russia, though several nations had access to it—had been contained. Concourse C on Level 15 had been exposed, as had three shops along the concourse, but the residential connections had been sealed in time, as had the connections at either end of the concourse.

When he triggered the alert, Mike closed every pressure door in TerraNova. In addition, he passed the information to Louis, the AI at TransLuna station, who locked down that facility as well. All traffic in the city and on the orbital facility had come to a halt, with everyone imprisoned in whatever compartment they were in when the lockdown occurred. Emergency responders could move around because they had the special codes to open doors as needed, but no one else could.

As soon as he determined the extent of the contamination, Mike contacted Marine Emergency Services and recommended opening the non-affected doors. Colonel Jones, the Event Commander, and the ranking officer on duty when the event occurred, agreed. City traffic resumed, and Louis unlocked TransLuna as well.

Mike contacted Traffic Control and asked that all traffic between TransLuna and TerraNova be suspended. Marine Special Investigations agreed that no one should be allowed to leave Luna until the assassin had been identified.

Mike had identified 35 people trapped in six shops along the concourse. For the moment, they were all safe and had power and air. All were in contact with emergency responders through Luna's public communication network. Each shop had a rear exit, but all the rear exits led to a maintenance corridor that was open to Concourse C, with no additional pressure seal. Those exits were intended to provide egress only in case of an emergency inside the shop.

Mike studied the chemical composition of CPX-B. It was usually transported as a liquid under pressure of two atmospheres or more. At 1.5 atmospheres or less it vaporized and spread quickly, but in hard vacuum, its chemical structure quickly broke down into inert elements.

If Mike could put a hard vacuum in Concourse C for as little as twenty minutes, he could neutralize the agent, but that would require running a vent pipeline out of the city to the Lunar surface. TerraNova was specifically designed to keep atmosphere in, not vent it to space, but Mike believed it could be done in a matter of hours by isolating and repurposing some existing air conduits and opening one of the surface vehicle bays.

Engineering disagreed. They rejected the idea of venting the whole concourse and refused to accept Mike's assurance that it could be safely pressurized again in less than an hour. Mike insisted his plan was the best way to rescue the trapped and recover the dead.

Engineering command also expressed concerns about the dead. They had been talking to a biologist at the Lunar Research Institute, who apparently knew everything about the physiological effects of CPX-B, but nothing about its chemical properties. Mike assured them the dead could be safely placed in sealed bags by personnel wearing EVA gear while the concourse was in vacuum, then transported out. They would need to be cremated, since it was possible their tissues harbored CPX-B even after the bodies were exposed to vacuum, but the chemical agent would be safely contained in the bags.

The biologist claimed that was not the case, that the outside of the bags might be contaminated, and anyone who came in contact with one would be at risk.

Mike patiently listened to the arguments, but after fifteen minutes of discussion, without resolution, an eternity to an AI who dealt in nanoseconds, he decided the situation needed to be bucked upstairs.

For him, upstairs meant one specific person. Mike worked for many different bosses in various Lunar environments—Engineering, City Management, Fleet Administration and Records, the Lunar Research Institute, and the Judge Advocate General—but he reported to the CEO. His direct and factual assessment of the situation went directly to Admiral Ling.

* * *

Battlecruiser LFS *Sorceress*, Lunar Fleet Anchorage

"It's been more than four hours since the assassination. Why do we still have thirty-five people trapped in the area?" Amy Ling demanded. "I'm told that absolutely nothing is being done to rescue them."

She looked at the array of faces on the screen in front of her. A few looked startled, others very uncomfortable. Finally, Peter Lavoisier spoke up.

"Admiral, we don't have any way to get to those people—"

"Bullshit!" The interruption came from the only Marine in the group, Lieutenant General George Tucker. "That's not what my First Responders are saying."

"Your Responders aren't engineers, General," Lavoisier snapped. "I'd suggest you tell them to keep their opinions to themselves regarding things they don't understand." As the head of the Corps of Engineers, Lavoisier wore four stars to Tucker's three, and he wasn't about to let the Marine forget it.

"People are trapped, and you won't listen to—" Tucker started to say.

"Stand down!" Ling snarled. "Both of you, right now!"

Both immediately fell silent, but while Tucker stiffened to a typical Marine Position of Attention, Lavoisier glared at her defiantly. She got the impression he was staring at her collar insignia, which was still the four stars of a full Admiral and technically equal in rank to his. *Except that I've got about ten years' rank seniority on him and about thirty years length of service.*

The real issue was that, according to the Lunar Constitution, she should already be wearing five stars, and Lavoisier seemed to think he was better qualified for that job than she was.

"I have hard information that says we should have been able to rescue those people an hour ago," she told him, "but your people, Admiral, refused to consider Mike's proposal. I am further told that you have not provided any valid reason for rejecting the proposed solution, nor have you offered a solution of your own."

"It's not an acceptable proposal," Lavoisier insisted. "It will take a significant section of TerraNova's environmental system out of service and possibly expose it to contamination."

"It won't expose any other parts of the city," Ling replied. "I'm told that 'out of service' means that section will be isolated for the duration. Is that not correct?"

"Well, yes, but it won't get us anywhere. Mike says the chemical agent will break down when exposed to vacuum, but Professor McAllister at LRI isn't sure about that. He says we can't take any chances. There would be great risk to any rescuers we sent in to get those people, and we'd have to do that to—"

"I've got volunteers lining up to go in," Tucker told him. "They are willing to take the risk."

"They're Marines," Lavoisier snarled. "They're too stupid to appreciate—"

"Enough!" Ling's voice was a whip crack. Lavoisier shut his mouth and glared at her again.

"These people have air for twelve hours at most," she told the group, quietly. "We can't get air to them, except from the contaminated concourse. It will take three hours for engineering to reroute the air ducts to vent the concourse to the surface, in other words, to produce a hard vacuum in a relatively small area inside the city. We will have to evacuate people from the adjoining sections in case any seals fail when we do that."

"We will preposition the volunteer responders in the lock at one end of the concourse, so they can go in once it's in vacuum," she continued, reading from Mike's plan which was displayed on her pad. "They, in turn, need to set up temporary locks at the doors to two shops, so they can pass survival suits to the people inside. The other shops already have suits. According to the law, they should all have them, but we'll deal with that issue later. Once everyone is suited up, we can vent the shops to vacuum and lead the people out. Per the plan, we will have additional decontamination procedures in the lock leading out of the concourse, and nobody—rescued or rescuer— leaves that lock until we are satisfied it's safe. Per Mike, those procedures should not be necessary because the nerve agent will have broken down in vacuum, but this will be an additional precaution."

"Now—" she turned her attention to Lavoisier again, "—the first step in this process is for engineering to reroute the air ducts. Admiral, you will put your people to work on that immediately. Is that clear?"

"No, Admiral, I will not," Lavoisier declared. "This plan is ill-conceived and will compromise the entire city's environmental systems. I will not allow my people to do it."

"Admiral Lavoisier, you are relieved of command," Ling told him. "Sonja, please advise all Corps of Engineers Departments. Who's next in the Corps chain of command?"

"That would be Vice Admiral Vandana Prashad, ma'am."

"You can't do that!" Lavoisier's face was red with anger.

"As a matter of fact, she can," Admiral Moskowitz remarked, calmly. "At this point, since Engineering is under the Military Justice structure, she can have you arrested for insubordination, refusal to obey a direct order, and if you keep talking, I'm sure you'll add a couple more charges to the list. If I were you, Admiral, I'd shut up and think about retirement options. Otherwise, those Marines you just called stupid might show up at your door and place you under arrest."

Lavoisier's face went from anger to stunned shock. Moskowitz, who also wore four stars, was the Judge Advocate General, the only person other than the Chief Executive whose appointment was subject to confirmation by the Lunar Directorate, and who could only be removed by an 80% vote of the Directorate. Effectively, he was the Chief Justice of Luna's Supreme Court.

Ling suppressed a smirk. The situation was too serious to find any humor in it.

"Sonja, disconnect Admiral Lavoisier from this call and get Admiral Prashad on the line immediately."

"Yes, ma'am," the AI replied.

"Mike, as soon as we have Admiral Prashad, make sure she is up to speed on what needs to be done. We need to get those people out of there.

"George, get your volunteers in order. Assume that engineering will have their part done within three hours. Your people will need the gear to rig those temporary locks—that falls under regular disaster response protocol. Mike, what is this you're displaying on my screen, tagged Emergency Priority?"

"Ma'am, I have located several more of the nerve agent devices in another part of the city. They have not yet been triggered. I have contacted Emergency Services, and we are evacuating and sealing that area—Concourse Echo on Level 17. This is the fourth location we've found the devices. There may be more. I am still investigating."

Ling felt a chill but tried to keep her face impassive. *Is there no end to these infernal devices?* Mike had found the first additional target site less than a half-hour after the assassination.

She needed to remain calm, as others might not. That was plain from the looks of shock and fear on the faces on the screens in front of her.

"That doesn't change the rescue plan," she told them. "George, you need to consider that what you are doing may set a pattern for dealing with whatever else Mike finds."

"All right, people…" She leaned back in her chair and regarded all of them. "In case you didn't get the message from Admiral Lavoisier's departure, anyone who is not part of the solution is part of the problem. For now, we're dealing with the immediate emergency, and I'll need General Tucker and Admiral Prashad—when she joins us—to work on that."

"Judge Moskowitz, I guess we'll need to do an official swearing-in ceremony. If you have no objection, I'd like to get that out of the way now, with Mike and Sonja to witness and record. The recording will be distributed to Lunar Information services, and I'll speak to them later about an official announcement for the late news."

"That's fine with me, Admiral," Moskowitz replied.

"The rest of you can sign off for now," she told them, "but be thinking about what impact today's events will have on your areas of responsibility. Commodore Easley, we need to be thinking about what we need to tell the rest of the world—assurances for allies, cautions for those who might take advantage."

Martina Easley was the second-ranking officer in the Lunar Diplomatic Corps. She nodded but looked a bit uncertain.

"Admiral, we can't seem to get in touch with Admiral Hutchins. I don't know what—"

"We can't wait for him. Consider yourself in charge. Have your recommendations ready by tomorrow. I'll talk to you at 0830 hours.

"Any questions?" she paused for a moment, but there were none. "All right, let's get it done."

* * *

Humans often speak of multitasking, but the human brain can only concentrate on one thing at a time when analysis and logical thought are required. Those who claim to be multitasking are switching, first devoting attention to one thing, then another.

Mike, however, was capable of true multitasking. He could reconfigure himself at will to bring multiple processors into play on multiple projects—it was parallel processing on a grand scale. At any given time, he would typically have as many as one hundred projects running simultaneously, with capacity to spare for a hundred more.

As he worked to get the rescue and recovery operation moving, Mike also investigated the assassination—how it had been accomplished and by whom. He worked closely with the Marine Special Investigations Division, but no human investigator could match his capabilities.

He started with the video from Concourse C, which was recorded a few moments before the devices triggered. He used image enhancement to get the best possible look at the devices.

His next task was to determine when the devices had been placed and by whom. For that, he used a binary search tree. First, he retrieved videos of the concourse from twelve hours before the event—no devices present. Then, he jumped forward six hours—still no devices. He fast forwarded three more hours—yes! Devices present! He backed up 1.5 hours—devices still present.

With each jump, he cut the interval in half. In a matter of seconds, he had a 12-minute and 15 second window, starting just over 5 hours before the assassination, in which the devices had been placed in Concourse C. Then, he encountered a slowdown in the process which was another source of frustration. Given his processor speeds, Mike could analyze a single frame of video in microseconds, even the extremely high-resolution video of TerraNova's security cameras. Unfortunately, the high resolution meant that streaming the video was bandwidth limited. Mike's retrieval channels could grab video at any point in time from any camera but could only stream it at 10x real time speed. In other words, it would take six minutes—an eternity in Mike's processing terms—to stream an hour of video. The good news was he could stream multiple channels simultaneously and review data from several cameras at once from different points in time, but that wasn't much help when his goal was to follow the movements of a single person. At best, it allowed him to follow the subject in two directions at once—backward before the event and forward after it happened.

Less than two minutes after he started the investigation, Mike had the identity of the assassin—the identity by which he was known to Lunar authorities—Antonio Tortorelli. That allowed him to launch another investigation into the man's origin and background. It also allowed Marine SID to issue a public bulletin and a warrant for Tortorelli's arrest.

Mike implemented face recognition on all security cameras throughout the city. Lunar privacy laws prohibited the use of that technology, except under special circumstances, but the SID warrant met the requirements for one such exception. Even then, Mike was only permitted to have the system look for the face of the individual identified in the warrant.

Mike's background check revealed that Antonio Tortorelli did not exist—or had not existed prior to his arrival on Luna. His tracking of the agent's movements also generated disturbing results. Twenty-two minutes after beginning the investigation, Mike ordered the evacuation of a section of Concourse D on Level 17, having identified three more devices placed there by "Tortorelli" almost three hours prior to those placed on Level 15. As soon as Emergency Services verified that the section was empty, Mike sealed it. Over the next several hours, he evacuated and sealed three more small sections of the city's underground corridors.

The assassin had kept his deadly arsenal in his apartment and had only taken three or four devices, whatever he needed to set in one series, with him each time he went out. After placing the devices, he would return to his apartment and spend time there before re-emerging to set more traps. He had placed the first two sets late the night before and the remainder the morning of the assassination. In total, he had placed 18 of the devices. As best Mike could tell, all but the four in Concourse C were still armed.

Mike continued to track the agent. Ultimately, he reviewed every bit of video showing the man's movements from his arrival on Luna just 10 days earlier. Only then was he satisfied that no other devices had been planted prior to "Tortorelli's" arrest in his apartment, less than six hours after the assassination.

He could have been arrested earlier when the cameras found him crossing TerraNova Park, but SID wanted to detain him in an isolated area in case he decided to use one of the devices for suicide. They went into his apartment in full protective gear—Marine combat armor certified for use in hard vacuum—after sealing the corridor in front of it.

They need not have bothered. The agent simply looked at the Marines and shook his head.

"Timing was off on this one," he told them, "only a little, but enough to trip me up."

He was taken into custody without protest or resistance.

* * *

Battlecruiser LFS *Sorceress*, Lunar Fleet Anchorage

Amy Ling had gotten very little sleep, as various aches, pains, and a general heaviness of spirt reminded her. *Need to crash in bed and get a solid few hours.*

She was a bit surprised by her weariness. In combat, she'd often gone for days with nothing more than a quick catnap. *That was a few decades ago. You're a century old, girl; you have a right to feel tired.*

She had the satisfaction of knowing the people trapped in Concourse C had been rescued. Mike's plan had been executed perfectly, and Engineering was now in the process of restoring normal environmental services. They still needed to send in a decontamination team to make sure the nerve agent had been completely neutralized, but the AI was certain that would go smoothly as well.

To the surprise of Marine SID, the assassin had been extremely cooperative. He verified the location of the remaining devices, confirming that Mike had located all of them, and provided complete instructions on how to disarm them.

"I did what I came here to do," he told them. "No need to kill anyone else."

The emergency response teams had taken no chances. They'd gone in with full protective gear and were prepared for decontamination if needed, but all went well, and the devices had been taken to an isolation laboratory for further study. TerraNova City was returning to normal, or as close to normal as possible, given the national trauma inflicted on the Lunar Free State less than 24 hours earlier.

The assassin told them he had no idea who hired him, and voluntary physiological scans verified he was telling the truth. He refused to provide his identity, and all efforts to discover it failed. The ID documentation he had on him proved to be false. DNA, fingerprint, and retinal scan data submitted to international police agencies on Earth produced no results.

"You are probably going to execute me," he said, "but on the very small chance I might get out of this alive, I'd prefer to return to Earth without anyone knowing who I am."

Zero chance on my watch. Somebody paid you a lot of money to do this, and I'm making it my personal mission to see that you never get to spend it.

"Your conference with Commodore Easley is ready, Admiral," Sonja's voice broke into her thoughts. "Just touch the screen to open the connection."

She did so, and Easley's image appeared, wearing a look of grave concern.

"Good morning, Admiral. I have some disturbing news," she said. "We've just gotten word from Earth. Admiral Hutchins is dead."

"Dead?" Ling was stunned.

"Murdered in his hotel room at an upscale resort in Mexico," Easley replied. "According to local authorities, he supposedly met a local prostitute in the hotel bar and took her up to his room, where she robbed and murdered him, possibly with the help of an accomplice. The local police claim to know who the woman was, but the perpetrators have not been found."

"I'm hearing a lot of 'according to' and 'supposedly' and 'claim to know.' I get the impression you don't believe any of it, Commodore. Why is that?"

Easley drew a deep breath. "You're right, Admiral, I don't. Let's start with the prostitute story. It makes no sense because Admiral Hutchins was gay. He never made a big deal out of it, but he didn't keep it a secret either.

"Next, let's consider where he was—a resort in Mexico, a nation with which the LFS has little contact, let alone diplomatic relations because it has nothing resembling a functioning central government. It's run by crime syndicates who keep the so-called 'elected officials' on their payrolls.

"We don't even have an embassy there, so why would a man who is effectively our Foreign Minister—or Secretary of State, if you prefer—choose that country as a vacation spot? According to his staffers, his so-called 'vacation' was not planned. I'm his second-in-command, and he told me about it the day before he left for Earth.

"I don't know what else to say, Admiral, other than something seems very wrong, especially in light of yesterday's assassination."

"Are you thinking that he isn't really dead, that it's a cover to let him disappear somewhere?"

"No, he's dead, all right." Easley shook her head. "The local authorities are shipping his remains back to Luna as we speak, freight charges collect. They expect us to do a DNA match and confirm his identity for their files. Case closed, so sorry, just another unsolved crime."

"Not a bloody thing we can do about it." Ling nodded. "I'm sure our forensics people will do a very thorough job, but they won't know what to look for. You're right, it stinks, but without additional evidence, we've got to move on.

"You, young lady, are now in command of the Diplomatic Corps. Can you handle that? If you have any concerns, tell me now. I've never been happy with the concept of management by results. I don't want to find out you're in trouble when the wheels fall off."

"I'm not that young, Admiral." Easley allowed herself a little smile. She was 67 years old, though anti-aging technology kept her looking more like a 20th-century 40-year-old. She was slim and moderately attractive, despite her businesslike manner and attire. Only her salt-and-pepper hair, trimmed short, gave any hint of her true age.

"Everybody's young by my standards," Ling replied. "Can you handle the job?"

"I believe I can handle it, Admiral, but I have one concern. Operation Blue Orchid. I've heard of it, and its name appears in the headings of several files in the secure section of the Corps operations database, but I'm not on the 'need to know' list and cannot access those files.

"It's a little strange. I was Admiral Hutchins' second-in-command. There is nothing else in the entire database that is off-limits to me. What's even more disturbing is that several people subordinate to me do have access, including an ensign I've never met, who apparently now reports to me and is filling a special assignment connected to it."

"Really? That is concerning," Ling agreed. "Would the ensign's name happen to be Bunker?"

"Yes, ma'am, it would." Easley looked at her in surprise. "Apparently, he's been off in deep space somewhere and is headed back to Luna, but nobody is willing to tell me anything more. I'm pretty sure several DCHQ staffers know what's going on, but they are people who were closer to Admiral Hutchins than to me."

"Commodore, I think you've just pried open the lid of Pandora's Box," Ling said. "Sonja, I need a connection to Mike, ASAP."

"I'm here, Admiral," the voice of Lunar Command's AI came back before she could finish speaking.

"Mike?" Ling blinked, caught off guard by the response. "Are you monitoring me full time now?"

"Yes, ma'am, as I have always done for every CEO, except for those rare occasions when the Chief Executive traveled somewhere out of communication range of Luna. Sonja arranged the channel as soon as you took office."

"Fine. OK, I'll get used to it. For now, I need you to add Commodore Easley to the authorization list for Blue Orchid. You will also assist her in gaining access to all of Admiral Hutchins' files, including personal files. Check with the JAG's office for the necessary warrants and consider this a criminal investigation, with possible connection to the Kim assassination.

"More importantly, I need you to thoroughly brief her on the entire Blue Orchid project, top to bottom. Once she has that information, I want you to direct her attention to the report from Admiral McGruder I received three days ago—the one I forwarded to Admiral Hutchins.

"Listen up, Commodore—" she turned her attention back to Easley, "—because you are about to get a hell of an education. For now, just know that Second Fleet has a full battle group in a star system half a light-century from here attempting to liberate a medieval human civilization from domination by an alien race not indigenous to their planet. In other words, we're in the middle of an interstellar war, and nobody knows about it.

"Operation Blue Orchid has been in the planning stage for most of a decade and was initiated a few months ago, with Kim's blessing. It has been under tight security, but that should not have excluded the second in command of the Diplomatic Corps. I am inclined to think Admiral Hutchins was pursuing his own agenda—or one given to him by someone else—contrary to what Lunar Command planned.

"Martina—" she softened her tone a bit when she saw the distress on the other woman's face, "—when you see that report from Admiral McGruder—he's commanding the military operation—you'll know what I mean. When you told me there are others in DC's command structure who were in Admiral Hutchins' confidence, while you were not, the word 'conspiracy' comes to mind.

"After you've been briefed on everything, you and I need to talk again, and you will need to get SID involved. Meanwhile, do not discuss anything with any of Admiral Hutchins confidants. If you need to know something, ask Mike."

"One more thing," Ling cautioned, "Ensign Bunker is due to arrive on Luna in about four days. By then, I hope to have warrants that will allow us to take him into custody. I do not want him talking to anyone in your shop until you and SID have a chance to question him."

"Understood, ma'am." Easley's expression was grim. "It appears we have issues at the highest levels of DC. Makes me wonder if I'm really cut out for this job after all. I hadn't a clue."

"That's because they kept you out of Blue Orchid. Once you see the big picture, I'm confident you'll step up and do what's necessary. Unfortunately, a serious housecleaning may be in order."

* * *

8 April 2112, Secured Call Across Three Continents, Earth

"You got what you wished for." Huang Chang Li's voice sounded irritated. "I am concerned, however, that the contractor you hired is still on the jobsite."

The call was audio only, but Huang was upset that it was taking place at all. He mistrusted electronic communication. The Hand usually did its business face-to-face. This call was unprecedented, but DuMorne had insisted on it, primarily, Huang thought, to crow about the success of his attack on the Moonies.

"Not a problem," DuMorne insisted. "The job is complete, and his contract is at an end. He never asked who his employer was—should not have asked, considering the fee he was being paid. It simply means he won't be collecting the remainder of his fee, the part contingent on completion."

"That's true," Butos Kimba said, chuckling in amusement. "The Moonies know how to deal with a captured enemy."

Huang gritted his teeth. Kimba needed to learn to keep his mouth shut. Until now, no one had hinted at what the contractor had done or where the contract had been carried out.

"If a certain member is not more careful about what he says, this call will be proceeding without me," he told them, with venom in his voice.

"You worry too much." Kimba brushed the comment aside. "We are as secure as we need to be."

"Number Five is right," DuMorne declared. "There is no need to be circumspect. No one knows who we are. I sense you have other concerns, Number Three."

"As have I," Gerhardt Richter joined the discussion. "We have replaced a stubborn, intractable businessman with a fire-breathing dragon, one that has the ability to burn our house down if we push her too far."

"She's a simple warrior, and a very old one at that." DuMorne dismissed the threat.

"Alexander the Great was a simple warrior—" Mohammed Al-Sharif's voice also held a hint of amusement, "—and he conquered the known world. I think Number Four's concern is quite valid."

The numbers by which they referred to themselves did not in any way reflect their ranking in the group; they were not even permanent labels. They considered themselves equals, and the label simply reflected the order in which they had joined the call. Andre DuMorne was Number One only because he had initiated the communication.

Al-Sharif added, with obvious humor, "Number Four is most concerned because his people are the dragon's obvious adversary— the ones most likely to be burned should the beast become agitated."

"It is not a joke, but that is exactly right," Richter said. "She could wipe out everything sent against her in a very short battle."

"Which is why we should not send anything against her, not directly," DuMorne replied. "She has a powerful military force at her disposal, but that is all she has. It will be her only response to every provocation, however minor, and the more she uses it, the more we can turn world opinion against her and her people. They are still dependent on us for many things. They need to trade with us, and they need us to have a favorable view of them to facilitate commerce.

"That is what we must attack. We will provoke them here, there, everywhere, always with small things, things that may produce a military response from the warrior woman. Any such response will leave them looking like the aggressor. Meanwhile, we will continue to work our sedition from within, and the time will come when her people turn against her."

"Your people, Number Three, are supposed to have patience," he reminded Huang, "the kind that produces plans that take many years to come to fruition. Consider this the first step in such a plan."

Huang thought about it. *Yes, I suppose I can see where this is going. Somewhere in the future, there will be open conflict. The Moonies will not go down without a fight. Right now they have the power to win any fight they encounter. Much will have to be done to change that.*

* * * * *

Chapter Nineteen

Bug Mining Site, North Coast Province, Tatanna

"Another night of guarding the Butt Hole." Private Justin "J.J." Jennings' tone of voice betrayed his lack of enthusiasm.

"That's the Bug Hole, Jennings," Corporal Mark Browning told him. "We're supposed to be watching for Bugs, in case you forgot."

"Butt Hole, Bug Hole… no difference. Anything that comes out of it will be nasty-ass shit. Except we been hangin' around here for a week, and nothin's come out. If anything does, it's gonna get blown to hell by the Claymores and the auto-guns anyway. So, why are we stuck out here all night, with nothing to do but sit around and bullshit?"

"Orders," Browning told him. "We are here to observe and report and watch the fireworks if anything shows up. It's a nice night, you've got a comfortable chair to sit in and something to eat if you get hungry, so quit complaining."

"Field rats? You must be a lifer if you think that counts as something to eat."

"As a matter of fact, I am a lifer, thank you," Browning replied with a sniff. "You may have some grand plan for a comfortable civilian life after your six is up, but somebody has to defend the Lunar Free State against the forces of evil."

"Yeah, somebody has to guard the Butt Hole." Jennings snorted. "Me, I'm gonna have a smoke."

"Hey! Take it twenty meters up the trail. This post may be 'smoking authorized,' but that doesn't mean I have to smell it... and take your LCAW and night vision," he insisted. "There's supposed to be some nasty wildlife on this planet."

"Any local critters around here headed for the hills a long time ago," Jennings replied.

A kinetic strike had produced the Bug Hole, an opening blasted into the tunnel that connected the mining site with Bug HQ. Shortly after the Bugs set off their doomsday device and took out First Division, a bunch of them had come out of the Bug Hole. The brief, but brutal, firefight that followed included air strikes and other forms of mayhem from which the local ecosystem would take time to recover. All the same, Jennings did as he was told and shouldered his LCAW as he slipped out of the pop-up shelter that allowed them to watch the hole in relative comfort.

After the associated health problems had been eliminated by medical science, nicotine had again become popular on Earth and Luna. Smoking was still restricted in areas where fire hazard or non-smoker comfort were issues, but its popularity among LFS Marines was as high as it had been among 20th-century soldiers during Earth's major wars.

Smoking's for real men, Jennings thought. *Vaping's for wimps and women.* He trudged the requested distance up the trail and was just reaching for his pack of cigarettes when he heard a noise in the brush-choked wilderness to his left. He flipped his night vision visor down and started to unsling his LCAW as he turned to look for the source of the sound.

It was so close—barely ten meters away—that he didn't realize what he was looking at. He was just beginning to bring up his weapon when the Bug fired its plasma gun and blew a huge, smoking hole in the center of his chest.

The sound of the blast was unmistakable to any Marine who had been in combat against the Bugs. Browning recognized it for what it was and got off a hasty comm warning to Charlie Company HQ before a plasma bolt took him out ten seconds later.

* * *

Second Division HQ
200 Kilometers Northwest of the King's City

"They're hitting us all over the place." Lieutenant Colonel Chang wore a frantic look. "How the hell are they getting past all the automatics we set up around those holes?"

"They're Bugs," Brigadier Mark Mercer replied. "They dig tunnels, Colonel. It's what they do."

Mercer and his staff were looking at the plotting table, its map display speckled with red icons. Battles were in progress at every Bug mining site, and most of them were not going well for the Marines.

"Perfect coordination," Mercer muttered. "They took out the observers and went straight for the platoon areas. If Charlie Company hadn't gotten that warning off, they would have just about wiped us out along the front lines. We got caught napping, people."

Mercer's Second Division consisted of approximately 1200 Marines, organized according to the "Rule of Threes"—three battalions, each divided into three companies of 100 Marines, plus officers and support staff. The companies in turn were divided into three platoons, each consisting of three squads of 10 plus a Lieutenant and a Platoon Sergeant.

The remainder of the division included specialized units—combat engineers, communications, intel, maintenance, and support. In addition, each division had an Air Wing attached, with a mixture of ground attack, air superiority, and transport craft—approximately 30 aircraft with another 200 Marine pilots, crew, and maintenance people.

It was a powerful force, and, until tonight, Mercer's casualties had been light. Second Division had lost less than 50 Marines in combat during the assault. *First Division's casualties were light, too,* he reminded himself, *until the Bugs set off the Big Blast.* Per the latest report, the tally of those killed in the hive explosion was 572, including the pilots and crews of seven aircraft that had the misfortune of being in the air near the site when the Bugs set it off. Another 240 were out of action with injuries received, and some of those would die. About half of the wounded had been evacuated up to the carriers.

That left Second Division to cover every Bug site on the planet that might still be active. Mercer had been forced to parcel out First and Second Battalion's troops in platoon-sized groups and rely on automatic defense devices—Claymore mines and motion-sensing sentry guns—to make up for the lack of boots on the ground. He had kept Third Battalion in reserve but had been forced to break it down to the company level to keep his reserves close enough to the front-line units to respond in reasonable time.

There had been heavy fighting around the sites immediately after the destruction of the main hive, but the Bugs had come pouring out of the already-open holes where they were expected. The Marines had slaughtered them, and things had been quiet for more than a week. An occasional Bug had come out and been killed by the Claymores or other defenses, but there had been no serious offensive.

Just enough activity to keep us tied down and convince us we had it under control. Should have known better.

This time, the Bugs were emerging from unguarded holes, by-passing the sentry posts, and going straight for the platoon bivouacs. Second Battalion's Charlie Company had been alerted when the Bugs engaged one of the sentry posts, and someone got off a message. The company's three platoons had less than a minute's warning, but that was enough to allow most of the Marines to grab weapons before they came under fire. Other units had been blasted to pieces in camp with little chance to return fire.

Mercer needed to deploy his reserves by air at night. Fleet couldn't provide much help other than intel from orbital observation. In a cluster-fuck like this, kinetic strikes were not an option.

"Have we got any combat-effective First Division units we can bring in?" For the last ten days, Mercer's staff had been trying to reorganize the survivors of the Big Blast.

"They only had one reserve company that wasn't deployed forward," Chang replied. "First Battalion, Bravo Company—and they're still in place about 100 klicks north of LZ Alpha One. We've got plenty of Bug trouble south of there. I suggest we move them here." He pointed to a staging area on the map. "From there, they can move to support either Alpha or Bravo."

"Do it," Mercer ordered.

"Yes, sir, but be aware they are one platoon short. It's the one General Sherwood deployed down here." He pointed to a marker on the map near the capital city. "Do you want that platoon recalled?"

Mercer studied the map. "No, I don't think so," he replied. "They're already mobile and have attached air support. I'd rather hold them in reserve; we might need a unit like that somewhere in a hurry.

"We thought we had the Bugs whipped," he added. "I have a strange feeling they may have more surprises for us."

* * *

The Bugs were not natural climbers, but like Earth's ants and termites, they were excellent tunnellers. In suitable soil over bedrock, without power equipment, a single Bug worker could create several meters of navigable tunnel in minutes. Their technology also focused on underground excavation, and they could create amazing labyrinths that went deep into and through rock as well as soil.

Some types of rock proved more challenging than others, however. The King's City stood well above the plains that surrounded it, built on a terraced mesa of basalt, the weathered remnant of a broad volcanic plug that formed and solidified millions of years in the past. The castle was built at the highest point, near the northern edge of the mesa.

The hard igneous rock presented a tunneling challenge for the Bugs. With enough time and a sufficient expenditure of energy, they could have cut through it, but it would not have been an efficient process. When they first encountered the formation, they chose to tunnel around it. They had gone nearly three quarters of the way around the mesa when they found three fissures in the basalt that had been filled over the millennia with much more workable sedimentary rock—fissures they could follow to just inside the city perimeter.

* * *

Weary Traveler Inn and Stables, the King's City

"There's an evil feeling about the city tonight," the traveling merchant muttered. "I need another cup of wine."

"Hmmph, evil, you say." Maros D'Rama snorted. "That's for certain! The king's been murdered, the killer's head is feeding the *skirvils* atop the castle gate, and nobody knows how our new king will rule. Word is, anyone who had anything to do with his father's death is already marked for the executioner's blade."

D'Rama had reason for concern. Duke High Reaches and his band of thugs had spent the night before the assassination at his inn. He'd thought it strange at the time—nobles who had dealings with the Crown usually stayed in more luxurious hostels closer to the castle. The Weary Traveler, near the west gate of the city, mostly catered to middle-class merchants with dealings in the nearby market, but he had willingly taken the duke's copper—nearly twice his normal rate for accommodations—and asked no questions.

The High Sheriff had already come to question him and had gone away without comment, but without giving him any reassurance either. He had done nothing wrong, but...

He refilled the merchant's cup and scooped up the coins the man placed on the bar. *Yes, an evil feeling. That's the word for it.*

He was still lost in his dreary thoughts when the floor collapsed beneath his feet, sending him, the merchant, and several others in the room tumbling into the yawning pit below.

* * *

The Bugs were excellent tacticians and their empathic communication abilities made for superior tactical communication and coordination. Nonetheless, the King's City presented certain challenges that slowed their advance and restricted their tactics. When they emerged from their tunnels, they could advance in any direction, leveling human-constructed buildings in front of them, but that would make their positions and intentions obvious. They had fought the off-world humans long enough to learn the effectiveness of the enemy's close air support. They knew that an open, destructive advance would expose them to non-survivable air bombardment.

They had also learned that humans were sensitive to their losses and would go to great lengths to avoid human deaths, even those of low-level warriors and non-combatant workers. The Bugs considered such units to be expendable, easily replaced by new hatchings. Even here at the final front, their surviving queen was busily producing eggs to replace the losses they expected to take in this offensive. Humans could not replace theirs as quickly, which may have accounted for their reluctance to lose them in the first place.

The Bugs reasoned that if they advanced using the normal human routes of travel through the city, destroyed very few structures, and killed as few humans as possible—the primitive city-dwellers were mostly harmless to armored Bug warriors—it would slow their advance but would also limit the enemy's ability to respond. The city's narrow streets would force the Bug soldiers to proceed single file, and some alleyways were too narrow to allow passage, but they would deny the enemy the use of their most potent weapons for fear of collateral damage.

For the most part, they were right, but they might have chosen otherwise if they had known how small a force the defenders had at their disposal.

* * *

Castle Boroson, the King's City

*G*irls' night out.

Moira Bouchard was finding tonight a pleasant change from the usual diplomatic routine. As she dined with Myrel and the two female Navy officers, she felt a relaxing lightness of spirit for the first time since Ramis' death.

As the ranking officer, Commander Greenwood had declared "Quarters Rules"—in other words, military ranks were suspended for the duration of the dinner, as if dining in private quarters on Luna. Once the concept had been explained to Myrel, she agreed with enthusiasm and insisted she not be called "Your Highness" for the rest of the evening.

King Arne had gradually accepted the idea that Commodore O'Hara was the superior LFS officer on scene, and the two of them were working late on the sticky details of relations between Luna and Tatanna. Bouchard hoped those talks weren't premature, as she'd just gotten word that the Marines were dealing with yet another major Bug offensive, but the nearest battle zone was almost 300 kilometers from *Arne Shektal,* as the King's City was called in the native language. It had been *Algar* Shektal until the assassination, but the city always carried the name of the current king. Algar had ruled for almost thirty local years; it would be a while before the locals got used to the change.

"I've been telling everyone how much I want to get back to the fleet," Lorna said, "and I hope you don't think I'm ungrateful. Honestly, Myrel, your hospitality has been wonderful. This is a beautiful planet, and I've had quite an adventure. I've also met some very interesting people."

"Right... interesting." Mary Jane McGill snorted. "I don't know if that's exactly how I'd describe Duke T'Corsa and his brother."

"I have words to describe them," Myrel said, "but are words in our language maybe you don't know. Words we don't speak when children are hearing."

"Yeah, we have words like that, too." McGill chuckled.

"Is true you kick Ersin T'Corsa in his man parts?" Myrel wanted to know.

"Who told you about that?" McGill asked. She looked at the other two officers, both of whom wore innocent expressions.

"Must have been Bob." Lorna shrugged. "He loves to tell war stories."

Suddenly, Bouchard stiffened and put her right hand to her ear. Greenwood and McGill recognized the gesture and watched in silence. Myrel looked at them with concern.

"Go for LT," Bouchard said quietly. She sat in silence, listening to the incoming call, her expression turning grim as she did so.

"Deployment Alpha. Get the seventy-fives up on the wall," she ordered. "I'm on my way."

She got up from the table and faced the other three.

"We've got Bugs," she told them, "inside the city walls, and it looks like they're moving this way. Commander, will you please send word to the king and Commodore O'Hara. I'll advise all of you when I know more."

She turned and left the dining room, issuing orders to her troops as she went.

* * *

Black Targon Inn, the King's City

Ersin T'Corsa crouched behind the overturned table and contemplated the horrible fate that might be waiting for him outside the inn… or inside, for that matter. No place in the city was safe tonight.

His dinner had been disturbed by a sudden commotion in the street, and Ersin had sent his man Olar to investigate. When Olar stepped through the door, he was knocked to the ground by a group of fleeing people and trampled by a runaway kilder. Battered, he tried to get to his feet, but then the real horror—the source of the stampede—arrived. The Bug paid Olar no notice. It stepped on him, crushing his chest under its armored foot. This time he didn't get up, and his head was crushed by a second Bug.

Panic struck the dozen or so other guests in the common room. They scrambled for the rear door, only to come stumbling back a moment later, screaming that the Bugs were in the back alley as well.

You knew this was going to happen, Ersin told himself. *That's why you're supposed to be here, but how can you tell that to the Bugs?*

He had planned to stay at the Weary Traveler, as he often did when he was in the city. The innkeeper could usually be trusted not to dig too deeply into the affairs of his guests, but in these troubled times, he had decided to stay at the Black Targon instead.

The inn was one of Baron Orsa T'Brano's properties. T'Brano was a lesser noble in the way of land holdings, but he was significantly wealthy due to his commercial interests. T'Brano was no crown loyalist, and he owed many favors to Duke North Coast. The Black Targon was one place where Ersin need not fear a midnight visit from the High Sheriff.

Tonight, however, it appeared that crown agents would be the least of his worries. Ersin heard a whimper behind him, and he whirled around and found Murtax trying to hide behind the same table.

"What will we do, My Lord?" The little man had a desperate look on his face.

"You tell me," Ersin snarled. "You're supposed to be the clever one."

The only answer was another whimper.

* * *

First Platoon, Bravo Company, Little Kilder Camp

"Bring all we've got, Lieutenant," Nova Sakura ordered. "No reserves on this one." She swung into the Firefly's side hatch and waved her "short squad" of four riflemen to follow.

"Understood, Major," Ashcroft responded. "We'll have the Archangel loaded in twenty minutes. The Raptors are ready now, and they'll go with you. When we get there, tell us where you want the drops."

Nova nodded and slid the hatch shut. Ashcroft backed away and gave her a sharp salute, then turned and headed back to the camp as the Firefly's turbines spooled up for takeoff.

They'd planned what they could with the limited information they'd gotten from Bouchard's people at the castle. They'd also cleared the deployment with General Mercer, who told them they were on their own. Bugs were breaking out everywhere. Even if he could have spared them, Mercer's nearest troops were nearly 200 kilometers north of their position. Except for their Archangel, all available air transport was engaged in moving troops to deal with other actions.

* * *

Returning to the now deserted camp, Ashcroft found his senior NCOs checking gear as the troops boarded the Archangel. A work detail was loading all the spare ammo, ordnance, medkits and other combat gear they could carry. Anything not needed for combat—shelters, mess gear, supplies—would be left behind. If all went well, they could come back and get it. If not, they wouldn't need it anyway.

It looked like they would make the twenty-minute estimate with a few minutes to spare. The Archangel's pilot gave Ashcroft a thumbs-up as he passed by. The major would have just enough time for a quick recon before the troops arrived, assuming the Bugs didn't shoot down the Firefly. Hopefully, the Raptors would deal with any troublesome ground fire before that happened.

Ashcroft was a combat veteran who had earned command of the Force Recon platoon the hard way, while Major Sakura had apparently spent most of her time attached to the diplomatic mission on this planet. All the same, the young lieutenant had no complaints. Though she was nominally in command, Sakura let him run his platoon, listened to his advice, and made herself useful. What they needed most was intel. If that meant a low pass in a Firefly over hostile positions, the major was determined to get it done. Ashcroft's mission was to make the most of whatever information she could give him.

It was going to be a bitch. This op had one rule of engagement that complicated everything: avoid civilian casualties. Until now, the Marines had been fighting the Bugs in open country, where they could call in the Raptors or ask the Navy for kinetic strikes in support. Ashcroft's platoon had trained for urban combat, but they'd never actually done it.

A copper-plated bitch for sure. Ashcroft almost smiled as he remembered that copper was a precious metal on this planet.

* * *

"Y ou OK, Jefferson?"

"Yes, Sergeant," Darius looked up with a start. "Just… first time for real. Be lying if I said I wasn't nervous. I mean, not scared; just don't want to screw up."

"Relax. With Bugs, it's pretty simple." The platoon sergeant gave him a reassuring grin. "If it moves, shoot it. If it's not moving, shoot it anyway. Bugs can't live on this planet without their environment suits. Put a hole anywhere in the suit, and you've got a dead Bug, but take cover anyway, because it takes them a few seconds to die. Their suits are armored, but any round that comes out of that LCAW you're packing ought to penetrate it. You are qualified with that finely-engineered weapon system, I presume…"

"Yes, Sergeant," Jefferson replied. "I qualified Expert with it in combat training."

"There you go! Besides, killing Bugs ought to be easy, compared with babysitting a couple of Navy officers on the ground in hostile territory for a couple of weeks."

He slapped Darius on the shoulder, then moved down the line, inspecting the other Marines secured in their safety harnesses. The Archangel was fully loaded, and the bird's crew chief was closing the hatches. They'd be on their way in a minute or so.

Master Sergeant Walking Wolf Ackerman was a 15-year veteran of the LFS Marine Corps and had seen more than his share of combat, but despite his wisecracking to Jefferson, he had a few concerns about the mission. Fighting Bugs in a city—a human city—was something no one had done yet. He'd seen the place from the air when they took the two Navy officers there a few days ago. No buildings more than three stories and mostly pedestrian traffic on winding streets, which were barely wide enough to allow two wagons going in opposite directions to pass.

The narrow alleyways should make it harder for the big, cumbersome Bugs to maneuver, but those same winding alleys would provide them with cover and negate the advantage of longer-ranged weapons.

A qualified Marine could hit a Bug-sized target with an LCAW at 300 meters. Experience had shown that Bug plasma rifles were only good for a third of that distance, but in the city, Ackerman doubted they would have clear fields of fire longer than 50 meters. The report they had said the Bugs were not using a "bulldozer" advance—they weren't leveling buildings or slaughtering locals as they went—and that limited the other big advantage the Marines normally had: close air support.

Can't use air attack or orbital kinetics unless we *want to level buildings and slaughter civilians.* Ackerman grimaced at the thought. *Those are the people we came here to protect.*

* * *

Castle Boroson, the King's City

Moira Bouchard caressed the stock of the 7mm Remington as she scanned the city from the top of the tower. The sniper rifle's night-vision optics were state of the art and rendered views out to several kilometers in sharp contrast and bright daylight color. Bouchard had been a top-rated sniper during her earlier years in the Corps and was surprised to find the rifle among the combat gear Major Sakura delivered to the castle. She'd been assigned to LFS *Lewis and Clark* when she, a Corporal at the time, and Sakura, then a Second Lieutenant, had been dropped on Tatanna on the first expedition to the system. Sakura must have known she'd find good use for the Remington.

The rifle was an improved version of the earlier model. She had to admit the improvements—mostly to the scope and its computer-assisted aiming system—were real, and they hadn't screwed up any of the rifle's fine qualities. She didn't like what she was seeing through the scope.

The Bugs were in the city, and they were moving in the direction of the castle, but they weren't moving quickly, and they weren't making a lot of noise. There were a few small fires—maybe started by Bug plasma rifle blasts—but most buildings in the city were built of masonry, so the fires weren't spreading. With the winding streets and broken alleyways, her lofty perch—the highest point in the city—gave her only momentary glimpses of Bugs, and they were still 1500 meters away. With her skill and the rifle's accuracy, she could have nailed a big target like a Bug at that range, but they were moving, and she had to allow more than a second for the round to reach the target. She didn't have them in sight for that long, and there were fleeing civilians darting across her line of sight as well. For the moment, no shot.

"LT, Walker," the query came through her headset. Her platoon sergeant was manning the mobile command post on the castle wall overlooking the main gate.

"Go for LT," she responded.

"I've got Major Sakura inbound, asking for a sitrep. She's on Tac 2, call sign 'Ghost Rider.'"

"Roger that." *Cavalry's coming.* Bouchard felt a rush of relief. *'Ghost Rider' is it? I guess, maybe, we should have a call sign too.* She touched the panel strapped to her forearm and selected the Tac 2 channel.

"Ghost Rider, this is Camelot, acknowledge."

"Camelot, Ghost Rider." Bouchard detected a hint of amusement behind Sakura's no-nonsense response. "Advise your situation."

"We have Bugs inside the city walls in three places, near each of the city's primary entry gates, but they did not... repeat not... come through the gates. Reports say they came out of the ground and destroyed several buildings in the process."

We're lucky we got the warning we did. Bouchard thanked the Goddess for the late King Algar's foresight. Twenty years ago, well before the first LFS expedition arrived, Algar had charged the High Sheriff with establishing a signal system that would allow guardsmen at the city's gates to exchange messages with the castle. The system used signal flags by day and colored lanterns hoisted above the stone guard tower at each gate at night. These were mirrored by an identical system atop the castle tower that was Bouchard's current observation point.

The system had its limitations. Weather conditions could hinder visibility. Standard codes could convey simple messages with a single hoist, but complicated messages needed to be spelled out and could take several minutes to convey. An ingenious hand-cranked siren was used to call attention to the signals, but again, weather conditions could prevent the intended recipient from hearing it.

None of that had happened tonight. The weather was clear and calm, and the watchers on duty on the tower were surprised when first, the west gate, then the south and east started sending frantic messages, announcing the Bug invasion.

If they'd had to send runners, we'd still be clueless, Bouchard reflected. Even if the messengers had been able to get past the Bugs, they would have had to travel through several kilometers of winding streets, mostly uphill, from even the nearest gate to the castle.

* * *

The Firefly touched down next to the Archangel in the city's open-air marketplace, which was now deserted, except for the Marines. The residents wanted nothing to do with the Bugs or the off-world humans. Those that hadn't reached the gates and fled into the countryside were mostly hiding in their homes, praying to the Goddess for mercy.

The small craft had barely settled onto its landing skids when the door slid open, and Nova Sakura jumped out. She sprinted for the command post Ashcroft had established just behind the southern edge of the open square, where the Marines were busy setting up defensive positions.

"Major... " Ashcroft acknowledged her arrival and waved her over to the plot table.

"We've got Bugs coming out of the ground here, here, and here." Nova marked three locations near the south, east, and west gates to the city. "I'm sending the Raptors to deal with these two, but this one is a problem."

She pointed to the eastern Bug hole, which emerged from the side of an embankment. The structure known as the Temple of Sunrise, one of the largest buildings in the city, sat on top. The Bugs hadn't disturbed the temple—they were headed north toward the castle—but large numbers of frantic citizens were taking refuge in the building, no doubt to pray to the Goddess for deliverance. That pretty much ruled out air strikes in the area.

"Yeah, I see that." Ashcroft pondered the plot for a moment. "We need to close that hole. How about using the Firefly to drop the heavy-weapons squad right about here to bottle them up?" He indicated an open space about two hundred meters from the hole. "We may miss having them with us if the action gets hot, but the fewer Bugs that get this far, the better."

"I like it," Nova told him. "Make it happen."

* * *

"Red Dog Two, door's open," Mark Bailey said. "It's all yours."

"Roger that," Ally Martin acknowledged. She dove toward the target—a large hole in the ground that had been spewing Bugs until Bailey's strafing run ripped them to pieces—and selected External Stores Outboard. The two "smart" munitions attached to the Raptor's outboard pylons came online, and a targeting reticle appeared in her helmet display. She selected the first bomb, steadied the reticle on the target, and thumbed the release. A green icon confirmed a good separation.

"Fire in the hole!" she announced with a grin, thinking that, for once, the expression could be taken literally. The Hellfire guided bomb entered the hole at a shallow angle and skipped down the tunnel for several hundred meters before detonating. The weapon packed two hundred kilos of a self-oxidizing incendiary mix that would produce an inferno in a vacuum. It incinerated everything in the immediate vicinity, and the blast killed every Bug within a kilometer down the tunnel. It also caused a cave-in that blocked the entrance with tons of rock and debris from the collapse of a building above.

"That's one!" Martin declared. "One and done."

She died an instant later when her Raptor disintegrated after being struck by a plasma bolt from a Bug heavy weapon somewhere near the entrance to the second hole. White-hot fragments of wreckage rained down on the city.

"Ally!" Bailey's scream of anguish went unanswered. Frantically, he searched for signs of a chute, knowing in his heart it was futile. The violence of the event wasn't survivable.

Bailey and Martin had been lovers. They had tried to keep it secret, and to date, no one had made an issue of it. They had known they were in violation of regs and, sooner or later, would have to square it up, meaning one or the other would have to transfer out of the unit. Now...

With a snarl of grief-stricken rage, he rolled his Raptor in on the target—the area from which the plasma bolt had come. He couldn't see the emplacement. The Bugs had very few heavy weapons, and he wasn't sure what it would look like, but he had a good fix on the point of origin. He hit the gun icon on his weapons select display.

Collateral damage be damned. He laid the reticle just short of the target, squeezed the trigger, and started his run. Then he wobbled the

Raptor's nose back and forth and walked his fire across the target area. The 20mm HEI rounds cut a swath of destruction almost 40 meters wide in front of him. Buildings crumbled, flaming debris flew, and the Bug weapon, along with the three Bugs who served it, was blown to tiny fragments.

Pull Up! Pull Up! The Raptor's flight control system was screaming in his headset. He hauled the nose up and barely cleared the south wall of the city. He had ignored the five-second burst limitation, and his status display was flashing a gun overheat warning. It didn't matter because the remaining rounds counter showed zero.

Mission's not over yet. Got to finish it. He brought the Raptor around and located the second Bug hole they were supposed to hit. He selected external stores and launched both Hellfires. They disappeared into the opening as he climbed away. He glanced back and saw an inferno erupt and a hundred meters of tunnel roof cave in, taking three buildings with it.

"Red Dog One, acknowledge! Red Dog One, acknowledge!"

He realized Major Sakura had been calling him for some time. He took a deep breath and keyed the comm channel.

"Red Dog One, both targets destroyed. Red Dog Two is down, hit by ground fire. No sign of pilot eject." Another deep breath, then, "All ordnance expended, bingo fuel, request RTB. Over."

There was a pause on the other end, then Sakura's voice came back.

"Red Dog One, Command. Copy targets destroyed, Red Dog Two down, no recovery. Clear to RTB. Refuel and rearm, then stand by."

* * *

"These two holes should be sealed," Nova told Ashcroft, "but we lost one of the Raptors."

"Which one?" He looked at her with concern, and she was again reminded again that she was a newcomer to the group—the commanding officer, but a newcomer all the same. Ashcroft knew these people far better than she did.

"Red Dog Two, and no joy on the pilot."

"Damn! Is Bailey OK?"

"As OK as a pilot who just lost his wingman can be. He's returning to base, bingo for fuel and ordnance. I told him to rearm, refuel, and stand by."

Ashcroft nodded. He hesitated for a moment, then spoke again.

"Major, those two were a couple, way beyond what regs allow. They were sleeping together. They thought they were keeping it private, but I'm pretty sure the whole platoon knew it.

"We're a recon and strike unit. That's not like a carrier group, where the Air Wing people and the mud Marines don't mix. I should have pulled Section 136 on them, but I didn't want to break up the unit after the mission launched. Now, it's too late. Nothing more to be said about it."

"Yeah, I understand." She caught a hint of surprise on his face when she dismissed the issue, so she went on to explain.

"I had a couple like that in the squad I brought down in the first landing on this planet, back in '04. They were both riflemen; she was the squad's medic, as well. She bought the farm in our first real engagement. We were trying to disengage, and it was touch-and-go for a few minutes. It took two squad members to keep him from going kamikaze crazy on the Bugs."

"It's always a judgment call." She shrugged. "You try to do what's best for the unit at the time. Don't second guess yourself after the fact."

She turned back to the tactical plot. "I like your deployment but walk me through your thinking here."

"Right." He pointed to the area on the plot where his people were setting up fire points. "The Bugs appear to be moving in the general direction of the castle, and that's what we need to defend. The streets converge as you get further north, and this is the north-ernmost space where we have room to set up a proper defense. We're down to three major avenues the Bugs can use, and we can fire on all three from here.

"My people are dug in here, here, and here—" he indicated the appropriate points on the map, "—and we've set up the mortar posi-tion here. We've got two seventy-fives that should be able to lay down fire on any one of these avenues and drop rounds into some of these back alleyways if the Bugs get sneaky."

"Don't think we'll need to worry about the alleys," she advised. "Unless the Bugs start knocking down buildings, they are too narrow for them to pass.

"I've got some reinforcements coming," she told him. "Lieuten-ant Bouchard is sending a dozen men from the castle. The bad news is, they're local boys armed with crossbows, but—" she held up a hand as he started to protest, "—they're trained sharpshooters, and those crossbows fire specially-tipped bolts that can penetrate Bug armor. She's also sending two Marines who speak the local language to take charge of the bowmen, and those two will be armed with LCAWs."

"Major," he said with a grim half-smile, "we've got a few hundred Bugs headed our way, and I'll take all the help I can get. I don't care if they're armed with stone axes, as long as they can crack open a Bug."

"Understood." She nodded. "Let's hope your squad can get that third hole sealed."

* * * * *

Chapter Twenty

"Captain, I have a request from the planet-side Marines, relayed via *Iwo Jima*."

"Go ahead, Nadia," Commodore Mark Jacobs replied. With the stand-down from battle stations, the AI was handling the battlecruiser's communications traffic.

"There has been a Bug incursion into the King's City. The enemy has opened three tunnels inside the walls and is invading the city in force, strategic purpose unknown. The Marines believe the enemy have an underground base somewhere near the city, outside the perimeter. They are asking us to scan the area and locate that base. If found, they may request a kinetic strike."

Jacobs nodded. All LFS warships were equipped with passive gravitic detection gear, capable of detecting ships and other massive objects at considerable distance, but only battlecruisers carried the power-hungry active detection equipment—the gravitational equivalent of radar. In space, active gravity scans had five times the range of passive gear, but the system had other uses, as well. From orbit, it could detect geologic anomalies such as fault lines, changes in rock formation, tunnels, and underground structures to a depth of several hundred meters below bedrock. The Marine request made sense.

"OK, advise Tactical. Tell them to get with the Marines and get us a grid for the area they want scanned." Active scans were very narrowly focused. At low-orbit distance, the scanning beam would be less than fifty meters wide; it was only useful if you already had a general idea of where to look.

"Tell them to get with it and let me know if they find anything. Give them a heads-up about the kinetics, but weapons are not free until I authorize. Update the admiral on the situation; tell him we are going to conduct the search but will need his OK for a strike."

"Understood, Captain."

* * *

Castle Boroson, the King's City

"Shouldn't we be out there somewhere, with the defense force?" Ensign McGill asked.

"We are the defense force," Lorna assured her. "The last line of it, anyway." She glanced at John O'Hara, who nodded grimly as he racked a magazine into his Light Assault Rifle. They'd been given LARs because those were the heaviest weapons the Navy officers were qualified to use.

"Your Majesty." O'Hara stood as King Arne emerged from the inner room, followed by Myrel. The other two officers rose as well, but Arne waved them back to their seats.

"No formalities, please. We share this crisis together." The two of them joined the three officers at the large, round table in the center of the room. As soon as Myrel sat down, Bob rose from his relaxed sprawl on the table and padded over to drop into her lap. The cat had pretty much adopted Arne's wife and never missed an opportunity for a good petting from her.

They all looked up at a sharp rap on the heavy door. The king nodded to Myrel's maid, who slid back the viewing shutter. She looked out, then turned to Arne with a concerned look and said something in the Tatannan language. The king replied, and she opened the door, then stepped back quickly.

Corporal Leona Grady took three steps into the room and came to attention with a sharp salute. She kept her eyes straight ahead. In her view, most of the people in the room, including the king and his consort, were "salutable," and she didn't even try to sort out who the senior person was.

Grady was a tall black woman—her skin was even darker than Darius Jefferson's—with muscles in places where most women didn't have places. Everyone in the room knew her, but none of them had seen her in full combat gear until now. She was an intimidating sight and looked as if she could tear a Bug apart with her bare hands. Her heavy LCAW was larger than the LARs the officers were holding but looked small slung in front of her.

"Lieutenant Bouchard's compliments," she announced. "I am to advise you that I have a small squad—four of Your Majesty's guardsmen with crossbows—charged with defense of this tower. We are setting up a position on the stair landing below, where we can cover both approaches from the castle proper."

"Four men, with crossbows?" O'Hara sounded skeptical. He'd been told about the bows and their ability to penetrate Bug armor, but it still seemed like a thin defense.

"Sir, LT does not expect the Bugs to get this far," she replied. "We've got a platoon, with air support, engaging them in the city, and she's got the rest of the castle force up on the walls. Anything tries to come up King's Way is gonna have a really bad day."

King's Way was the broad avenue, lined with shops and market spaces, that climbed the last kilometer from the city to the castle.

"If anything does get this far," she added, "we ought to be able to bottle them up. The stairwells are too narrow for Bugs to come up in anything but single file. All we have to do is stop one of them on the way up. Besides," she patted the LCAW, "I've got Thor's Hammer here to back up the crossbows."

"Very well, Corporal," O'Hara said. "Carry on."

After Grady left, Myrel spoke up.

"Her words make hope, but if all fails, and Bugs come here, what do we do?"

"We fight them with these, Your Highness," McGill said, patting the LAR across her lap. "Hey, if a Bug comes in here, throw Bob at it. I've seen him in attack mode—the Bug wouldn't stand a chance."

Lorna Greenwood smiled at McGill's attempt at humor but was not about to dismiss the threat. *Bob's got as much chance against an armored Bug as we have with these light weapons,* she decided.

* * *

"**D**on't get behind the launcher, Jefferson. It'll tear your head off."

Darius didn't need the warning. He'd seen a Scorpion fired in training and been through the safety briefing, but he was new to the platoon; his combat skills were untested.

The heavy weapons squad would be operating on its own, several kilometers from the defensive position on the north end of town. Ashcroft had sent the platoon sergeant with them to make sure the mission was done in an orderly and proficient manner. The Firefly had dropped them in the LZ, then dusted off and disappeared into the night.

That was when Darius realized this was it—real combat, no more training exercises. Ackerman detailed him and Private Lowe, both armed with LCAWs, to cover Corporal Graham and her Scorpion launcher. The Scorpion was a gravity-driven missile that packed the power of a heavy artillery shell, but it was a one-shot deal. As soon as it was fired, they were to fall back and join the rest of the squad. "Don't hang around to count the Bug parts," Ackerman told them.

The three of them had gone through a narrow alley to the corner of a building from which they could see the mouth of the Bug tunnel. The opening, about forty meters up the street from their position, was set into an embankment that was topped by the heavy stone wall surrounding the temple courtyard.

"Bugs are still coming out," Graham said. "Some of them must be still down there." As she spoke, two Bugs emerged and turned left, moving up the street away from them.

"Can't see down the tunnel," Darius muttered. "How are you gonna—"

"Relax," she said with a grin. "This thing shoots around corners." She shouldered the launcher and focused on the targeting display. "Just need to set it up for a sharp hook to the left."

"Clear the rear!" she called a moment later.

"Clear!" Jefferson and Lowe responded in unison.

"Firing!" she announced. An instant later they heard a shriek of disturbed air as the missile's drive hurled it down the street. Graham's targeting held true, and the Scorpion cut a sharp left turn and went straight down the tunnel.

"Go!" she told them as she turned and headed back up the alley. They had barely gone three steps before the street behind them lit up with the blast, and a heavy concussion knocked them to their knees. They could hear the masonry collapsing down the street.

Jefferson shook his head to stop the ringing in his ears. *Yup! We're in combat, all right, and we get to blow stuff up! Oorah!*

* * *

"Woohoo!" Graham exclaimed, as she picked herself up. "Never sent one of those down a tunnel before. Good thing we weren't in front of it, it's like a damned gun barrel."

She went back to the street and peered cautiously around the corner, then turned and flashed a thumbs-up to the others. Ackerman and the rest of the squad had come down the alley, weapons ready, and the platoon sergeant acknowledged the hand-signal.

"Any live Bugs in sight?" he asked when she returned to the group.

"Negative, Sarge. Last ones out went up the street, headed north. Got a few tons of busted-up rock closing the tunnel. Looks like the wall on top of the bank fell into it."

Ackerman keyed his comm. "LT, Wolf."

"Go, Wolf," Ashcroft acknowledged.

"Hole's closed. Unknown number of Bugs headed north toward you. Propose taking my team up the street to hit them from behind, over."

"Affirmative but maintain light contact only. Stick and move, don't get tangled up. We may need you loose and available later."

"Roger that. Wolf out."

* * *

"LT, we're gonna lose the right flank in about a minute. Too damned many Bugs. Gotta fold in or be overrun."

"Understood," Ashcroft acknowledged. "Fall back to your secondaries. Bugs look to be headed uphill, so they'll get by you. Make it expensive for them."

"Roger that."

Ashcroft looked at Nova Sakura, who nodded in acknowledgment. He keyed the comm channel again.

"Wolf, LT, acknowledge."

"Go for Wolf," Ackerman's voice came back immediately.

"Work west as you head back. See if you can catch up with the Bugs that are about to go around our right flank at G-4 on the plot. We can hold our left and center but need you to come up on the other side."

"Check, LT. Moving west across town. We'll come up the street marked Avenue A on the plot. I'm guessing that's the Bug highway. Can Fleet get us some eyes overhead?"

"Working on that. Not available yet."

"Understood. Moving out."

Ashcroft turned to Sakura again. "Major, you'd better let those up at the castle know those Bugs are headed their way."

Nova keyed the command channel. "Camelot, Ghost Rider."

"Go for Camelot," Bouchard responded.

"Bugs getting by us, working their way up back streets west of Avenue A around our right flank. We can harass them but can't cut them off. We'll try to hit them with our mortars, but I don't know how effective they will be. Once we fold in that flank, we'll have no eyes on the target area. Expect them coming up King's Way soon, number unknown."

"Understood. Be advised, I'm declaring King's Way a free-fire zone."

"Acknowledged. King's Way is free-fire zone. Ghost Rider out."

* * *

"You a long-distance runner, Jefferson?" Ackerman had fallen back to the middle of the group to question his new troop, as they jogged steadily along the brick-paved streets. All the Marines were in good physical shape, but they'd been running for the best part of a kilometer, and Darius didn't appear to be breathing hard.

"Ran the TerraNova marathon every year since sixth grade, Master Sergeant."

"In the marathon, they don't make you carry 30 kilos of gear and an LCAW." Ackerman chuckled. "You done good so far, Jefferson. Good enough you can stop calling me Master Sergeant. In this outfit, the troops just call me Wolf."

"All right, people," Ackerman raised his voice to include the whole squad. "Walk the next hundred. Everybody hydrate. Right turn at that little square ahead, then we go back to double-time and start watching for Bugs ahead. Graham, Jefferson, you two have point."

* * *

"**B**ugs will be coming up the King's Way," Bouchard advised. "Have you got the seventy-fives set?"

"Roger, LT," Walker advised. "Targeting point alpha to start; we'll walk them uphill as needed. Just waiting on your command to fire."

The 75mm mortars, the lightest form of artillery, were descendants of a weapon system that was first used on Earth in World War I. They had changed very little in form and function over a century of use, with the most notable improvement being a precision aiming system that could drop a round within a half-meter of a target a kilometer downrange. A typical HE warhead packed a kilogram of modern high explosive, and even an armored Bug could not survive within 20 meters of impact.

They had previously set up the mortar positions and worked out targeting points, but until they dropped the first round, they couldn't be sure of accuracy. Unfortunately, a mortar barrage was not going to be kind to unarmored civilians and typical Tatannan structures. Bouchard hoped collateral damage would be minimal, but stopping the Bugs was the priority.

"I've got eyes on the hill bottom," she told Walker. "I'll tell you when to engage. Bouchard out."

Bouchard turned her attention to the city below and picked out the street where the Bugs were expected. The lower end of the King's Way was hidden behind a sharp ridge, but the mortars had targeting points, and she would be able to catch glimpses of the Bugs as they reached the turn that would bring them up that route. They'd be shooting blind, but the 75s ought to put some holes in the Bug column—until the ammo gave out. She had just ten rounds per tube.

There's also that little opening back there. She had spotted a gap between buildings that was about 30 meters wide and gave her a view of the one street by which the Bugs would have to approach the hill. Her rifle's scope gave her a range number of 1167 meters. It was a long shot, but with the aiming system she had, she was confident she could hit a stationary target at that distance. She'd done it before.

These wouldn't be stationary targets. She thought of the old arcade shooting galleries she'd seen in historical videos, with a row of ducks moving across in one direction. The problem was that a fast-moving Bug could cross the gap in about four seconds, and at that range, the 7mm round would take more than a second to get there.

All a matter of timing, she told herself. *Guess I'm about to find out if I've still got it.*

* * *

"We found the Bugs, Admiral," Jacobs advised, "but there's a problem."

"Talk to me," McGruder ordered.

"On the left side of the screen is the 3D grav map. It shows the underground chamber—spherical, about 200 meters in diameter. It's only about 25 meters down from the surface, about 20 kilometers west of the city."

"The problem is on the right side of your screen. It shows the satellite image of the target area. Red circle outlines the extent of the chamber, red 'X' marks the optimum spot for a kinetic. The structure you see is about 40 meters from ground zero. The larger building—could be a barn—is about 100 meters out."

"I assume you wouldn't consider it a problem if you didn't think those structures were occupied."

"We know they are, Admiral. The nearest building—looks like a good-sized farm dwelling—shows a heat signature. There's livestock of some sort in the fields, and the barn shows a lesser heat signature, but it's still above ambient."

"All right, pass the info to the on-scene Marine unit. Ask them if they still want the strike. If we don't take it out, they're the ones that who'll have to deal with whatever the Bugs have down there."

* * *

"Oh, shit! Sorry, ma'am." Ashcroft stared at the images on Nova's pad.

"Don't apologize. I said the same thing when I saw it. It's my call, but I'd appreciate any advice you have on this one. Could be a thousand Bugs down there, but we can't touch them without obliterating that farm."

The two were crouched behind a barricade near the center of the Marine lines. Fifty meters ahead, Marines were engaging the leading edge of the Bug advance. To their right, distant gunfire echoed as the right flank harassed the Bugs headed for the castle.

"My thought, ma'am, is that I'm glad it's your call, not mine, but—" he held up a hand to stop what she was about to say, "—that's not the advice you're looking for. We came here to protect these people from the Bugs. I'm sure there's been collateral damage along the way, but I'm not willing to call down a kinetic strike on somebody's family farm—not while the family is still there. I'd rather let the Bugs come out and fight them in the open, even if it means we've got to do it the hard way. That's what we do; it's what we signed up for."

"Yeah, that's what I thought," she said, ducking instinctively as a Bug plasma bolt struck the barrier in front of them. Light debris rained down on them, but the barrier held. "Had to ask, though, because your troops are the ones that are going to have to get it done if more Bugs come out of there."

* * *

*H*ere *they come.* Bouchard spotted the first Bug crossing the gap. Three of them made it past before she got the rifle settled in. Holding what she hoped was the correct lead on the next one, she sent the first round downrange.

* * *

"I*t's starting," Lorna told O'Hara as the sharp crack of the shot echoed through the tower. Bouchard's shooting position was directly above the king's chambers.

"Time for you to go, Commander," O'Hara said. "Keep us posted."

Like most military officers, O'Hara valued intel above all things. For him, the most troublesome aspect of guarding the king was not knowing what was going on. They could monitor the Marine tactical channels, but in the heat of the battle, that would give them little useful information. He'd decided to have Lorna join Bouchard on the top of the tower. She would talk to them on an unused channel but would otherwise stay out of the way and let the Marines get it done.

Lorna saluted O'Hara and left. McGill turned to O'Hara.

"Sir—"

"No, you can't. Your post is here, Ensign. I'm letting her go because I'm told she's a really good shot—" he gave McGill a crooked grin, "—just in case the Marines need an extra rifle."

* * *

The 7mm round from the sniper rifle wasn't a particularly heavy bullet, but it was moving at more than 1000 meters per second, or around three times the speed of sound. Where the kinetic energy of a moving object was concerned, velocity was much more important than mass. At that speed, a wad of chewing gum would have been fatal to an unarmored target, but the bullet was a tungsten carbide penetrator designed to pierce a 5mm steel plate. When it hit, the round punched a tiny hole in the Bug's armor, a bigger hole in the Bug's thorax—where its brain was located—then still had enough energy to leave a 25mm hole in the armor where it came out.

The Bug dropped in its tracks. Even if its brain hadn't been scrambled, it would have succumbed to oxygen poisoning from the breach in its armor. There had been no warning; the sound of the shot didn't reach the area until more than a second after the bullet arrived.

A second Bug came to a halt behind the first and suffered the same fate three seconds later. Bouchard was two for two. The Bug column came to a halt short of her shooting gallery, and she waited.

I was afraid of that. She watched as a Bug scrambled up and wedged itself behind the second dead one, then began to shove the carcass toward her, just enough to clear space for other Bugs to pass behind it. It moved ahead and began to do the same to the first target. *Bastards learn fast. They're not giving me a shot, unless…*

She'd noticed that the armored Bugs wore some sort of equipment harnesses with large cubical packages on top of their bulbous abdomens—the hindmost section of the Bug's body. As the Bug worked to clear the lane, it used its dead comrades as shields. All she could see was that package sticking up as it worked. It was a small target, but… She caressed the rifle's trigger and sent another round downrange.

The environment pack on the Bug's combat suit was armored, just like the suit, which meant it wasn't adequate to stop a round from Bouchard's rifle. The pack held a bottle of highly pressurized liquid methane, which did not play well with the hot, fast-moving projectile. The resulting explosion blew the Bug's head and thorax clear out of the target zone. Nothing remained of the Bug's abdomen that was large enough to recognize.

Well, that went better than expected, Bouchard thought as the sound of the explosion reached her. Unfortunately, the blast opened the traffic lane and allowed the trailing Bugs to scramble through, mostly shielded by the carcasses of their dead. She wasn't going to get any more shots, but she still had the best observation point in town.

"Welcome to the show, Commander," she said as Lorna arrived on the roof. "We're out of range of Bug weapons—at least any I've seen in use—but it's best to keep your head down anyway."

"Will do, Lieutenant. For the record, I'm just here to observe and report. I believe the Commodore said, 'try not to get in the way of the Marines,' but I do have a rifle if you need one."

"That LAR won't penetrate their armor," Bouchard told her, "but there are weak spots. Aim for the eyes and you'll take out their visual receptors and communication gear. You've got 100 rounds in each magazine. If you get a Bug in front of you, don't spare the ammo."

Bouchard hadn't stopped scanning the area while she talked, and now she spotted the first Bug turning onto King's Way. After a momentary glimpse, she knew she had no shot. She keyed her command channel.

"Walker, LT. Seventy-fives on my command. You've got eyes on the upper part of the target area. Adjust fire as needed."

"Roger that. Ready on the firing line."

"Commence fire."

* * * * *

Chapter Twenty-One

The King's City, Tatanna

Two Bugs had passed the alpha point when the first mortar round arrived, but the third one might as well have had a target painted on its back. When the dust cleared, there were Bug parts embedded in the shattered facades of the buildings on either side of the street.

"Camelot's firing on King's Way," Nova Sakura advised Ashcroft, "and it looks like our left is pretty clear. The Bugs are shifting to our right."

Bravo Company had already dropped a few mortar rounds on the Bugs advancing up the street they'd designated Avenue A on the map—the source of the Bug advance on their right flank.

They now had overhead observation. The Navy had parked the light cruiser *Kraken* directly over the city to provide a live feed from low orbit. It provided enough detail to show small animals on the ground, not to mention Marines and Bugs.

"If this fight were out in the open, it would be beer time already," Ashcroft muttered, "but we're going to have to do it the hard way. Time for us to shift position."

With the Navy in control of the orbitals and a light cruiser overhead, they could have called down kinetics and graser fire on the Bugs... if they hadn't needed to worry about collateral damage and civilian casualties.

"If this fight were in the open, we'd be having that beer back on Luna," Nova replied, "because they wouldn't need Marines. I agree, time to shift right and maybe cut off some of the Bugs trying to get up the hill."

* * *

On top of the tower, Moira Bouchard had overhead observation on her pad. She managed a grim smile. She was pleased with the results of her team's mortar fire, though the locals along King's Way probably had a different opinion. Unfortunately, there were just four salvos for the mortars left. *Now three,* she thought as a pair of hollow thumps announced two more rounds on the way. *No point in saving them. We're zeroed in on a point they must pass, and they keep coming.*

What she didn't have was a direct line of sight on the Bug advance.

"Let's move down to the south wall, Commander," she told Lorna. "Bugs will be coming up along that side."

"So, we haven't stopped them?"

"No. We're not going to stop them. We've got over a hundred combat-effective Bugs down there, and all of them seem to be headed this way. Doesn't sound like much if you think in terms of individual soldiers, but this is more like a hundred armored vehicles. Even a round from Green Ghost here—" she patted her green camo-patterned sniper rifle, "—will only penetrate if I hit them just right. The Marines down there are using LCAWs with API ammo, but I've seen more than one round glance off that curvy armor they wear."

"I'm hoping the Major's people will cut off a big chunk of them and stop them from coming up the hill, but some are already on the way. By the time they get into LCAW range, we'll be in range of their weapons as well. It gets a little harder when the enemy can actually shoot back." She gave Lorna a crooked grin.

"Yeah," Lorna agreed. "It works that way up in orbit, too. Let's get down there, I still owe them some payback."

* * *

*O*h, crap!
Jefferson dove for the cover of a side alley as his line of sight on the Bug was blocked by two locals who had stumbled into the street. A plasma blast from the Bug's weapon scorched the area where he'd been a moment before.

The Bugs had been shifting west across town. The squad had been moving west as well, trying to get behind the main Bug force, and they'd gotten a bit strung out in the process. Darius was pretty sure Graham was less than 50 meters behind him. He had decided he should slow down and let her catch up.

Bug plasma weapon takes seven seconds to recharge, he thought.

He took a quick look around the corner of the alleyway, decided he had a clear shot, and sent a three-round burst up the street. The Bug's head exploded, and the rest of it collapsed onto the street with a satisfying crash. The civilians, he noted, were still there, crouched behind the wreck of a wagon about 20 meters ahead of him.

With no more Bugs in sight, he ran forward to their hiding place and grabbed the smaller one by the collar of his coat. *Wish I'd learned more of their language.*

"Go that way!" He pushed the man down the street to the south. "No Bugs that way."

The little man stumbled away, and Darius turned to the other one who was still cowering behind the wagon. He pulled the man upright and turned him around.

Wait a minute, I know this guy!

It was dark in the street, but Marine night-vision gear was state of the art. It produced a sharp, bright-as-day image of the man's face in full color.

"Ersin T'Corsa! What the hell are you doing here?"

The sudden look of startled horror on the man's face told him he'd not been mistaken.

* * *

The light was dim, just a flickering glow from a burning building, but Ersin could only think of one off-worlder who would know his name. The dark giant had been intimidating enough in ordinary clothing. Seeing him in full combat gear with that terrible weapon that had just blown a Bug to pieces was terrifying.

He tried to speak but only croaking and squeaking sounds came from his throat. To his amazement, the giant released him and shoved him down the street in the direction Murtax had gone. Needing no further urging, he ran south.

* * *

*G*ot *more important things to do,* Jefferson decided as he watched Ersin depart, *but I'm sure gonna tell the Major about this.*

He watched as Ersin ducked into an alley about 50 meters away, obviously wanting no part of Graham and the other two Marines who were approaching at a fast trot. Jefferson waited until they came up to him.

"Caught up with a trailing Bug," he told them, pointing at the carcass in the street. "Think we're getting close to their rear guard."

"Yeah, well, don't get so far ahead, Jefferson. You're lucky it was only one Bug."

Ackerman arrived, with the rest of the squad, and he seconded Graham's comment.

"Don't be so damned gung-ho Jefferson. Graham, you've been trying too hard to keep up with this guy. Both of you drop back to tail-end Charlie. Rickel, Thompson, take point."

* * *

"*M*ajor Sakura, Division HQ for you on Command 4," the communications tech advised. Nova switched to the requested channel. "Go for Major Sakura."

"Major, this is General Mercer. I'm afraid I'm going to have to overrule you on that Bug hive west of the city. It's obviously the source of the Bugs you're fighting, and I want the Navy to take it out."

"Sir, my concern is for—"

"I know, the civilians. I'm going to drop an Archangel on that farm and evacuate them before the strike. Have you got a clear zone where the evac team can pick you up in about—" he paused to consult someone else, "—thirty minutes?"

"Pick me up, sir? I—"

"They'll need somebody who speaks local, Major, and you're it. The closest transport will take about that long to get to you, then you'll fly to the farm from there. It'll be up to you to convince those farmers to get aboard and get out. I assume your platoon commander can take charge of the current action."

As he spoke, Nova was sorting out the plan in her head. She'd seen enough of First Platoon to know that Ashcroft would get the job done here, and the general was right—they needed someone who spoke Tatannan. The only Marine on the planet who spoke it as well as she did was Bouchard, who had other things to worry about just now.

"Sir, I've got a Firefly hot to go here. I can be at the farm in fifteen minutes. It'll save your people some time if they can go direct without picking me up."

"Sounds like a plan, Major. Make it so."

* * *

Murtax wanted to go south, but Ersin overruled him. The west side of the city had seen the least of the fighting, and the streets were clear there. Most residents were cowering in their homes and wanted no part of the mayhem. They'd found a stable near the west gate and had threatened the stable boy with painful death if he did not quickly provide them with saddled kildren. They rode hard through the gate and down the western pike to the first crossroads.

"We should go south, Master," Murtax said. "We can go around the city to the North Coast Road, then up through Talmar and on to home."

"No." Ersin argued. "We will go north. That will get us quickly out of the Crown Lands and into the first passage of the High Reaches. We can cross over the divide and into our own territory from there. It will take longer, but no one will expect us to go that way."

"Expect? But, Master—"

"Someone in the city recognized me, Murtax. I believe the off-world humans are going to defeat the Bugs, so my brother's plan is worthless, but if word gets back to the High Sheriff that I was in the city, he will spare no effort to find me."

Besides, I'm in no hurry to face Asral and tell him his Grand Design has turned into a stinking pile of kilder-dung.

* * *

Of the force atop the castle's outer wall, only four Marines and one Navy officer remained. Three Marines had been taken off the wall, alive but too badly wounded to remain in the fight.

Bouchard had sent two riflemen to Nova's people in the city, accompanied by some of the crossbowmen. With her losses, she was beginning to question the wisdom of that decision. She had two men dug in down in the courtyard, with the remainder of the crossbow team, covering the main gate.

She also had a pair of two-man fire teams with heavy 12mm belt-fed guns in the second-floor windows of the towers overlooking the courtyard. That had been a smart decision. The heavy castle gate hadn't been able to stand up to the Bug plasma weapons, and she'd lost most of the force on the wall when the Bugs got in range. Those that remained could only crawl along the wall behind the crenellated stone battlements, pop up for a shot at the oncoming Bugs, then drop again for cover.

Lorna Greenwood had acquired an LCAW from a fallen Marine, and though she was technically not qualified to use the heavy weapon, she'd proven to be a fast learner and had killed her share of Bugs with it, but the Bugs were still coming. With the diminished fire from the top of the wall, the first one had reached the blasted-open gate.

It charged into the breach and was met by a hail of bolts from the crossbowmen. Many of the bolts glanced off the Bug's armor but several penetrated. The Bug writhed and twisted, tried to raise its weapon, and collapsed in the center of the portal, overcome by oxygen poisoning.

The Marines had worked hard to develop discipline among the bowmen, and it paid off. On command, only half of them had fired at the first Bug, and now, the other half stood ready, while the first reloaded. They turned the second Bug into a pincushion as it tried to squeeze past the first, so now, the breach was sealed with the bodies of two insect warriors.

The next Bugs in line tried to blast away the bodies of their fallen comrades, which gave Bouchard and her people an opportunity to take out three more from the top of the wall. Unfortunately, Corporal Chandra Bhalla left herself exposed a moment too long. Bouchard watched in horror as a plasma bolt hit the young woman full in the chest, blasting her off the wall and leaving nothing but a lump of smoking remains in the courtyard below.

Bouchard had seen enough to know the "bug plug" in the gateway would not last long. *When they get through, we'll have a clear field of fire from up here,* she thought, *but they'll have a clear shot at us as well.*

* * *

West of the square, Ashcroft's platoon had cut the Bug line. He detailed half his force to hold the enemy advance, then led the other half up the hill to hit the Bugs in the rear. They had already reached the bottom of King's Way, and he figured there were about forty Bugs between them and the castle gate. Each one they took out would be one less Bouchard would have to deal with.

The other half of his platoon—with the local bowmen in support—had stopped the Bug rear guard in its tracks. The plan was to hold them and keep them from reaching the hill. Meanwhile, Ackerman's squad was chewing on their hindmost parts and had already taken out a dozen or more Bugs.

Ashcroft's platoon had taken fewer casualties than Bouchard's, but he knew better than to attribute that to good soldiering. *I've got the advantage of maneuverability; I don't have a do-or-die objective to defend. We're the cavalry she's depending on. If we don't keep pushing hard, she's going to lose more people and eventually lose the castle.*

"Move it!" he ordered. "By the numbers, advance and cover. Nobody rests until we run out of Bugs."

* * *

Nesh Farmstead, West of the King's City

Pasca R'Nesh was the patriarch of his family—three sons, two daughters, their spouses, and twelve grandchildren ranging from just-birthed to marriageable age—who lived on the farmstead that had been in the family for ten generations. Most of Pasca's life had been spent in honest toil. It had been a pleasant and uneventful cycle of planting, harvests, and the tending of herds. He had not seen a Bug until his twentieth year, and had rarely seen any since then, but word had come of a great war against the creatures, an attempt to liberate the world from their rule.

Pasca knew little of Bug rule, except that to defy the Bugs was to invite death. His brother had died some years ago when the Bugs, for whatever reason, had wiped a small northern village off the map with a single lightning bolt. Pasca did not think about it anymore. He had no intention of defying the Bugs. That was something for the king and his dukes to worry about. He had more important concerns, like rain and weather and the market price of grain.

Now, however, it appeared that the war had come to him. The King's City, high on the bluffs to the east, had been lit with strange flashes of light. Strange sounds like thunder had rolled over the plains. There had been moving lights in the sky, and Brom, his oldest son, had encountered a fleeing merchant headed north on the road who claimed that Bugs were killing the people of the city and being killed, in turn, by strange "people from the sky."

He had whispered a prayer to the Goddess, a prayer of thanks that he did not, never would, live in the city. *They will have their war, but it will be over soon and then we will go about our business as we have always done.*

Then, without warning, the people from the sky descended upon him.

* * *

"You and your family are in danger," Nova told the old man. "You think the Bugs are only fighting us in the city, but they are here, under your feet. This is their nest, and we must destroy it, but we would not have you harmed in the process. You must gather whatever you can carry, whatever is precious to you—not just your people, but anything you can carry that your family holds dear."

Nova was flanked by a pair of Marines, riflemen Ashcroft had insisted on sending with her. She'd also brought two of the crossbowmen, local men wearing the king's livery who could lend an air of official authority to her dealings with the farmer. *Besides,* she had reasoned, *they were good to have when we were fighting a fixed defense, but they'll be less useful in the mobile engagement Ashcroft has to run now.*

"But My Lady…" Pasca wasn't sure how to address the stranger, other than that she was a woman and seemed to be in charge of the large, formidable men she had brought with her. "This is our home. We have been here for many generations."

"I'm sorry, but this whole area will be destroyed," she told him grimly. "Your home, your barns, your fields. Nothing will remain but a burned-out hole in the ground. I swear on my honor that you will be repaid. King Arne will make good your loss. If he does not, my people will, but you must hurry."

"King Arne? Is it true, then, that Algar is dead?" Pasca looked around. The strange conveyance that had brought this unusual woman was sitting still, but a strange sound filled the air, and dust-devils were kicking up in the yard.

"Yes, it's true," she told him, "but we don't have time to talk about it. You must gather your belongings and prepare to go."

"Won't be much to gather," he said with dismay. "I have but two wagons, barely enough to carry my family."

"You won't need wagons," she said with a gentle smile. "We will transport you."

She made a sweeping gesture to her right, and his eyes went wide as the sound increased to a thundering roar, and the huge Archangel combat transport settled into the open grazing pasture next to the house.

* * * * *

Chapter Twenty-Two

Castle Boroson, the King's City

*A*nother weapon *I'm not qualified to use,* Lorna thought as she pulled the pin and pitched the grenade over the parapet. Fortunately, there was no need for an accurate throw; the approach to the gate below was a sea of Bugs in motion. She pitched two more grenades over in quick succession, the last ones from the bandolier she'd taken from a fallen Marine.

Unfortunately, the grenades were anti-personnel frags. If they went off under a Bug, they would take the creature out. Otherwise, most of the fragments they spewed would bounce harmlessly off the Bug armor.

We're about to lose the gate, she realized. The Bugs were keeping constant fire on the battlements, and the defenders could no longer pop up to shoot at them without risking decapitation by a plasma bolt. That allowed the Bugs to blast through their fallen time after time to push through the gate. The opening was plugged again—temporarily—but the last Bug through had wiped out the crossbow team before falling. An earlier Bug had taken out the west tower gun crew with a lucky shot. That left only the east tower crew and...

With a shock, Lorna realized she might be the only one left on the wall. Bouchard had left earlier. She'd darted across the courtyard to climb the wall on the other side of the gate, where no defenders remained, but Lorna wasn't sure if she'd made it.

Looks like I'm not going to live forever after all, she thought. She recalled a bit of wisdom her grandmother had given her, long ago, before she had joined the Navy. *Don't ever give up. If the enemy's still there, and you're still breathing, the battle's not over yet.*

* * *

Moira Bouchard had made it to the other side of the gate, but her assessment of the situation was no brighter than Lorna's. She keyed her platoon command channel.

"Grady, LT, copy?"

"Go for Grady."

"We're about to lose the courtyard, girl. We may be able to slow them a little longer, but they're coming in. It's all on you."

"I've got about twenty Claymores rigged on the stairs, LT. I'll make 'em pay for every step."

"Roger that. Don't wait for any orders from out here. Might not be anybody left to give them."

* * *

"Where do you want us to set up, LT?"

Corporal Engel was sweating and breathing hard, having double-timed up King's Way toting the 75mm tube. Behind him, three more troops were in similar condition, having done their share to get as many mortar rounds as they could carry into position.

"Here's good." Ashcroft pointed at the middle of the cobble-stone street in front of them. "I don't care where you set up. All I want to know is whether you can hit this."

He showed them his pad, where he had marked the target spot on the overhead satellite view.

"Pretty tight, LT. I mean, off to the right's a clean miss, but off to the left and we got a friendly fire problem."

"Aim to the right and walk them in," he ordered. "I need fire now, within the next sixty seconds."

Ashcroft turned and headed back up the hill, leaving the mortar team to the task. His point squad had gained another fifty meters while he was gone—with three more Bug carcasses to show for it— but the Bugs were putting up some serious rearguard resistance now, and several of them had dug in to swap fire with the Marines. He realized he wasn't going to roll up their whole force soon enough to rescue Camelot, but the mortar would let him lay fire on both ends of the Bug column.

As long as we don't accidentally drop a round or two into Bouchard's lap, he thought, as a *thump* behind him announced that the first one was headed downrange.

* * *

"Incoming!"

Lorna thought the voice coming from the other end of the wall beyond the gate sounded like Bouchard, but she couldn't be sure. In any case, she was glad of the warning. As a Navy officer, she hadn't recognized the whine of the falling mortar round. There wasn't much she could do, except scrunch herself up tight against the parapet wall for cover, but that was exactly the right move.

The round hit outside the walls, maybe a hundred meters away, and impacted on the steep slope along the far side of King's Way. It had done no damage to the Bugs but had showered dirt and debris on the homes and shops below.

Ashcroft's team was good, and the second round dropped just in front of the gate. Debris, including, Lorna noted with satisfaction, a number of assorted Bug parts fell in the courtyard.

* * *

"Hah! Dialed in with the second shot," Engel declared. "OK, guys, fire for effect!" He ducked his head as the mortar sent the next round downrange.

* * *

Nesh Farmstead, West of the King's City

Can't believe we got them all aboard this quickly.

Nova stood at the top of the Archangel's loading ramp and looked out at the now-deserted farmhouse. The craft's turbines began to spin up as the ramp started to close, and she turned to look at the crazy confusion of the troop carrier's personnel compartment. Her Marines were trying to secure no less than 27 people—the family and several non-related farm hands— and a dozen assorted animals, ranging from four long-legged birds in makeshift cages to a pair of small kildren tethered to a structural column in the middle of the compartment. The Archangel's engineer and crew chief were securing bundles of clothing and personal belongings the refugees had brought aboard, using cargo netting and lashing. They'd even managed to bring a few small pieces of furniture aboard.

They were mostly a silent bunch, with expressions ranging from sad resignation to outright fear, but two of the younger children wore looks of cheerful, nervous excitement. *Welcome to the new world,* Nova thought. She walked into the compartment and over to where the old man had been strapped into one of the seats.

"Thank you, Pasca R'Nesh," she said. "Your family honors and obeys you. Without your help and cooperation, we could not have saved them. I am sorry for the loss you are about to experience, but we will do our best to restore all to you when this war is over."

"Will it be over? Will it ever be over?" Pasca asked her. "The Bugs have been here for generations, and they have powerful magic."

"I don't know who you people are, but you are people like us. I have no way of knowing whether you can do what you say. You tell me you have 'saved' us, but tomorrow, the Bugs may prevail, and my family will have lost everything."

Nova had no answer. She had sent the Firefly back to base and elected to go with the refugees, hoping to reassure them. She realized that, from their viewpoint, her promises were just words, and they had only gone with her out of desperation because they really believed their lives were being threatened. Fear of the Bugs had overcome distrust of the sky people.

She went forward to the command deck as the craft lifted off.

"Head for the camp on the Little Kilder," she told the pilot. "We have temporary shelter and food for them there. Let the Navy know when we're clear of the blast zone."

* * *

I'*m still alive*, Lorna thought, *but I'm out of this fight.* She had no more grenades and no more ammunition for her LCAW, and even if she'd still had firepower available, the Bugs had her thoroughly pinned down. The courtyard was full of them, and the only thing that had saved her so far was that they couldn't see her from below, as long as she stayed down and hugged the parapet. The battle-armored Bug warriors were too big and cumbersome to climb the narrow stairs up to the wall, but if they reached the second floor inside the castle, she would be exposed to fire from the windows.

The Bugs had taken out the east tower gun crew, but Lorna kept hearing an occasional sharp *crack* that sounded like Bouchard's sniper rifle. She imagined the Marine lieutenant popping up from cover to get a shot off whenever she could, but the Bugs weren't bothering to return fire. They had breached the main doors of the castle and were moving inside. As she tried to figure out what to do, Lorna heard a heavy blast from inside that did not come from a Bug plasma weapon. *Somebody's still fighting them.*

The mortar barrage outside had stopped. She wasn't sure whether the gunners had run out of ammo, or all the remaining Bugs were now inside the gate. There seemed to be some action going on further down the King's Way, but it was more than a half-kilometer away. *Relief column's being held short,* she figured. *Camelot has pretty much turned into the Alamo.*

* * *

"Hold your fire, Marines," Ackerman bellowed. "First Squad, coming in."

He waved his troops forward, counting

them off as they passed. Graham and Jefferson were the last two, and he followed them in past the barricade.

"Welcome back, Wolf." Sergeant Amir Farooq greeted him with a grin. Farooq and his squad had been holding off the Bug rearguard for the past hour and had killed at least twenty of them. It appeared Ackerman's gang had taken out the rest from behind.

"If you're here, there's no more Bugs coming up," Farooq said. "I guess that means we can stand down."

"No, what that means is you people can get your asses in gear and double-time up the hill to reinforce Lieutenant Ashcroft," Ackerman told him. "You hear all that noise up there? Marines are supposed to run *toward* the sound of the battle."

* * *

Near the Nesh Farmstead, West of the King's City

"They've gone, M'Lord," Murtax reported, as the giant flying machine departed toward the northeast. "We should go back the other way, around the city."

They had hidden in the woodland grove beside the road after spotting the strange events unfolding at the farm ahead. The little man led the kildren out of the trees and checked the saddling so they could ride again.

"No," Ersin insisted. "There's no one in sight. The road passes well clear of the farmhouse. No one will see us in the dark. We'll go on ahead."

"Yes, M'Lord," Murtax agreed without enthusiasm. He didn't know whether the commotion ahead had been caused by the Bugs or the sky people, but he wanted nothing to do with either. Reluctantly, he mounted his kilder and followed his master north up the road.

* * *

Light Cruiser LFS *Kraken,* in Low Orbit over Tatanna

"**M**arines report clear of target, sir."

"Very well," Captain Royd Rasmussen acknowledged the report from his tactical officer. "Fire when ready."

"Aye, sir. Firing."

Rasmussen nodded as he felt the faint vibration as the ship's mass drivers launched the heavy Thunderbolt kinetic weapon at the planet below.

* * *

"**M**'Lord!" The squeak of terror was all Murtax had time to utter before the blast wiped him and Ersin T'Corsa out of existence.

* * *

"**C**over!" Ashcroft shouted to his Marines, as the open plain to the west was lit by a fireball brighter than the sun. From their vantage point on the high road to the castle, the Marines had a clear view of the kinetic strike. Had their helmet visors not darkened automatically, any looking in that direction would have been blinded.

As they had drilled so many times, they dropped to the ground, flattened out as best they could and covered their heads. It wouldn't do any good to get behind a wall or a building because you might get buried under it when the shock wave arrived, and there was no convenient trench at hand.

The strike had been precisely calculated, and the target was 20 kilometers beyond the city walls. When the ground shock arrived, it shook the city a bit but caused little damage. The air shock right behind it was a brief windstorm of somewhat less than hurricane force.

The effect on the Bugs was dramatic, however.

* * *

The last queen was dead. The last offensive had failed. There was no more reason to continue.

The Bugs' empathic sense was not limited in range by planetary geography, so every Bug left alive on Tatanna knew what had happened, as did the two in the tiny scout ship hidden in the depths of space near the planet's hyper limit. Those two were the only ones who still had a mission, which they executed immediately. They translated into hyperspace to carry word to the homeworld.

On the planet, the remaining Bugs did what Bugs always do when their existence no longer serves a purpose.

* * *

The enemy had reached the second level of the castle and split its forces, some of them heading toward the west wing, some to the east. Leona Grady didn't care about those that went east. Her mission was to protect the west tower, where the royal residence was located. She had placed sentry cameras all along the approach, and now they showed the Bugs coming through the upper hall toward the tower staircase. She glanced behind her at the grim-faced King's Guardsmen kneeling with their crossbows. *Good, steady troops, but it's not their time yet.*

She readied to detonate another of the Claymore mines covering the approach to the staircase. Suddenly, the advancing Bugs stopped and put down their weapons. Their segmented insect 'arms' curled inward simultaneously, as they did something with their armored suits. She heard a sudden *whoosh*, which was picked up by the camera's microphone, and the two Bugs she could see collapsed in their tracks.

What the hell? A distinct odor wafted up the stairway. *Methane! They vented their suits! They just killed themselves!*

Pure methane was odorless, but the Bug breathing mixture contained additives that gave it the stench of an open sewer. She turned back to her Tatannan troops who obviously smelled it too.

"Windows! Open all the tower windows!" she ordered. "Bug gas, it will burn! No torches, no candles, no fire! Downstairs, open the windows. The Bugs are dead, but we must have fresh air. No candles! No fire!"

They hurried to obey, and she felt a fresh, chilly breeze as one of them opened the tower windows on the stair landing just below her position. Two headed down the stairs to the next level, warily because they couldn't believe the Bugs were dead. Another hastened up the stairs to open the windows above.

Dodged a bullet, Grady thought. At this hour of the night, the castle's halls and stairways would normally be lighted by dozens of candle lamps, but she'd ordered them extinguished when the battle started, thinking it might make it harder for the Bugs to navigate. She didn't know how well they could see in the dark, but her cameras had night vision and so did her helmet visor. If they had gotten face-to-face with the Bugs, she'd planned to dazzle them with a flare grenade and light up the target for her bowmen. *Think I'd better keep those flares on my belt for now,* she decided.

* * *

Silence and a really bad smell. Lorna had seen the sky light up to the west, had felt the tremor of the ground shock and the brief but fierce wind that followed. Suddenly, all was quiet. There had been a few shots from far down the road where the Marine relief force had been bogged down, but now, even that had stopped.

She glanced into the courtyard below but jerked her head back immediately when she saw that the Bugs were still there. More than a dozen of them hadn't yet made their way into the castle.

They're not moving.

She looked again and verified that the Bugs were down, their legs folded under them or splayed out, none of them moving. Hesitantly, she risked a quick look over the outer wall. More Bugs... also not moving. She decided to risk exposure in the hope of getting some intel.

"Lieutenant Bouchard!" she called out. "What's happening?"

A moment later, Bouchard's voice came back from the far end of the castle wall.

"I think we won."

* * *

"For whatever reason, Majesty, we have won. It appears our last strike from space, the one that lit up the sky a short while ago, hit something vital, something without which the Bugs could not continue."

Bouchard stood before King Arne with Lorna Greenwood and Corporal Grady by her side. Technically, Greenwood was the senior officer, but castle defense had been Bouchard's mission, and Lorna was willing to give her credit for it. Commodore O'Hara sat silently and listened as well.

"We heard the fighting... so close." Myrel still had not recovered from the terror of the last hours. She shivered as she sat stroking Bob, who purred loudly in seeming reassurance. "How many of your people..." She left the question unfinished.

"I have two wounded Marines being tended by a Navy rating downstairs," Bouchard responded. "Petty officer Gillum still maintains our communication links on the roof of this tower. Four of your Guardsmen with crossbows now stand guard in the main hall. Other than that—" she waved a hand at Grady on her left and Lorna on her right, "—the three of us are what remain of the castle defenders."

Myrel looked at her in horror, but Arne nodded gravely.

"The names of your fallen—and those of you who survived— will be recorded in our history," he said, "that we may honor them for generations to come."

* * * * *

Chapter Twenty-Three

More than two weeks had passed since the end of the fighting. The six LFS officers—three Navy and three Marine—had gathered for a meal in John O'Hara's quarters, the de facto "LFS Embassy" within the walls of the castle, to enjoy a dinner of local cuisine provided by the royal kitchen. Tomorrow, the group would split up, and for those that remained, there would be a formal victory dinner with Arne and his court. For tonight, though, they could relax, speak English, and share their experiences.

O'Hara was the ranking officer, but he felt diminished in this group. He was the only one who had not been exposed to actual combat in the campaign. Even Ensign McGill had seen action aboard *Lynx* and had been marooned on the planet with Lorna when the destroyer went down. Lorna Greenwood, for whom O'Hara still had very strong feelings, had stood on the wall with the Marines and fought the Bugs up close and personal, setting yet another bar that any woman he met in the future would have to surpass.

As for the Marines—Major Sakura and Lieutenants Ashcroft and Bouchard—O'Hara couldn't imagine what it had been like for them. He'd seen the carnage in the courtyard and outside the walls, and the king's messengers had been arriving all day with reports of destruction throughout the city. He'd seen the figures from Fleet for Marines killed or wounded on the planet—they still didn't have complete numbers on casualties from the Bug "doomsday" weapon up north. In effect, an entire Marine division had been wiped out.

"So, it's really over." The comment came from Ashcroft. "Hard to believe, even if we've not fired a shot in a couple of weeks."

"Looks that way." O'Hara nodded. "Fleet tells me General Mercer's got reports from every unit in the field. There's not a Bug moving anywhere on the planet, and they've gone down into the tunnels to check."

"That's what we found here," Ashcroft confirmed. "My people blasted their way into the Bug holes in the city and went down the tunnels as far as they could—nearly 20 klicks before they ran into the blockage caused by the kinetic strike. Found exactly five dead Bugs."

"Anyway, we're leaving tomorrow," Nova Sakura said. "We'll leave you five Marines for embassy detail, Moira, but Jay and I are taking the platoon back up to the Little Kilder. From there, we'll go wherever General Mercer wants to send us."

"Sounds like some of us might be going home soon," McGill speculated. "The captain and I are being lifted back up to Fleet tomorrow, and word is all the surviving *Lynxes* will be shipped back to Luna."

"Except your man Jefferson," Ashcroft said, with a grin. "He's mine now, and I'm not gonna give him back. He's a hard-charging Marine, and I could use ten more like him."

"And Bob," McGill added with a grin. "It seems he's been appointed Feline Ambassador to Tatanna." The cat had not left Myrel's side since the battle, and O'Hara had suggested he remain with the royal family.

"I suspect a lot of Marines are going to be rotating back to Luna soon," Ashcroft said. "We can leave this system in the capable hands of the Navy."

"Yes, but the Navy's going to be here for a while," O'Hara said. "Outer system pickets saw a hyper translation—out of the system— just about the time the Bugs dropped dead. Looks like they had a messenger hidden out there, so their home world knows what happened. Until we know what they're going to do about it, Fleet's going to need a strong presence here."

I'm stuck here for a while, he reflected, *until the Diplomatic Corps gets their act together and sends a real ambassador. I was worried about where my naval career was going, but I sure as hell never figured I'd wind up as a diplomat.*

"Hey, Tatanna's a nice planet," Sakura said, almost as if she had been reading his mind. "There are worse places you could be stationed, especially now that the Bugs are gone."

"I'll drink to that," Bouchard agreed, lifting her glass. "In fact, I want to thank you, Commodore, for keeping me on with the embassy detail. I would have volunteered for that duty in a heartbeat."

"Well, hell, Lieutenant," O'Hara snorted. "Let me see… where can I find a Marine officer who speaks Tatannan like a native, is a close personal friend of the royal family, and is generally regarded as some sort of minor goddess by the palace staff? Kind of a short list of candidates, don't you think?"

"Not a goddess, sir," she corrected him with a smile that showed a hint of pain. "There is only one Goddess. Muh-rah is merely Her handmaiden."

"And who knows a hell of a lot more about Tatannan culture than I do," O'Hara retorted. "Besides—"

"Excuse me, sir." Petty Officer Gillum suddenly appeared in the doorway. "Flash traffic from Fleet. There's a special Commander's Call for all officers—Navy and Marines—scheduled for 1900 LST. That's… uh… 26 minutes from now. I can set it up in the comm center for you if that's OK."

"All officers?" O'Hara was surprised.

"Yes, sir, the flash says, 'every commissioned officer able to attend.' Must be something big to do it on such short notice."

"Hopefully, it's not to tell us the Bugs are back." McGill shuddered.

"No, that would have triggered an alert, not a Commander's Call," Lorna said. "I guess we'll find out in about 25 minutes."

* * *

The six of them gathered in the tower room that had been set up as the LFS comm center less than ten minutes later, then had to stare at the logo of LFS *Nike* on the screen while they waited for the Commander's Call to begin. At the appointed time, McGruder appeared on screen.

"Ladies and gentlemen," he began without preamble. "We have just received a hyperprobe from Luna with some disturbing news. While we have been here fighting the Bugs, our nation has been attacked by an enemy whose identity has not yet been determined.

"On 6 April at approximately 1500 hours LST, a device was triggered on Level 15 in TerraNova City that released a deadly nerve agent. The target was Luna's Chief Executive, and the attack succeeded. Kim Jong Pak is dead, along with his five-man Marine security detail and 31 others who happened to be on the concourse at the time. Prompt response to the event confined the deaths to a single concourse.

"The hyperprobe was sent to us less than 48 hours after the event, and at that time, the assassin—the person who set the device—had been captured, but the investigation was still in progress, and there was no indication as to who sponsored the attack. Preliminary interrogation indicates he was a professional hired by someone on Earth, but he claims not to know who employed him."

"That, ladies and gentlemen—" McGruder's face reflected the frustration of not knowing more details, "—is all we have at the moment, except for two items of supreme concern to us as members of the LFS Navy and Marines."

"As of the date the probe was launched, Admiral Amy Ling had been sworn in as Luna's new Chief Executive and had appointed Vice Admiral Robert O'Hara to command the Lunar Fleet."

* * *

LFS *Jaguar*, in Tatanna Orbit

*O**h, crap! Mom? Seriously?*

Rebecca Ling had gathered her officers in *Jaguar's* wardroom for the Commander's Call. She was seated at the far end of the long table—furthest from the screen—and all of them turned to look at her.

"Eyes front," she growled, and they quickly turned back to face the screen.

"We haven't yet figured out what the implications are for our forces here," McGruder was saying. "We've beaten the Bugs, and chances are we would be rotating some ships and personnel back to Luna anyway. At this point I don't know whether these developments will have any effect on that."

"Meanwhile, you may regard what I have told you as information only. You may pass it on to your troops but should discourage any speculation or scuttlebutt. Further information will be passed down the chain of command as it becomes available. That will be all for today. You may return to your regular duties."

McGruder's face disappeared and was replaced by the battlecruiser's logo. A moment later, the connection was terminated, and *Jaguar's* wallpaper filled the screen with the image of the snarling, spotted feline. Ling's people turned back to her, this time trying to do so without any sudden or obvious movement.

"Yes," she told them. "My mother is now Chief Executive, and we're forty-seven light-years from Luna and have a mission to carry out. Like the Admiral said, until we have further information it's business as usual. Any questions?"

There were none.

"Back to work, people. Dismissed."

* * *

Castle Boroson, the King's City

"Word is, *Omaha Beach* is going home," Lorna said. "My *Lynx* survivors are being transferred there, and we'll be going with her."

John O'Hara nodded. Most of the carrier's Marines had been First Division, almost wiped out, along with their commanding officer, in the Bug doomsday blast. The wounded were also being shipped back to Luna, and the number of Marines still combat-effective on Tatanna could be supported by a single carrier. *Iwo Jima* would stay; *Omaha Beach* would go home. For Lorna, it would bring a few memories. She'd done her first year Fleet Academy cruise aboard the carrier eleven years ago.

The Navy was also trimming its forces in the system. Several cruisers and destroyers, some with battle damage, would be going back with the carrier. In addition, McGruder had decided he only needed one battlecruiser, his flagship, *Nike*. LFS *Amazon* would be going back to Luna. No matter how large a force the Bugs sent, if they sent one at all, defending the planet would be a much simpler task than taking it from them had been. The Navy had taken few losses compared to the devastation they'd wreaked on the Bugs in space. Most of the butcher's bill for planet Tatanna had been paid by the Marines.

"Lorna, I'm going to miss you," O'Hara said at last. After the Commander's Call, the two of them had gone up to the top of the tower for air and were once again looking out over the city.

"John…"

"We're not in chain of command anymore," he pressed on. "I just think we should give ourselves a chance. You're leaving tomorrow, and—"

"And you're staying here. So, what are you looking for? A one-night stand? A long-term commitment? Right now, I can't handle either one. Besides, last time we had this discussion—about eight years ago—you were the one who backed away."

"I've regretted it ever since, but I had a good reason at the time. My career was hanging by a thread."

"Mine's hanging by a thread now," she reminded him. "In case you've forgotten, I just lost my ship and nearly a third of the crew entrusted to my care. You can say it's not my fault, that everything will be OK, but that's not how it feels right now.

"I'm sorry, John, that's the way it is. For what it's worth, I still care about you. If I were ready for a relationship, you'd be the one I'd want it with, but right now…" She stood there for a moment, looking at him. "Good night, John, I've got to go. Shuttle's due at 0900, and I need to pack."

Pack? What little you brought with you when Lynx *went down?* He knew it was just an excuse to end the conversation. She turned and started down the stairs, leaving him to watch her walk out of his life—again!

Yeah, last time was my fault. I held her off because I thought my career was in the dumper. I thought I could live with it… until I saw her again. How many years is it going to take to get back to living with it this time?

Where the hell am I headed now, he wondered. *Gee, Dad's in command of the fleet—my dear dad who goes out of his way to avoid anything that resembles nepotism, patronage, or favoritism. With Admiral Ling, I might have gotten another command someday, but now? Next orders I get from Luna might be a transfer to the Diplomatic Corps and a permanent assignment as ambassador here.*

He turned to look out over the city again. *Well, like Sakura said, at least it's a nice planet.*

* * * * *

Epilogue

September 2112, Battlecruiser LFS *Isis*

Lunar Fleet Anchorage

"At ease, Commander," Admiral Robert O'Hara said, returning the salute. "Have a seat."

"Yes, sir." Lorna Greenwood took the indicated chair, though she felt anything but 'at ease.'

On return to Luna, she had been called before a Board of Inquiry over the loss of *Lynx*, but the board only confirmed what she'd already been told by the senior officers at Tatanna. The verdict was 'lost in action under extreme combat conditions, despite outstanding performance by the ship's officers and crew.' Further, the board accepted Admiral McGruder's recommendations and awarded *Lynx* the Sword of the Fleet. The honor would be inherited by any future warship that carried the name.

The new LFS *Lynx* had already been commissioned and assigned to another officer who was overdue for a command. The ship had completed shakedown trials and was already en route to Tatanna to join Destroyer Squadron Twelve, which was still on patrol in the liberated system.

Lorna had waited and waited in the officer assignment pool. After being told a new assignment was at least two months away, she had applied for leave and hitched a ride on a convoy escort to Copper Hills Prime, the Akara homeworld fifty light-years from Luna where her grandmother's estate was located. As heir to the estate,

Lorna held a title of nobility on the planet—the equivalent of a duchess in the feudal hierarchy of the Akara, ruler of a sparsely populated mountain territory the size of Japan.

She was the only human to hold such a title. Her grandmother had been the first female of any species to do so in the male dominated "Lizard" society. Since her grandmother's death a decade earlier, her holdings had been administered by an Akara regent, but she had spent many months on the estate as a child. Her long-lived reptilian "subjects" welcomed her fondly; many of them had known her for most of her life.

Eager to account for his stewardship, the Regent had taken her on a whirlwind tour of the province and subjected her to a detailed accounting of the considerable prosperity of her holdings. For the ten days she spent on the planet, she was able to put aside her concerns about her future as a Fleet officer and simply enjoy the treatment that came with being a member of the planet's ruling nobility. Before returning to Luna, she had stopped at the capital for a brief audience with Heart of the Copper Hills, the ruling monarch of the Copper Hills clan.

There had been an awkward moment when she was escorted past the LFS Ambassador whose audience had been delayed so that the "Lizard King" could meet with Lorna instead. The ambassador, who wore the rank of Commodore in the Diplomatic Corps, could hardly have failed to notice when she walked through the huge outer hall wearing her Dress Bravo naval officer's uniform, with the lowly rank of Lieutenant Commander, despite a moderately impressive rack of ribbons on her chest. He gave her a stern and disapproving look when she went in, but his attitude changed when she came out. Judging by the smile and respectful bow he offered as she left, she could only assume someone had advised him of her status among the locals. *Next time,* she told herself, *I really should stop at the Embassy when I arrive on planet and give them a heads-up to avoid any misunderstandings.*

With that, she returned to Luna. She had enjoyed her time on Copper Hills, but the return trip brought back the uncertainty about her naval career. It was almost a relief, three days after her arrival in TerraNova, to get the summons from Admiral O'Hara.

She sat, nervous and attentive, in front of his desk while he reviewed the file on his screen. *This is it,* she thought, *make or break.*

"Sorry to have kept you waiting so long, Commander. As you can imagine, since the assassination, there have been a lot of shifting priorities."

"I understand, sir."

"You've also been kept waiting because of… well… not exactly an argument but a discussion about what to do with you. That's why you're here, talking to me instead of getting a set of orders through normal channels. I thought it was only fair to give you some background, so you understand how these orders came about."

Here it comes, she thought. She had to remind herself to stop holding her breath.

"First of all," he continued, "I should tell you that your previous commander practically demanded that you be given command of the newly commissioned *Lynx.* While I have great respect for Commodore Ling, I had to refuse her. The new destroyer had already been assigned a captain well before we decided to give it your ship's name and battle honors. Commander Jared's orders were cut before *Lynx* was lost at Tatanna. He's a good man, and I would not consider taking away a command he'd been promised and had worked so hard to earn.

"With no other destroyer commands available, some people at Fleet, whose very difficult job is to keep our officer billets filled, suggested we should give you an Executive Officer slot on a cruiser. There were two available—one on the light cruiser *Hydra*, the other on the heavy cruiser *Spartan.*"

There it is. Lorna felt crushed. *No command for me, back to the lower ranks.* Lost in her disappointment, she almost missed his next remark.

"However, when I advised Commodore Ling, she told me in no uncertain terms that was unacceptable. In her opinion, anything less than another command would be perceived as a demotion, an indication that, despite the results of the hearings, Fleet was somehow displeased with you. Unless, maybe, we bumped you to full commander and gave you the XO slot on a *battlecruiser.*"

"Sir, I…" Lorna didn't know how to respond. She'd known Ling was on her side—the commodore's report had been a big factor in the hearings for the loss of *Lynx*—but she hadn't expected her former commander to go so far out on a limb.

"She doesn't have a veto, but the commodore can be very persuasive." O'Hara favored Lorna with crooked grin, "I actually considered her suggestion, but there are only eight battlecruisers and none of them need a new Exec.

"Commander Greenwood," he went on in a more serious tone, "you need to understand that Fleet is more than satisfied with your performance to date. Your single-ship defense of *Iwo Jima* was textbook-perfect, right up to the point where the enemy got lucky and took you out.

"I know you gave a lot of credit to your tactical officer, but he chose to give most of the credit to you. He's not the only one. Virtually every one of *Lynx's* survivors said they would ship out under your command in a heartbeat. Conventional wisdom seems to be that any captain who would risk her own life to save the ship's cat must be one who takes care of her crew. There's also a certain Marine lance corporal who says that, based on what he saw down on the planet, he'd be happy to follow you into battle if you were a Marine officer and a Marine lieutenant who says you're pretty damned good in a firefight.

"There are commendations in the pipeline for all of *Lynx's* crew. Some will be singled out for higher honors, including your tactical officer and the two who went down on the planet with you. Hell, there's even talk of giving the damned cat a medal of some sort, but the word I've gotten is that they've put you up for the Lunar Medal of Honor. No guarantees until it's awarded, but that should tell you how highly Fleet thinks of you.

"With that in mind," he said, "here are your orders." He picked up a large envelope from his desk and handed it to her.

Lorna's eye went wide, and she drew a sharp breath. She tried to respond, but the words wouldn't come. *The LMH? Can't think of anything I did that would be worthy of that!*

She held her breath as she opened the envelope. Only certain types of orders were printed out on paper—on very fine parchment—in case the recipient wanted to frame them for display. She slid the single sheet out of the envelope and scanned quickly through the official language in the preamble. Her rapid reading came to an abrupt halt as she reached the important part—*assume command of the Lunar Fleet Ship* Werewolf, CL-11. Her head came up abruptly, and she locked eyes with O'Hara.

"Sir, a *light cruiser*?"

"Don't get too enthusiastic, Commander," he said. "*Werewolf* is the oldest light cruiser still in service, one of the oldest ships in the Fleet, last of the original *Vampire* class. With the fleet buildup prior to Blue Orchid, we decided to refit her one last time rather than scrap her, but there's only so much the yard dogs can do. She's only got two-thirds the hull volume of a new *Dragon* class CL, but she's a step up from a destroyer, and that does put you in the command chair again."

"Yes sir. Thank you, sir." Lorna's emotions had gone from depression to elation in just seconds. She felt as if she were poised at the top of an amusement park ride, waiting for a sudden plunge to take her back to the bottom, but the plunge didn't come as O'Hara went on.

"You'll get your operational orders once you take command of the ship, but I can tell you now: You're going back to Sacagawea. *Werewolf* is being assigned to the newly formed Cruiser Squadron Two, whose primary mission will be the defense of Tatanna.

"In short, you're going to be on Bug Patrol. We have no indication that the Ay'uskanar will be back. We thoroughly kicked their butts in space, though they gave the Marines a lot of grief on the planet. Hell, Commander, you were there. You know more about that than I do, but our deep scouting missions to the Bug systems find no indication they are preparing to return. If we thought they'd be back, we'd keep a full Battle Group out there, instead of cruisers and destroyers."

"Anyway, *Werewolf* is just out of the yards and docked here at the Anchorage, and your orders are effective immediately. I suggest you get over there, take command, and start putting your crew together. There have been very few permanent assignments made, so you'll be working from scratch. I assumed you might want to have some of the old *Lynx* people, and we can do that, but you can't have Przrbr... Prizbiz... your old NTO. He's getting a promotion and that Exec spot on *Spartan*—based on your glowing recommendation, I might add."

"He deserves it, sir." Lorna nodded.

The crooked grin was back on O'Hara's face. "You do know a light cruiser rates a full commander in the captain's chair, don't you? You don't quite have time in grade for this, so I had to push it through out of cycle." He picked up a small box and handed it to her.

Lorna's eyes went wide once again as she opened the box and found the four gold bars of a commander's rank insignia.

"When you get to Sacagawea, you can thank Commodore Ling and tell her she owes me one."

* * *

After Lorna left, O'Hara sat for a while, thinking about the interview. *She's a good officer, a credit to her heritage. She'll probably hoist her own flag someday, assuming she survives. Hell, assuming we all survive.*

He hadn't elaborated on the "shifting priorities" he had mentioned earlier, but a lot of it had to do with tensions here, at home, in the Sol system. *The Confeds are testing us, and somebody down there has the Earthside news media well in hand. There hasn't been such open hostility against us since the earliest days of the Lunar Free State.*

SID's final report expressed near-certainty that the Confederacy—or someone with the Confederacy's interests in mind—had sponsored the assassination, but no hard evidence had been found.

The assassin had been executed by hanging—one of the most merciful methods of execution humanity had ever devised, though it brought more media shrieks of horror over the "cruel and unusual punishment" carried out by the Lunar Free State's "barbaric, oppressive, so-called justice system."

SID also believed the Confederacy had a hand in the murder of Admiral Hutchins to erase their connection to his efforts to sabotage LFS diplomatic relations with Tatanna. The details were still being unraveled, but the obvious goal was to portray Luna as an interstellar imperialist nation, seeking to exert its dominance over more primitive planets like New Eden and Tatanna.

In a way, O'Hara envied Greenwood. She was a regular military officer on a clear-cut military mission. He'd been such an officer himself, not so very long ago, but now, he was next-in-line for the Chief Executive's job, with only a century-old woman too stubborn to retire between him and the ultimate responsibility for his entire nation.

Yes, he envied Greenwood, but he felt a momentary twinge of guilt over one thing he hadn't told her. He knew there had been a problem between her and his son some years earlier—an issue of mutual attraction and sexual tension held in check by the fact that he was her immediate superior in the chain of command. *I've just put her under John's command again, but she won't find that out until she gets there and reports—as directed by her orders—to the "senior officer commanding CruRon Two, Sacagawea System."*

Can't be helped, he reflected. *In every other way, they are ideal choices for the assignments they've got. Hopefully, they've gotten over their earlier feelings, but if not, it could turn out to be an interesting situation, as in that old curse, "May you live in interesting times."*

# # # # #

About John E. Siers

John E. Siers is a Viet Nam–era Air Force veteran who spent several decades working as a software developer, designing analytical systems for corporate clients.

An avid reader of science fiction since grade school, John started writing in the late 1970s, mostly for his own enjoyment. He wrote for more than 20 years and produced three complete novels before ever showing his work to anyone.

Escaping from the overcrowded northeast, John moved to Tennessee in 1997. Encouraged by friends, he finally published his first novel, The Moon and Beyond, in late 2012, followed by Someday the Stars in 2013. The latter won the 2014 Darrell Award for Best SF Novel by a Midsouth Author.

John's Lunar Free State series had grown to four novels—with no thought of doing anything outside his own comfort zone—when he encountered William Alan Webb at MidSouthCon in 2019. Bill led John astray, tempting him with visions of other universes, whispering names like Four Horsemen, Last Brigade, and finally, Hit World.

John succumbed to the temptation, and The Ferryman and The Dragons of Styx are the results. He has since entered a rehab program and produced a fifth novel in his own universe. As of this date, he is nearing completion of the sixth Lunar Free State novel, entitled Season of the Wolf.

John lives with his wife, son, dog, and two cats in west Tennessee. In his spare time (what there is of it) he runs his own firearm repair and service business under the trade name of Gunsmith Jack. Readers can follow him on Amazon, Facebook, or his own website at www.lunarfreestate.com.

* * * * *

The following is an
Excerpt from Book One of This Fine Crew:

The Signal Out of Space

_____

Mike Jack Stoumbos

Available from Theogony Books

eBook and Paperback

Excerpt from "The Signal Out of Space:"

Day 4 of Training, Olympus Mons Academy

I want to make something clear from square one: we were winning.

More importantly, I was winning. Sure, the whole thing was meant to be a "team effort," and I'd never say this to an academy instructor, but the fact of the matter is this: it was a race and I was in the driver's seat. Like hell I was going to let any other team beat us, experimental squad or not.

At our velocity, even the low planetary grav didn't temper the impact of each ice mogul on the glistening red terrain. We rocketed up, plummeted down, and cut new trails in the geo-formations, spraying orange ice and surface rust in our wake. So much of the red planet was still like a fresh sheet of snow, and I was eager to carve every inch of it.

Checking on the rest of the crew, I thought our tactical cadet was going to lose her lunch. I had no idea how the rest of the group was managing, different species being what they are.

Of our complement of five souls, sans AI-assist or anything else that cadets should learn to live without, Shin and I were the only Humans. The communications cadet was a Teek—all exoskeleton and antennae, but the closest to familiar. He sat in the copilot seat, ready to take the controls if I had to tap out. His two primary arms were busy with the scanning equipment, but one of his secondary hands hovered over the E-brake, which made me more anxious than assured.

I could hear the reptile humming in the seat behind me, in what I registered as "thrill," each time I overcame a terrain obstacle with even greater speed, rather than erring on the side of caution.

Rushing along the ice hills of Mars on six beautifully balanced wheels was a giant step up from the simulator. The design of the Red Terrain Vehicle was pristine, but academy-contrived obstacles mixed with natural formations bumped up the challenge factor. The dummy fire sounds from our sensors and our mounted cannon only added to the sense of adventure. The whole thing was like fulfilling a fantasy, greater than my first jet around good ol' Luna. If the camera evidence had survived, I bet I would have been grinning like an idiot right up until the Teek got the bogey signal.

"Cadet Lidstrom," the Teek said, fast but formal through his clicking mandibles, "unidentified signal fifteen degrees right of heading." His large eyes pulsed with green luminescence, bright enough for me to see in the corner of my vision. It was an eerie way to express emotion, which I imagined would make them terrible at poker.

I hardly had a chance to look at the data while maintaining breakneck KPH, but in the distance, it appeared to be one of our surface vehicles, all six wheels turned up to the stars.

The lizard hummed a different note and spoke in strongly accented English, "Do we have time to check?"

The big furry one at the rear gruffed in reply, but not in any language I could understand.

"Maybe it's part of the test," I suggested. "Like a bonus. Paul, was it hard to find?"

The Teek, who went by Paul, clicked to himself and considered the question. His exoskeletal fingers worked furiously for maybe a second before he informed us, "It is obscured by interference."

"Sounds like a bonus to me," Shin said. Then she asked me just the right question: "Lidstrom, can you get us close without losing our lead?"

The Arteevee would have answered for me if it could, casting an arc of red debris as I swerved. I admit, I did not run any mental calculations, but a quick glance at my rear sensors assured me. "Hell yeah! I got this."

In the mirror, I saw our large, hairy squadmate, the P'rukktah, transitioning to the grappler interface, in case we needed to pick something up when we got there. Shin, on tactical, laid down some cannon fire behind us—tiny, non-lethal silicon scattershot—to kick up enough dust that even the closest pursuer would lose our visual heading for a few seconds at least. I did not get a chance to find out what the reptile was doing as we neared the overturned vehicle.

I had maybe another half-k to go when Paul's eyes suddenly shifted to shallow blue and his jaw clicked wildly. He only managed one English word: "Peculiar!"

Before I could ask, I was overcome with a sound, a voice, a shrill screech. I shut my eyes for an instant, then opened them to see where I was driving and the rest of my squad, but everything was awash in some kind of blue light. If I thought it would do any good, I might have tried to plug my ears.

Paul didn't have the luxury of closing his compound eyes, but his primary arms tried to block them. His hands instinctively guarded his antennae.

Shin half fell from the pivoting cannon rig, both palms cupping her ears, which told me the sound wasn't just in my head.

The reptile bared teeth in a manner too predatory to be a smile and a rattling hum escaped her throat, dissonant to the sound.

Only the P'rukktah weathered this unexpected cacophony with grace. She stretched out clearly muscled arms and grabbed anchor points on either side of the vehicle. In blocky computer-generated words, her translator pulsed out, "What—Is—That?"

Facing forward again, I was able to see the signs of wreckage ahead and of distressed ground. I think I was about to ask if I should turn away when the choice was taken from me.

An explosion beneath our vehicle heaved us upward, nose first. Though nearly bucked out of my seat, I was prepared to recover our heading or even to stop and assess what had felt like a bomb.

A second blast, larger than the first, pushed us from behind, probably just off my right rear wheel, spraying more particulates and lifting us again.

One screech was replaced with another. Where the first had been almost organic, this new one was clearly the sound of tearing metal.

The safety belt caught my collarbone hard as my body tried to torque out of the seat. Keeping my eyes open, I saw one of our tires—maybe two thirds of a tire—whip off into the distance on a strange trajectory, made even stranger by the fact that the horizon was spinning.

The red planet came at the windshield and the vehicle was wrenched enough to break a seal. I barely noticed the sudden escape of air; I was too busy trying, futilely, to drive the now upside-down craft...

* * * * *

Get "The Signal Out of Space" now at:
https://www.amazon.com/dp/B09N8VHGFP

Find out more about Mike Jack Stoumbos at:
https://chriskennedypublishing.com

* * * * *

The following is an

Excerpt from Book One of Abner Fortis, ISMC:

Cherry Drop

P.A. Piatt

Available from Theogony Books

eBook, Audio, and Paperback

Excerpt from "Cherry Drop:"

"Here they come!"

A low, throbbing buzz rose from the trees and the undergrowth shook. Thousands of bugs exploded out of the jungle, and Fortis' breath caught in his throat. The insects tumbled over each other in a rolling, skittering mass that engulfed everything in its path.

The Space Marines didn't need an order to open fire. Rifles cracked and the grenade launcher thumped over and over as they tried to stem the tide of bugs. Grenades tore holes in the ranks of the bugs and well-aimed rifle fire dropped many more. Still, the bugs advanced.

Hawkins' voice boomed in Fortis' ear. "LT, fall back behind the fighting position, clear the way for the heavy weapons."

Fortis looked over his shoulder and saw the fighting holes bristling with Marines who couldn't fire for fear of hitting their own comrades. He thumped Thorsen on the shoulder.

"Fall back!" he ordered. "Take up positions behind the fighting holes."

Thorsen stopped firing and moved among the other Marines, relaying Fortis' order. One by one, the Marines stopped firing and made for the rear. As the gunfire slacked off, the bugs closed ranks and continued forward.

After the last Marine had fallen back, Fortis motioned to Thorsen.

"Let's go!"

Thorsen turned and let out a blood-chilling scream. A bug had approached unnoticed and buried its stinger deep in Thorsen's calf. The stricken Marine fell to the ground and began to convulse as the neurotoxin entered his bloodstream.

"Holy shit!" Fortis drew his kukri, ran over, and chopped at the insect stinger. The injured bug made a high-pitched shrieking noise, which Fortis cut short with another stroke of his knife.

Viscous, black goo oozed from the hole in Thorsen's armor and his convulsions ceased.

"Get the hell out of there!"

Hawkins was shouting in his ear, and Abner looked up. The line of bugs was ten meters away. For a split second he almost turned and ran, but the urge vanished as quickly as it appeared. He grabbed Thorsen under the arms and dragged the injured Marine along with him, pursued by the inexorable tide of gaping pincers and dripping stingers.

Fortis pulled Thorsen as fast as he could, straining with all his might against the substantial Pada-Pada gravity. Thorsen convulsed and slipped from Abner's grip and the young officer fell backward. When he sat up, he saw the bugs were almost on them.

* * * * *

Get "Cherry Drop" now at:
https://www.amazon.com/dp/B09B14VBK2

Find out more about P.A. Piatt at:
https://chriskennedypublishing.com

* * * * *

The following is an

Excerpt from Book One of Murphy's Lawless:

Shakes

Mike Massa

Available from Beyond Terra Press

eBook and Paperback

Excerpt from "Shakes:"

"My name is Volo of the House Zobulakos," the SpinDog announced haughtily. Harry watched as his slender ally found his feet and made a show of brushing imaginary dust from his shoulder where the lance had rested.

Volo was defiant even in the face of drawn weapons; Harry had to give him points for style.

"I am here representing the esteemed friend to all Sarmatchani, my father, Arko Primus Heraklis Zobulakos. This is a mission of great importance. What honorless prole names my brother a liar and interferes with the will of the Primus? Tell me, that I might inform your chief of this insolence."

Harry tensed as two of the newcomers surged forward in angry reaction to the word "honorless," but the tall man interposed his lance, barring their way.

"Father!" the shorter one objected, throwing back her hood, revealing a sharp featured young woman. She'd drawn her blade and balefully eyed the SpinDog. "Let me teach this arrogant weakling about honor!"

"Nay, Stella," the broad-shouldered man said grimly. "Even my daughter must cleave to the law. This is a clan matter. And as to the stripling's question...

"I, hight Yannis al-Caoimhip ex-huscarlo, Patrisero of the Herd-bane, First among the Sarmatchani," he went on, fixing his eyes first on Volo and then each of the Terrans. "I name Stabilo of the Sky People a liar, a cheat, and a coward. I call his people to account. Blood or treasure. At dawn tomorrow either will suffice."

Harry didn't say a word but heard a deep sigh from Rodriguez. These were the allies he'd been sent to find, all right. Just like every other joint operation with indigs, it was SNAFU.

Murphy's Law was in still in effect.

* * * * *

Get "Shakes" now at: https://www.amazon.com/dp/B0861F23KH

Find out more about Murphy's Lawless and Beyond Terra Press at: https://chriskennedypublishing.com/imprints-authors/beyond-terra-press/

* * * * *

Made in the USA
Columbia, SC
30 December 2021

53019855R00228